COWBOY WITHIN
CHALLENGES AND REWARDS

LIAM LENHART

ISBN 978-1-966012-21-4 (paperback)
ISBN 978-1-966012-22-1 (hardcover)
ISBN 978-1-966012-23-8 (digital)

Printed in the United States of America

Dedicated to my kids
And to cowboys keeping the American dream
And way of life alive

PROLOGUE

The Twisted Live Oak Ranch dramatically changes Luke Anderson's life. The Cowboy Code guides wranglers' lives and reveals ways to help Luke combat his anger, hatred, and overall contempt for daily routines and people. Luke's loathing for horses erodes after constant daily rides. He shows signs of becoming an expert rider like the cowboys. And Hope Cooper.

Chester Kinkead and Hank McIntyre teach Luke to trust certain people and consider remaining on the ranch. Hope and her daughter Faith could have the greatest impact on Luke's maturation.

Luke struggles with new physical, emotional, and psychological conflicts along with long-buried sentiments. His honest introspection into past failures could result in a happier outcome and lasting love. Luke faces the ultimate decision whether to stay for true love or risk losing everything if he returns to Chicago.

CHAPTER

ONE

Hope lays her naked body on Luke and begs. "Luke, I'm yours. Enjoy my moist satin blossom all you want."

Luke jolts awake and looks around. *'It was a dream? It seemed real. What the hell was that about?'*

The raven-haired buxom beauty's kiss full of lustful passion leaves Luke confused about Hope. *'I've only been here three months and I'm hiding in a barn full of horses I wouldn't be caught dead around before. That kiss shook Hope too. Why? Why did I fight those guys instead of running?'*

Hope avoids Luke by letting Beth bring Faith to visit Chester. *'How do I explain why I kissed Luke? How do I face him again? I'm not sure I can. I shouldn't but I'm startin' to have feelin's for him.'*

Hope forced Beth to swear not to repeat their conversation and is restless at night. *'What made me kiss Luke like that? Or at all? It felt good holdin' him. His kiss made me feel somethin' I ain't never felt before. I felt alive. I felt butterflies. Wyatt never did that to me. Are Jubilee and JeniMay right? Am I tempted by Luke because he doesn't chase me? Why did Ben say Luke could find a reason to stay? If I start something with Luke and he still leaves, I don't need more heartache. Why would Luke stay?'*

Faith's acceptance of Luke concerns Hope. She's unaware Faith's creating an emotional bridge with Luke even he hasn't detected yet. *'Why doesn't Faith fear Luke? What if this all ends badly?'*

Hope's past heartbreaks fuel her low self-esteem regarding men. Owning a successful equine clinic doesn't eliminate a negative self-image and her achievements and intellect serve to intimidate many men who can't see past her outer beauty. *I'm nothin' but a sex trophy. I'm not like Holly. I want a lifetime love. Could Luke honestly be interested if he still wants to leave? What would Beth say?'*

"Beth, can we talk? I need your advice."

"Sure."

"What if I do have feelings for Luke? He still plans to leave."

"Whoa. Breathe. Slow down. Focus on what's possible. Stop worrying 'bout what might not happen. Luke's bustin' through your walls. Y'all're scared. I get it. Luke could choose to stay. What if everything goes right as rain? Faith's riskin' that chance already."

"Why isn't Faith afraid of Luke?"

"Luke's genuinely kind and honest with Faith. Without bein' asked, right?"

"I've never asked him to be nice. Why is he different?"

"Faith must sense somethin'. Talk to Luke. Y'all gotta have some reason for kissin' on him like ya did. Wyatt was your last real love. Maybe love's knockin' at the door again. Luke does look at y'all like Ben looks at me."

"Wyatt's the past. Nobody compares to Ben." *'Beth mentions Wyatt after I think about him, why?'*

"Are you blind? It's obvious Luke cares about you. Hell, he fought five guys to save you. Joe would've left you for dead."

"I don't think love's in the cards for me 'n I can't handle another broken heart."

"Faith'll grow up seein' you live half a life and probably do the same."

"Don't say that, Beth. I'll teach Faith to make better choices."

"Who's gonna teach you first?"

"Can we talk again later? Jubilee texted and wants to go to the gym."

TWO

Chester declares, "I figured you'd be the idjit to run the tractor into the barn. Not those two dumbasses. How ya doin' with this?"

"Good. I guess."

"I stuck Jesse 'n Jake with Danny 'n Kyle repairin' barbed wire fencin' today."

Chester notes Luke's shirt is soaked through with sweat before inspecting his work. "Scooter's taughtcha well."

"Scooter teaches well even if he talks funny."

"Y'all ain't standin' on solid ground in Texas to say that."

"Fair enough. So Jake and Jesse drove the tractor into the rodeo barn?"

"Yep. Ben said Jesse was tauntin' Jake for losing women's attention to you. Go git somethin' to drink 'n eat. Then clean this up."

"Shouldn't I clean this up first?"

"Naw. It'll keep. The horses are in the pasture."

Luke reaches the Live Oaks by the driveway just before a sizeable branch splinters nearby ahead of a gunshot a microsecond later. *What the hell was that?*

Chester emerges from the barn to see Luke squatting and apprehensively searching down the driveway before hearing a dirt bike speeding off in the distance.

Chester approaches looking concerned. "Were you shot?"

Luke touches his left temple area and feels blood. "No. The branch splintered."

Chester's call brings Bob to listen to Luke's explanation before quietly investigating and finding nothing conclusive. The tire tracks simply end by the road. Luke, y'all got any enemies?"

Luke ponders Bob's question. *'Could Hope want me dead?'* "Hope?"

Chester retorts, "That's not funny."

"I'm not being funny."

"Hope wouldn't do that."

"She's acting odd lately."

"Hope'd do her own shootin'."

Bob queries, "Am I missin' somethin'?"

Chester simply states, "Thankfully nobody knows what happened." *'Who'd shoot at Luke? And why?'*

Luke follows Chester to the rodeo barn to clean his cut before hearing a sport's car arrive. *'That's not Colt.'*

The driver revs the engine before shutting it off.

"Who the hell's doin' that on my ranch? They'll spook the horses."

Luke notices a long-haired woman step out of the black Ford Mustang Shelby GT500.

"Oh shit! She's back."

"Who's back?"

Holly runs from the house screaming. Chester groans, "Trouble! Meet me in the office in a moment."

Chester furiously stomps towards the women hugging and speaks to them before entering the house. He lets the screen door slam shut.

"Is that my cue?"

Luke approaches Holly and her brunette friend.

"This is my best friend, Jazzy. Jazlynn Moore. She's a professional bodybuilder."

Luke guardedly tips his hat.

"This is Luke."

"Nice to meet you, Jazlynn. *She's got an awfully hungry look in her eyes.*'

"Call me Jazzy. Shoot, cowboy, y'all can call me anythin' anytime y'all want."

Luke hears Jazlynn's Texas drawl through her suggestively laced invite. *'I understand Chester's assessment now.'*

"Damn. Holly, I've forgotten how good cowboys look."

"Find your own. This one's mine."

"Yours? Nah. Y'all ain't fixin' to settle down with one yet."

Luke examines Jazlynn's five-foot eight inch muscular yet rather feminine physique. She's barely clothed in a pink sports bra and black low-rise athletic shorts revealing her belly piercing and several decorative tattoos on her arms, ribcage, and legs. Her long straight hair is dark brown until halfway down where it's dyed dirty blonde. *'Jazlynn's actually quite attractive. Hot even.'*

"I've got work to do. Nice meeting you, Jazlynn."

"Jazzy. I'll be around. A lot."

Luke tips his hat again and enters the house. *'Is Jazlynn worse than Holly?'*

Chester unexpectedly interrogates Luke. "Y'all sure you know nothin' 'bout that shootin'?"

"Nothing."

"Don't be hidin' nothin'. People are at risk." *'Luke doesn't reveal much of anything personal.'* "Let the real person out or it'll tear ya apart."

'Chester sounds like Hank.'

"Look, y'all showed up here with no usable skills. Now you're fixin' stuff. Learn from your past to shape your future. Figure out who ya want to be. I think y'all got a god-lit fire burnin' inside ya but you gotta control it 'n take it in the right direction."

Chester pauses. "Y'all could become a cowboy yet by the looks of the barn repair."

Luke feels a newfound satisfaction and recalls the Cowboy Code stating to take pride in one's work. *'Three months ago I wanted Chester or Hope to shoot me dead.'*

THREE

Chester enters the riding barn in a foul mood the next morning while Luke mucks stalls.

"I didn't fight in a world war so politicians could flush this country down the toilet today. Those bastards care only 'bout themselves. This government can't run shit 'n those D.C. bozos work for us. Not the other way 'round. Why's everyone forgot that? To top it off, I've gotta deal with Holly's worst influence."

Scooter motions Luke to remain quiet.

Chester thinks, *'That hussy'll distract my men 'n git someone hurt again. Millie, I wish y'all were still here. I miss ya.*

Scooter fills Luke in after Chester rides Waylon out of sight. "Chester's mood's all cattywampus this time of year. It's best to leave him alone. We lost Millie this time last year. He's missin' his son. And Jazlynn's back. And the state of the country he loves has gone to shit."

"I understand Chester then." *'I'm that way in September when I lost my parents.'*

"How so?"

"I just do." *'Chester was molded in a different time like my dad was. They're cut from the same cloth. I was raised to think the same way with the same values, morals, and integrity. People took care of themselves and each other. They didn't depend on the government. The government's not supposed to rule us like a tyrant.'*

Chester searches for solutions and processes problems on rides. Luke finds good and bad memories emerging from dark corners of his mind and seeks peace in his room. Hank's conversations create emotional conflicts which interfere with Luke's idea of returning to Illinois.

'I've made a lot of poor decisions and mishandled bad times. Should I stay here? Or go back?'

Chester's shrewdly alluded to the possibility for Luke to remain on the ranch of his own volition. He's encouraged Luke's growth and maturity while cultivating useful skills. Holly stirs things up by inviting Jazlynn to breakfast. Her reputation and conduct around men is worse than Holly's. Chester issues a stern warning when he sees her.

"Act up in any way 'n I'll throw you off my ranch."

"Chester, I like it rough."

"There's somethin' seriously wrong with you."

Holly attempts to quell Chester's worries. "Grand-daddy, Jazzy'll be with me. She'll behave."

"Ha. I'll believe that when I see it."

Jazlynn smiles, *'New pleasure targets.'*

Holly grumbles after breakfast. "Jazzy, Luke's drivin' me crazy. Grand-daddy threatened to shoot him dead if he hooks up with me. So he's tryin' to avoid me."

"Maybe he'd rather hook up with a gym bunny."

Holly's concerned Jazlynn's right. "Don't try stealin' Luke 'til I've had him."

"We've shared guys before. I don't follow rules. Neither do you. Who cares who gets him first?"

"I've worked too hard this time. I'm gittin' tangled up with Luke first."

"I have needs too. I'm not competin' for a while."

Jazlynn's light brown eyes reveal her perpetually scheming thoughts. Her muscular physique and dominating personality intimidate competitors without detracting from her feminine charms.

"I'm gonna go to the gym too, okay."

"Are ya gonna just look pretty or actually work out?"

"Both. By the way, y'all won't believe what happened the other day."

"Try me."

"Hope kissed Luke."

"What? No way. Hope? She's a born again celibate after her divorce."

"Yup. She flaked out 'n hates Luke for breakin' Ben's jaw 'n nearly shot him twice."

"No shit. That's messed up. But so is Hope. Does she still work out?"

Chester contemplates an observation. *Luke's more onry when Hope 'n Faith don't visit. Why?*

Havoc ensues when Luke's assigned to learn desk duties for guests. He's constantly fending off Holly and Jazlynn's flirtatious advances until Chester summons him to the office.

"What was I thinkin'? Saddle up horses."

Luke hears the TV after leaving the office. *Why's that on?*

Hope's watching a movie with Katie. A woman's voice sings about taking someone broken, scarred, and bruised just the way they are after expressing she's not in need of saving. Katie notes the despondent looks Hope and Luke give each other. Chester's booming voice ends the moment.

"Those horses ain't gonna saddle themselves."

Chester sees Jazlynn enter before Luke leaves. "Watch your ass. Leave Luke 'n my wranglers alone."

"Your men watch my ass 'n Luke's a tall glass of iced tea I'd like to drink."

"I said watch it."

Jazlynn further frustrates Chester, "Luke might like my lovin'."

Hope's disturbed by Jazlynn's disrespectful attitude. "Y'all best obey Chester. His ranch, his rules."

"Bless your heart, Hope. Honey, I'm gonna do to Luke what Holly ain't yet. Better 'n more often too."

Jazlynn returns to Holly while Chester follows Luke to the barns. They hear a rough running engine and turn to see an old, rusty, two-toned red over white pick-up pull up to the house.

'Who's drivin' that piece of shit here?'

Chester instantly recognizes the scraggily bearded man wearing a beat up cowboy hat. "You've gotta be shittin' me. That sonofabitch dares step foot on my ranch after our last run-in."

Luke notices the stranger's slightly bow-legged. Chester rushes towards the man and hollers "Get off my ranch."

"That's no way to greet your grand-nephew."

"There ain't nothin' grand 'bout you. I disowned you years ago."

"Our bloodline still shows us as kinfolk no matter what you say or do, Chester."

Katie hears Chester's angered tone through the closed window and peers between the blind's slats. *'What's he doin' here?'*

"We ain't been kin for a long time. You and your daddy screwed that up."

Randy Kinkead smirks after Chester gruffly addresses him. "Is that so? Gimme what's mine. Y'all won't see me again."

"You'll get nothin'. Get off my ranch or I'll call the sheriff to bring ya somewhere familiar."

"Fine, have it your way. For now. I'll be back for what's mine."

"Y'all'll get a double-barreled load of buckshot if'n ya return."

Randy's crooked grin indicates Chester's threat is meaningless. "We'll see 'bout that."

Scooter approaches Luke, "Dia duit."

He sees the two men, "Thank goodness neither has a gun. They'd be shootin' it out."

"Who's that?"

"That's old trouble."

"What did you call me? Dee what?"

"It's pronounced Dee-ah-gwit. It's an Irish way to say hello."

Luke watches Hope step onto the deck with her gun drawn and force Randy to leave.

"Think he'll be back?"

"Unfortunately, yes."

Hope leaves but returns with Faith for supper.

FOUR

Luke's restless that night. *'Hope's affecting me even more than Jini did.'* Hope's warm electrifying kiss fills Luke's mind with thoughts like a floral garden's springtime bouquet fills the air. *'This ranch is changing my outlook and attitude. I never opened up to Linda. I was too ashamed to try. Something's pushing me to open up to Hope. Faith's got me feeling things I've never felt. Am I supposed to stay here?'*

Chester and Ben meet in the office. "Teach Luke the ranch operations. Educate him on all aspects of what we do."

"If he'll listen."

"Somethin' tells me he might."

"Yes sir."

Ben's surprised when Luke appears open to his guidance. *'Luke's settlin' in better than I expected 'n he's pickin' up what we're teachin' him. He's learnin' to ride pretty good already. Maybe his insults hide who he really is.'*

Luke's begun embracing Hank's advice about opening up after some deep reflection. Beth's pushing Hope to talk to Luke and joins her at the gym to discuss her options. Jazlynn and Holly enter and disrupt Beth's quiet consultation between sets. Jazlynn sours the atmosphere immediately by attempting to turn her workout into a competition with Hope.

"Y'all best watch out. I'm stronger now."

Jazzy's still bitter I've whooped her ass so many times.'

Hope finds a newly hired deputy introducing herself to Chester, Ben, and Luke the next day. Luke's well-meant attempt to tease Hope backfires.

"Holly mentioned Jazlynn outworked you at the gym yesterday, Hope."

Hope bristles, "Y'all weren't there. You don't know what happened. God, I hate you."

Luke responds half-heartedly, "Yeah, I remember."

Chester's about to question Hope's harsh attitude when a Live Oak sends fragments everywhere. Luke shouts for everyone to get down before the sound of a dirt bike's engine is heard departing.

'Who's shooting at us? Or me?'

The deputy scrambles to her squad and races down the driveway just ahead of screeching brakes and a crashing sound. The deputy's car returns a few moments later with a lone male in the back seat. She looks a bit shaken while the guy's laughing at her.

"Y'all ain't seen someone killed before, have ya?"

"Shut up."

The deputy gets out of the squad, "This one's lucky he's alive. A semi crashed into his buddy's pick-up pulling a trailer with the gate down. Looks like he pulled out in front of the truck and got hit head-on."

Luke quickly deduces what happened previously. *'The bike disappeared into the trailer.'*

The deputy's frazzled state by the crash scene has left her unfocused and hasn't properly secured the shooter. He escapes the squad and pulls a knife and lunges towards Hope. Luke recognizes the man's intent on killing someone and Hope's the closest to him. Luke intercepts the deadly threat mere feet from Hope while the guy lets out a banshee-like yell. Hope freezes while Luke rushes in. The knife's blade glides across Luke's arm before his fist swiftly strikes the guy's throat. The impact viciously throws the assailant backwards before falling to the ground and writhe in pain. He emits a dreadful gurgling sound while his eyes wildly stare at Hope and Luke. He brings his hands to his throat before going motionless and silent. The deputy moves in.

"He's dead."

Hope's stunned. "You killed him?"

Luke receives disbelieving expressions from everyone and hear him state, "Arrest me. Take me to jail."

"You saved this woman. You acted in self-defense."

Hope stares at Luke. *'Luke saved me again. After I told him I hate him.'* "Luke, I don't know what to say."

Luke snarls, "Save it, Hope. I heard you loud and clear. Officer, can I go back to work?"

"I'll need a statement. Where can I find you?"

"In one of those barns."

Ben walks with Luke. *'What do I say? Why did Hope say she hates Luke? Could Luke've killed me?'*

The men saddle horses for a bachelor party trail ride.

"Luke, double check Holly's scribble and make sure we got the right head count."

Ben comprehends Luke could've killed him and needs a few moments alone to process it. Luke's unhappy to enter the guest office until seeing Holly push a male guest away from her.

"Get away from me, asshole."

"You were throwing yourself at a stupid cowboy. C'mon, I enjoy your type every trip. I'll get you fired otherwise."

"Fat chance. You're harassing his grand-daughter."

They turn to see Luke's hostile expression.

"She said no. Respect that."

"Hey, it's the stupid cowboy. This doesn't concern you."

Luke nonchalantly approaches the obnoxious guest. "I'm not having a good day."

"Touch me and I'll sue you and the ranch."

Luke grabs the man's arm and menacingly twists it behind his back. "Unfortunately for you, I don't work here. I'm a convict on work release. Let's go for a little walk and talk."

Luke glares at Holly while escorting the guy outside. His eyes shoot daggers at her. Ben sees Luke re-enter the barn and motion for him to leave and nods his acknowledgement.

"Where are you going? Hey, stop this asshole. I'll sue if he hurts me."

"I just watched him kill a man. Y'all gotta survive first."

Fear grips the man stronger than Luke's hand.

"It's a shame when people don't listen on ranches. Injuries happen that way. Some don't survive. Catch my drift?"

"Are you threatening me?"

"Naw. Just warning this ranch could hurtcha."

The man's smug expression evaporates after realizing something could happen and look like an accident.

"So, you gonna take me to the train station?"

"Seriously? You're referring to a fake TV show?"

"Whatever. I'll find a hick girl in Austin later."

"Don't bet on it."

"This state's full of them."

"Possibly. But we escort groups so you don't get lost. I'm one of tonight's guides."

"We don't need babysitters."

"You're proving different."

Luke issues a command once Ben returns with Jake. "Get ready for the ride. Or find somewhere other than the desk to hang out."

Cody leads the remainder of the group and warns them. "No macho shit while you're in the saddle."

Jazlynn's following them and heads straight towards Luke and throws her arms around his neck to kiss his lips before he can react.

"My hero. Let's go on a date tonight."

"I'm working Jazlynn."

"Call me Jazzy already. Unless sex kitten works better."

Luke sees the guy's side-eyed glance and smirk. "Who needs the babysitter?"

"I'm all yours, cowboy."

Hope and Chester enter to check on the foal and find Jazlynn's arms around Luke.

'Of course Jazzy's all over Luke.'

Luke looks at Hope while stepping back from Jazlynn. His eyes express confused sadness.

"Luke, we need to talk."

"I'm busy."

Jazlynn adds, "Yeah, with me."

"No Jazzy. With work."

Hope feels helpless when Luke departs. *'Luke saves me again and I shit all over him. I ruined that chance to talk.'*

Ben hugs Hope. "Are you okay? That coulda ended different out there."

"Yeah. Thanks to Luke. He's so mad at me."

"Whatcha expect? You said you hate him."

The deputy notices Luke's stained shirt sleeve after finding him in the rodeo barn. "Are you okay?"

"I'm good. I did the right thing, right?"

"Yes."

"So there's no repercussions?"

"No sir."

'From the law anyway.'

Hope returns to Chester's side. "Why was Randy here?"

"He thinks I owe him."

"Do you?"

"Nope."

"He oughta be in jail. Let's check the foal then I wanna say hi to Holly. She's at the desk, right?"

Chester responds heatedly, "She better be."

Hope enters to hear Holly talking to Jazlynn. "Luke took that guy outta here for botherin' me."

"Yeah, well, I just kissed Luke in the barn."

Hope steps into view, "Guests are off limits. Holly, you weren't leadin' one on were you?" *'Why do I feel jealous?'*

Hope's glare shifts to Jazlynn. "Guests are off limits to you too. And so is Luke."

Holly comments, "Luke's pissed the guy was hittin' on me. I'm winnin' him over."

Hope worries, *'Did I push Luke towards Holly 'n Jazzy?'*
"I didn't lead the guy on. He saw me with Luke and tried his luck."
"Stop hittin' on Luke!"
"Luke's fair game, sister."
Jazlynn quips, "I'm glad I'm an only child."
Hope envies Holly's boldness. "Quit makin' trouble, Holly. First Ben, then Colt's friend at the barbecue, now a guest. You're draggin' Luke into your messes. Stop signaling guys here. Save it for the saloons."

"That's ironically rich. You haven't sent signals for years. Then ya kiss Luke."

Holly's cutting remark irritates Hope. *'Is Holly right?'*

Jazlynn's statement infuriates Hope. "I'm sendin' Luke signals. I want more than kisses."

Hope responds angrily, "I'll beat your ass like I did when we were kids."

"I'll whoop your ass now. I ain't that little girl anymore."

Hope exits furiously with thoughts crossing her mind. *'Am I sendin' any signals? What signals? Why? And to who?'*

Hope glimpses Luke in the pasture on horseback and catches her breath. *'Did I ruin my future?'*

FIVE

Ben enters Chester's office after supper. "Intense couple of days, huh?"

"That's an understatement."

"Why was Randy here?"

"Money. Same as always."

"Think he'll be a problem for the guest? Again."

"He's breathin'. He's a problem."

"Why was he even here?"

"Bob said he got released for good behavior."

"Randy can't even spell that let alone act it. His pappy gittin' shot should've turned him 'round. A bad tree produced a worse apple."

"Jazlynn's makin' things worse too."

Ben asks, "Should I run her off?"

"No. Holly'd probably follow her."

"Luke's at least becomin' useful. But did we see the real side of him today? A killer?"

"He's no killer. Luke's a protector like a sheepdog watchin' over the herd. I sent him to Austin to get away from here."

"One guest ain't happy 'bout that. He upset Holly somehow 'n Luke sent him a message with southern inhospitality."

"Didn't Hope have supper plans with Beth?"

"Beth cancelled to help a friend. Hope did ask where Luke was."

"Interestin'." *So why did Hope say she hates Luke?*

Hank shares his assessment with Chester after discussing the deadly incident with Luke the following morning.

"I've reassured Luke he acted properly to save Hope. I told him he had no recourse and made the right decision. He's troubled. And rightfully so but don't bring it up."

"Killin' a man ain't somethin' you put behind ya. I hope you're right. I hope Luke's okay."

"Luke's mentally 'n emotionally tougher than I first thought. He'll process this through and I can help him."

Chester gathers the wranglers for a short meeting. "Welcome to the first day of summer."

"Hasn't summer already been here?"

"Welcome to Texas, Luke. Summer heat arrives early. Y'all're goin' out with Danny 'n Kyle to mend fences. Severe storms are comin' this afternoon. Watch the skies."

Danny warns, "Our thunderstorms are legendary. They sing songs 'bout 'em."

Kyle adds, "Chicago storms ain't got nothin' on ours."

White cotton-ball clouds float harmlessly overhead while they prepare an old grazing area for the Longhorn. Avian chirps and chattering breaks the silence. Luke notices Danny and Kyle seem subdued.

"What's eating you two?"

"KOKE-FM's playin' some hip-hop rapper 'n callin' him country."

"We're losing our only good country station to a poisoned mindset."

Luke ponders their depressed responses. *I'll admit I like their real country and Red Dirt music. I don't like rap or hip hop either. It's too degrading to women and black people. Makes them seem like they don't matter.*

Luke's thoughts change direction. *'Can I live with killing a man? Even if I had to? Hope hates me but I promised to protect her. I'll stay as long as necessary. For Faith's sake. It's strange I miss Hope when she's not here.'*

The morning breeze becomes gustier before lunch. A faint smell of rain mixed with Texas florals drifts in. Luke comments, "Hey, the birds got quiet."

"Yeah. So?"

"That means storms are close."

The trio scrutinizes dark clouds approaching from the south.

"Shit! That's movin' fast. How'd y'all know about the birds?"

"We get storms too. The birds do the same thing."

"We should've used UTV's instead of horses."

Luke studies the ominous clouds. "That's coming in fast."

Brilliant bolts of lightning discharge from the dark clouds and strike the ground. Kyle commands, "Mount up! The horses are gettin' skittish."

"Shit, we waited too long."

Luke questions their urgency. "It's a thunderstorm. Big deal. We'll get wet. It's not the first time."

"This storm'll pound ya with golf ball sized hail. You're horse'll throw y'all off."

"Hurry up. Mother Nature's gonna pummel us."

Luke's horse instinctively races to stay ahead of the storm. He peers over his shoulder to see the weather's catching them. The trio barely reaches the barn ahead of a blinding bolt of lightning crackling as it hits the ground nearby. A deafening clap of thunder rumbles across the land to spook the horses and drown out the intense sizzle of nature's electricity. Guests stand inside the barn after a shortened trail ride and marvel at the storm's power. Raindrops pound the corrugated roof alongside more long rumbles of explosive thunder. Luke silently observes it all.

'Rain's louder on a metal roof. But soothing.'

Danny, Kyle, Billy, Jack, Cody, and Ben speak softly to calm the nervous steeds in their stalls. Luís, Henry, Jake, and Jesse are doing the same in the rodeo barn. Guests edge closer to the barn entrance to watch lightning dance across the wide open sky until opaque walls of rain fall to obscure the countryside.

'Kyle's right, I wouldn't want to get caught in this. Dad, we used to watch storms like this, right?'

Pea-sized hail thumps the roof and covers the ground in a frozen white blanket. The barn shudders during rumbles of thunder to add to the rhythm of large raindrops and hail in a chaotic cadence.

Luke remarks, "Texas thunderstorms are something y'all. I hope Faith's okay. She hates storms."

Cody whispers to Ben. "Interestin'. Luke's worried 'bout Faith?"

Billy addresses Luke. "Hey, y'all just said y'all."

Luke frowns. "Great I'm broken. I can't return to Chicago this way."

Billy grins. "Chicago won't miss ya. You're stuck here."

'Does everyone know about the missing person's report?'

Chester's alarmed after answering his phone. "Ben, run the show. Hank's in the hospital."

Luke's negatively impacted while helping the guys escort guests to their quarters once the storm eases up before returning to the barn.

"Cowboy Up! Check the Longhorns. Saddle up."

'The Cowboy Code makes more sense.' "Is this riding for the brand?"

Jack's cinching his saddle next to Luke. "Y'all're pickin' more up than I thought you would, city boy. Doin' what needs doin'. That's what we're gonna do now."

Luke dons a black oilskin duster and mounts his horse. Ben looks over at him.

"Y'all good?"

Luke nods before joining Jake, Jesse, and Henry. Ben calls out, "Let's ride."

They push the scattered Longhorn to a secure paddock in the rain. Luke notes, *'It's a lot cooler now.'*

The storm knocks power out to parts of the area so guests remain on the ranch and enjoy Katie's cooking. Hope and Faith arrive for supper.

"We lost power."

The skies clear to reveal a beautiful sunset while Katie updates Hope on Hank's situation.

"Maybe it's good the storm knocked the power out at home."

The guys debate between rodeo and baseball after supper. Hope's retired from the rodeo circuit and played ball when she was younger. *'I'll watch either. Luke's focused on Faith.'*

Jake's the last to enter and releases a long loud fart. "I feel so much better."

"Jake! Disgustin'!"

Hope follows Faith out of the room and suggests they go outside to enjoy the rain freshened air. The guys choke and cough and cuss Jake out before breaking into laughter in the horrid invisible cloud and toxic smell permeating the room.

"Shit. It's like Mars in here. No oxygen."

Jake quotes his favorite movie line. "More beans Mr. Taggart?"

Luke responds first, "Hell no. You don't need any."

Hope and Faith finally return. Hope starts fussing with her hair. "I should cut my hair. I'd look more professional with shorter hair."

Luke speaks without thinking, "No! Short hair wouldn't suit you. You're beautiful with long hair."

Hope's stunned gaze at Luke after his honest exclamation precedes her blushing.

"Sorry. You hate me. I'll shut up. Do whatever y'all wanna do." *'Hope doesn't want my opinion.'*

Faith objects immediately. "Momma, Luke's right. Y'all're beautiful with long hair. You didn't let me cut my hair last year. You said what Luke said, remember?"

Hope stares at Luke before addressing Faith. "Maybe you're right, Pecan." Hope glances at Luke. "I'll keep my hair long. Especially if y'all like it this way." *'Did Luke show interest in me? After what I said to him? Would Luke stay for me?'*

Everyone wonders if Hope's talking to Luke or Faith. The group's further baffled by Hope's extended second glance towards Luke. Chester enters to shift attention away from Hope.

"Hank's one pissed off sonofa, oh, hi Faith. The staff overreacted. Hank tripped on a table leg. I knew he was alright when he cussed out the prettiest nurse in the room."

"Hank's alright then?"

"Yes, Luke, Hank's fine. Madder'n hell 'bout bein' treated like an old man though."

Hope retorts, "Hank is an old man. Like you."

"Watch it daughter or y'all're outta the will."

Chester smiles, "Oh, Hope, I have a surprise for ya."

A man walks through the doorway dressed like he's worked on the ranch.

"Wyatt?"

"Hello darlin'. I've missed y'all."

Hope's shocked to see Wyatt and doesn't react during his prolonged hug in the sudden silence. Faith finally asks, "Who's this, Momma?"

"Um, an old friend from long ago." *'What's happenin'?'*

"We were more than friends."

Hope's eyes dart around until noticing Luke's confused expression. The guys welcome Wyatt with high fives and slaps on his back.

"Where the hellya been, Wyatt?"

"Arizona. But I'm movin' back to Texas."

Hope quietly asks, "Why've ya been in Arizona?"

"My wife 'n I ran her family ranch."

Hope visibly stiffens.

"Pardon me. Ex-wife. Still gettin' used to that."

Wyatt looks into Hope's eyes, "I married the wrong girl. Hope, you're as beautiful as ever."

'This can't be happening. I need to leave.' "I'd like to stay but I need to take Faith home. Can we catch up tomorrow? If you're still here."

"I'd love to catch up. I'm not goin' anywhere. I'll see you tomorrow."

CHAPTER

SIX

Chester spots Luke in the pre-dawn darkness. *'Luke's fightin' demons by the looks of it.'*

Luke relives the moments of killing the man. *'I had no choice. He'd've killed Hope. Faith would lose her mom. I had to. He got what he deserved, right? I need to talk to Hank again. Hope hates me so why does she want to talk? Who's Wyatt?'*

Chester lets Luke talk with Hank and notices he's exhausted when he re-enters the office. Luke hands the phone to Chester.

"Hey Hank, let me call ya back in a moment." Chester ends the call. "Did Hank help ya?"

"Yeah."

"Y'all look like somethin' else is buggin' ya."

"The guys told me Hope planned on a life with Wyatt. Hope's told me she hates me but wants to talk." *'Why should we talk? I've never had a chance with Hope.'*

"That was a long time ago."

"Where do you need me?"

"Saddle horses for the big trail ride. Holly's leadin' this one 'n bringin' Jazlynn along."

"Great."

Chester calls Hank back after Luke leaves. "Whaddya think 'bout Luke?"

Hope walks in unexpectedly. "Did you invite Wyatt here?"

"Nope. He was in the driveway last night. Y'all're actin' like it's a bad thing."

"I never expected to see Wyatt again. Not after the way he left me."

"Wyatt couldn't refuse that offer."

"He didn't even say goodbye."

Wyatt's done pretty good for himself. Champion bull rider turned champion bronc buster."

"He took care of himself. We talked 'bout forever together. Then he was gone."

"Wyatt had a dream to chase. But he's back. What does that mean?"

"I don't know. I'm gonna check on the foal."

Hope's plans to talk with Luke go awry when Jazlynn enters the barn first. Hope remains out of sight.

"Luke, come ridin' with me. Or maybe y'all wanna ride me instead."

Hope steps into view and rolls her eyes after Jazlynn's seductive invitation.

"Somethin' botherin' ya, Hope?"

"You. Jazzy, you bother me. Trouble happens when you're around."

"Well bless your heart. I hear y'all got a man killed here."

"Shut up, Jazzy. I'll knock the vamp outta you."

"I'll beatchur bitchy ass."

Chester enters, "No fightin' on my ranch. Take this elsewhere."

Hope's startled, "Sorry Chester. I'll finish and head to my next client." *Dammit, I really wanna talk to Luke.*

Chester addresses Jazlynn. "Y'all bring that up again Jazlynn 'n y'all'll never step foot here again."

Hope and Jazlynn's combative exchange piques Chester's curiosity. *Hope's upset Jazlynn's flirtin' with Luke. Interestin'. Come to think of it Hope stresses when other women talk to Luke now. This is new.*

A voice calls out. "Hope? Are ya in here?"

Wyatt strides confidently up to Hope. "This place sure brings back fond memories, don't it?"

Luke notes, *'Hope's caught off guard Wyatt's here.'*

Jazlynn jumps at the opportunity to irritate Hope again. "Well, Hope's one true love returns to roost. Wyatt, y'all reclaimin' Hope?"

"Jazlynn, you've changed 'n yet ya haven't. Howya doin'?"

"Never been better."

Wyatt's attention returns to Hope. "Could we go somewhere 'n catch up?"

"Her bedroom's got a vacancy. Wanna fill it?"

Chester angrily orders, "Zip it, Jazlynn. One more comment 'n y'all're done."

Luke unexpectedly interrupts, "I'll go on the trail ride with Jazzy 'n Holly."

Hope's noticeably concerned expression changes when Colt walks in and shoots a condescending glance at Luke. Colt's arrogance disappears when he sees Chester.

"Hello darlin'."

Jazlynn's elated. "This keeps gettin' better."

"CJ? What are you doin' here?"

"I wanna ask you and Faith to supper. Who's this? Wait. Wyatt, is that you?"

"Howdy Colt. Am I missin' somethin'? Hope, you datin' Colt?"

"What? No!"

Chester senses Luke's aggravation during the newly developing situation and scrutinizes Hope's response. *'Luke's antsy to leave. Hope's unhappy to see Colt 'n unsure 'bout Wyatt bein' here.'*

"I'm not sure about supper, Colt."

"Don't let me stop you, Hope. I have a business call this evenin'. I'd like your number though."

Wyatt kisses Hope's cheek after entering her number in his phone. "I'd like to get back what we had. I miss you."

Wyatt directs a sideways glance at Colt before exiting the barn. Holly enters with guests and observes Wyatt momentarily then makes a beeline for Luke. *'Wyatt still looks good.'* "Luke, wanna join us?"

Chester shocks Hope, Holly, and Jazlynn, "Luke, be an extra trail guide today."

Hope's astonished until Colt regains her attention.

"I'd like to take you to Luby's. It's still Faith's favorite, right?"

"Y'all remember Faith likes Luby's?"

"Of course."

"Um, okay, sure, we can go to Luby's tonight."

Colt steps in like he's going to brush Hope's hair back only to tickle her instead. Hope giggles. "Stop. Y'all know I don't like bein' tickled. And not here."

Hope glimpses Luke's expression. *'Why does Luke look upset?'*

"You've never minded before."

"It's not proper behavior. *'Luke might get away with it though.'*

Chester interrupts, "Hope has work to finish."

Hope's relieved to have an escape from an uncomfortable predicament.

"Alright. See ya later, darlin'."

Colt casts a wicked smile towards Luke. *'That dumbass'll learn his place 'round me.'*

Chester contemplates what's unfolding. *'Hope got nervous 'round Colt. Does she know 'bout his comments? Nah. She'd beat him for those.'*

Chester sees Hope's annoyed Jazlynn and Holly surround Luke. *'Hope's not actually jealous, is she?'*

Jazlynn slips her hand into Luke's back pocket. "You can slide up in me as easy as this."

Hope's stomach knots up during Jazlynn's boldly crude sexual advance. *'Luke deserves someone better than Jazzy. But would he settle for me?'*

Luke's honestly spoken admission confuses everyone. "Something bad happens to ruin something good happening."

Hope wonders, *'What's Luke insinuatin'?'*

SEVEN

Luke sees Hope's truck after the trail ride. *'I thought Hope left.'*

"Cody, didn't Hope leave?"

"Hope's with Wyatt."

"Who's this Wyatt guy anyway?"

"Right. Y'all weren't here for that."

Cody explains, "Wyatt 'n Hope were hot 'n heavy on the rodeo circuit years ago. Even talked about gettin' hitched."

"Oh."

"Wyatt's Hope's first real love. Her first heartbreak too, I think. He left her without a goodbye to become a champion bull 'n bronc rider."

Luke mulls through thoughts while working. *'Why did Wyatt really leave Hope? Should I consider Holly? Or Jazzy? Wyatt's obviously back for Hope. Maybe I should head north.'*

Luke's sent to the office that evening but Chester signals him to remain quiet. Luke hears Hope's voice.

"Faith didn't enjoy supper tonight."

"That's a shame. Luby's is one of Faith's favorites."

"Faith didn't like CJ bein' there. She asked why Luke couldn't go. Colt got pissed at that."

Luke refrains from laughing. *'Serves him right.'*

"Luke'd never be allowed to go to Luby's, right?"

Chester ponders Hope's inquiry. *'Why's Hope askin' that if Wyatt's back?'* "Do ya wanna take Luke?"

"What? No! That's ridiculous. You'd never let that happen."

Chester glances at Luke. "How 'bout I treat you 'n Faith tomorrow. We ain't been there in a while."

"Faith'd love that. Colt mostly ignored Faith after gettin' her food. He was so bowed up when Faith mentioned Luke. I thought that was odd."

"I'll see you tomorrow."

Luke's indignant snort amuses Chester. "Faith disrespected Colt to his face."

"Y'all ain't got the right to judge." *'Although you know Colt well enough.'* "Tomorrow's ride is a bunch of inexperienced riders. Keep 'em safe."

"We'll watch over 'em sir."

"Danged if y'all're soundin' more Texan every day."

Luke frowns. *'Is that good?'*

Faith's comment brings a grin back. *'Good job, Faith.'*

The next day's trail ride is uneventful and all return to enjoy lunch poolside. Cody realizes Holly hasn't put towels out and calls her.

"Holly, where's the towels?"

"They're up at the house pool. I'm stuck here with a guest problem."

Luke offers to retrieve the towels. *'Hope danced sexily at the barbecue. Why am I thinking about that?'*

A woman's voice disrupts Luke's thoughts. "Hey Luke, play with me."

Jazlynn's tanning topless so Luke diverts his eyes.

"Don't be shy. Look at me like ya wanna. I'm all yours."

Luke looks at Jazlynn's half naked body involuntarily. "Cover up. Families are here." *'Jazzy's hot.'*

Jazlynn slips her thong off. "Here's the whole package."

Luke grabs the towels but glances at Jazlynn's naked physique before leaving. *'Am I crazy for not hooking up with Jazzy?'*

"Y'all know ya want me, Luke."

'Jazzy could be right.'

Ben intercepts Luke at the guest pool. "Chester needs you in the office."

Luke worries Jazlynn has something to do with the reason. *'Good, Jazzy's not here. I'm crazy to pass on her. It's more crazy I'd rather find a serious relationship again.'*

Chester greets Luke on the deck and notices movement down the driveway.

"That sonofabitch is back."

Luke notices the truck peripherally. "I take it you don't want him here."

"That's an understatement. That asshole waltz's in like he owns the ranch."

"Why does he think that?"

"Because he's from my brother's side of the family."

Randy haphazardly parks across the driveway and gets out. Chester furiously shouts, "Get that wreck off my ranch."

"I want what's mine, Pop's. Then I'm outta here."

"You'll get nothin' from me."

"You owe me old man. You stole from my daddy 'n he's dead."

Luke detects pained anger in Randy's voice.

"Your daddy's dead for stickin' his nose where it didn't belong. Like y'all're now."

"I oughta help you reach the great round up in the sky sooner."

Luke responds to Randy's threat. "Back off, asshole. Or start digging for six and lay down. That's where I'll put you."

Chester hears the dark sinister fury in Luke's voice. *'Luke hides his menacing side well. Until he needs to show it. He carried out a deadly attack without warnin'.'*

Randy's not intimidated and bumps Luke. "I've heard worse from tougher 'n I was last one standin'."

'Randy's been drinking.'

Luke's hand swiftly chops Randy's throat to double him over gasping for air. "That's your only warning. You won't walk away next time. Don't make me lose my temper."

Randy hisses his threat before staggering back to his truck. "I'm not done here. With either of you."

"You ain't too smart, are you?"

Chester glances sideways at Luke. *'Would Luke retaliate like he says?'* "You good?"

"Yup."

"Alright. Moving on. There's a couple wantin' to go the bass pond. The woman's gonna propose and wants it on camera. Here's her phone. I guess they met while fishin'. Give 'em space afterwards. Ben's prepping horses for all y'all."

Luke fills Chester in afterwards. "The poor guy was clueless at first. She had a ring he could put on her finger. He was shocked. I wonder how I'd react if a woman proposed to me?"

"Y'all got another task. Change 'n wash up. Meet at my truck in fifteen minutes."

"Now?" *'Chester's taking Hope and Faith to dinner soon.'*

Chester's waiting when Luke returns. "Sit in back."

"The back? Why?"

"Don't question me. You're my entertainment tonight."

"I don't wanna be your entertainment."

"Shut up! Sit down, 'n belt in."

Faith bursts from the house when Chester pulls into the driveway.

"Grand-daddy! I'm happy we're goin' to Luby's together."

Faith's loud shriek causes Hope to come running. "Faith, did you fall? Are you okay?"

Hope's heart skips a beat noticing Faith hugging Luke. "What's goin' on, Chester?" *'How should I feel about this?'*

"Luke earned a night off."

"Uh-huh. Interestin' timing."

'Hope's not upset by Luke's presence.'

"Colt ruined last night."

"Faith, that's rude. Colt tried bein' nice to you."

"No Momma. He doesn't ever play with me or help me like Luke does."

Chester comments, "Luke does help ya 'n share time with you."

"Yeah, he does."

Hope stares into Faith's innocent blue eyes while Chester winks at Faith.

"Yup. Luke plays with y'all instead of workin' for me."

"Faith, Pecan, Luke helps you but he's not stayin. Colt lives here. Luke's nicer than I thought but he doesn't live here."

Chester retorts, "Luke could stay."

"Don't start, Chester."

Luke responds, "Faith, your mom'll be happy when I leave. That's clear." *'I'm not sure I can stay now.'*

"Momma, Colt doesn't look at you like Luke does."

"How does Luke look at me?"

"Like he really cares about you, Momma."

Faith's revelation reddens Luke's cheeks. *'Am I showing something I can't hide anymore?'*

Chester notes Luke's uncomfortable reaction in the rearview mirror. "Don't forget, Wyatt's back too."

Hope's stunned and shifts in her seat. *'Why would Faith say that? Is it true?'* "Chester, you're puttin' the cart in front of the horse." *'Luke happily gives Faith attention. Colt barely acknowledged her last night. That was a debacle.'*

Chester and Hope worry when Luke steals green beans off Faith's plate at dinner. Luke uses them as a bug's antennae and walrus tusks to make Faith laugh hysterically. Surrounding tables find her laughter contagious along with Chester and Hope.

'Faith really does get along with Luke. Few can take food off Faith's plate and not get yelled at.'

An older couple stopping by the table amuses Chester.

"All y'all make a lovely family."

"You have a beautiful daughter."

Hope's shocked when Chester responds, "They do make a nice family, don't they?"

Luke glances at Hope before they look at Chester. Hope's dismayed Chester alludes they're a family in front of Faith and admonishes him on the way to the truck.

"Have you lost your mind? Why would you say that? In front of Faith?"

Faith didn't hear them. She was laughing."

"Thank God for that."

Hope peeks at Luke but looks away when he looks at her. *'Could Luke make a good dad? Or a good husband? What about Wyatt?'*

Luke grills Chester once they're alone. "Why did you tell that couple we're a family? Hope hates me. She doesn't want me here. It was stupid to say in front of Faith."

"Faith didn't hear them. It was easier to agree instead of embarrassing her."

"So you were protecting Faith?"

"Faith seems to like you. You must have some redeeming qualities."

"Hope's pissed. Again. I can't win with her." *'Even if she may have what I'm looking for in a woman.'*

Luke watches the blazing sunset and dwells on thoughts. *'Why does Faith like me? I enjoy helping her.'*

Katie steps outside for a deep, relaxing breathe of evening air and enjoy the various shades of reds and oranges blending with gray, purple, and black hues in the clouds.

"Hello Luke, beautiful sight, huh? Smell that? That's Texas."

"I do smell something other than horses, Longhorns, and Jake. What is it?"

"That's Texas Sagebrush. It's a spicy bitter smell. It stays around as long as the weather stays warm."

"So forever?"

Katie chuckles. "It can get cold here. We burn Sagebrush indoors to help kill airborne bacteria from time to time. It grows all 'round here. Look for small soft silver or gray-green leaves and lavender to purple flowers."

"It smells oddly nice. I've never smelled anything like it before."

"Maybe y'all'll stay in Texas longer than you planned then?"

'Why isn't Faith afraid of me? Why does Hope hate me so much? She planned a life with Wyatt. And now he's back. Would Hope even consider me? Could I stay for Hope?'

EIGHT

Chester allows guests to work alongside his wranglers to better understand the hardships of cowboy living not necessarily shown in movies or TV shows.

"There ain't nothin' romantic about cowboys sweatin' in high heat or freezing their balls off to push cattle or mend fence in all weather conditions."

Watching guests attempting cowboy tasks amuses Luke. *Did I look like that?*

Ben reveals Chester's true intention. "People don't push through perceived physical and mental limitations to succeed so they fail. Cowboys don't make excuses. We simply push through barriers and obstacles to accomplish the task. Triple digit heat, rain, even cold 'n snow doesn't stop us. The job needs doin'. No excuses. Y'all've learned that."

Luke's martial arts' training and gym workouts conditioning has gained respect from the wranglers. *I'm not who I was anymore.*

Chester notices Hank's mood's improved and questions the desk nurse after a visit.

"That young fella's visits've been good for Hank."

'That old coot 'n this young punk are becomin' fast friends. Who's helpin' who? I wouldn't've seen this comin' if it were lit up on a billboard.'

Hank checks on Luke's emotional and psychological condition at the ranch. Hope's surprised to see Hank and Luke sitting on the deck when she arrives to check on the foal. Cody greets her on the way to his truck.

"Hey Hope, how ya doin'?"

"Why's Hank sittin' outside? It's too hot. Why's he here?"

Hank's visitin' Luke."

"Why?"

"Rumor has it Luke's a good influence for Hank. They get along."

"Luke? A good influence? How?"

Cody smirks, "Luke did save you. Helped Faith. He's gettin' to be a pretty good wrangler."

"That doesn't make him a good influence."

"We might've misjudged him. Like people misjudgin' I'm a genius."

"Nice try, Cody. Y'all ain't stupid but you're no genius. Are ya still tryin' to convince people soy milk is real milk?"

"It is."

"Not even close."

"Damn. I lost a bet to Luke."

"I hope you didn't bet much."

Hope walks to the deck and says hello to Hank but leaves without saying a word to Luke. *I don't know what to say to Luke. Chester's comment and Wyatt's return have thrown a wrench into my plans. I loved Wyatt but I never thought I'd see him again. And how do I really feel about Luke?'*

Hank notices a sparkle in Hope's eyes during her glance at Luke. *'That look said what Hope can't.'*

Luke mutters, "I'm going back to Chicago."

Hank grunts and points towards Hope. "That's a damn good reason to stick around."

Luke rolls his eyes. "She acted like I didn't exist. Hope hates me. Some guy named Wyatt's back."

Chester steps outside before Hank can respond.

"Luke, Scooter needs help."

"Yes sir. Have a good chat with Hank."

Luke eyes both men. "Crap, I'm sounding like that Irish windbag now."

Hank and Chester laugh.

"He goes on and on about kissing the Blarney Stone for the gift of gab. He already talks too much."

Hank comments after Luke walks away, "Everyone's rubbin' off on that boy. Our words 'n phrases."

Chester thinks, *'Luke wouldn't sound like that sittin' in jail.'*

"Luke mentioned Wyatt's back."

"Yup. He showed up two days ago. Said he's movin' back to Texas."

"Wyatt hung the moon for Hope back then. How's Luke reactin' to Wyatt?"

"He ain't reacted one way or 'nother 'bout Wyatt."

"Yet."

Chester tells Hank about the dinner outing. "Hope 'n Luke protested me sayin' they made a good family but not in a heated way."

"Interestin'. Perhaps telling even. I believe Hope's becomin' open to the idea of a relationship again. I think Luke's got somethin' to do with that."

"Hope's still cold towards Luke 'n he still plans to leave."

"Luke ain't been given the right reason to stay. At least not yet. He still wants to punish himself for his past. Hope's rowin' the same boat. Neither's moving towards positive changes. I think I've just figured out a major piece of the puzzle 'bout Luke's life and who he is. I'm gonna talk to Hope in a few days."

Faith's unhappy when Hope starts spending time with Wyatt and grows cold and distant to Luke. "Momma, why can't I see Luke?"

"It's complicated Pecan. I need answers to questions."

"What answers?"

"Wyatt's part of my past before you." *'I'm not sure if he's meant to be part of my future or not.'*

"I still wanna see Luke."

"Honey, Luke's only here 'cause he hurt Ben. He'll be leavin' soon."

"I'm gonna ask Luke to stay. He's nice to me. Like really nice. Not pretend nice. Can I see him?"

Hope dwells on Faith's intentions, descriptions, and question. *'Luke has been genuinely nice and honest to Faith. And maybe me too.'*

Hank calls Hope several days later. "Hope, why are ya avoidin' Luke?"

"I'm not avoidin' Luke. I'm spendin' time with Wyatt. I'm protectin' Faith. Luke's leavin', Wyatt's returnin'."

Hank speaks bluntly, "Hope, shut up 'n listen. After years of bein' a psychologist, I read people rather well. Luke's workin' through problems just like y'all are. I'm gonna partially break my agreement with Luke to explain a few things to you."

Hank divulges certain information to Hope then asks, "Do you trust me, Hope?"

"Of course I trust you. But understand my position. Wyatt's return has to mean somethin', right? Luke's passing through. Wyatt's said he's back for good 'n he missed me. Faith needs someone who'll stay."

"Faith's fine 'round Luke."

"I don't trust Luke."

"Luke killed a man to protect y'all. That's twice he's rescued you. How well do you know Wyatt now?"

"I know Wyatt well enough still. We loved each other. I might still love him." *'I think.'*

NINE

Chester catches Beth while she visits Ben at the ranch. "Beth, take Luke with you today."

"That's a bad idea, Chester."

"It's Hank's idea."

"Hope's gonna be pissed."

"Take him anyway."

Hope's outraged to see Luke in Beth's truck. "What's he doin' here?"

"Ask Chester 'n Hank. I said it's a bad idea."

Hope phones Chester. "What the hell are ya doin', Chester? Y'all're wreckin' our girl's day."

Hope tells Beth. "I'm drivin' too."

Luke knows his presence agitates Hope. *'Why did Chester think this would be a good idea?'*

Hope stops to pick up a client's feed order. Luke offers to help.

"Get away from me. I'm capable of doin' this myself. I wish Wyatt were here. Stay in Beth's truck or I'll actually shoot you this time."

Beth observes Luke's dejected return. *'Hope burned Luke like fire through paper. What's her deal?'*

Two young men pass Hope while she loads the truck bed. One guy moves ahead to turn and push his friend into Hope. The second guy grabs Hope's breasts and gropes her for several seconds. Hope's too shaken by the unexpected occurrence to react. Everyone expects Luke to beat the two men but he remains in Beth's truck while they laugh at their juvenile prank.

The second guy announces, "Her tits are as real as they're big."

"Yeah? And her legs go all the way to Heaven."

Beth yells out, "Luke, why aren'tcha beatin' those assholes?"

Luke answers edgily, "Hope said she'd shoot me. She doesn't want my help. She'd let Wyatt help."

Beth realizes Luke won't disobey Hope's order. *'Hope's her own worst enemy.'*

Hope's silently admonishing herself. *'What's wrong with me? Why did I tell Luke not to help me? I want Luke to beat these assholes. I keep hurtin' Luke. I'm so tired of bein' treated like an object instead of a person. Luke's never done that. Would Wyatt 'n I still work?'*

Beth approaches the two men and slaps the first one before kicking the second one in the groin. She rotates and punches the first guy's nose to bloody him before returning to stare at Luke. "Y'all ain't the only one who knows karate. You just hit harder."

Luke does step from the truck to send the two men running off while Hope watches Faith walk over to Luke. *'What could Faith possibly be thinkin' right now?'*

"Why didn't you help Momma?"

Faith's question clearly demoralizes Luke.

"Your mom's mad at me. She told me not to help her. I didn't want to disrespect her wish. It may've been the wrong choice but I don't want to make things worse."

Hope hears Faith's tone and Luke's answer. *'How do I explain this so Faith'll understand?'*

Hank's words come back to Hope regarding Luke's life before the ranch. *'I hurt Luke for no reason. I've set a bad example for Faith. What's wrong with me?'*

Luke briefly approaches Hope. "This wouldn't've happened if I weren't here. This is my fault. I'm goin' back to the ranch. And I'll leave as soon as possible."

Hope speaks up while Luke backs off. "I don't know if I can trust you. I need time to sort things out."

"I probably won't be here when you do. But Wyatt's back anyway."

Luke's statement strikes deep emotionally and reduces Hope to tears. *'What's the right decision?'*

Beth calls out while Luke walks away. "Luke, wait, I'll have Ben pick you up."

Hope ponders Luke's final words during the remainder of the day.

TEN

Beth confronts Hope at the ranch. "What's wrong with you? I can't wrap my head 'round yesterday. Stoppin' Luke from helpin' ya. Why? What were y'all tryin' to prove?"

"I didn't know those assholes would show up."

"You didn't fight 'em. You made Luke feel like shit. In front of Faith. Is this about Wyatt?"

"I froze. Beth, I froze. I thought about the first attack. It's complicated. I don't wanna talk here."

"Tough shit, honey. We're talkin' 'bout it now."

"I don't want to."

"You turned Luke into a gelding. He's a mustang. Your need for control of everything neutered him. I did what he shoulda done. Faith's disappointed Luke let her down. That hurt Luke more than any punch. He said y'all're mad at him. Again. Why? What's wrong with you? Luke's a decent guy 'n you're bein' unfair to him."

Hope hesitates before her confession. "I'm startin' to feel somethin' for Luke."

"What? Hatred? That's all I see. Ben said Luke's more determined to leave. I wonder why?"

"Why is Luke here? Why did Wyatt come back? What if Wyatt came back for me?"

"The Lord works in mysterious ways. Y'all best figure it out. Before Luke leaves."

"I'm afraid. Nothin' good seems to last."

"Thanks. So our friendship won't last?"

"You know what I mean."

"I'm not sure I do anymore. Ben mentioned Luke's revealed a wicked sense of humor after your kiss. Coincidence? What about that kiss. You ain't showed interest in men for years. Then this. What if Luke has feelin's for ya? Ever consider that? He hasn't pushed you away."

"Luke's said he's leavin'."

"You're pushin' him to. Nobody's asked him to stay."

"That kiss, it made me want him. Really want him. But I could get Wyatt back."

"Kiss Luke again. He might could stay for that. Wyatt's back but is he what he was?"

"I kissed Wyatt the other day. It felt good. Sorta like old times. But also different."

"Honey, y'all got decisions to make. Right quick."

ELEVEN

Wyatt overhears the guys talking about Hope's incident and Luke's inaction and confronts Luke outside the riding barn. "Hey jackass, why didn't you help Hope yesterday?"

"That's none of your business."

"Hope is my business."

"You left her once. You could leave her again."

Wyatt attempts to intimidate Luke. "Do y'all know who I am? I'll mess you up."

Luke laughs, "You definitely don't know who I am. I'm gonna help Katie."

Chester initially sent Luke with Katie to H-E-B as punishment only to realize the food bill dropped considerably. Katie informs him Luke finds the best deals.

"So Luke's punishment pays me dividends."

Luke's more open with Katie on shopping excursions after learning she's trustworthy with their conversations. He stops at one particular aisle.

"I need something extra today."

"Should I add it for the future?"

"Nah. One time's enough."

Katie notes Luke's mischievous gleam when he returns with a bag of soy beans.

"Whatcha fixin' to do with that?"

"It's a surprise."

Katie's eyebrows rise up. "If you say so."

Cody had questioned Katie about soy milk. *'Luke's gonna poke fun at Cody. Soy milk's a plant-based product and not real milk.'*

Katie benefits from Luke's company because the female employees go out of their way to help Luke find items. Katie's amused when one assistant manager who doesn't like her always bags groceries for Luke. *'She's so smitten with Luke. Any of these ladies would say yes before Luke finished askin' them out.'*

Luke excuses himself during supper and motions to Katie when he re-enters with the bag of soy beans hidden from sight.

'What's Luke up to?'

"My glass is empty." Luke sets the bag down in front of Cody. "I'd like more milk please."

Cody's cheeks turn beet red while everyone bursts out laughing. Jake's comment worsens Cody's discomfort.

"Finally! Now will ya shut up 'bout soy milk bein' real milk? Cows make milk. Not plants. Even I know that."

Hope laughs at Luke's prank which embarrasses Cody further.

"Are you sidin' with the enemy, Hope?"

"Hey, the enemy's right."

Luke hears Hope's wording. *'Hope thinks I'm the enemy.'*

Hope winks at Luke. *'Did I just do that?'*

Luke thinks, *'What was that?'*

Katie reconsiders Luke's disinterest at H-E-B after Hope's unusual gesture. *'Is that why Luke's so coy at the store?'*

TWELVE

Luke's wicked sense of humor matches his cutting insults. His quick wit and rapid thinking reveals itself more each day. Jake's been the ranch jokester but finds himself challenged and overwhelmed to retain his title. Cody complains to Ben on the way to the barn the next morning.

"That wasn't cool. I'll get even with Luke. He embarrassed me in front of everyone."

Ben rubs his jaw. "Luke gave ya beans. I got a broke jaw. Cowboy up buckle bunny."

"I can ignore his insults but he made me look foolish."

"Y'all brought it on yourself."

They enter the barn.

"Cody, what's wrong with this picture? Luke's already cleanin' stalls."

"Clearly, we've entered an alternate universe."

Ben smirks, "Nobody's beaten me in years."

"Chester might let me leave sooner."

Cody jokes, "Yeah 'n take all our redneck wisdom back north."

"That'd fit in a thimble."

Ben chuckles, "Luke's too quick for ya, Cody."

"Honestly, I'm not sure if the ranch has hurt or helped me."

Luke shifts to feeding and shares an apple with Bullet. *'I'm not telling these guys how I really feel.'*

Ben reviews Hope's reaction at supper. *'Why did Hope wink at Luke?'*

Chester and Ben discuss Luke after lunch.

"Luke's improvin' every day."

"He still annoys the guys when possible."

"Luke's a real enigma, Ben. I thought he was nothin' but a dumb-assed, arrogant, troublemakin' city boy. But he's turned into a pretty good cowboy. He shows leadership 'round guests."

"Luke's surprised the heck outta me. Savin' Hope after she nearly shot him, helpin' Faith with math."

Chester reveals, "Hope winged him on his second day."

"I'm amazed he's survived Hope's temper. Luke defended Holly as well."

"Yeah. And now Holly's chasin' him even more."

"I can't figure Hope out. She's different 'round Luke. She hates him but seems to like him too."

"And Wyatt's back."

Chester considers Hank's early assessment of Luke. *'Hank saw Luke for who he is.'*

Ben becomes Luke's next target. He starts calling him 'Tiny' instead of Scooter's choice of 'Big Ben' because he towers over Scooter. Luke's nickname is an antiphrasis styled moniker to honor old west movie characters he grew up. Ben turns Luke's joke around when he introduces himself to new guests.

"I'm the ranch foreman, Ben. I'll help y'all enjoy this week. Y'all can call me 'Tiny' like the old west cowboys with silly nicknames."

Scooter's livid so Luke suggests a nickname for him as well. "We could call y'all Festus."

"Keep your ideas to yourself, laddie."

Scooter bitterly complains to Chester.

Chester chuckles, "Honestly, I like it better."

Scooter walks off in a huff. Later, several male guests approach Ben before supper.

"Settle a debate for us."

"If I can."

"We say you're the toughest cowboy here."

"And we heard someone might be tougher. Who's right?"

Ben smiles. "I did bulldoggin' for years butchy'all gotta watch out for the cowpoke leanin' against that there fencepost."

Ben points at Luke chomping on a piece of straw while scanning the horizon.

"Him? No way! He's smaller than you."

"That cowboy'd knock y'all out with one punch."

"You're lying."

"Wish I was. He broke my jaw 'n knocked me out with one punch."

"That can't be true."

"You could find out yourself. I wouldn't recommend it though."

"Um, no that's okay."

Several women overhear Ben. "Is he dating anyone?"

"That cowboy's a tumbleweed rollin' through. The wind'll blow strong 'n send him on his way."

"Well, we'd like a date with a real cowboy."

Hope enters to check on guests before locking eyes with Luke for several seconds and turning away. Luke's gaze remains fixed on Hope.

"Y'all can ask but that cowboy's heart may not be for sale anymore."

Ben's turn of phrase confuses the women who happily walk towards Luke. Two male guests notice Hope.

"Now that's a smokeshow."

"That smokeshow'll burn ya for sayin' that."

"I'd like to handle that country girl's booty."

Ben studies Hope while the women fawn over Luke. *Hope looks concerned.'* "That's my little sis 'n that cowboy might be interested in her. So watch it."

Hope appears relieved the women seem disappointed while departing but tenses up when Wyatt shows up to hug and kiss her. *'Did Luke see that?'*

Hope notices Luke's looking at her until Wyatt heads for the guest office. Ben wanders over to greet Hope.

"Evenin' Hope. Looks like you 'n Wyatt are gettin' closer again."

"I'm not sure about that."

"Luke sure gets the ladies attention, don't he?"

"Ben, Luke knows he can't date guests, right?"

"Technically, Luke's not an employee. He can date anyone he wants. Hell, he could date you."

Hope responds instantly. "Why would you say that? Do you know something?"

Ben's amused and shrugs and shakes his head before Hope walks away. *'Huh, Hope didn't fight me on that or put me in my place.'*

Luke notices Hope and Wyatt holding hands from time to time during the evening. *'I guess Hope's made her choice.'*

THIRTEEN

Chester's presented with a unique opportunity at the end of June. "Ben, I'm takin' Luke somewhere today." *'Luke's not such a royal pain in the ass anymore.'*

Chester mystifies Luke after breakfast. "Clean up and wear somethin' nice."

Luke returns to find Chester by his truck. *'What does he have in store for me?'*

"Where are we going?"

"You'll know when we get there. I hope."

Chester pronounces certain road names, "We say things different 'round here. It separates tourists from Texans."

Chester lets several miles pass. "Do ya wanna be a bee or mosquito?"

Luke groans dramatically and slouches in the passenger seat. *'Terrific! Another speech. And I'm stuck. I oughta jump out.'* "Why would I want to be either of those?"

"Because one's a positive producer 'n the other's a negative nuisance."

"They're both nuisances in my book since they both sting."

Chester's responds testily, "Northern schools don't teach basics. Bees' sting. Mosquitos bite."

Luke's agitated and remarks, "We learn plenty up north. I see so many stories about southern people doing stupid things."

"Don'tchy'all believe much of the news nowadays. Most're spittin' out opinions for ratin's. No truth or facts. Texas has a lot of good schools 'n teachers. Don't change the subject."

Luke scowls dejectedly. "I'm in no mood for a lecture."

"Tough. Y'all gotta lotta learnin' to do."

"Alright smart man of all knowledge, am I supposed to be a bee or mosquito?"

"Shut your mouth 'n I'll tell ya."

Chester starts explaining, "Y'all're a dumb-assed mosquito. Ya show promise of becomin' a bee. Mosquitos are a negative nuisance. They're Satan's evil gift that steals your blood to make more mosquitos 'n spread filthy diseases. Bees on the other hand, they're positive and productive. They build hives, a community, like we build houses 'n neighborhoods. They work together to gather nectar and pollen to produce honey. They help nature pollinate plants which wouldn't survive otherwise 'n only take what they need but give back more. Like me owning land I won't sell to developers so people enjoy a simpler, tougher lifestyle for lifetime memories."

"They sting you."

"Only to defend the hive from threats. They don't sting for the fun of it. Bees die after stingin' ya. Hornets 'n wasps sting repeatedly."

"I know that. How does any of this apply to me?"

"Let me explain so even your thick skull understands. Mosquitos indiscriminately steal blood like criminals steal belongings 'n money. Some people die during the crime like people die from diseases from mosquito bites."

Luke rolls his eyes. "How are bees better?"

"Listen 'n learn somethin' useful."

"Excuse me oh wise one."

"Bees mind their own business unless threatened. They don't look for trouble or create trouble 'n only attack to defend what's rightfully theirs like we defend our loved ones 'n property."

"Okay, I kinda see your point. Why do I want to be like a bee?"

Chester's brow furrows. "You want to be productive for society 'n have a positive impact instead of bein' a taker and a destroyer. I grow cattle, horses, and jobs on my ranch. I help guests create memories and even find peace of mind. If someone threatens that, well that's where a double-barreled shotgun, my forty-five, and Winchester rifle enter to stop 'em dead. Just like crushin' the mosquito tryin' to steal my blood. I'll stop a criminal from spreadin' more poison by makin' 'em dead as dead can be within the laws provided by God 'n country. You of all people should know that."

Luke recalls Chester's picture of the coat of arms. *It said 'I'll Defend'.'*

Luke contemplates his own life. *'Saving Hope's the first time I've put someone ahead of myself. I didn't do that with Linda. I thought I did.'*

Chester interrupts Luke's thoughts. "My wranglers work hard 'n show guests why we enjoy our way of livin'. It's not just a paycheck to them."

'Chester's the bee protecting his hive. It produces for society. He'll defend the ranch against anyone trying to steal or threaten it. Chester acts hard-assed but actually cares about people and puts their needs first when necessary.'

Luke mulls over Chester's words to songs on KOKE-FM. "What did the guys call this music?"

"This is real country music. Fiddle, steel guitar, and singers with a twang. Nashville's callin' pop music country now. Don't get me wrong, they're good songs 'n good singers but mostly it ain't country. Some Red Dirt and traditional musicians are breakin' through 'n makin' a mark in Nashville. People remember truer versions of country music."

"Red Dirt, that's it. They support each other too."

"Nashville's pushin' money makin' happy fluff. Real traditional 'n Red Dirt's real life in a song. KOKE-FM plays Merle 'n Waylon 'n Emmylou 'n Patsy 'n Cash. All the traditional musicians. I prefer older traditional country. Today's Red Dirt has attitude, tells real stories people can relate to and it's more gritty. Bob Childers started it outta Stillwater in a house called the Farm. Texas developed its own style with steel guitar 'n fiddle."

"How do you know so much?"

"I read a lot. So do my wranglers."

Luke recognizes Chester's pointed reference to his insult the guys couldn't read. Luke spots a billboard promoting a snake farm in New Braunfels. "You won't see that in Illinois."

"Why? Too sophisticated for northerners?"

Luke mistakes Chester's playful dig as an insult.

"What? No smart-assed comeback?"

Luke angrily spits out his retort. "You think I'm stupid because I didn't go to college or have money, don't you?"

Luke's bitter tone and resentful accusation agitates Chester and provokes a heated response.

"Don't put words in my mouth I ain't spoke. I didn't go to college either. People mistake me for a poor hick cowboy since I wear Wrangler's 'n simple button-downs 'n say y'all. I ain't fancy. I laugh at bein' misjudged 'n walk away. People see what they wanna see. You oughta try projectin' a different image. Or are you an asshole who hates the world 'n thinks it hates you back? Guess what? The world don't care about you. Some people might if ya treat 'em right."

Luke realizes he shifted into attack mode like usual. *'Did I misunderstand Chester?'*

Chester states, "I've got more money than Colt but y'all'd think he's richer with his fancy car, thousand dollar suits, and eight hundred boots."

Luke focuses on his shameful reaction while Chester calms down before revealing personal information.

"I was born in nineteen thirty 'n joined the Marines in '44 by lyin' 'bout my age. I wound up in the Fifth Marine Division on a god-forsaken island and saw a lot of buddies die. We took the most losses outta six thousand men on that eight square mile hell rock. I returned without a physical scratch but spent five years in a whiskey bottle until Millie saved me from myself. We married in nineteen fifty."

Chester struggles to compose himself after reliving painful memories. "My daddy was good with the herd but not financially. I learned from his mistakes, asked questions to successful ranchers, and grew the Twisted Live Oak into what you see. I sold part off to pay debts off but still own thousands of acres of beautiful Texas land. The school of hard knocks educated me but I'm blessed to watch cowboys 'n cowgirls ride from my deck until I die. Or when I retire."

Chester's last comment piques Luke's curiosity. "You'd actually retire?"

"Yup. I'd sell the ranch 'n move to Mexico to open a tequila bar."

"Seriously?"

"No! I ain't sellin' why I get outta bed every day. Besides, I drink whiskey. Tequila makes me sick."

Chester's next remark sounds frustrated. "People get jobs they can't wait to quit but retire with no idea what to do next 'n die from boredom or lack of purpose. Me, I own somethin' that don't remotely resemble work. I enjoy runnin' the ranch so guests live out dreams. I'll be buried on the ranch next to Millie and …"

Luke considers his life after Chester pauses. *I definitely haven't built a successful life. Linda pursued a career to support her dreams and goals. I used tragedies as excuses to avoid making better decisions. I've hid from life. No wonder Linda cheated. I rejected management opportunities from the pet store and gym.'* "I've made so many bad decisions I'm not sure I can make good ones anymore."

Luke's confession surprises Chester. *'Luke shared something personal.'* "Every sunrise offers the chance to make good decisions. If you use a positive mindset." *'Hank said Luke's more troubled than trouble.'*

Luke hesitates to ask his next question. "Who's gonna take over at the ranch?"

"Holly's not interested. Or responsible. I'm reconsidering my options."

Luke grins during while remarking. "Holly'd rather spend money you make."

"Watch it buster! Holly's still my grand-daughter."

"I'm not being disrespectful, sir. Holly's not interested in managing a business."

"I gave more attention to Hope early on. I didn't do a good job with Holly. Both girls were handfuls in different ways."

"Aren't they still?"

Chester smiles, "Yup."

"You miss your wife, don't you?"

"You never stop mourning loved ones you've lost. Memories help create reasons to get up every day. You keep livin' to keep loved ones alive too."

Chester's words hit Luke hard. *I miss my parents.*

Luke's saddened expression switches to end his dazed moment. "You were at Iwo Jima, weren't you?"

Chester's shocked by Luke's deduction. "How'd you know that?"

"My dad was navy. He had a picture of the flag raising on Iwo."

"People don't usually know that happened near the beginning of fightin'."

"I do. My dad told me stories about battles. I wish I still had that picture."

"Why don'tcha?"

Luke's response stumps Chester. "I don't wanna talk about it."

Chester wonders, *'Luke's dad comin' up makes him sad every time 'n he's sad about losin' a picture. Why? I wish Luke'd fill in gaps 'bout who he is.'*

FOURTEEN

Chester pulls into a parking lot on the corner of Houston Street and Bowie Street. "Welcome to San Antone."

'Why am I here? He can't be bringing me to visit his friend, can he?'

Chester pays the parking fee and hands Luke the keys. "Put the receipt on the dash 'n lock the truck."

Luke does as instructed and returns to Chester.

"Y'all didn't wanna steal my truck?"

"Nope. I'd only steal Hope's truck to escape her attitude."

Chester chuckles and begins walking west on Crockett Street. *'Luke's distracted.'* "Relax. Enjoy the sights."

Luke's suspiciously surveying the area. "Don't worry, I'm taking everything in."

"We're here to enjoy today."

Chester's startled to feel a gun shoved into his back.

"Do what I say 'n you'll walk away."

Chester's voice conveys his fear. "Y'all can have whatever ya want."

"You got that right."

Chester glances at Luke. *'Luke's calm now.'*

Luke speaks up, "Don't hurt us mister."

Chester hears Luke's frightened tone.

"You'll get what you deserve." *Idiot. Wearing a vest to hide your gun on a hot day. This guy's nervous.*

"I want your valuables. Now."

Chester moves slowly. "I'm reachin' for my wallet. Don't shoot."

A gunshot thunders out and Chester feels an impact against his back and falls to the ground. He lies motionless on the sidewalk. Luke reacts during the terrifying seconds and viciously beats the thug and knocks him out.

"Dumbass."

The man lies next to Chester's seemingly lifeless body. A second man turns to run prompting Luke to give chase and pounce on him and drive his head against the pavement to subdue him. Several men help restrain the dazed and bleeding man. Luke returns to Chester and hears a low angered voice.

"I coulda been killed. What were ya thinkin'?"

"Hush up. That asshole shifted his gun away when I made him think I was scared too."

"Like y'all knew he'd do that."

"Possibly. I didn't like his attitude."

"You crazy sonofabitch! You couldn't know what he'd do 'n I'm bettin' he hates your attitude more."

"I calculated possibilities and probabilities."

Chester watches Luke inform the police what happened. *Luke's actin' like he's in charge of the scene.*

Luke's ability to remain calm during life-threatening situations baffles Chester. *Katie's verbal rebuke unnerved Luke but this didn't bother him.*

They continue along Crockett Street and turn at the corner. Luke observes a gated whitish limestone rock wall partially shielded behind medium heights Live Oaks. A childlike wonder overcomes Luke once he notices Alamo Plaza's famous structure. Reddish brown mortar streaked with gray markings break the white limestone's color pattern and the sight of the Alamo leaves Luke initially speechless.

"This is the Alamo! This is the actual Alamo!"

Chester's please by Luke's reaction. *Luke respects this place.*

Luke's wide-eyed reaction is the polar opposite to his recent steely-eyed expression.

"The Alamo is a Texas icon. Like cowboys ridin' horses 'n Longhorn cattle."

"Can we go inside?"

"That's why we're here. I visit several times a year to pay respects to those who helped create Texas."

Luke marvels, *'This is unexpected.'*

"The Alamo helped shape the country as well in its own small way."

An open gate in the stone wall to the left of the main wooden doorway serves to let people in. Luke thinks about the hundred and eighty nine men who perished on March 6, 1836 defending freedoms they sought.

"Somewhere 'round fourteen people, mostly women 'n children were allowed to leave along with a slave named Joe."

"I thought everyone died here."

"Nope. Santa Anna ordered no prisoners but a few lived to tell the horror that happened within these walls."

Police deter any damage occurring to help preserve a revered part of American history. Chester questions Luke abruptly after entering the grounds. "Y'all didn't really know that guy was following us, right?"

"My training…let's just say I had a lucky hunch. Like a cowboy."

"You really don't like talkin' 'bout yourself, do ya?"

Chester receives silence. "I'll get answers one way or 'nuther."

Luke's alarmed. *'Chester seems certain he'll get information. How?'*

They enter a section known as the Long Barracks. Luke respectfully touches the wall while Chester rents an audio device to let Luke learn about the artifacts on display. They leave the Long Barracks and walk the Alamo's hallowed grounds and examine several cannons placed at certain spots. Luke notes the Live Oaks and other plant life as well as a narrow waterway containing large colorful Koi lazily swimming around.

"It looked different during the battle. The waterway was here but otherwise it was just open area."

"It's smaller than I imagined."

Chester leads Luke to the church entrance. "Take your hat off."

Luke studies a diorama of the Alamo from 1836 in the starkly lit interior.

"This is what it looked like."

Luke takes in the reverence of the chapel's atmosphere until Chester leads him outside again.

"Let's sit 'n relax."

Luke's struck by an odd thought. *'I feel oddly at peace where so much bloodshed and death happened. Men fought 'n died here which inspired others to continue fighting. It's not like when I visited my parents' graves.'*

People wait for others taking pictures. *'I'm used to everybody pushin' and shoving their way through.'*

Chester finally breaks the silence. "Let's find somethin' to eat."

They head west on Crockett and turn left at Losoya Street.

Luke thinks, *'This isn't like Chicago.'*

Music's heard nearby and Luke spots a sign for an Irish pub. *'I recognize that song. 'Can't You See."* Luke smiles, *'I can now.'*

Luke laughs about his first night in Austin.

"Somethin' funny?"

Luke shakes his head. *'Chester won't want to hear about my first night with Holly.'*

They pass a stuffed Longhorn at the entrance of the Lonestar Café.

Chester remarks, "I think I know this guy."

Luke laughs heartily while reading the sign warning people not to touch the ragged and worn nose.

'Only Faith gets Luke laughin' like that.'

The hostess eyes them warily since people ignore the sign. Chester leads Luke down a stone stairway at Commerce and Losoya to the San Antonio River Walk. Luke takes in the sights, smells, colors, and sounds of restaurants, stores, and hotels lining both sides of the river.

FIFTEEN

People explore San Antonio's River Walk's energetic atmosphere where delicious aromas and lively music merge with an impressive color palette. Chester stops by a man singing a song.

"Focus on the words, Luke."

The song expresses the difficulty to be humble when you're so good looking. Chester drops a couple dollars into the guitar case and comments, "I inspired that song. Mac Davis sang it better."

Luke's disbelief is quite apparent.

"What? You don't believe me?"

"Would you believe you?"

Street artists offer face painting and caricature drawings as souvenirs for tourists underneath bridges. Others sell trinkets and toys. Chester guides Luke across the river on an arched stone pedestrian bridge while tour guides slowly navigate boats along the waterway. They explain particular sites along the River Walk system. They reach a Mexican restaurant and get greeted by the owner.

"Would you like your usual table, Mr. Kinkead?"

"I'd like to sit by the water today, Manuel. And call me Chester already. We've known each other too long for formalities."

Manuel Sanchez nods and ushers them to a table next to the river and waves his best waiter over. He speaks in Spanish. "Their meals will be on the house."

"That's not necessary."

Manuel cuts Chester off. "I'll treat you to your meals, Mr. Kinkead, Chester." He glances at Luke. "I can because of you."

"Manuel, this is Luke. He's new to the Twisted Live Oak."

"Ah, sí, he's the headache."

Luke shoots an annoyed look at Chester.

"He ain't wrong."

Manuel extends his arm to shake Luke's hand. "Chester's the reason I'm doing so well."

Chester attempts to interrupt Manuel but fails.

"Mr. Kinkead helped me move from a terrible corner in Austin and my business has grown since then."

Chester shakes his head. "Your cookin' got you here."

"Mi familia, my family's so very thankful for all you've done for us. Your generosity has helped us put our children through college."

Manuel's voice reflects his gratitude.

"Please enjoy your meals. Let Juan know if there's anything you need."

Juan acknowledges Manuel in Spanish before speaking clear English to take their orders.

"Order whatcha want, Luke."

"Okay. I'll have the Enchiladas. Chicken."

"Double that, Juan."

Chester studies Luke scanning the area and people during lunch. *'Luke's not payin' attention to the pretty women. He's shown lots of interest in Hope when he's around her. What's goin' through his head?'*

Luke's thoughts would shock Chester.

'What would it be like to come here with Hope and Faith? Is that even possible?'

Juan's appreciative for Chester's generous tip. "Gracias señor. Papa'd like to see you before you leave."

Chester walks inside and returns to find three women talking to Luke. "Y'all need a moment, Romeo?"

"No. Ladies, thank you for the compliments."

Luke tips his hat before facing Chester.

"Let's walk around."

Chester watches the women leave. "Didja get a date?"

"Why would I do that?"

"They seemed interested."

Luke chuckles. "They were complimenting me for taking my Grand-pappy out for lunch."

"No they didn't."

"Yup."

"Y'all told 'em we ain't related, right?"

"Nope."

"Do I need to whoop your ass?"

Luke's triumphant smile frustrates Chester. Luke shifts his attention to the diversity of colors, sounds, and smells so Chester motions to a boat launch.

"C'mon, we'll take a tour. The guide'll explain the area to ya."

Luke learns the River Walk covers around twelve blocks. The guide instills his sense of humor but gets serious when informing passengers no building can cast a shadow on the Alamo. Luke's fascinated by the optical illusion of a building appearing flat even though it's not. He observes couples and families enjoying the River Walk and visualizes being with Hope and Faith. *How often have they been here? Would they ever want to come with me? Why am I even considering this?*

Luke stops mid-thought. *Hope's not interested in me. Not since Wyatt's back. That's clear. Do I even want to stay?*

Chester notices the time. "Thirty Five'll be backed up. We'll go ride Tower of The Americas in Hemisfair Park and stay for supper. Y'all can view the city from above."

Luke recalls how sparsely populated the area was in 1836. They return to the River Walk and Chester chooses Saltgrass Steak House for dinner.

"Order anything you want."

Both men order steaks and beers and leave contentedly full. Chester's inquisitive expression prompts Luke's question.

"What now?"

"You didn't know those men followed us, right?"

"Really? I got lucky. Leave it at that."

Chester merges onto I-35 North to Austin and pulls over. "Follow the signs for 35 North to Austin. Wake me when we reach Austin."

Chester dozes off and mumbles, 'Y'all ain't gonna find any place like Texas."

Luke settles into the driver's seat. *'Is Chester right?'*

They pass the Buc-ee's in New Braunfels which Chester pointed out going to San Antonio. He mentioned it has the largest convenience store in the world and one hundred and twenty fuel pumps. *I feel alive and connected in Texas. Not like Chicago. Life's an adventure here. I don't have any painful reminders either.'*

Luke listens to a song titled, 'Steal You Away' by Randy Rogers and thinks, *'Could I steal Hope from Wyatt?'*

Chester shudders, whimpers, and mutters in his sleep.

'What's that all about?'

Chester wakes near Austin and directs Luke back to the ranch. Luke speaks before exiting the truck.

"Thanks for today. It was a good day."

"It was a good day. You're welcome. 'Cept you nearly killin' me."

"Your breathing. Quit whining like an eight year old."

Chester realizes Luke's quoting from their first day. "Shut up."

Luke heads for the bunkhouse with a smile. The men walk in opposite directions but become closer even though it won't become fully evident for some time. Luke wonders about Chester's restlessness. *'Was that from the war?'*

SIXTEEN

Hope enters Chester's office. "Ben? Where's Chester? I wanna take him to lunch."

"Chester took Luke to San Antone."

"What? Luke should be workin'."

"Hope, I stopped tryin' to figure Chester out when I stopped tryin' to figure you 'n Beth out."

"Funny. I'll find out tomorrow."

"Good luck with that."

"Chester's sneaky but I've learned how to get information from the best."

Ben grins. *'You do interrogate rather well.'*

Wyatt notices Hope exit the house. "Let's go for a ride."

"Don'tcha have work to do?"

"Nah. I'm free right now."

"Um, alright."

Hope and Wyatt head out for a short ride but Wyatt stops once they're out of sight. He dismounts and asks Hope to do the same. Wyatt moves in to kiss Hope.

"I've been wantin' to do that again."

Hope's receptive to Wyatt's kisses while his hands wander around her body.

"No. Not here. We could be seen. I need to go."

Hope returns to the barn. "Scooter, I need to leave. Could you take care of Patsy?"

"Sure. Y'all okay?"

"Um, yeah."

Hope's thoughts spin so she invites Jubilee and JeniMay to lunch. *'Beth's spoilin' Faith today. Chester's doin' god knows what with Luke. Wyatt's actin' like we're already together. I hope the girls'll help make sense of all this.'*

"I'm glad y'all could join me."

"What's up? Y'all sounded upset."

"Chester took Luke to San Antone."

Jubilee's suspicious of Hope's true intention for lunch. "Are we gonna talk but not talk 'bout Luke again? Who cares what Chester does?"

JeniMay comments, "Yeah. Chester can do what he wants, right?"

"Sure. Except with Luke. He should workin' at the ranch."

Jubilee and JeniMay roll their eyes. "Here we go again. Who cares? Y'all're so focused on Luke."

"JeniMay's right. Does it matter what Luke's doin'? Or does it matter to you?"

"What?! No! I told you already. Luke doesn't matter to me. Ben does though."

"Hope, y'all've been alone too long. Luke's affecting your focus. We help when we can because we love you but…"

"Letchur guard down. Let someone in. You deserve someone special. What about Wyatt?"

"What are you talkin' about?"

JeniMay explains, "We're talkin' 'bout findin' love, Hope. Joe cheated on you. He wins the longer you stay closed off. You're everything a guy wants. You're beautiful, kind, giving, and loyal to the end. I'm wonderin' if y'all like Luke. Not hate him. Luke's not a bad guy."

"He's not a good guy either." *'Am I just kiddin' myself anymore?'*

"I disagree. He's not interested in me. I tried. I asked him point blank at the barbecue. Y'all know what he did? He looked straight at you the way Wade looked at me."

Jubilee adds, "Luke does look at you like a man in love."

Hope argues their observations. "Y'all're crazy. I don't like Luke 'n he don't like me."

"Jubilee's got a point. I've seen Luke look at you. He may not show you since y'all keep shootin' at him. Or threatenin' to anyway."

"And tellin' him y'all hate him."

"He treats Faith so good. She enjoys bein' with him."

"Faith's never acted that way around anyone 'cept the guys at the ranch."

"Faith knows who she can trust."

"What's happenin'? I ask you to lunch and y'all're givin' me a lecture about love. I think?"

"Hope, you protest too much about Luke."

"And too loud. It's time to rethink life 'n love."

"Can we change the subject?"

"You started it. Jubilee, should we stop talkin' about Hope's love life? Or lack thereof."

"Hmmm. Nope."

"Funny. You two're real funny."

SEVENTEEN

Hank hears details about San Antonio the next morning. "Luke didn't know we'd get robbed, right?"

"Chester, Luke's rather perceptive but doesn't let on."

"He couldn't possibly know that."

"I've got Luke somewhat figured out. He's a runner or protector dependin' on his circumstances. Emotionally, he runs from challenges. Physically, he'll protect whoever needs protectin'. I'd like to talk to Luke 'n ask certain questions for his reaction."

"Billy's runnin' a guest into town. He can drop Luke off."

Luke's confused until Billy pulls into the parking lot. "I'll be back in a bit."

A young new nurse greets Luke. "Hello handsome. Are y'all here to see me?"

"No, Monique, he's here to see me. Or wouldja rather visit with Monique?"

Luke stammers, "Uh, no. Thank you, um, Monique."

Hank's amused by Monique's flirtatious greeting. "Let's findja a safer spot."

"Howya doin', Hank?"

"I'm good. Y'all're soundin' more Texan. Anything exciting happen lately?"

Luke eyes Hank suspiciously. "Nope. Oh wait, Chester's gonna stop drinkin' whiskey."

"Yeah?" Hank chuckles, "When hell freezes over."

"You know something."

"Perceptive. I might've heard about San Antone yesterday."

Hank spies Monique eyeing Luke. "Monique's pretty, ain't she? And single."

"Yeah? So? Don't try settin' me up with her. I'm leaving, remember."

"You made a promise even if Hope's not readily available with Wyatt around."

Hank notes Luke's physical reaction to Hope being unavailable. *'That got his attention.'*

"Y'all might stay for someone else."

"Don't start again. Hope's happy Wyatt's back."

Hank listens carefully. *'Luke sounds sad.'* "It's early. Too early to tell. Or give up. Have you ever had an Iceberg moment?"

"A what?"

"I read 'bout why the Titanic sank so fast. The hull was compromised by an uncontrolled fire in a coal room. An unreported explanation stated the ship was travelin' fast 'n reckless to use the coal up 'n put the fire out."

"That's news to me."

"It was never confirmed. It's based on crew reports. Have you let poor decisions affect your life?"

"Hank, you know my life story."

"Yup. But y'all ain't mentioned a moment that if ya slowed down 'n made a different choice it would've changed everything instead of recklessly moving full steam ahead."

Luke ponders Hank's query. "Jini was my iceberg moment. I should've asked her to stay."

"I'm not so sure."

"My life would be different. I wouldn't be here."

"Possibly. Remember when I told you God had a plan y'all ain't understood yet."

"Then it would've been passing on the dojo."

"Maybe. But Jini could've prevented that from happenin' and she still could've left ya."

Luke struggles to absorb Hank's message.

"I believe hittin' Ben's your iceberg moment."

"How?"

"If you'd've slowed down 'n held your temper you wouldn't be here now. You're so focused on leavin' y'all ain't slowed down to notice possibilities at the ranch. Thinkin' smart separates success from failure."

Luke sighs. *'Don't bet on it.'* "Wyatt's changed all that." *'I've wondered if the ranch could be a place to live. If Hope would want me to stay? Faith too.'*

'Luke immediately thought of Hope.' "Poor decisions'll sink your life."

"Y'all walked me into that, didn't you? Making me think about my future now?"

"I'm tryin' to figure out what you were thinkin' yesterday."

"How'd you hear about that?"

Hank grins. "Chester told me this morning. But it was on the news yesterday. You do attract trouble."

"You think I find trouble?"

"If'n it ain't findin' y'all first."

Luke smiles at Hank's half serious joke.

"Your training saved Chester. How'd y'all recognize those guys?"

"The guy looked nervous. He was sweatin' in a leather vest in summer to hide his gun."

"How'd you keep Chester from gettin' shot? He said he felt the gun in his back."

"The guy pointed the gun away when I acted scared. Subduing him was easy. Same for the second guy."

"Deception. Smart. Actin' weak to avoid gettin' shot."

"Yeah. Something like that."

"Thanks for keepin' Chester safe. He can't believe you knew."

"This stays between us, alright. I don't want people knowing that side of me."

"Y'all don't want anyone knowin' any side of you."

"I'm shy, what can I say."

Hank grins, "Not buyin' it. What if you didn't find true love before? Maybe it ain't happened yet."

Billy's knock prevents further conversation. "We need to get back to the ranch."

Luke's left wondering, *'What's Hank saying?'*

EIGHTEEN

Hope barges into Chester's office unannounced determined to get answers.

"Y'all're actin' more like Holly. Did we have a meetin'?"

"Why'd you bring Luke to San Antone yesterday?"

"First, he didn't try stealin' my truck."

"Funny. Ha ha."

Chester recognizes a fact, *Hope didn't lead with the robbery attempt. Good, she ain't heard about it.*

"I tried a different tactic to learn more 'bout Luke."

"He could've run off."

"Only to get away from you."

Chester's crooked little smile irks Hope.

Hope blurts out, "Did he say that? Did Luke talk?" *Am I the reason Luke wants to leave?*

Chester notices Hope's expression sour. *That got Hope's attention.* He returns to his paperwork. "You seem bothered I took Luke to San Antone."

Hope's response exposes some interest. "Didja learn anything? Does he want to leave because of me?"

Chester pretends not to hear her.

"Well?"

Chester partially answers, "Somethin' bad happened to Luke. He ain't handled problems well. Hank's talkin' to him now. Billy dropped him off."

Hope sounds disappointed. "Luke's not here?"

"Y'all're awful interested in someone ya hate. Ain'tcha gittin' back with Wyatt? He missed an assignment yesterday 'cause of y'all 'n forced Ben to lead a trail ride Wyatt was supposed to."

"Wyatt said he wasn't busy."

"Hope, y'all know we're always busy in season."

'Wyatt lied to me.' "It sounds like you didn't learn anything yesterday. I'm lookin' out for Faith's well-bein'. Since she likes Luke."

"Luke's not so bad actually." *'Luke saved my ass instead of runnin'.'* "His past is a minefield of problems 'n issues. Stop attackin' Luke 'n give him a chance. Faith is."

Hope painfully vocalizes her heartbreaking experiences. "Give Luke a chance? Right. Like givin' the modeling agent a chance? Or what about the last man I gave a chance to? Wyatt already left me once. Where's my happy ending? I'm not lookin' to get hurt anymore."

Chester listens to Hope's anguished tone. *'Hank might be right 'bout Hope's emotional state.'*

Hope thinks, *'Why do I think about Luke so much? I'd like him to hold me again. And kiss me. Why's Wyatt really back?'*

Hope's feeling bouts of jealousy due to her deepening attraction to Luke and worries when other women flirt with him. She's confided with Beth to make sense of it all. *'Can I find the strength and courage to admit how I feel? Or is that a sign?'*

Chester notices a key detail he's overlooked. "Hope, are y'all wearin' make-up?"

Hope stiffens and inhales. *'How do I explain this?'* "I showed Faith how to apply make-up this mornin'."

Chester challenges Hope's implausible explanation. "Lordy, Lordy! Faith's eight! She don't need to know 'bout that yet."

Hope blushes and nervously glances at the clock. "Look at the time. I have a client in Bertram."

"I'd walk ya out but I've got paperwork."

Hope timidly laughs and fidgets with her necklace. "I doubt anything'll happen."

Chester struggles to recall when Hope last wore make-up. *'Hope's actin' stranger by the day. Why did she come here?'*

Hope spots Billy's truck from the deck and hears a heavy rhythmic thumping near the rodeo barn. *'What's that noise?'*

Hope halts once she finds the source of the noise. *'Oh my!'*

Luke's on the opposite side of the metal fence facing away from Hope.

'Luke? Whoa!'

Luke holds an axe in his left hand. He's wearing his white straw cowboy hat to shield his eyes from the blazing sun but his shirt's slung over the fence. Luke's bare torso glistens with sweat trickling down to his jeans in the sweltering heat. Hope's awestruck by the sight of Luke reaching for another large log for the chopping stump. Luke's pre-dawn workouts and daily physical labor have kept him in excellent shape. His thick brawny back muscles flex with every movement and his well-defined sinewy shoulders resemble cannon balls. Luke raises the axe overhead and effortlessly swings downward to splinter the log with great force. He tosses the pieces aside and stacks two logs and splits both with one swing then makes them smaller for the Christmas in July bonfire.

'That's amazing.'

Hope's mesmerized by Luke's physique and spellbound by his lean, muscular body with his wide shoulders and back narrowing to his trim waist. She's seeing him shirtless for the first time which has her swooning like a teenaged girl. *'Luke's built like action movie heroes.'*

Hope snaps out of her trance and realizes Luke might see her standing there. *'I'm actin' like a love-sick girl.'*

Hope turns away but glances over her shoulder to admire Luke's physique again. Luke senses the movement and spots Hope walking away.

'Great. Hope's checking to see if I'm working.'

Hope realizes Luke's seen her and hurries to her truck. *'I'm so embarrassed Luke caught me staring at him. I get why Holly's after Luke.'*

Hope fights the urge to return to spy on Luke again and dwells on new thoughts. *I didn't realize Luke was in such good shape. That's why he fights so well. He keeps breakin' down my barriers. Why? This ain't love. It's primordial lust. I'm not ready to let anyone in again or get hurt, right? I'm so confused.'*

Another set of eyes observed Hope watching Luke. Luke's summoned to the office after a police officer arrives to drop off a large manila envelope to Chester. He pulls his shirt on and buttons it before entering the house and knocking on the open office door.

"Come in. Y'all can have this back."

Chester hands over Luke's wallet.

"You're giving my wallet back? What's the catch?"

Luke's distrustful tone amuses Chester. "No catch. You've earned some trust after yesterday's incident. Not one word about that though, got it?"

Luke acts confused. "Did something happen yesterday?"

Chester's glad Luke understands. "Good. Only Hank knows 'bout this."

"Yeah, I know."

Luke slowly opens his wallet and reverently pulls an old worn picture out. *'Mom, Dad.'*

Chester notices Luke's hand shaking while bittersweet memories flood his mind. Luke removes a second picture and studies it briefly before tossing it onto Chester's desk.

"You can throw this out."

Chester reaches for the picture of a long-haired blonde. "Y'all sure you don't want it?"

Luke answers resolutely. "Yeah. I'm sure."

Chester flips the picture over. *'Linda.'*

"Alright. How's the bonfire supply comin' along?"

"Nearly done. It'll be good 'n dry."

"Good."

Luke exits clearly happier while Chester slides the picture into a drawer. "I guess Linda's not gettin' a fourth proposal."

NINETEEN

Isolated thunderstorms disrupt guest events leading up to July Fourth. Luke shares a thought with Ben while much needed rain brings short-lived relief from triple digit extreme heat.

"I understand the expression a snowball's chance in hell better."

"Texas summers. High heat. No rain or strong storms."

Luke thinks, *'This ranch brought a different kind of storm to my life. No shelter from it either.'*

Guests enjoy a local Fourth of July parade in the morning before spending the afternoon and evening at a festival with rides, games, food, music, and fireworks. Luke's subdued while surrounded by happy people talking, singing, and yelling on rides or at games. Jake and Jesse flirt with every passing girl while Jack, Billy, Henry, Danny, and Kyle try winning prizes between food booths. Luke overhears Jake flirt with one particular girl who mentions she has a boyfriend but has an identical twin whose single. Jake asks, "What does she look like?"

The girl rolls her eyes and walks away.

'Good Lord, Jake. Really?'

Ben and Beth and their daughters watch Cody lose money trying to win Jubilee a stuffed animal. Ben approaches with a ten dollar bill.

"Watch 'n learn, Cody. Jubilee, pick which one y'all want."

The booth operator accepts Ben's money and hands Jubilee a prize. "What the hell?"

Ben grins, "Learned that raisin' our daughters."

The guys notice Luke turn down women asking him to go on rides.

"Is Luke afraid of rides? Or Texas women?"

"Both? Neither? Who knows? Hope's the only Texas woman Luke should watch out for."

Luke's muted attitude shifts once Hope and Faith arrive and Faith jumps into Luke's arms causing Chester to quietly comment to Hope.

"Faith's eyes are as big as Moon Pies."

"I said Luke might not be here today."

"Why wouldn't he?"

"I don't know."

Hope watches Luke hug Faith. *'Luke treats Faith so well. Would he do that for me too?'*

Wyatt surprises Hope from behind when he wraps his arms around her.

"Momma, I wanna spend today with Luke 'n play games 'n ride rides."

Wyatt whispers, "I'd like to ride you 'n play games again."

Hope pushes away from Wyatt's wandering hands. "Excuse you. You may be back but I'm not ready." *'Luke has a better chance right now.'*

Hope addresses Faith's request. "Pecan, today's our day for fun."

Luke tenses up. *'I'm not getting between Hope and Faith. Or Hope and Wyatt.'* "Faith, I'm okay alone. Spend today with your mom."

"Momma, Luke shouldn't be alone today."

Luke becomes despondent. *'This sort of reminds me of my parents last day.'*

Hope nods her approval. *'I can't disappoint Faith.'* "Okay."

Faith moves between Hope and Luke and reaches for their hands. "Let's go play games."

Hope sees Wyatt shoot Luke a dirty look while joining Cody and Jubilee at a game booth.

"Faith, Hope, join us for some fun."

Jubilee points towards a stuffed bear. "Cody'll win one for you."

Faith notices a stuffed animal at a nearby tent. "Luke might could win me that pink elephant."

Hope watches Faith's eyes light up while asking for Luke to win the prize.

"Me? What about Cody?"

Wyatt steps up, "I'll win it for ya, Faith."

"No, I want Luke to win it for me."

Faith's insistence irritates Wyatt. Hope intervenes, "Okay, Luke'll win ya this one. Wyatt'll win ya the next one."

"Momma, I want Luke to win me prizes today. Or Cody."

Hope glances at Wyatt. "Sorry."

"Whatever."

Luke steps up to the ring toss booth. "Here goes nothin'."

His first toss misses. Wyatt subtly ridicules Luke. "Can't throw, can ya."

Luke scores on two special pegs to win the elephant and glances at Wyatt, "Guess again."

Faith cries out, "Yay! You did it. I knew you could. Thank you, thank you, thank you."

Beth observes Luke gravitates towards Faith while Wyatt distances himself. *'They're opposite.'*

Luke playfully holds the elephant out of reach over Faith's head before lowering it to kiss Faith's cheek and let her grab it. She hugs it tightly.

Beth whispers to Hope, "It's nice seein' Faith engagin' 'n laughin' with someone not from the ranch."

"Momma, look, Luke won it for me."

"I see, Pecan." *'It is nice Luke plays with Faith. I could get used to him bein' 'round too.'*

Cody asks, "What's next Faith?"

Faith heads to the baseball toss. "This."

Beth and Ben's daughters walk up and hug Hope.

"Courtney, Trish, I can't believe I babysat you two."

Beth asks, "Hope, do you see a prize to win too?"

Hope's confused so Beth points at Luke.

"Heard Luke put on a show for you."

Hope blushes. "What? How would you know?"

"Please, the ranch has eyes everywhere."

"Ben!"

Ben's smirk confirms Hope's guess.

Wyatt's concerned Luke's becoming competition. Cody approaches the counter and takes the balls but turns to hand them to Luke.

"Y'all might be better at this."

Beth remarks, "Cody you were a pitcher."

Luke understands Cody's reference.

"Luke's better 'n me."

Hope realizes Cody's alluding to the barbecue. *'Oh. When Luke defended Holly.'*

"Luke, win me another prize. Please."

"I'll try."

Luke's first throw bounces off the bottom left bottle. Wyatt scoffs.

"Y'all can't knock a bottle down."

Luke glances at Wyatt before glaring at the carnival worker. He hurls the next ball and shatters the bottle revealing the cement filling inside.

"I believe the young lady deserves the biggest prize here, don't you?"

The man nods and hands Faith the largest bear.

"Wow! Thank you, Daddy! I love it."

Hope's mortified. *'Chester's wrong. Faith heard that old couple.'*

Wyatt laughs, "As if."

Beth notices Hope's dismayed expression.

"Hey, Hope, y'all okay?"

"No. I'm not sure. No. I don't know."

"Faith's just excited Luke won the bear."

Wyatt overhears Hope's hushed response and Beth's reply. "Faith's gettin' too attached to Luke. He's not stayin'. I don't wanna see Faith hurt."

"Interestin' Faith called Luke Daddy. Maybe it's a subconscious message?"

Beth's question forces Hope to consider possibilities. *'Would a dad be Faith's real prize? Faith needs a good man in her life as a role model.*

Someone who'd protect her from harm. And teach her things I can't. Luke ain't that person though, is he?'

Hope approaches Luke. "Can we talk? Alone."

"Yes ma'am." *'Here comes I hate you.'*

Hope starts, "Faith didn't mean to call you that."

"I know."

"She's excited about the bear."

"Hope, I get it. I'm not her dad. Y'all don't trust me. Hell, y'all don't like me. You're uncomfortable I'm here. I'll leave. Wyatt'll win Faith's prizes. You want him anyway."

Hope's stare concerns Luke.

"Good Lord, Luke, you really are startin' to sound like us."

"Blame Hank and Chester. They think they can make me Texan or a cowboy which ain't possible."

"You're only Texan if y'all're born here or we grant you the right to say that. Would that be so bad?"

Faith interrupts them. "This is awesome. Thank you, Luke."

"You're welcome. You deserve it."

Faith struggles to hold the bear with her right arm. She motions with her left index finger for Luke to bend over so she can kiss his cheek. "Y'all're the best, Luke."

"Thanks. You're even more the best."

Luke mumbles to Hope. "I saw your face when Faith called me Daddy. I'll stay away like you want."

A man taps Hope's shoulder after Luke walks away.

"Hey there darlin'. Let's spend time together today 'n tonight."

Beth rushes over. "Her boyfriend's over there. He just got outta jail for attempted murder. Yeah, some guy tried askin' her out before. He's still in bad shape."

The man notices Luke stops to look back and hastily retreats. Hope glares while Beth laughs.

"Beth! What's wrong with you? Why would you say that? And point to Luke?"

"Didja wanna get to know that guy? No. So I chased him off. You're welcome."

"You're unwell. You know that."

Wyatt approaches. "I'd've scared him off. I'm more likely to be Hope's boyfriend."

Beth laughs, "No offense, Wyatt, y'all ain't scary. Luke, on the other hand, is."

Hope speaks up. "Why say that with Faith here?"

Wyatt questions Beth. "Why'd y'all say Luke was in jail?"

"Because it's true. It makes the story better. Luke's more ornery 'n keeps the riff raff away. Mostly. Hope, you're welcome."

Beth grins when Hope throws her hands into the air and returns to Faith. Men approach Hope while Wyatt's next to her so she needs to shoot them down. Beth's telling look irritates Wyatt. Faith spots Luke at a concession stand and runs to him. Hope, Ben, Beth, and Wyatt watch two women and a man arrive at the same time.

"No ring, Cara. Ask him out."

"Is that your daughter? Want help raising her?"

"She's not mine. She belongs to someone else."

The guy steps up to Luke. "You one of them molesters? Run little girl."

The man grabs Luke's shirt to throw him to the ground but only tears his shirt when Luke reverses the move and slams the guy down and knocks the air from his lungs.

"I'm not a pedophile! Asshole!"

Cara intervenes, "Whoa, hold up cowboy. Jimmy's drunk 'n misunderstood me askin' you out."

Luke brings Faith to Hope while his shirt's hanging off his shoulder. Women gaze at Luke's exposed torso with great interest. Wyatt's frustrated by Beth's pointed observation.

"Hope, Luke's a hunk. Wowser! Maybe Luke'll steal your heart's attention away from Wyatt."

Faith further irritates Wyatt. "Momma, that girl was tryin' to be Luke's girlfriend. Right Luke?"

Hope gazes at Luke's exposed chest and shoulders. *I could get used to seein' that.'*

Faith adds, "Momma, you could be Luke's girlfriend. Then he'd stay."

Beth fuels the fire. "Yeah, Hope, you should be Luke's girlfriend."

"You're not helpin', Beth."

"Or am I?"

Luke's attention is diverted by women shouting. Hope's eyes follow Luke's.

Hope stammers, "Those are the guys."

Beth insists, "Do what y'all wanted to before."

Ben sees a young man grab at a woman's chest.

Beth explains, "They did that to Hope."

Ben angrily replies, "Why wasn't I told?"

"Don't worry honey, Luke's about to right a wrong. Right, Hope?"

Hope glances at Beth and nods at Luke. Faith questions Hope.

"Momma, Luke's gonna beat them up, right?"

Beth smirks, "This'll be fun to watch."

Wyatt watches Luke march off like a runaway freight train towards the laughing men and unleashes his anger on them. He's merciless and leaves them bloodied on the ground. Luke turns to check on the women before issuing a warning.

"Y'all do this again 'n I'll break your hands. For starters."

Luke heads off into the crowd forcing Hope to chase him through the people.

"Luke! Stop! Where're ya goin'?"

"They won't bother anyone again. I won't bother you either. You don't want me or my help."

"Luke, I was wrong. I do appreciate what you just did. Faith does too."

"Butcha don't trust me. You spied on me while I chopped wood. You don't trust I'm doin' the work."

Hope blushes when Luke confirms seeing her. *I wasn't spying. Can I admit I was admiring you?'*

"Go back to Wyatt. He came back for you." *'Maybe I should go back to Linda. Or stay for Jazzy.'*

Luke seeks refuge in the crowd until Ben finds him.

"Figures I'd findja by the food. Faith's sad y'all ain't with her. Hope ain't as happy as she could be either. What did ya say to her?"

"Nothin' but the truth. She's got Wyatt 'n Faith makin' her happy."

"I'm not sure 'bout Hope 'n Wyatt. His leavin' hurt her. You gonna do the same? To Hope 'n Faith?"

"Ben, I…"

"Don't disappoint Faith."

"Fine. For Faith."

Luke returns to the group with Ben. Faith runs to hug Luke.

"I thought you didn't like me anymore. I wanna go on rides with you. Please."

Faith's blue eyes implore Luke to stay.

"Faith, I love you. I'll go on all the rides with you."

Luke notices everyone's staring at him, especially Hope. "What?"

Hope moves closer. "Stay with Faith today. Please."

"I will for Faith's sake."

"Luke, I know you work hard. You could stay at the ranch. Wyatt 'n I aren't set in stone."

Images of Linda kissing Robert flash through Luke's mind. "I don't stay where I'm not wanted."

Hope's green eyes shine while locked on Luke. *'I wish I could be honest with you.'* "You said you love Faith. She's so happy. Thank you."

Ben hands Luke an oversized t-shirt. Several women whistle and admire Luke while he changes which frustrates Hope. Danny and Kyle get invited to sit in with several bands to show off their impressive six string skills. One musician compares them to Flatt and Scruggs and Roy Clark.

TWENTY

Luke notices Hope holding Wyatt's hand during his time with Faith. She even dances with Wyatt while Danny and Kyle are on stage. *'Hope looks pretty set to me.'*

A drunken college-aged kid puts his hands on Hope and slurs rude comments about what he'd do with her. Wyatt shoves him away.

"Get off my girlfriend."

"She's mine now."

Wyatt knocks the guy down with a solid punch only to get hit from behind by a second guy with an arm cast. Luke hears a dull thud and sees Wyatt drop to his knees in a dazed state before Luke delivers knockout blows to each man.

"His cast is rigged."

Police arrest the drunken offenders while EMT's assist Wyatt before taking him to the hospital for further observation. Peace returns until a noisy, motley group of boys settles near the Twisted Live Oak spot to watch fireworks. Hope speaks up after they start swearing loudly which upsets Faith.

"Please quiet down. Or go somewhere else."

"We'll sit where we want."

"Yeah. It's a free country."

The boys laugh and make obscene gestures and comments to Hope. They laugh more when Cody intervenes.

"Momma, should we move?"

A stern voice answers Faith's question. "No! Y'all ain't moving. They are."

The lead boy speaks, "My dad's a lawyer. We'll sue 'n I'll own you."

Luke closes in to grab the boy's throat and presses his fingertips against the jugular vein. "Any more pressure and you won't see fireworks. Or tomorrow. I don't own anything. The girl don't need to hear your crude remarks little guppy."

Another boy asks, "Are you threatenin' us?"

"Not yet."

Luke shoves the boy into his friends and watches them scatter to avoid his wrath. Hope's confused why Luke's so forceful while protecting Faith.

'Luke's not Faith's dad but acts like it. He's protectin' her. Could Luke be a real choice? Am I avoiding the truth in front of me? Could Luke be good for me? I didn't correct Wyatt sayin' I was his girlfriend.

Beth misreads Hope's baffled expression. *'Great. Hope's upset at Luke again.'*

"Why're y'all upset, Hope?"

"I'm not upset, Beth."

Luke crouches down in front of Faith. "Are you okay?"

"Yes Luke. Thanks for gettin' rid of those boys."

"I'll take care of you while I'm here."

Hope hears Luke's comment while he backs off and requests, "Luke, sit with us. Faith'll feel safer."

Chester sarcastically harasses Luke. "Sit down. Quit blockin' my view."

Katie listens to Hope's appeal. *'Is Hope willin' to give someone other than Wyatt a chance after all?'*

Luke snuggles with Faith. "Nobody'll bother you now." He glances at Hope. "If that's okay."

Hope's eyes convey a deeper emotional message than her slight nod. Faith brings her hand up.

"Pinky swear. You can't break a pinky swear. It's bad luck, right Momma?"

"Right, Pecan." *Faith's pinky swearing with Luke. She only does it with me.'*

"I won't break our pinky swear. Unless Chester or your mom runs me outta Texas."

'I'm confused. Is Luke sayin' he's stayin'? Oh God, what if he stays?'

Faith sits in Luke's lap for the start of the fireworks. "I'll sit with Momma too."

"Good idea, Faith."

'Luke's provin' to be better for Faith than some men who've known her longer. Why would Luke stay?'

TWENTY-ONE

Faith sets off to find Luke on the Fifth while Hope visits Chester at the ranch.

"How's your day goin', Chester? How's Wyatt feelin'?"

"I'm good. Wyatt's concussed 'n restin' in the bunkhouse."

Luke's holding Faith's hand entering the office. "I believe this youngster belongs to you."

Hope looks at Luke. "Did I hear a twang in your voice?"

"I heard it too, Momma."

"Y'all're soundin' more 'n more like y'all belong here."

Chester winks at Faith and counters Hope's point. "I don't think I want him here. He's still a pain in my keister 'n givin' me headaches 'n trouble. He's hoggin' my time with Faith."

"Grand-daddy, Luke's nice to me. That counts, right?"

"You bring up a valid point for consideration."

"Chester, I'll be back 'n forth between other ranches these next few weeks. Beth'll bring Faith here."

Luke's expression sours. *I didn't consider Hope could have boyfriends at other ranches.*

Ben enters with an announcement. Wyatt passed out tryin' to walk to the house. The doc said he'd need to be watched for symptoms."

"Hope, couldja look at Wyatt 'n tell me whatcha think?"

"Chester, I'm a vet, remember."

"Hope, you've mended my men for years, remember. Look Wyatt over 'n tell me somethin'."

"Fine."

Hope returns to report. "Wyatt got released too soon. That's his fault though. Watch him closely."

"You mean babysit him."

"Sure, yeah."

"Couldja check him out when you're here?"

"I guess so."

Luke speaks up. "I've got work to finish. Faith, good seein' you again."

"Can we play when I'm here?"

Luke smiles, "Yes ma'am. Bitsy."

"You haven't called me that in a while."

"Is it still okay?"

"Yes, but only you, Luke."

Luke's final glance at Hope is telling that he's troubled while Faith hugs him. He tips his hat and returns to saddling horses. The guys joke during the task. Hope and Faith appear with apples so Billy gets Hope's attention with a joke.

"Billy, keep your day job. You're a better cowboy than comedian."

"Hey, comedy clubs have a two drink minimum so everyone sounds funny."

Hope pokes more fun, "How big 'n strong are those drinks 'n how far is the audience from the stage?"

"Ouch."

"Shakespeare declared all the world's a stage but somehow y'all belong in general seatin'."

"Oh, you're tellin' jokes now?"

Luke nervously attempts to joke with Hope as well. "So, Hope, do you come 'round here for unbridled fun often?" *That was stupid. Why did I say anything?'*

The guys erupt into laughter.

"Luke, y'all made Billy sound funny."

Billy exclaims, "Don't bring me into it. I'm not that bad."

"Hope grew up here. She's always here for the horses."

Hope's perplexed. *'Was Luke tellin' a joke or flirtin' with me?'*

"Sorry. I took comedy lessons from Billy. That was stupid."

Hope gazes at Luke. "You meant well. I think? Right?"

"Yes darlin'. I meant well."

The barn goes silent. Luke recognizes his blundered response and escapes before Hope makes a cutting remark. Luke's self-inflicted embarrassment humors the guys since Hope despises being referred to as darling by anyone. Hope continues saddling Patsy and Dottie to go riding with Faith while all eyes are on her. Outwardly, she seems unfazed. Inwardly, Hope's emotionally dizzy.

'What did Luke mean by that? Did I like Luke callin' me darlin'?'

Luke's disposition darkens while Hope's away and becomes short-tempered. It worsens after Hope visits the ranch long enough to check on Wyatt and departs again. Chester informs Hank of Luke's volatile behavior.

"Luke's professional 'round guests 'n happy with Faith but he's onry otherwise."

"Chester, it's soundin' like Luke's missin' Hope. Wyatt's a probable threat. Could Hope be Luke's Millie or Sally?"

"That's a stretch ain't it? Y'all think Hope affects Luke that much?"

"Luke's happy when Faith's around. Faith's an extension of Hope. Luke 'n Hope's emotional scars dictate their present actions. Those painful relationship failures affect any future possibilities."

"Are ya sayin' fear keeps 'em apart? It's tellin' how Hope 'n Luke look at each other now."

"Perhaps. I'm tryin' to figure out certain aspects of Luke's past. He hasn't opened up enough to answer some questions. How's Wyatt doin'? Heard he got banged up."

"He's concussed but he'll live."

Hope pulls up the next day and takes a puppy from the passenger seat. Luke holds the door as he exits the house so Hope can keep the squirming pup in both arms.

"Where's Chester?"

"In the kitchen. Join me for sweet tea."

Hope asks Luke, "Why aren'tcha with guests?"

"Hello to you too."

Luke follows Hope into the kitchen. She sees an empty space where the dishwasher had been.

"What happened?"

Luke returns to washing dishes.

"The dishwasher gave up the ghost last night. New one's on the way. What've we got here?"

Hope sets the energetic pup down next to Chester. "This little guy interrupted my work."

Chester detects a trace of perfume while Hope's next to him and notices she's wearing make-up again. *'Does Hope have a date with Wyatt?'*

Luke's also noticed Hope's transformation. *'Hope probably did that for Wyatt. She's naturally beautiful. That sweet scent's makin' me wanna hold and kiss her again. It's almost too much to resist.'*

Hope states, "I found him yesterday. He's a little banged up but okay otherwise."

Chester subtly watches Luke steal glances at Hope. *'Hope hasn't bothered to gussy up for years.'*

"Luke, this cur dog reminds me of you when y'all first arrived."

Hope responds indignantly. "He's no cur dog 'n you know it."

"Do I want to know what a cur dog is?"

Luke's question is answered by Chester's evil smirk.

"There's some Golden for sure."

"Couldja keep him a couple days? I'll find a better home soon 'n I have what y'all need in the truck."

"Sure. The Twisted Live Oak ain't the same without a dog. We can take naps together."

Chester puts the pup down and he trots to Luke and lies across his feet.

"I'll walk him so he's ready for those naps."

"That'd be mighty helpful."

Luke smiles. *'I miss the customers and their pets.'*

Hope's shocked the pup stays by Luke. "He was skittish around men yesterday."

"Sounds like you on Luke's first day."

"I was angry. Not skittish."

Chester remarks to Luke, "He sure seems to like you." *'The pup accepts Luke like Faith 'n Bullet.'*

Hope's astounded when the pup rolls over for a belly rub while Luke scratches his ears.

'This dog must trust Luke to do that.'

Chester grins knowing Hope's studying Luke while he's preoccupied.

'Animals know who they can trust. Luke's hair's grown out. He's not shavin' every day either. He's more rugged lookin'. And handsome.'

Hope's perfume saturates Luke's nostrils when he inhales deeply to retain the sweet aroma longer. Chester watches and wonders why Hope's brought the pup to the ranch.

'Hope knows people who foster animals. Is she here for a reason other than Wyatt?'

Hope states, "I'll check back in a couple days. Someone might take the pup in."

Chester notices Luke's happier while Hope's around. *'There's a definite connection.'*

Luke cares for the pup without instructions from Chester.

"I'm impressed. I thought I'd need to teach ya how to do everything."

"I've spent five years at a pet store. I know what to do. I've watched customer's pets while they're on vacation too."

Chester pauses. *'Luke opened up. I know more than he's aware though. Maybe he'll share more if I stop pushin' for information.'*

"People trusted you with their pets?"

"Yup. Shocking. And no wallets got taken."

"You got it back."

"Yeah. After savin' your dumb ass."

"That helped you earn it back."

"Right. Earning my own wallet back. Not buying what you're selling."

Hope returns and meets Chester by the riding barn. "I found a temporary home. It's not ideal but I'll take the pup off your hands. Has he been any trouble?"

Luke questions Hope's decision. "Won't that stress the pup? He could stay here. I'll take care of him."

Hope challenges Luke. "I don't think that's a good idea."

Chester realizes a fact. *'Hope's unaware Luke's caring for the pup alone.'* "The little guy can stay here."

Luke's next question surprises Hope. "Chester, could I keep him?" *'I enjoy taking care of him.'*

Chester's sly smile precedes his observation. "I knew y'all were gettin' attached. Sure. Why not?"

"I disagree, Chester. Luke's not stayin'. What happens when Luke leaves?"

"The dog stays. There's no downside."

Hope's incensed expression conceals her emotions. *'Do I want Luke to leave? I can't risk another heartache. I don't need Faith hurt.'*

Luke disrupts Hope's thoughts. "I think I'll name the puppy Austin. He's as lively as the town."

Chester's comment rubs Hope wrong. "Y'all're closer to bein' a cowboy."

Luke challenges Hope visibly annoyed eye roll.

"You still don't think I could be a cowboy, do you?"

Hope vehemently disputes Luke's question without thinking. "Bless your heart. It ain't that easy. No city boy's gonna be a real cowboy. Cowboys aren't afraid of horses. You're a pretender. Real wranglers work this ranch."

Hope finds Luke physically and emotionally attractive while battling inner turmoil which emerges as unchecked fury. Her fiery outburst disguises inner thoughts and emotions. *'Do I fully trust Luke? He's adapted to ranch life better than I thought he could. He's not committed if he still wants to leave. What if I ask him to stay?'*

Luke's seething over Hope's judgmental attitude. *'Everyone still condemns me for no reason. Nothing's changed.'* "You don't know a damn thing about me. You haven't learned who I am." *'Hope's beauty is skin deep. She's so uncaring.'*

Chester infuses unwanted humor. "Y'all need to kiss again 'n make up."

"She can't handle romantic connections."

Hope slaps Luke's cheek. "How dare you. I'm leaving. I'll come back to see if the pup's still alive."

"Austin'll be alive. For the record, I could easily become a cowboy. It's not the outside appearance. It's whatcha do and how you do it. Like takin' care of others 'n having pride in your work. It's not about where you're born. And I can be trusted. With Austin. And Faith."

Luke storms off before Hope responds. Chester notes her flustered condition.

"Is he abandoning the dog? I'll be back in a couple days."

Hope's oblivious that Luke's capable of caring for the pup. Chester reacts disapprovingly to her harsh statements.

"I agree with Luke. He set you straight, didn't he?"

Chester's critical tone baffles Hope.

"Why's Luke mad? It's true. He's not a cowboy. He didn't even like horses. He's not from Texas."

'Hope's not seein' Luke's changin' 'n growin'.' "I thought I raised you better. You continue judging Luke without knowing all the facts. You could give Luke an honest chance to show what he's made of."

Chester's irritated statement confuses Hope. "Why're ya mad at me? I need to return to work. I will check on the pup."

Chester emphasizes, "The pup's name is Austin. I like it."

Hope ponders Chester's wrath. *'Why's Chester mad at me? I didn't say or do anything wrong. Luke acts like the guys but it's an act. He's not attached to the ranch or ranch life like us. Why is Luke getting to me? Why him? Why now? I really wanted to kiss him instead of slapping him. Maybe I should spend more time with Wyatt.'*

TWENTY-TWO

Hope stops at Beth's to figure things out.

"I don't know why Chester's mad at me. I feel like I let him down somehow. I hate disappointin' him. He's done so much for me 'n Faith."

"You spoke your truth. But is it the real truth? Could there be another reason you attacked Luke?"

"I didn't attack Luke."

"Really? You slapped him. You insulted him. Why do you lash out like that with him?"

Hope apprehensively asks her next question. "How'd y'all know Ben was the one for you?"

Beth answers immediately. "Honey, that's easy. I felt butterflies the moment I saw Ben. He was and is the most handsome cowpuncher I'd ever seen. Love at first sight."

Hope's momentarily silent. "I felt that with Wyatt. I didn't with Luke. But am I fallin' for Luke?"

Beth moves in to hug Hope as tears fall down her cheeks.

"I'm confused. I don't know what to do anymore. I don't want my heart broke again. I'm not sure I know what love is. Wyatt's the closest possibility."

"You were smitten with him."

"My last choice nearly destroyed me. Faith and all y'all saved me."

"Hope, you can't hide from life. It happens anyway. You don't control life or love. They just happen."

"Have I wasted the last eight years?"

"No, not at all. You healed. You've grown. But y'all built your walls thicker 'n higher. Life's still ahead of y'all. It looks promisin' if you ask me whether with Luke or Wyatt."

Luke returns once Hope leaves and sits on the kitchen floor so Austin can crawl into his lap. Austin's reddish coat resembles a Golden Retriever. His tail curls prominently into a half-circled arc and his legs and fur are longer to indicate he's a mixed breed. His elongated snout is nuzzled against Luke's side. Chester chuckles, "You two've taken to each other right quick. We'll find the cowboy within y'all yet."

"Hope doesn't think so. Have you met anyone and felt like you were meant to be together?"

"Yep. I married her as fast as I could."

"What? Whoa. That's not what I meant. I mean Austin. It feels right to keep him."

"Are ya sure that's what you mean?"

"Yeah."

"If you say so. Hope's wrong 'bout you bein' a cowboy."

Luke forgets Hope's threat to check on Austin. He enters the kitchen two days later before his next assignment. Katie returns with an empty tray.

"Howdy Luke. I brought Chester a sandwich. Y'all need somethin' too?"

Luke's startled and acts like he's someplace he shouldn't be. "Sorry Katie. I needed a snack."

Katie's amused by Luke's apology. "Relax. You don't wanna be hungry while ya work. I think Chester's got something for you. There's an envelope with your name on his desk."

Luke's puzzled. *'No one knows I'm here.'*

He knocks on the open office door and watches Chester become distressed and stammer and stutter.

"Um. Oh, um, uh, Luke, I didn't think you'd be here now."

Luke stares at a large manila envelope with his name boldly printed on it. "Is that for me?"

Chester acts like he's been caught with something he shouldn't have. "Luke, you gave me no choice. This may've been a mistake."

Chester's partial explanation confuses Luke. "What? Can I see that?"

"I know how your parents died. You've never mentioned a sister."

Luke can't discern Chester's message.

"You forced my hand. I needed information. I know why you're so onry and closed off."

Luke's slow to react until anger builds after understanding Chester's words. "You investigated me? You betrayed the little trust I had in you."

Chester's brazenly selfish act causes Luke to storm from the office and shatters Luke's growing trust in him.

"Luke!"

Luke aggressively swings the screen door open and breaks it off its hinges to land on the deck. He passes Hope without making eye contact. Hope's outrage switches to alarm when Chester hurriedly exits the house.

'Somethin's wrong.'

Chester's words confirm Hope's fear. "Luke. Stop. We need to talk 'bout this."

Hope turns to follow Chester rushing past her. "Chester, what's wrong?"

Luke's resolutely striding down the driveway until the sheriff's car appears. He halts and looks back to shout incredulously at Chester. "You called the sheriff?"

Chester's just as surprised. "No. I didn't."

Luke's glare shifts to Hope. *Bitch. She'll do anything to get me arrested.'*

Bob's perplexed by the driveway scene. "What's goin' on here?"

Luke fiercely answers, "I'm leaving this hellhole."

Chester notes Hope's trepidation as Luke heads down the red gravel driveway again. *'Hope's afraid.'*

Bob inquires, "Is Luke finished here?"

"That's not it. There's somethin' I need to make right with Luke."

Bob unholsters his pistol. "Luke, stop. I'll shoot y'all for resisting arrest."

Luke raises his right hand and extends his middle finger without stopping.

"You're disregarding a direct order."

Bob begins squeezing the trigger.

"No, Bob, don't shoot Luke."

Hope's panicked voice surprises Bob and halts his action after hearing her caring appeal. Bob loudly reveals why he's at the ranch.

"Hope might be in danger."

Luke spins around to forcefully growl out his questions. "Why's Hope in danger? How? By who?"

Bob's stunned by Luke's aggressive interrogation.

"I'll explain everything inside. Luke's involved also. Whether y'all like it or not."

Hope notices the envelope when they enter the office. *'Luke Halsey Anderson.'*

Luke's next question focuses Hope on her impending trouble.

"How's Hope in danger?"

Bob speaks directly to Luke. "Hope's ex-husband might've been involved in her attack."

Hope's face pales while collapsing into the stuffed brown leather chair by the door. Luke involuntarily moves closer.

'That shook Hope.'

"One suspect's facin' two counts of attempted murder and rolled over for a deal. He mentioned Joe hired them to eliminate you but might've fled to Mexico."

Hope buries her face in her hands and leans forwards and begins crying. "He's gonna kill me."

Luke pushes thoughts of Hope's cold, standoffish behavior aside and kneels beside her to put his arm around her. Luke disregards the envelope when Hope presses into his comforting hug. Her emotional dam breaks and she soaks his shoulder with tears until regaining some composure.

"Who'll protect Hope?"

Bob's perplexed. "Lord knows you're capable of protecting Hope."

"Chester's ended that possibility, sheriff."

Chester responds, "We need to discuss that."

Luke cuts Chester off in a low heated tone. "We're done talking."

Their exchange dumbfounds Hope. She stands and locks eyes with Chester. "What's wrong with you two? Why's Luke leaving?" *'Why's Luke leavin' when I need him most?'*

Pure hatred tinges Luke's response. "Y'all wanna explain, Chester?"

"What's Luke talkin' about?"

Chester slides the envelope towards Hope and sits down. She studies Luke's full name. *'Halsey? That's odd.'*

Hope's unaware Luke's middle name honors a great World War Two admiral. Her eyes dart between Chester and Luke while pulling the paperwork out.

"Is this what I think it is?"

Chester sighs while Hope re-examines Luke with a sympathetic gaze. *'This made Luke furious.'*

"You investigated Luke? He didn't tell you anything so y'all decided to find out anyway, right? Luke, I'm sorry. I understand why you're angry."

Luke replies bitterly. "You knew about this."

"NO! No. Chester did this to me but for a better reason."

Hope turns and glares at Chester. "But not this time!"

Luke snaps. "I don't care. I'm leaving. That's it."

Katie hears the commotion. *'It's pretty intense in there.'*

Luke walks to the door. Hope's voice sounds small and weak.

"Luke, this is why I carry a gun."

Luke opens the door but doesn't exit. *'Hope's never sounded like that.'*

"My ex-husband threatened to kill me after our divorce. He said I embarrassed him. I've lived in fear he'd carry out his threat but also harm Faith. She matters most to me. Along with everyone at the ranch."

Hope pauses, "And I do mean everyone."

Luke thinks, *'Hope means Wyatt.'*

Hope's confident nature evaporates. Her adverse attitude towards Luke vanishes during her anguished revelation. Luke steps into the hallway. *'Hope's had difficult times too.'*

Luke faces Hope and gazes into her distraught emerald eyes as tears roll down her cheeks. Luke's stern expression vanishes.

"If. And I do mean if. If I stay, it's only until your ex is caught. I won't let Faith get hurt."

Relief washes over Hope after hearing Luke's assurance to honestly protect her and Faith. Chester sees a twinkle replace the sadness in her eyes and a slight smile form on her lips.

'Hank's on to somethin'. Hope 'n Luke can't admit how they feel for each other.'

Hope approaches Luke to speak softly. "Thank's for stayin'."

Luke thinks, *'What am I getting into?'*

Hope hugs Luke but he doesn't immediately hug her back.

Chester ruminates, *'I need to clear things with Luke right quick.'*

Luke states, "I've saved your ass once or twice. What's one more time?"

Hope cheerfully hisses and giggles until more large fear induced tears escape her lively green eyes again. "I appreciate you stayin'."

"Yeah, well, ya got Wyatt too."

"Luke, I want you protectin' me 'n Faith."

Hope's sweet yet strong Texas drawl captivates Luke. A male voice quietly sings about seeing miles and miles of Texas in his loved one's eye's on Chester's radio while Hope stares into Luke's sympathetic hazel eyes. Luke thinks, *'I might understand what he means.'*

Bob adds, "We'll patrol your neighborhood more often."

"Thanks Bob."

Bob informs Luke, "No missin' person's report on you yet."

Luke's eyes cloud over. Hope sees how the disconcerting news affects Luke. *'Poor Luke. He's been forgotten. Like my parents forgot me.'*

Luke dwells on Bob's news. *'Guess I don't matter up north.'*

Hope queries Chester. "Could Luke 'n I spend some time alone?"

"Take all the time you need."

Hope gazes into Luke's eyes. "Can we ride? And talk?"

TWENTY-THREE

Luke's drawn in by Hope's pleading eyes. "We can ride 'n talk."

They saddle Patsy and Willie. "Chester's right. You like ridin' to sort through things, don'tcha?"

Hope gets defensive. "What else has he told you?"

"Nothin' else. You secrets are safe. Don't worry."

Cody questions Ben while the pair rides off. "Hope still hates Luke, right?"

Billy adds, "Yeah, what's that about?"

Ben shrugs while thinking, *'Hope might be gettin' serious 'bout Wyatt unless there could be somethin' buildin' with Luke.'*

Luke breaks the uncomfortable silence. "It's strange riding with you instead of guests."

"Thanks. That's not very comfortin'."

Luke observes, *'Hope sounds less frazzled already.'*

Hope asks bluntly, "Luke, can I really trust you?"

Luke notes Hope's shimmering eyes. "My answer probably won't matter if you're asking that." *'Is there a deeper reason? I've saved your life 'n you still don't trust me.'*

"You say y'all're leavin' still. You were leavin' today. You act like the ranch is a virus you need to escape from."

"I'm vermin trying to escape a hostile environment."

Hope states, "I was mad at you."

"I promised to stay until Joe's caught."

Luke's tone prompts Hope's next question, "Can you keep that promise? It could take a while."

"I've got nowhere to go."

"Faith needs your protection too."

"I'm aware of that. Y'all got Wyatt to help you too."

"Wyatt can't keep me safe like you can. Why do you care about Faith so much?" *'Faith's one reason I want trust you.'* "Faith's not your daughter but you treat her as such. Why?"

"I like Faith. She makes me feel…"

Luke goes silent. *'What does Faith make me feel?'*

Hope wonders, *'What? What does Faith make you feel? How do you feel about me? What are you hidin'? Who am I to ask that?'*

"Why won't you open up, Luke?"

Luke shrugs.

"I thought I knew the man I married. I said yes as fast as possible when Joe proposed which pissed Colt off. We tried datin' but Colt was fixin' on joinin' the navy to fly jets. I didn't want another relationship with someone who wouldn't be around all the time. I tried that during my rodeo career."

"Wyatt?"

"Yeah. Joe said 'n did all the right things a girl likes. I thought he loved me. He worked with his dad's construction company and did the same to other women when he travelled to oversee projects in other towns."

Hope pauses and Luke processes her past. *'Hope reacts like she does because of that. She had genuine heartbreak too.'*

"I understand why y'all hate me."

"I don't hate you." *'Not anymore.'*

Luke raises an eyebrow. "Hope, your life is none of my business. Remember."

"Y'all're willin' to protect me 'n Faith. You should know certain things."

"What do I really need to know?"

Hope's eyes widen. "You're usin' y'all more."

Luke frowns, "You people broke me."

"You broke Ben first."

"Ouch. True. But still."

"Chester might be right. Y'all could become a cowboy yet."

"I distinctly remember an irate woman declare this city boy'd never be a cowboy."

Hope recalls Chester's angered outburst. *'I was wrong. Luke's changin' for the better.'*

Luke misinterprets Hope's silence. "Sorry, I shouldn't've said that."

"I might've been a little wrong."

"Are you admitting you were wrong about me?"

"I'm sayin' I didn't have all the facts right."

Luke chuckles, "That's not what I heard. Why haven't you remarried? You can pick any guy."

"I've never been lucky with guy's 'n love."

Luke's expression challenges Hope's statement.

"That didn't come out right. I'd only try if I knew he's the right one."

Luke smiles, "You'd get picky for your second marriage? Should've tried that the first time."

"I don't trust most men. They're nothin' but trouble. Holly could care less. You know that."

"Holly approached me. I got so drunk that night I don't remember getting to the ranch. I passed out before anything happened."

Hope's relieved. *'JeniMay 'n Jubilee were right. Holly didn't sleep with Luke.'*

"Why did you marry Joe if he cheated on you?"

Hope's defensive after Luke's erroneous assumption. "I didn't know Joe was cheatin' till I was pregnant. He accused me of trapping him."

"Trap him? You were married."

"In a one-way love. God blessed me with Faith to get through a dark time. She was the reason I got out of bed every mornin'. I was so broken. I cried for days after signing the divorce papers. I felt like I failed."

Hope wipes back tears and Luke recalls how he felt to lose his parents.

'I felt lost and broken too. Hope's marriage died like my parents did.'

"It wasn't your fault. You weren't a failure."

"Joe made me feel otherwise."

"I can't imagine cheating on you. You've done well to keep living."

"My pathetic life probably bores you. You've lived other places in big cities."

"It's not all it's cracked up to be. The Hill Country offers a lot and you've built a life here." *'Should I open up? Hope won't wanna hear about my life.'*

'Is Luke bein' honest?' "Sometimes I've been the windshield. Mostly, I've been the bug."

Luke locks eyes with Hope. *'I'm nervous.'* "Maybe I should share something too. Hank's pushing me to open up more. Chester stole my life though."

"That was wrong. Chester went too far to protect the ranch."

"I didn't give him a choice. I'm pissed but I'll deal with that later."

"Don't hurt Chester."

"Hurt him? It goes against my training. I saved his sorry ass."

Luke realizes he broke his promise.

"How did you save his ass?"

Luke's silent momentarily. *'Better yet, how do I save my own ass now?'*

"By getting Faith off Waylon so she wasn't hurt. You'd probably kill him for letting that happen."

"Maybe. What training?"

"I, uh, I, well." *'This opening up ain't going well so far.'*

"You've seen me fight. I'm a highly trained black belt who can hurt someone with one punch. Or worse."

"You mean you can kill someone."

"Yes."

"Like you did to save me. Again."

Luke looks away to avoid answering.

Hope wonders, *'What's Luke hiding?'* "How many people have you killed?"

"Only one." *'With my hands.'*

"You beat those guys rather easily. Bo too."

"I don't wanna talk about it. It brings nothing but trouble."

"You don't like fightin'. Why? The guys love talkin' 'bout fights."

"No one wins a fight. Both sides lose when control is lost. Fighting's necessary for self-preservation and protection. Not for ego boosting."

"Whoa. Philosophical. You're not like the guys at all. I kinda like that."

"Do you really understand?"

"I think so. I'm glad I talked them outta tryin' to whoop your ass."

"Wait. What? They were serious?"

Hope realizes she's opened a can of worms best left closed. "Um, never mind. Forget I said anything."

"No, it's good y'all stopped 'em. It would've ended badly. Worse than Ben."

"Why did you hit Ben?"

"You don't know?"

"No."

"We disagreed on my score for riding Bullet."

"That's not the reason."

"Ask Ben. He'll explain it."

"I'll find out. I always do."

Luke shifts the conversation's direction. "Chester said he knows how my parents died. I'm to blame."

Hope's shocked, "What do you mean?"

"My choice was a circus. They didn't make it home. My uncle died a few years later."

"Luke, how was that your fault?"

"I don't want to talk about it. Hank is helpin' me see things differently."

"Trust Hank. He's a retired psychologist." *'I get Hank and Chester's message better now.'*

"That's why the old coot knows what to say."

"You didn't know that?"

"Nope."

"I'll listen too. If ya wanna talk to me."

"I want to believe you. Maybe when I'm ready."

Hope recalls Hank's message. *'Now I know why Hank told me to talk to Luke. He's guarded like me. He's gone through hard times.'*

Luke decides to test Hope. *'Let's see if Hope'll really listen.'*

"My girlfriend 'n I dated for four years until she cheated on me. I thought we'd get married."

'I wasn't expecting Luke to share anything like that. At least he can commit.'

"It's my fault. Linda turned me down. She wasn't ready when I proposed."

'What woman wouldn't want marriage after four years? Luke's handsome. And nice.'

"That must've hurt."

"It did. It still does."

'Luke's not the same person anymore. We do have things in common. I've clearly misjudged him.'

"Is Linda why you haven't hit on me?"

"What?" *'Hope expected me to hit on her?'*

"Never mind. That was a stupid question." *'Would Luke stay after Joe's caught? Could I take a chance with him? Instead of Wyatt?'*

TWENTY-FOUR

Luke catches Hope glancing at him while riding.

"What's wrong? Go ahead. Make fun of me."

Hope blushes, *'Damn, Luke caught me starin' like a shy school girl.'*

"Nothin'. You're doin' everything right. Without fear."

"I understand horses now. A pony threw me when I was a kid 'n bit my arm."

"I remember seein' a mark on your arm. You got bit?"

"Yeah. I was scared 'n ran off into the crowd. My dad found me though."

"You scared? I can't imagine that after seein' ya fight."

Luke stops his horse. "Hope, there's a lot you don't know about me. You may not like most of it."

"You're a mystery. I don't know you that well. Like I know the guys."

"And Wyatt."

"I'm not sure I know Wyatt anymore."

"I know I'm not handy like the guys here. I'm a small fish in Chester's pond."

Hope wonders, *'Why does Luke think so little of himself?'*

"Have you ever been married, Luke?"

Hope's question emotionally wounds Luke.

"Sorry, I don't know why I asked that."

"No. I've never been married."

"You were engaged, right?"

Luke sighs, "I wasn't engaged either. She never said yes."

"Was your girlfriend…"

"Ex-girlfriend."

"Sorry, ex-girlfriend. She was the only one special enough to propose to? Never mind, of course she was. She's the only who made you feel that way?" *'That sounded stupid. I sound stupid. I shot Luke so he'd never propose to me.'*

Luke wonders, *'Did Hank mention Jini to Hope?'* "There was one other person but I pushed her away. Let's change the subject."

Hope hears sorrow in Luke's voice. *'Luke's been hurt like I have.'*

Luke gazes into Hope's eyes. *'Hope's eyes remind me of Jini's the first time I saw her.'* "I don't know why I told you any of that. It's not like you care. Or that you should. You nearly shot me dead after prejudging me before knowing anything."

"I did judge you. You judged me too. We're strangers so we don't trust each other. Maybe we can change that."

"I guess it's possible. I don't matter up north. Maybe I should stay here. You know Wyatt came back for you. I've got no one."

'Luke's hurt knowin' he's been forgotten.'

Hope smiles warmly, "Stayin' might be good for ya. Y'all're not a terrible disruption anymore." *'Chester could be right 'bout gettin' to know Luke better.'*

Hope bites her lower lip and brushes her hair back. Luke studies her words and actions. *'Is Hope showing interest in me? Wyatt did return for Hope. Could something happen with Hope if I stayed?'*

"Faith thinks you're special. She hasn't acted this way 'round a stranger before."

"She's a great kid."

"Faith trusts you 'n wants to see you all the time."

"You don't trust me though? I don't blame you. I showed up a tired, drunken mess 'n broke Ben's jaw. Hard to trust someone you hate. Plus y'all nearly blow my head off."

"I don't hate you."

Luke's eyebrow rises.

"Alright, I did hate you. I may've over-reacted a little. *I'm never livin' that down.'*

"A little?"

Hope's lips curl upward mischievously. "Fine. I over-reacted a lot. But you hurt Ben. He's my big brother 'n protector. I promise not to shootcha again if you behave."

'It's easier talkin' to Hope than I thought. I wonder if I could've talked to Linda like this. Would it've mattered? Would she still cheat? How did Hank put it, maybe God put me on a path I wasn't ready to understand yet? Is this my path? Here? Hope?'

Hope examines Luke. *'Chester's makin' a cowboy outta Luke. He rides like one.'*

Luke interrupts Hope's thoughts. "Would Joe try hurtin' you or Faith?"

Hope shudders, "Joe was furious. He threatened to kill me. We should head back."

Luke's surprised when Hope nervously kisses his cheek once their horses are in their stalls. "I learned that from Faith."

Luke grins, "Faith's a good teacher."

Hope relaxes. "Thanks for stayin' to help me and Faith."

"You're welcome."

Hope's show of affection baffles Scooter. Hope exits the barn and spots Chester on the deck and heads straight for him.

"Leave Luke alone!"

"Yes ma'am."

"He's been through a lot 'n he's hurtin'. He needs time to figure things out."

Chester grins after Hope walks to her truck. *'Wyatt's got competition.'*

TWENTY-FIVE

uke's mood darkens to match his furious expression and aggressive approach once he catches sight of Chester.

'Incomin' storm.'

"We're gonna talk when I'm ready."

Chester nods. "The door'll be open."

"What did you say on my first day? Don't put a bird feeder where ya don't want bird shit. Your investigation is a bird feeder comin' back to bite your ass now. I'd leave but I promised to help Hope."

Chester's agitated his own words are being used against him while reviewing Hope's reprimand. *'Bullet sensed Luke's pain. Hank might be right 'bout Hope 'n Luke bein' positive influences on each other. I have a ranch to protect.'*

Colt's corvette and a Harley Davidson head up the long driveway as Hope reaches the gate so she reverses course. *'Why's Colt here? Who's driving the motorcycle?'*

Holly exits Colt's car and Jazlynn appears from under her helmet. She shakes her hair loose so it flows freely down her back over a leather vest and sports bra. A nine millimeter pistol is tucked into her workout leggings waistband. Holly hugs Colt. "It was fun to go shootin' and workout today."

Jazlynn beelines towards Luke and kisses him while throwing her arms around him before he reacts. She smiles when Hope turns around and drives away.

'I can't compete with Jazzy or Holly.'

Luke watches Hope depart. *'Hope saw Jazzy kiss me. I wish she stayed. I'd've hugged and kissed her to send a message.'*

Hope travels overnight to Fort Worth to help another veterinarian. Beth's at Hope's house for when Faith wakes and to inform Chester of the unexpected development.

"Mornin' Chester. Hope's in Cowtown. Faith's stayin' with Ben 'n me. Hope said to leave Luke alone even if Jazzy's takin' care of him. Whatever that means."

"Hope missed Luke cussin' Jazlynn out."

Luke becomes nastier during Hope's absence and lashes out at Danny and Kyle while they goof off.

"Will you two idiots grow up already? Figure out your life."

Chester theorizes with Hank. "Luke's professional 'round guests and happy to see Faith but off the rails moody alone."

"Hope's affectin' Luke's behavioral twists 'n turns."

Jack quizzes Ben for answers. "What set Luke off?"

"I have no idea."

Luke dwells on Hope's personally disclosed information. *'Katie was right. I misjudged Hope. I didn't know certain things. Hope's had a tough life and may've made some bad choices like I did. Is that what draws me to her? We can understand each other.'*

Holly learns about Luke's private ride with Hope. *'Hope's not movin' in on Luke. I'll derail any chance she has.'*

Luke barges into Chester's office while Holly pleads for a day off to go to Austin with Jazlynn.

"Grand-daddy, we want to go town."

"Hell no! You two get into more trouble than she's worth 'n y'all've got work."

Luke rudely addresses Holly. "Shape up, Holly. You work like the rest of us here. Get out so I can straighten this asshole out."

Luke's abrasive verbal attack stuns Holly. "How dare you talk to me like that! Grand-daddy, tell Luke he can't talk to me that way."

"Luke's right. Y'all got work." *'Luke sounds like a ranch foreman, not an unwilling ranch hand.'*

Holly's disgusted glare shoots daggers at Luke.

"God, I hope she stops chasing me now."

Chester shrugs. "Probably not." *'Holly's not one to get bossed around by anyone. Even me.'*

Luke snarls his next words while imposingly pounding his clenched fists on Chester's desk.

"You stole my life from me."

Luke's venomous indictment brings Chester's inner Marine out. He sits back and responds to Luke's verbal broadside.

"I had no choice. You were uninvited, unknown, broke Ben's jaw, rode my prize buckin' bronc. Y'all ain't opened up to ease suspicions. What would you've done in my boots?"

Luke's intense glare precedes his response. "How about starting a civil conversation instead of always threatening jail as a consequence?"

Chester tries staring Luke down but blinks and looks away. *'It's like challenging an angry canebrake rattler.'* "You didn't seem like a civil conversation was possible."

Luke's reply drips heavily with sarcasm. "Obviously."

"I like things simple. I hate complications. Especially unnecessary ones. You're a major complication. That report showed y'all've had challenges 'n didn't handle 'em well. Regret thrives on a troubled past. Opportunity builds a better future. Moments are meant to be experienced in the present. Stop livin' in the past. Everybody dies but not everyone lives."

"I don't want a lecture."

"Tough. A bad attitude and poor choices got you here. A positive attitude 'n better choices'll help ya succeed."

Luke opens his mouth but closes it after Chester's unexpected diatribe throws him off.

"Y'all got somethin' to say, say it."

"What about Holly?"

Chester rubs his chin stubble. "Holly's anythin' but simple but she's family." *'She might be more complicated than Luke.'*

"Hank's tellin' me to open up more. Even with you. You stole that. I don't easily trust people. Too many people've let me down after losing my parents."

Luke's second reference that his life's been stolen rubs Chester the wrong way.

"I have a ranch 'n people to protect. I might've made a mistake here."

Chester's conciliatory tone is interrupted by Hope.

"What's goin' on here?"

Hope texted Katie for a late breakfast before picking Faith up. Katie sees Luke angrily enter Chester's office and calls Hope to inform her of Luke's moodiness.

"I'm nearly there. Chester's stupid stunt pissed Luke off."

Hope's piercing green eyes lock onto Luke. Chester watches Luke's aggressive posture transform while his angry glare softens.

'Huh. Hope's timing is perfect. Luke was about to go ballistic.'

"Are you alright, Luke? Is he botherin' you?"

"More like the other way around, Hope."

"I'm not talkin' to you."

"Excuse me."

"I'm sorry I wasn't here to help."

Hope's presence tempers Luke's fury. His narrowed eyes widen."

Chester notes, *'Hope's soothin' Luke's attitude. Like Millie did with me.'*

Hope's eyes possess a shimmering new energy.

'Even Wyatt hasn't made Hope happy like this.'

Chester speaks up, "Luke, figure out who 'n what's important. Keep what matters 'n let the rest go."

Hope listens to Chester's message. *'I've never heard Chester say that before. Is that just for Luke?'*

Chester continues, "Don't forget your past, you'll repeat mistakes. This Confederate flag reminds us when right 'n wrong nearly tore this country apart."

Luke's astonished to learn Chester's reasoning for the flag. *'I was wrong. Chester has that flag to remember a terrible part of our history we overcame.'*

"Time 'n love are our most precious gifts. Time can't be controlled, borrowed, or saved."

Hope contemplates Chester's message while he continues.

"Time gains value as we age. Live life where and how you want 'n chase your dreams to avoid regrets."

Hope thinks, *'I've listened to Chester all my life. What's Luke's thinkin'?'*

"What if I don't wanna live here? Or do this?"

Hope's overcome by a sickening feeling in her stomach.

"Keep your promise to Hope. Y'all can leave once Joe's caught."

Chester's last words stop Luke's heart and knot his stomach. He's searched inwardly since Hope's conversation opened his eyes to new possibilities. *'Can I really leave here? And Hope 'n Faith? I can picture my life with them now. Hank's made it clear Linda 'n I would've failed eventually.'*

Hope's stance becomes rigid. *'I can't trust Luke. Or any man.'*

She crosses her arms over her waist. "I'm gonna pick Faith up. I miss her."

Hope's rapid exit dumbfounds Luke. *'Dang it. I had questions for Hope. Her answers'll help decide if I stay or not.'*

Hope rushes past Katie while raising one hand to her mouth.

'Hope looks sad. Or sick. What happened in there?'

Hope's rebuilding walls with every step. She hears her name while nearing her truck.

"Wyatt, why are you really here?"

"I came back for you, Hope. For us. I wanna try again."

"I need to get my daughter. I'll think about it."

Hope's confused during the drive to Beth's.

TWENTY-SIX

Katie calls Beth after Hope's hasty departure. "Hey Beth, Hope's headed your way but she looked sick, or sad. Check on her, okay." "I will."

Chester walks Luke out of the office. "I think the good Lord's made ya better 'n what you've settled for. I've had plenty of days I got rode hard 'n put away wet. Struggles challenge us to figure out who we are, what we're made of, what we're capable of accomplishing."

"Life's beaten me down hard."

"You've hid from life 'n avoided challenges which could grow ya." *'I did after the war.'* "Turmoil drives a person towards success or failure. The strength of your character determines the outcome." *'Luke could consider stayin' on 'n callin' the ranch home.'*

Sorrow tinges Luke's response. "I've always known I haven't tried as hard as I could. I never felt motivated. I ignored good influences."

"Y'all oughta start workin' smarter, not harder."

"I'd like to be better. For myself and for someone else too."

Luke's self-awareness impresses Chester. *'Is Luke thinkin' 'bout someone in particular?'*

Katie hears their conversation. *'I don't hear any reason for Hope leavin' like she did.'*

Chester adds, "Luke, you're stronger than you realize."

Luke recalls his sensei's advice. *My life would be so different if I listened to him.'*

"Life'll move ya sideways or backwards sometimes to help ya move forwards again."

"I'm not sure I can make good choices anymore. I've made so many bad ones." *'I've really screwed my life up.'*

"Today presents opportunity for change 'n tomorrow's a new start for sure. Life's changin' for ya already. Maybe someone's part of that change."

"Who? You?"

"Nope."

"You mean Hank."

"Not Hank either."

'Who does he mean?'

"Luke, you're disciplined to stay fit. Apply that to your life overall."

"I haven't set those goals." *'I see that clearly now. Could Hope be part of my life? Is that who Chester meant?'*

Luke's reaching for the door when Katie steps into view.

"Ma'am. I need to get back to work. I hear the owner's a hard-assed son of a bitch."

Luke's devilish grins induces Katie's chuckle. *'Not to me.'*

Wyatt approaches while Luke opens the door and the two men size each other up while Chester steps outside.

"Hiya Chester. I'm good to return to work. Where wouldja like me?"

"Find Ben. See where he needs ya."

"Yes sir. I forgot somethin' in the bunkhouse then I'll find Ben." *'Soon, I'll trade the bunkhouse for Hope's house.'*

Luke looks back at Wyatt while walking to the guest houses. *'I really wish Hope hadn't left.'*

Katie questions Chester. "Luke's not the guy y'all wanted to kill some months ago, is he?"

"Nope."

Katie points at Wyatt. "Is he the same?"

"Not sure."

TWENTY-SEVEN

ope, didja miss Faith that much?" *'Somethin's wrong.'*
Beth examines Hope's moist reddened eyes. Hope sniffles, "Yeah.
I missed Faith. Where is she?"

"She's out back with my daughters."

"I'd like to get her home. I'm tired."

"You look upset. Come inside. Faith's good to stay longer."

"I'd rather go home."

Beth examines Hope. "What's wrong, Hope? Don't tell me nothin'. It's written all over your face. I know you too damned well. Did somethin' happen up north?"

"No. That went well."

"Did Chester upset you?"

Hope neglects to recognize Beth knows she stopped at the ranch first.

"Don't be silly. Chester didn't upset me."

"Then what's got you goin'? Did Luke or Wyatt do somethin'? Should I tell Ben?"

Hope looks down. "Luke didn't do anything."

"What's goin' on? I don't believe you."

Hope stares at Beth. "Luke's leavin' after Joe's caught."

Beth states, "Aha. Luke is involved. Luke could stay if y'all'd be honest with him. He's always said he'd leave. Wyatt poses a threat to any chance Luke has with you."

"How? I'm confused. I'm not sure how I feel about anything. Or anyone. I can't get hurt."

"Honey, that horse left the stables already. You're hurtin' anyway. You try not feelin' anything but guess what, you are. Talk to Luke. Talk to Wyatt."

"I did talk with Luke last week. I told him parts of my life 'n he shared parts of his with me."

"Hope, that's amazin'. You haven't shared anything with most anyone. That's tellin'."

"But Luke's still leaving."

"One talk won't change everything. Are ya sure that's what he said?"

"Not in so many words."

"So y'all're projectin' fear into a situation that might not exist."

"Luke asked Chester what could happen after Joe's caught. Chester told him he could leave if he wanted to."

"But Luke didn't actually say he'd leave. You're assumin' this."

"No. I know he'll leave the ranch. And me."

"Stop it, Hope! You're allowed to have a happy life. Whether it's with Luke or Wyatt."

"It'd be easier if I didn't feel anything."

"Safer maybe. Not easier. And you'd feel things anyway. Stay here 'n figure this out today."

"Okay. I don't really wanna be alone anyway."

Beth's phone rings. "Yes honey. Is everything alright?"

Hope's curious when Beth's silent for a moment.

"I see. I'll tell Hope. Love you more."

"Is somethin' wrong? Do I need to go back to the ranch?"

"Everything's fine. Ben let me know Chester officially hired Wyatt on."

"What does that mean?"

"Maybe it won't matter if Luke leaves."

Maybe it does. To me.

TWENTY-EIGHT

Scooter informs Chester that Luke and Willie are missing the next morning.

"Shit. The horses ain't ready 'n we've got an early mornin' trail ride. This'll set the day back." *'That bastard knows I'm a stickler for schedules. He better not've run off.'*

"Saddle Waylon up. I'll be back."

Chester returns with his .45 strapped to his hip.

"Are ya gonna shoot the lad?"

"I'm not takin' any chances."

Chester tracks Luke's horse through unused pasture to a stand of Live Oaks. *'There's Willie.'*

Luke's sitting against the far side of a tree so Chester swings Waylon around quietly to face Luke.

'I wasn't expectin' this.'

Luke stares up at Chester with a lost look. "I reckon I'm in trouble. I didn't finish my work."

"Y'all take your time. The others'll cover for you. Get your head straight." *'Is Luke comin' to terms with his past?'*

Chester's statement dumbfounds Luke while Chester rides off to allow him more time and space.

'Luke's hit a fork in his road and has tough decisions to make about his future.'

Luke comprehends the ranch can provide a positive environment for growth and maturation. He's become receptive to Hank and Chester's healthy guidance instead of avoiding it as in prior years. Linda may have shattered Luke's dreams but Hope offers a chance at a new beginning. Adverse forces are far away to allow Luke to delve into old habits and excuses.

'I never shared my past with Linda. I pushed her away. I thought it was too embarrassing. Hank's right, I'm punishing myself for an event beyond my control. I should try opening up here. Maybe even with Hope. I failed Linda by not talking so she'd understand who I was. What if I'm falling for Hope? I wasn't expecting that. I wasn't expecting anything here.'

Chester returns to the barn and calls Ben and Scooter over. "Discreetly pass the word, Luke needs time off."

The men nod and inform the others between tasks. They've watched Luke become a good wrangler. Midday, Scooter watches Luke return to the riding barn.

"What can I help with?"

"Saddles need removing. Horses need brushing."

Luke works silently after his inward exploration leaves him exhausted. Wyatt wonders aloud, "Luke can't hack life or ranchin', can he?"

"Y'all don't know him like we do."

"I've known guys like him."

Cody and Jack let Luke unsaddle horses alone. Luke's finally dealing with reality head-on instead of avoiding challenges now that his emotional dam has collapsed. Past mistakes flood his mind like flotsam.

'I'm more confused 'n lost now.'

Chester calls Luke to the office that evening. "You need to help Jazlynn at the gym."

"Why?"

"Holly made a valid point Jazlynn needs your help. I can't believe I said that."

"Why me?"

"She had a training mishap of sorts."

"Jazlynn has a trainer, right?"

"He's outta town 'n the gym's trainer despises Jazlynn's success. So y'all're goin' to the gym."

'I've missed the gym.'

Holly plans to go with Jazlynn but gets stuck at the ranch.

'Grand-daddy must've found out. He won't be around to interfere with me forever. The gym'll be something I can have in common with Luke.'

Jazlynn discovers Luke's a serious task master during sets and reps. "You can train me anytime. I'm impressed. Maybe we could shower together afterwards 'n call it cardio. Whaddya think?"

"Get serious, Jazlynn. Or I'm done. What's wrong with you?"

"Call me Jazzy already. Don't blame me wantin' to hook up with you. Y'all're a hunk."

"You use guys for your own pleasure. You have no self-respect or care what people think of you."

Jazlynn's demeanor changes after Luke's rebuke.

"Hey, sorry, I don't know you. That was kinda rude."

"Luke, can I tell you somethin' only my mom knows?"

"That's up to you."

Jazlynn takes a deep breath. "My dad 'n uncle abused me when I was young. They called me pretty but did things a little girl shouldn't know about."

"Jazlynn, are you making this up?" Luke studies Jazlynn's sad expression. "You're not kidding. Look, I'm not sure I'm the right person to tell that to. Doesn't Holly know?"

"No! Nobody knows. Please don't tell anyone. I thought it'd be easier tellin' a stranger. My mom was ashamed of me. She lost her husband 'n brother to prison. After they'd been raping me for over two years. They were supposed to be my protectors."

'I thought my family was bad. That's worse.' "You should talk to someone. It might help heal ya."

"It's easier lettin' everyone think I'm some bad-assed gym girl."

"A professional could help end your nightmare."

"I tried a shrink once. I still feel like it's my fault."

"It wasn't your fault." *'I sound like Hank.'* "I won't say a word. At least I understand you're throwing yourself at me outta habit."

"No. I might like you but can't say it."

'This is a new wrinkle to deal with.' "We need to finish. I've got work waitin'."

Holly witnesses Luke hug Jazlynn before they fist bump each other. Jazlynn heads towards Holly.

"Hey, that went well."

"Why did Luke hug you? What the hell's goin' on? You're not tryin' to steal my man."

"We had a good workout. That's all. Luke simply congratulated me with a hug. Relax." *'Maybe truth'll win Luke instead of deceptive games.'*

TWENTY-NINE

Wyatt steps up his attempts to win Hope over after her ride with Luke. Hope hears Luke's working out with Jazlynn and opts to observe them during their next workout.

'Luke seems more relaxed around Jazzy. What changed? Why didn't I think to invite Luke to the gym? Why can't I open up to Luke more?'

Luke works on final preparations for the Twisted Live Oak's Christmas in July party with Austin by his side. A snowmaking machine is set up in one tent for a wintery scene and allows guests to enjoy snowball fights, make snowmen, and snow angels. Ben scrutinizes Wyatt's continued focus on Luke's whereabouts.

'What's Wyatt up to?'

Wyatt kisses and hugs Hope when she arrives with Faith. Hope catches her breath. *'Wyatt's still handsome.'*

Luke exits the winter tent and witnesses their kiss and turns away. Wyatt tries for a second kiss. "I've missed ya darlin'."

Hope panics that Luke's seen them kiss so her reaction differs this time. *'Luke's good-lookin' too. And kind-hearted. Could I fall for him? Am I already?'*

Wyatt thinks, *'No wannabe's interfering with me gettin' Hope outta her jeans. She's hotter than ever.'*

Beth watches Hope's interaction with Wyatt. *'Does Wyatt see Luke as a threat?'*

Courtney and Trish join Beth ahead of Jazlynn's arrival on a Harley wearing torn jeans and a white tank top to reveal her fit physique. Jazlynn walks up to Luke for a hug and kisses Luke's cheek and then his lips. Beth and Hope notice Luke doesn't resist her. Beth wonders, *'Has Hope pushed Luke to Jazzy?'*

Hope also wonders, *'Am I losing Luke to Jazzy? What do I do?'*

Faith bluntly questions Hope. "Momma, why're you lettin' Wyatt kiss you? Don'tcha like Luke?"

"Your mom 'n I used to kiss like that all the time. Hopefully we'll do more again."

"Momma, I'm confused. You really really kissed Luke."

Wyatt looks at Hope. "Tryin' to make me jealous? He ain't competition."

Hope hears Wyatt's condescending tone. "Don't get snippy with me. What if I do like Luke?"

"Then I've been away too long 'n your standards dropped."

Faith speaks up. "Momma, I'm bringin' Luke to the snow tent."

"Okay, Faith, have fun."

Faith runs to Luke. "C'mon Luke, let's have a snowball fight."

Luke smiles, "Y'all know I grew up doin' this, right? I'm gonna win."

"No way."

Luke pretends to forget how to throw snowballs and lets Faith win. "Alright, alright, I surrender. You win."

Faith giggles, "Let's build a snowman."

"Okay."

Jake enters and shivers. "Whew boy. It's colder 'n a witch's…"

Luke glares at Jake. "Be real careful how you finish that sentence."

"I was gonna say it's colder 'n a witch's broom handle at Santa's North Pole workshop."

"Uh-huh?"

"Getchur head outta the gutter. Whaddya think I'd say. Sheesh. Y'all act like you're Faith's papa."

Jubilee and Cody hear Luke and Jake. Jubilee whispers, "It's not a bad thing if y'all ask me."

"I wanna show Momma our snowman."

"Okay Faith."

Faith and Luke exit the tent but go in opposite directions.

"Momma, come see what Luke 'n I did."

"Okay. Where's Luke?"

"He's checkin' on guests."

Luke sees Wyatt follow Hope and Faith into the tent. Jake intercepts them inside.

"Y'all gotta talk to Luke."

Hope's concerned. "Why?"

"He was tellin' me off 'bout her like he's her dad or somethin'."

"Why did he do that?"

"He told me to watch my mouth 'round Faith. Like I don't know that already."

Hope smiles. *'How should I handle this?'* "Luke looks out for Faith. He means well. I trust Faith with Luke." *'Did I say that out loud? Is it true?'*

"Y'all might as well be datin' Luke, Hope."

Jake's statement shakes Hope. *'Does he really mean that?'*

Wyatt shifts attention back to himself. "Faith, how 'bout you 'n I have a snowball fight? I've never done that before."

Faith anticipates Wyatt will play like Luke. Faith starts crying after Wyatt's first snowball hits her cheek. Hope worries, "Faith, are you hurt?"

Jake retorts, "Luke'd whoop Wyatt's ass if he were here."

Wyatt responds, "No chance that's happenin'."

Hope thinks, *'You have no idea. Or any chance against Luke.'*

Wyatt examines Faith. "She's fine. It's just snow."

Hope hears Wyatt's insensitivity. *'Wyatt has no idea how to handle kids. Luke does. Why?'*

Beth's amused when Luke hunts Wyatt down without warning and shoves him to the ground. "Hurt Faith again 'n I'll put a hurtin' on y'all a hundred times worse."

Wyatt jumps up to face Luke. "Leave already. Hope's my girl. I'll take care of Faith too."

"Maybe I oughta stick around so Hope has a better option."

Hank's arrival pulls Luke away to assist him alongside Monique. "How ya doin', Luke?"

"I feel like the world's crashin' down on me, Hank. But I feel like I belong too."

Hank chuckles, "You began feelin' when Linda broke your heart."

Monique quips, "I'd never break your heart."

"You don't know that. Never say never."

Luke's sage advice to Monique impresses Hank. "Luke, walk your own path in your own boots. Stop tryin' to fill your daddy's shoes. A god-lit fire'll carry y'all through hell 'n back."

Monique checks out the activities while Luke and Hank talk. People decorate pine trees, speed wrap gifts for prizes, decorate keepsake ornaments, string popcorn for length or for time, along with the snow tent events. Monique returns to ask Luke a question.

"Luke, wouldja dance with me later? I promise I won't step on your toes."

"I might. I don't dance."

Monique glances at Hank. "Y'all're right, Mr. McIntyre. Luke sounds more Texan now. And sexy."

Beth notices Luke blush and Hope's reaction when Monique leans against Luke. Beth walks over to Hope. "That could be you. If'n ya let it happen."

"I don't think Luke's interested in me."

"I wouldn't bet on that. Luke's always lookin' 'round to find y'all. Like now."

Hope turns and sees Luke looking at her.

"That doesn't mean anything."

"That's the look of an interested man. Be honest with yourself. Talk to Luke. And Wyatt."

Jazlynn approaches Hope and Beth. "Who's that girl movin' in on my man?"

Hope responds first. "Y"all've never wanted one man?"

"Hey, I might've found the right guy to change that."

Hope and Beth watch Jazlynn walk towards Luke. She verbally intimidates Monique.

"Y'all ain't tryin' to steal my man, are ya?"

Luke cuts Jazlynn off. "Jazzy, don't start. We're all here to enjoy the day. No trouble. Monique's assisting Hank."

Beth follows Hope when she walks away. "Where ya goin'?"

"I'm not stayin' to watch Luke hook up with Jazzy. Or the other girl."

"Hope, Luke's watched how many guys hit on you? And Wyatt's doin' it too."

"Luke's throwin' himself at Jazzy."

"He ain't exactly throwin' himself at anyone. Bein' unusually nice, yes."

Wyatt's tracking down Hope and hears them. "Who cares if Luke's with Jazzy? Hope, it's you 'n me again."

Beth cuts Wyatt off. "Hope ain't with you. Not yet."

Wyatt responds resentfully, "He's a fake. You're crazy to choose him."

Beth scolds Wyatt, "Y'all just got back. You left Hope. You don't own first rights to her heart. You went 'n married someone else."

Wyatt hates Beth mentioning that fact. "Shut up."

Billy eyes Wyatt on his approach to Hope. "All good here?"

Hope replies, "It's okay, Billy. Wyatt, I may have feelin's for Luke. I can't watch him tramp around with Jazzy. Or anyone else."

Hank observed Hope's hasty exit after Jazlynn's interaction. *'Interestin'. Hope's even walkin' away from Wyatt.'*

"Hope, Hank wants to talk to ya."

"I'll be there in a moment."

Beth chides Hope. "Y'all're more drama than my daughters."

Hope breathes deeply and exhales while walking to Hank.

"How are ya, Hank?"

"Oh, the usual. Old. But breathin'. So I'm good. The question is how are you?"

"Please don't psychobabble me today."

"Y'all might need it."

"Life's confusin' 'n wearin' me out."

"Life? Or Luke 'n Wyatt?"

Hope remains silent.

"Professionally speaking, I think someone's lassoed your heart and you're scared. You high-tailed it outta here after Jazlynn kissed Luke. And you were quite smitten with Wyatt once upon a time."

Hank's statements cause Hope to frown.

"Open up. It's time to live 'n love again."

"Why's everyone tellin' me that?"

"Everyone?"

Hope concedes and reveals her emotional quandary until Faith runs up to her.

"Momma, come quick. Luke's gonna do a horse trick."

Luke spots Hope guiding Hank over towards him and Waylon before placing his hand on the saddle horn and effortlessly jump up into the saddle without using the stirrup. The feat impresses everyone, especially Hope.

'I didn't know Luke could do that. I didn't know anyone to do that with Waylon.'

Hank notes Luke stalled before accomplishing his impressive performance so Hope would see it. *'The real show's about to start.'*

Wyatt states, "Anyone can do that." *'He ain't showin' me up.'*

The crowd watches Wyatt attempt to replicate Luke's accomplishment and fall flat on his back which induces roaring laughter.

"He got lucky."

Chester chuckles. *'This is gonna be one long hot summer.'*

Wyatt shows off rope tricks with the other wranglers later on and finishes by lassoing Hope.

"I dedicate this to my darlin', Hope. She's lassoed my heart."

Luke walks away while several women comment how sweet Wyatt's gesture is. *'Who am I kiddin'? I'm not competin' with Wyatt.'*

Hope notices Jazlynn follow Luke when he leaves. *'Was Luke showin' off for me?'*

Ben intercepts Hope when she's headed towards the rodeo arena while Luke's assisting kids in the chutes for the mutton busting event.

"Hope, Patsy's set to ride."

'*Shit.*' "Thanks Ben." '*Patsy gets antsy before this. I need to stay with her.*'

The arena is cleared out ahead of Hope riding in fast, wild, and hands free to demonstrate her riding skills. Beth meets her once she dismounts.

"I recorded all of it. FYI, Luke didn't take his eyes off ya. Wyatt, well, he was too busy talkin' to Jazzy 'n missed everything."

Chester amuses guests when he announces Christmas songs can be requested on a hundred degree day in July. Wranglers ask several guests to inspect targets set up in the nearby pasture at varying distances before Chester stops the music for the next demonstration.

"Welcome Hope back for some of the finest shootin' y'all're ever gonna see on horseback."

Hope exhibits expert rifle skills on the furthest targets while Patsy gallops through a pattern before switching to her pistol to fire at the closer targets. Luke's in awe along with the guests at Hope's shooting ability when the targets reveal only bullseyes.

'*Hope's definitely an expert marksman. She missed me on purpose.*'

Ben removes Patsy's saddle and Hope grabs a handful of mane to remount bareback and stand to show the close bond between rider and horse. The crowd applauds when Hope guides Patsy to the fence to step off and let Ben catch her in his arms. Wyatt corners Hope in Patsy's stall.

"Hope, y'all still ride 'n shoot better 'n anyone I know."

"Wyatt, you startled me. I'm surprised you noticed. How's Jazzy today?"

"I forgot you two despise each other. I was just catchin' up. I only have eyes for you. Jazzy's found someone else to make her happy."

"Didn't you make her happy also?"

"That was before you and you know it."

"I need to find Faith."

"Hope, I want a fresh start with you. One that can last this time."

Wyatt moves closer to kiss Hope and finds her letting him.

'*Should I let Wyatt waltz back into my life? I'm lettin' him kiss me whenever he wants. Do I still love him? What if I'm fallin' for Luke?*'

Wyatt holds Hope's hand while approaching Faith and Luke. Hope realizes Luke's staring at her hand and pulls it away.

"Momma, are you datin' Wyatt? Or Luke?"

Wyatt remarks, "We're gonna start seein' each other again. Isn't that great?"

"I like Luke. Momma, you like Luke too, right?"

Luke interjects, "Faith, your mom 'n Wyatt knew each other first. She wouldn't date me anyway."

Hope hears Luke's tone. *'Is Luke givin' up on me? Us? Would he actually date me? Beth's right, I should've talked to Luke already.'*

Luke asks, "Faith, can you help me pick out a song?"

"Sure."

Beth and Hope watch Luke and Faith walk to the DJ and see him nod before the next song begins.

"The Little Drummer Boy? Did Luke request this?"

"I don't know. Beth, couldja find out? Please?"

"Yeah. I'm curious too."

Beth approaches Luke. "Didja request this song?"

Luke answers immediately. "Yep."

"Why?"

"It shows God accepts everyone even if they have nothing to give."

Beth wonders, *'Luke sounds depressed.'*

Luke continues, "I've got nothing for anyone. Not here. Not anywhere. Hopefully God'll accept me."

Beth gleans important information to share with Hope. "It's Luke's request."

"Why this song?"

"He doesn't think he has anything to give anyone here. That's why he hasn't tried askin' ya out."

Wyatt grins, "I've got a lot to offer Hope."

Beth frowns, "Hope, it's Luke. Not you. He thinks he's got no worth here."

Wyatt leans against Hope. "Why are we still talkin' 'bout a loser?"

Beth harshly states, "Because Hope needs choices."

"He ain't stickin' 'round."

Hope thinks back to her conversation with Luke and Beth's news. *'Luke has worth. He offers more than he realizes. He can't see that.'*

Beth informs Wyatt, "Luke beat the shit outta five guys to save Hope. Can you do that?"

"You're lyin'."

Hope speaks up, "No, she's not."

Hank asks Luke to help before leaving.

"Luke, life's measured in moments, not minutes. Home's where ya decide it is."

"I feel close to my parents in Chicago."

"That feelin' travels with you. Memories too. Now go dance with Hope. She needs a new dance partner. That's an order."

"Um, yes sir."

Luke taps Wyatt's shoulder. "Hank ordered me to dance with Hope."

"So what."

"It's okay, Wyatt. I haven't danced with Luke yet."

Wyatt sourly releases Hope and glares at Luke. "I thought you don't dance?"

"I don't. But Hank said Hope needs a new dance partner. I'm not disobeying an old man's order."

Luke nervously stretches his arms out to place his hands on her waist like they're at an elementary school dance.

Hope giggles, "Luke, I don't bite."

Luke closes the gap and feels Hope shudder. "If you'd rather dance with Wyatt…"

"Shut up 'n dance. I need to take Faith home soon. She's exhausted, thanks to you."

Hope leans against Luke to continue their dance. *I'll enjoy this and hope we do it again.'*

Jazlynn boldly interrupts them. "Excuse me, Luke's my dance partner."

Hope spins around to slap Jazlynn's cheek hard enough to force her backwards. "You bitch! You wanna go? I'll mess you up."

Luke prevents further hostility by separating them. "Jazzy, go dance with Wyatt. I'll find you in a few minutes for a dance."

Jazlynn's infuriated by Hope's action and glares at her. "This ain't over. I'll get even."

Hope attempts to walk away until Luke gently pulls her back to him.

"Can we finish our dance? I'm enjoyin' it. I hope you are too."

Luke's gaze is fully locked on Hope. "Sure. If ya wanna. I am enjoyin it."

Hank hears about Hope's standoffish behavior when she stops visiting the ranch for several days and calls her.

"Hank, I'm too busy to visit."

"Come to my office, Hope."

"Hank, I'm kinda busy."

"Now! You 'n I are talkin'. Are you too busy to fix your life?"

Hope drives to Hank's. *I feel like I'm bein' called to the principal's office.'*

Hank's at the door when Hope arrives. "You, me, outside, now."

"It's too hot outside for you."

"I'm Texan. It's never too hot."

The sun beats down on the pair at an outdoor table.

"Hank, really, you shouldn't be outside."

"The heat ain't gonna kill me. You, on the other hand. Why're ya avoidin' the ranch?"

"How would you even know that?" *'The ranch has too many busybodies.'*

"I have sources. Why ain'tcha spending time at the ranch? Home?"

"I do work, Hank."

"You don't work twenty four seven. Out with it. Why?"

Hope pauses before confessing. "I'm embarrassed Jazzy got to me at the party. I hit her."

"Bullshit."

"Hank. What the hell?"

"Jazlynn's never embarrassed you ever. Irritated you, yes. I wasn't born yesterday. What're ya afraid of? Somethin'? Someone? Both? You might've shown possessive interest in Luke 'round Wyatt 'n Jazlynn. You're afraid of losin' either of 'em, or both of 'em, right?"

Hope hesitates before answering. "Yes."

"The good Lord ain't gonna let me live forever 'n I'd like to see you happy before I leave Earth. You might've found the right person to complete that puzzle."

Luke exits the house with a clipboard while Chester rocks on the deck.

"Luke, sit a spell."

"I've got a lotta work left."

"I know. I make the assignments."

Luke concedes and sits.

"I wanna share part of my life with ya."

"You don't need to."

"Yeah. I do. Y'all ain't a pain in the ass anymore."

"Thanks. I think."

"I'm fourth generation Texan. My Great-Grandpappy left Virginia 'n worked the Chisholm Trail to get this land. He died in a Longhorn stampede in eighteen-seventy nine. My Grandpappy was only ten but he and my Meemaw kept the ranch goin' through hard times 'n my daddy was good with the herd but knew squat about business. He had three daughters 'n two sons. I'm the last one livin'. My pappy saw my son born before passing in nineteen sixty-three."

"Where's your son?"

"He joined the Marines 'n died in a trainin' accident in April of '90."

"That's you 'n your son in those pictures."

"Yup. I got mean drunk 'n Millie threw me out to sober up and…"

Chester stops abruptly. *'The rest goes to the grave with me.'*

"I've got a constant reminder of Chester junior here."

Luke doesn't understand Chester's insinuation. "How?"

"Y'all're here 'cause of her."

"Holly?"

"Yup. Holly's a lot like Chet which hurts 'n heals at the same time."

"I'm sorry for your losses."

"You mean that, don'tcha?"

"Losing family's a hurt that fades but doesn't go away."

"Yep. Millie was fine wine, I'm cheap whiskey. We married in nineteen fifty 'n had seventy two blissful years plus growin' up together. Millie made me a better man. She loved me when she shouldn't've. Millie never knocked me down when I slipped up 'n always picked me up when I fell. We made each other feel like no one else existed."

"You and Millie raised Hope. That's why she's family too. What happened to her parents?"

Chester's resistant to answer. "We were raisin' Holly after Chet died. Her mom overdosed at a party. Hope wound up here 'cause her momma struggled to keep a job and abandoned Hope here."

"What about her dad?"

"Hope's dad's never been in the picture as far as Hope knows."

'Chester's uncomfortable tellin' me about Hope. Why?' "So Hope 'n Holly grew up without parents. Like I did. How often do you think about the war?"

"All the time. But I've learned to deal with those memories."

"I think about the accident that killed my parents."

"Millie did her best to help with my demons. She couldn't understand 'n never sympathized but she empathized when she could. Her love consoled me through dark days 'n years. Millie stood by me when she shouldn't've." *'I can't say why.'*

"Why are those called barns instead of stables?"

"The Twisted Live Oak was a cattle ranch but expanded to have milk cows too. Then I turned it into a dude ranch."

"That makes sense."

Chester hears Randy's rough rumbling engine and intercepts him as he steps from his truck holding a rifle.

"Get off my ranch."

Randy reaches into his truck and laughs. "Good. Your pet's here too. I've got somethin' special for y'all."

Randy brings a bullwhip into view. "This is yours. A round's chambered for Chester."

Luke moves in front of Chester. Randy flicks his wrist to crack the whip which strikes the ground at Luke's feet. Randy flicks his wrist a second time to tear Luke's sleeve. Luke grabs the whip mid-air on Randy's third attempt and yanks it from his hand and swiftly spins to send the handle back and hit Randy's forehead to stun him. Luke delivers a clothesline to flatten Randy before dropping down on him. Ben and Wyatt approach and witness Luke's actions and hear his statement to Chester.

"Bob needs to visit alone 'n leave with one more than he arrived with."

Chester grins. "Parroting my line, huh? At least you're listenin'."

"He's got skills. I'll give him that."

Chester glances at Wyatt. "Luke does come in handy."

Hope arrives while Randy's lying on the ground. Pure hatred resonates in her voice."

"What's he doin' here?"

'Hope really doesn't like Randy.'

Chester motions towards Luke. "Gettin' his day ruined. Hogtie him. Thank God he don't have kids."

Hope queries, "Luke, why do you have ketchup on your shirt?"

"I haven't touched ketchup today."

Luke looks down at his shirt.

"Your sleeve."

Luke tugs at the sleeve. *'Randy cut my arm.'*

Chester peers into Luke's torn sleeve. "Hope, this'll need stitches. Couldja patch him up?"

"I don't have anything with me."

"I'll take care of it myself."

"Nah, Hope'll fix ya up. Katie's got whatcha need in the kitchen."

"I didn't come for this. Let's get this over with."

"Sorry for bein' a problem."

Hope glances at Luke. *'You are a problem. One I might want stickin' around.'*

Katie's already set out the first aid kit when Hope enters with Luke. "I saw what happened."

Chester instructs Ben and Wyatt, "Follow me. How's the day goin'?"

Hope notes, "Katie, there's no rubbin' alcohol."

Luke snarls, "Who cares? Just stitch this."

Chester offers, "Use some whiskey." *'Why's Luke mad at Hope. Or is it Wyatt?'*

Hope catches her breath when Luke removes his shirt. *'I'll never get used to seein' Luke's body.'*

Chester hands Hope a whiskey bottle and notices she's admiring Luke's torso.

"This might hurt."

Hope pours a little whiskey on a towel and rubs Luke's bloodied arm.

"If you say so."

Hope threads a needle and wipes the blood away again before closing the cut. *'Luke's not flinchin'.'*

"Don't turn me into Frankenstein."

Hope frowns while Chester chuckles. *'Luke ain't gonna let Hope forget that.'*

"Shut up. Or I will."

Hope finishes and wonders, *'Does Luke feel pain?'*

Chester studies Wyatt examining Luke while Hope works. *'Wyatt seems bothered by Luke. Why?'*

Luke flexes and inspects Hope's work before she wraps gauze over it. "Thank God! It's still attached. Am I gonna live, doc?"

"Keep talkin' 'n ya won't."

Luke's small grin disappears after noticing Wyatt looking at him. "You need something Wyatt?"

"Nothin'."

"I need to change for the next trail ride."

Hope watches Luke leave shirtless. Wyatt steps close to Hope. "Let's have dinner tonight 'n talk. Just the two of us."

"I have Faith."

"Can someone else take her?"

Ben offers, "Beth 'n I could spoil her."

"Um, okay."

Hope pulls Chester aside. "Faith's askin' about Corpus."

"It's already booked."

"Good. I could use a couple days away from here. *'From everyone.'*

Ben states, "Wyatt, we got work to do."

Wyatt's quiet at first while they walk. "Does the ranch have a gym?"

"No. Why?"

"Luke's pretty fit for a ranch hand."

"Luke arrived that way. He's a gym rat. Now he's trainin' with Jazzy. Don't get on his bad side. He broke my jaw."

Wyatt speculates, *'How do I win Hope over without pissin' Luke off? He doesn't scare easily.'*

Chester stops Luke after supper. "Don't go lookin' for someone's respect that might not give it. Respect yourself. See how far it takes ya. Y'all'll live happier that way. The right people respect you. The rest can go to hell for all you care."

THIRTY-ONE

Chester enters Luke's room on the first Friday in August. "Get up. We've got somewhere to go."

Luke blinks and rubs his eyes when the light blinds him. Chester drops an old brown suitcase on the floor.

"What's that for? What time is it?"

"Pack 'n meet me in the kitchen."

"It's four in the mornin'."

Chester points down. "Pack."

Luke gets up and packs then trudges to the kitchen. He's grown accustomed to working before eating so Luke enjoys Katie's hearty breakfast.

"Where're we goin'?"

Katie's surprised. "Luke doesn't know?"

Chester casually sips his coffee. "Not a clue."

"Kinda mean, ain't it?"

"Maybe."

Chester informs Luke, "This weekend'll change your life so eat up."

Katie refills Luke's cup. *'Chester's up to somethin'.'*

Chester adds, "I've seen hard times 'n didn't always make the best decisions. I did choose to be tougher 'n beat the challenge. Success 'n failure are separated only by effort, desire, and direction put forth."

Luke hears a truck pull up.

"That's our ride. Ben'll take care of Austin."

Luke steps outside.

"Why's Luke here? Is your arm okay? I'll take the stitches out Monday."

"Luke's gonna be my guest."

Hope's pleasantly bewildered expression is revealed in the headlights. "Oh?"

Luke shrugs.

"Let's hit the road to beat traffic."

Chester sits up front and hears Faith's sleepy voice. "Hi Luke. I'm happy you're comin' too."

"Howdy Faith."

Faith's groggy smile precedes her question. "Have y'all ever been to the beach?"

"Here? No. Does Texas have beaches?"

Faith shakes her head. "Silly Luke. Yes, we have beaches."

"Then let's go have fun."

A thought occurs to Hope. *'Faith took to Luke immediately but resistant to Wyatt. Why? I wish I could be like Faith but I'm afraid to get my heart broke if Luke leaves. Wyatt 'n I had a strong bond but our evening didn't go well.'*

Faith leans against Luke and yawns and falls asleep again. Hope observes the scene after Luke dozes off with his arm around Faith. *'I wish it were that easy. I'd like that again. I envy Faith. She's lucky Luke's in her life. Maybe I am too.'*

Chester sees Hope's occasional glances in the rearview mirror and speaks low. "I brought Luke along so you can relax too."

"Thanks. I guess." *'Could this be my future? Why do I feel tense?'*

They pull into a hotel parking lot in Corpus Christi around nine. Hope walks alongside Luke while entering the building. Sweat trickles down Luke's cheek.

"Is it possible it's more humid here?"

Hope smiles. "I'm not sure where y'all're stayin if it's full."

Luke shrugs. "There's a bench out front. Or maybe the beach."

Hope's hesitant to ask her next question. "Why were you so angry when I was away?"

"I, uh, I, uh, I don't know." *I'm stunned Hope's asking.'* "Chester's stunt." *'Because I missed you.'*

"Was that all?" *'Katie seems to think it was somethin' else.'*

'Why's Hope asking? Does she think about me at all? Probably not, she's thinking about Wyatt.'

"When did your parents die?"

"Why?"

"Ben 'n Beth've lost their parents. Chester lost Millie. They get moody 'round that time. I wondered if that happened to you."

"My parents died in September. I get moody then." *'Does Hope think about me?'*

"I'm upset a lot in January. That's when I got abandoned."

"Really?"

Faith runs up with a key card but turns to face the sliding door which opens automatically. "Momma, look, I still open the door with my mind."

Hope glances at Luke. "It's tradition. Faith does this every year. Congratulations Faith. You still have mystical powers."

Luke playfully comments, "I opened the door with my finger."

Faith frowns, "No, Luke, you don't have any powers here. Just me."

Luke grins, "Excuse me."

Chester approaches and hands a key card to Luke. "You're bunkin' with me."

"Great. There goes my vacation."

Luke stops Hope before entering the elevator. "Can I get your opinion on something?"

"Sure."

"I didn't know who I was before so I never knew how to be me. I'm findin' out who I am here. Does that make sense?"

"I guess so. Y'all've gone through a lot here you wouldn't in Chicago." *'Like I am because you're here.'*

They step onto the elevator so Faith can push the button. She happily skips down the hallway to their rooms. Luke imitates her and clunks his boots skipping after Faith until nearly tripping halfway. Faith laughs hysterically while Hope debates if it's funny or embarrassing.

'Luke acts silly around Faith in ways I can't to make her laugh.'

Chester admonishes Luke. "Y'all, that was so wrong. Don'tcha ever do that again. I can't unsee that."

Faith pulls Luke to the balcony. "Isn't this great, Luke?"

Luke examines the beach, Corpus Christi Bay, and the aircraft carrier moored offshore. *'Dad.'*

Seagulls flock to the area searching for food. The salty air smells of washed up seaweed. Chester and Hope hear Luke explain what the carrier means to him.

"My dad's ship was bigger than that."

"Bigger? That ship's huge. Grand-daddy took me on it last year. I was so tired when we got off."

Hope quizzes Faith. "What should we do first?"

"The beach. Of course."

Luke grows apprehensive. "I don't have a swim suit."

Chester confirms, "I figured. There's shops nearby. Hope'll bring Faith to the beach. We'll meetcha there."

The men cross the parking lot to several stores so Luke can find swimsuits. Chester offers to buy him a couple t-shirts also. Luke picks out a plain white shirt with Corpus Christi on front and one with the aircraft carrier blended with the American flag. *'This makes me think of dad.'*

They return and head for the beach. Luke's wearing his jeans and button-down over the t-shirt and bathing suit. The sun heats the tan grainy sand and bakes Luke's feet like a pizza in the oven. Luke ducks to avoid low swooping gulls catching food from kids tossing fries into the air.

"Let's find the girls."

Chester leads Luke through the crowd. "Found 'em."

Hope's wearing an over-sized Longhorn t-shirt over her suit to prevent men from gawking and making lewd comments in front of

Faith. She catches sight of Luke in a sea of bikini clad young women. *'Should I take my shirt off? Would it matter to Luke?'*

Luke spots a brown pelican gliding above the small waves. *'I've never seen a pelican before.'*

Several white pelicans fly in formation until one dives below the surface. Hope removes her t-shirt to reveal a cobalt blue one piece suit highlighting her beautiful figure. Luke's attention shifts to Hope when several men whistle and make crude comments and notices Hope's flustered reaction. Luke removes his button-down while approaching Hope and Faith.

'Hope'd probably shoot me if I tried kissin' her.'

Luke gazes unabashedly at Hope while she's looking at Faith. She turns to see Luke looking so he looks out at the carrier. The U.S.S. Lexington is a floating museum for touring and learning about wartime battles which gave the ship the nickname 'Blue Ghost'. Chester notices Luke staring at the ship.

"We'll board her later and walk top to bottom."

"I'd like that."

Hope comments, "Y'all can take your jeans off if'n ya want to."

Chester watches her eyes glimmer with interest. *'This could work better than planned.'*

Hope keenly watches Luke take his jeans then his t-shirt off to expose his torso. *'Luke's body's so sexy. His arm makes him look tougher.'*

Hope would be shocked to learn Luke often still envisions himself as the pudgy teen. Several young women halt Hope's shy, hungry gaze with shouts towards Luke.

"Hey, don't stop. Keep strippin'. We'll pay you 'n make it worth your while."

Their suggestive requests catch Luke off guard and stares at the women in tiny bikinis. Chester watches Hope's expression.

'Hope's hoppin' mad. They ruined her moment.'

Hope glares at the college girls using more erotically indecent language to entice Luke. Chester's struck by two thoughts. *'Luke seems uncomfortable by their compliments 'n Hope's actin' mighty jealous Luke's lookin' at 'em.'*

A few more girls join to shamelessly hurl suggestive sexual offers at Luke. Hope's seething until grasping the fact Luke's free to walk over to the flirtatious women if he chooses to.

'We're not dating. I can't stop other girls from flirting with Luke. Maybe this is how Luke's felt when men hit on me.'

Hope worries when Luke waves to the girls. *'Could they win Luke over?'*

Luke turns around. "That was interesting."

Hope's angered expression erases Luke's grin.

'Is Hope mad at me?' "Did I do somethin' wrong?"

Chester's amused chuckle at Hope's animated eye roll is barely audible. *'Luke's smile disappeared quicker 'n brisket at the ranch.'*

"Let's look for seashells, Faith." *'Why can't I flirt like that?'*

Luke's confused. *'What the hell? Hope's shot at me. Told me she hates me. Then acts interested, I think. Until she's mad at me again. Or is it still?'*

Chester saves Luke. "C'mon, we'll tour the carrier. You won't get in trouble there."

"Um, okay."

"Hope needs time to cool off."

"The ship ain't that big."

Chester laughs and notices Hope's glance at Luke when he's looking at her. "I'm takin' Luke to Lady Lex."

'Luke's lookin' at me with a wanting look like at the barbecue.'

The women beg Luke to keep his shirt off while he pulls it on. "Keep it off. Take all of it off."

Luke's first impulse is to look until Chester speaks up. "Walk away. Don't look."

Hope rushes at the women once Luke's out of sight. "I'll rip your nose ring out and shove it down your throat."

One girl boldly challenges Hope. "Is he your boyfriend?"

Hope answers without thinking. "No."

"Then he'll be mine tonight. Y'all can't stop me."

Hope remembers Faith's nearby. "Stay away from him."

"He's fair game. He'd probably rather hook up with someone younger with no kids."

Her statement stings Hope deeply. *'Is she right? Is that why Luke ain't hit on me? And still wants to leave?'*

Hope returns to Faith with mixed emotions. *'What's Luke done to me? What if he doesn't like me? Is he bein' nice til he can leave?'*

Another thought terrifies Hope. *'What if Luke does like me? What if he does stay?'*

Hope tries clearing her mind to enjoy the beach with Faith. *'Why's Luke really here? He'll ruin another trip. Why couldn't it be just the three of us like usual?'*

Chester and Luke explore U.S.S. Lexington while Hope battles challengers and challenging thoughts. They start with the lower decks and work up to the flight deck and eventually the ship's island. Chester's impressed with Luke's knowledge of sea battles and the vintage war planes on board.

"Lady Lex steamed with us to Iwo. The Japanese thought they sank her four times only to find her still sailing. Tokyo Rose gave Lex her nickname, the Blue Ghost."

Luke adds another tidbit. "This Lex was originally built to be a different ship."

"I don't know 'bout that."

"CV-16 was supposed to be U.S.S. Cabot until CV-2 Lexington sank in the Coral Sea. They renamed the ship to continue Tokyo Rose's unsinkable 'Blue Ghost'.

"How do you know that?"

"Luke proudly smiles. "I read a lot."

Chester scowls. "Those old warbirds flew overhead at Iwo. They were a welcomed sight to us on the beach. Them and sixteen inch shells from battleships Missouri and Wisconsin bombarding inland. Those shells sounded like freight trains goin' over us."

The men head back to the beach to find Hope and Faith relaxing in shallow water.

"See. Hope's cooled off."

"Funny."

Faith sees Luke, "Momma, now can we get food?"

"Yes Pecan. We'll change 'n eat."

Hope trails behind Luke to see if he searches for the college girls. *'Luke's too busy talkin' to Chester. They seem better again.'*

Chester's amazed by Luke's knowledge of World War Two naval battles. "Your daddy taught you well."

"He taught me to enjoy history."

Luke checks on Hope periodically and smiles each time they make eye contact. Hope feels herself relax and tense up for the same reasons.

'Luke hasn't looked for those girls. He looks at me though. And Faith. What's gonna happen this weekend? Why does Chester treat Luke so differently?'

THIRTY-TWO

Several men pass Hope and Faith waiting outside the hotel's beachside entrance. They make vulgar comments before Hope's able to cover Faith's ears.

"I've got a pole y'all can swing around for hours."

"Your legs definitely go to Heaven."

"Corpus has a couple large mountains today."

"Grow up. Get lost. My daughter's here."

"Lose her. I wanna climb your mountains 'n explore your valley. You'll enjoy it."

"How dare you! I'd neuter all y'all if I could."

"Holster my pistol baby. Satisfy my needs, milf."

Luke slips through the door quietly and hears the men's degrading comments. Chester remains inside.

"Show the lady respect. Faith, go see Chester."

"This milf needs a real man's attention."

Luke coldly glares, "I guess miserable sand crabs like you are ruled out."

"Go find your own bitch. She's ours."

"Y'all think this is none of my business?"

"Yup. Vamoose, asshole."

Luke acts as if he's leaving. "Maybe you're right."

"Don'tcha dare leave me alone, Luke."

"Sorry guys. Unlike you, I'll listen to the lady."

Luke's fist impacts the most outspoken guy's jaw to lift him up before he crumbles in front of his friends. "Huh, one punch. Who's next?"

"Look mister, we're just havin' some fun."

"Find a different way someplace else."

Chester and Faith come outside. "Luke knocked the rank outta him. They won't hassle you again."

Hope's unsure how to feel or what to think. *Could Billy be right? Is Luke my knight in shining armor? Or is it Wyatt?*

Faith tugs at Luke's shirt. "Thank's for helpin' Momma."

Hope smiles, "Yes, thank you. You weren't gonna walk away, were you?"

"Not even if you ordered me at gunpoint."

Hope can't stop smiling on the way to Pier 99 for lunch. Her phone rings as they get seated. "Wyatt? Why're ya callin'? Is somethin' wrong?"

Hope listens quietly before getting irate. "Wyatt, we can talk when I get back. I'm with Faith 'n Chester."

Luke notes he's not mentioned. Hope's phone rings a moment later.

"Hello Sam. What's goin' on?"

Luke watches Hope's perplexed expression.

"First of all, that client's next week. Secondly, I'm with Chester 'n Faith."

Faith asks Luke for ketchup.

"Did Faith just ask Luke for ketchup? Is Luke there? I'd've come if ya needed a man on the trip."

"I'm not here with Luke."

"I'm confused. Is Luke there or not?"

"Luke's here with Chester. Not me."

"I'm confused."

"Sam, Faith 'n I are tryin' to enjoy Corpus with Chester. I'd like to order my food, goodbye."

Hope glances at Luke. *'I'm actin' like Luke's not here after he's just defended me.'*

Luke shields his aggravation by engaging with Faith. *'Hope's unable to tell those idiots I'm here. She's gotta have feelings for Wyatt.'*

Hope reads Luke's body language. *'Luke's mad. He must think I'm awful.'*

The waiter takes Hope's order while her phone rings again. "CJ, I'm busy. I'll call you later."

"Are you in Corpus with Luke? Your standards have fallen."

"How dare you insult me like that! How would you know Luke's here anyway."

"Wyatt helped me buy a horse. Sam's shoeing it. I'll fly there if'n ya want good company."

"Colt, this trip is for Faith."

"I could be there in two hours if you're that lonely."

Hope's frustrated. "Goodbye Colt. We'll be talkin' when I get back."

Chester's amused until realizing Wyatt's not at the ranch. "Wyatt didn't have permission to leave the ranch. He's got work to do."

Hope's agitated. "I'll take your problem over mine. I have three idiots to deal with 'cause of Luke."

"You'll find the right words. *Someday, you'll learn why Luke beat the shit outta those assholes.'*

"I'm glad Luke's here, Momma."

Hope glances at Luke. "It's nice Chester invited Luke to join us."

Chester's thinking, *'Wyatt, Colt, 'n Sam feel threatened Luke's here. Bringin' him's gettin' better by the minute.'*

Chester calls Ben. "Give Wyatt all the crap jobs when he returns to the ranch where he supposed to be."

Hope's phone interactions mute Luke's mood. *'Hope doesn't want me here.'*

Luke refuses to look at Hope.

'I hurt Luke with what I said. Or didn't say.'

Faith's energetic outburst after lunch elicits a weak smile from Luke.

"Luke, we're goin' to one of my most favorite places besides the beach."

Hope adds, "We can't get there fast enough, can we, Pecan?"

They arrive at Texas State Aquarium where Faith announces, "I'm gonna show Luke everything today."

"Stay with your mom, Faith. This trip is for you 'n her. I'm not complicating things more."

Hope cringes, *'Luke's mad for sure.'* "Nope. Faith's your guide today. That's final."

"Faith should be with you."

Hope smiles and her eyes sparkle. "Don't argue. Y'all'll be safer with Faith. So you don't get lost or fall in the shark tank."

"Is this a trick? I'm not getting between you 'n Wyatt."

Hope's concerned after Luke's comment. *'How do I answer Luke?'*

Chester hands Luke a map. "Here's a souvenir."

Faith guides Luke around all the exhibits and Chester pulls her aside when they finish.

"You've earned a visit to the gift shop."

Faith displays her cutest expression. "Grand-daddy, I'd like that stuffed dolphin."

"It's yours."

Hope states, "Faith's got you wrapped 'round her little finger."

"Yep. What would you like, daughter?"

"Nothin'. Dad. I'm past stuffed animals. I can buy my own gifts now."

Luke notes Chester's distinctly proud smile when Hope calls him dad. *'Chester likes Hope calling him dad.'*

Luke exits with Chester. "Faith's a young version of Holly at times, ain't she?"

Chester glares at Luke. "Don't ever say that again. Y'all almost gave me a heart attack."

Hope observes Chester's outburst. "What are you two talkin' 'bout?"

Chester responds. "Nothin' y'all need worry about."

Luke whispers, "For now."

Hope's irritated stare terminates Luke's smile. "Do I have to babysit y'all?" *'What are they up to?'*

Chester answers. "No ma'am. We're mindin' our P's 'n Q's."

Hope's wry grin indicates she's kidding. "I swear I'm here with three kids, not one."

Luke notes, *'Hope has the same devious smile like Chester.'*

They walk along Shoreline Boulevard. Hope sees Luke's focused on the carrier until they pass it. *'What's Luke thinkin'?'*

Luke speaks up, "Hey, there's something in the water."

Hope comments, "Faith, those are dolphins. They're sayin' hello to your dolphin."

Luke studies the water, "I count eight dolphins."

"Momma, that's one for each year old I am."

"Right, Faith."

Hope observes Luke. *'He's fascinated by those dolphins. Like he's never seen them before.'*

Luke smiles, "This is so cool." *'I feel a spiritual connection here.'*

Hope and Faith change and return to the beach, Chester sits in the restaurant to read, and Luke decides to swim in Corpus Christi Bay's calm water. They drive into downtown Corpus for dinner at Faith's choice. She tugs at Luke's sleeve, "Longhorn Steakhouse is one of my favorite places."

Chester pulls into La Palmera Mall and parks close to the restaurant. Luke comments on the restaurant's décor after being seated.

"This looks like your house, Chester."

"Because they have good taste."

Faith asks to go to the attached mall after supper. Chester replies, "We'll walk off our meals."

Hope pauses at the Victoria Secret's window display. Chester taps Luke's shoulder and points towards Hope. She blushes when she realizes Luke's noticed what's she's looking at.

'Great. What's Luke thinking right now?'

Luke ponders, *'I'm sure Hope's got plenty of sexy outfits.'*

Chester nudges Hope while Luke's by a jewelry display. "You drop Luke a hint?"

"That's not funny." *'No one's buyin' me a ring again.'*

Luke deliberates, *'What if I proposed to Linda with a ring? I wanted to shop for rings together. It doesn't matter now.'*

Chester hollers at Luke. "Y'all pickin' somethin' out for someone?"

Luke glances at Hope then Chester. "I was thinkin' about getting you 'n me friendship rings."

Chester frowns, "Shut up. You ain't funny."

Hope comments, "Oh, so it's only funny if it's about me?"

Chester barks out, "It's time to go."

Faith surprises Hope at the hotel. "Momma, watch the sunset on the beach with Luke."

"But Pecan, we do that."

"Share it with Luke tonight. We'll all watch tomorrow night."

"Um, are you sure?"

Hope and Luke exit the cool lobby and run into the college girls dressed in skimpy outfits.

"Hey handsome, come dancin' with us. We'll enjoy naked horizontal moves later."

"Yeah, dump the old lady 'n join us for real fun."

Hope's ready to confront them until Luke's words throw cold water on the situation.

"Sorry girls, the old lady's promised to watch the sunset with me. I'll stay here with a beautiful woman while y'all go have fun."

"Come find us when you're bored."

"I won't get bored."

Luke sees Hope's smug glare while the girls depart. *'What's that about?'*

Hope's heart palpates after Luke's complimentary explanation on how he's spending his evening. *'Wyatt's the last man to make me feel this way.'*

Hope leads Luke across the cool sand while he admires the Lexington bathed in a blueish hue to enhance the 'Blue Ghost' reputation.

"I didn't say anything inappropriate, did I?"

Hope's unable to suppress a smile. "You said the right things to those girls. Except the old lady part." *'I can't believe you chose me over them.'*

"I wanted to soften the blow of losing me to you."

"Let's dip our feet in the water then enjoy the Corpus sunset."

Hope leads Luke into the shallow water after he takes his boots off. *'I like Hope holdin' my hand.'*

Luke looks at their clasped hands and feels Hope's grip loosen and gently squeezes so Hope turns away.

'I can't let Luke see me smile like this.'

Luke doesn't see Hope's shy smile while tiny waves rhythmically lap at the shoreline. They return to the sand and admire the horizon emblazoned in the setting sun's glory.

"I'm surprised more people aren't here for this."

"I chased 'em away so you could enjoy your first Corpus sunset."

"Wait. Didja bring your gun?"

Hope's defensive until noticing Luke's mischievous glint in his eyes. "Oh. Y'all're makin' fun of me, huh? Ha ha."

Luke laughs.

"I don't have my gun. As far as you know."

"Fine. I'll behave. Maybe."

"Good boy. Y'all figured that out all on your own."

Luke enjoys the timeless, yet extravagant show Mother Nature provides while Hope positions herself to observe him in the reddening evening sky.

"I'm glad Luke shaved so I can see his rugged facial features in this light.'

Hope shudders recalling Luke's expression during the parking lot attack. *'Luke looked so fierce. Now he seems at peace with the world.'*

Luke misses Hope's measured observation but glances over to see the scarlet light illuminate the sparkle in her green eyes. *'Gorgeous.'*

A gentle breeze moves strands of hair across Hope's face. Luke brushes it from her eyes causing Hope to smile and look down. Her usual tense controlling mannerisms give way to a cheerful carefree attitude. Scattered clouds are shaded in pinks and purples along with the sunset's reddish colors until night consumes the remaining daylight. Chester studies the pair from the balcony.

'They're close but seem distant. Luke has Hope's full attention.'

"Grand-daddy, do ya think Momma's enjoyin' the sunset with Luke?"

"I think so. It's nice you let them do that."

The day's activities sap Faith's energy and make her yawn. "I'm gonna brush my teeth."

Luke watches Corpus Christi Bay darken once the fiery orb sinks beneath the horizon. "That's about the prettiest sight I've seen today. It's still second place though."

Hope's enticing Texas drawl barely veils her curiosity induced question. "What's first?"

Luke pauses, "I'll keep that to myself. For now."

Hope wonders, *Does Luke mean those college girls?*

"The guys play a song, somethin' 'bout a good day for sunsets. I get it now."

Luke's eyes radiate a strong spark of interest. Hope stands and pulls him up and kisses his cheek. *I can't believe I did that.*

Hope tries concealing her flushed cheeks. "Let's go thank Faith. That song's probably Roger Creager's 'Good Day For Sunsets'.

The twilight reveals Hope's blushed cheeks while facing Luke. *Hope's blushing.*

Luke looks at Lexington. *Goodnight Dad.*

THIRTY-THREE

Chester shushes Hope entering the room and points to Faith and whispers, "Faith sleeping. She saw the sunset, brushed her teeth, and flopped into bed."

Hope whispers and kisses Faith's forehead, "You're such a blessing."

"Faith hopes you two enjoyed the sunset together."

Luke remarks, "I did. Faith's a good girl." *I definitely enjoyed the sunset with Hope.'*

Hope adds, "It was selfless of Faith."

Chester makes a suggestion. "Hope, take Luke for a nightcap at Blackbeard's On The Beach."

Hope answers timidly. "Luke doesn't wanna do that with me. We can call it a night."

Luke pokes fun at Hope. "I think the old broad deserves a mom break."

Hope feels giddy but angrily retorts, "Watch it." *'Luke's askin' for more time with me. Why do I feel like this?'*

"We don't have to."

"Take me to Blackbeard's."

"Okay. We won't be gone too long."

Chester grins and winks. "Take your time, Hope." *'Wyatt returnin' shows me Luke's good to and for Hope.'*

Luke studies Blackbeard's lavender-shaded exterior and the interior's festive pirate-themed décor. He spots a set of Longhorns mounted on one wall. "What Longhorn lived a pirate life?"

"I've never thought about that before."

Hope orders a Margarita while Luke chooses Shiner Bock.

"Look at you orderin' a Shiner. You're gittin' more Texan by the day."

"I doubt I can drink my way to bein' Texan." *'I'd've been third generation Texan after my first night.'*

Hope's confused until Luke clarifies. "I drank so much my first night in Austin. I woke with a jackhammer splitting my head in two."

Hope worries, *'Will drinkin' with me remind him of Holly?'*

"I don't wantcha rememberin' bad times. Should we leave?"

"What? No. Hope, I'm simply saying I'm not drinking like that for a long time. Enjoy your Margarita. How 'bout a toast to a memorable time in Corpus."

Luke lifts his bottle and gently taps Hope's glass. "Oh, and to dodging bullets on my first day at the ranch."

"That's never goin' away, is it?" *'Has Luke forgot the lunch phone calls?'*

"Nope."

"Fair enough."

Luke keeps the conversation revolving around Hope, Faith, the ranch, and Hope's upbringing without disclosing much personal information. Hope realizes this while a song starts that catches Luke's attention.

"This is a pretty seductive song."

"It's Cody Johnson's, 'Nothin' On You'."

"He's gotta be singin' about someone special. You hear it in his voice. You've had someone sing like that to you, right?" *'Like Wyatt?'*

Hope's expression saddens. She looks away. *'No one's felt that way about me.'*

"I bet Wyatt's done it. I would if you were my girl. Except I can't sing, so you'd run."

Hope gazes at Luke. "Wyatt never did that." *'Would you really, Luke? Wyatt's sweet-talked me but that's all.'*

Luke shifts to a lighter subject. "How did you 'n Chester find this place?"

"Chester's Marine buddy recommended the hotel."

"Chester has a lot of friends, doesn't he?"

"He's had some good friends for years. Luke, why don't you talk about yourself?"

Luke's unprepared to answer Hope's directness. "Never mind. That was rude."

"No. I don't have much to tell. Nothin' interesting anyway."

"We should head back. They close soon."

"People leave when they get to know me."

Luke's unexpected answer throws Hope. *'Why would people leave?'*

Luke watches the bowstring arch styled bridge's vibrant colors changing hues and patterns while crossing the parking lot to the hotel.

"Faith loves watching the bridge change colors. Isn't it pretty?"

'Is Hope changing the subject already?'

Hope regains Luke's attention by the elevator. "Luke, I'd like to know more about you."

'Did I misread Hope?'

Luke attempts an awkward hug before Hope enters her room. "Goodnight Hope."

"Goodnight Luke."

Chester enters, "Are ya drunk? My girls make ya drink too much."

Luke's irritated glance is his only answer. *'I did enjoy having a drink with Hope.'*

Hope and Luke review their evening. Hope wonders, *'Should I let Luke into my life more? I might want him around. Does Wyatt affect my future?'*

Chester hears Luke whimper before his nightmare wakes him. Thoughts of Hope keep him awake. *'What does Hope want? Who does Hope want? I can't tell. She needs full control. That's apparent. We're similar but also very different.'*

Luke ponders Hank's lessons. *'Hank's taught me the right people influence my life positively. Hope does seem like a better choice than Linda.*

But could I rebuild a better life with Linda by trying harder with her. Like Hope's doing with Wyatt.'

Chester's reading on the beach after breakfast Saturday morning. Hope and Faith play along the shoreline. Chester mentally notes Luke's disposition being fully dressed and continually observing the carrier.

'Luke seems like he has a lot on his mind. Hope's actin' the same way. What happened last night?'

Red flags flap in the gusty wind causing rough waves which force Hope and Faith to remain near shore.

Waves constantly crash the shore with considerable intensity. Faith digs a channel so the water creates an inland river. Hope spots Luke wandering in the direction of the carrier and searching the sand.

'Luke's overdressed for the beach.'

Faith's brief shriek shatters Hope's tranquil moment and turns to find her floating farther offshore. Faith had moved into deeper water to bob up and down with the waves. Larger waves roll over her and push her under so the undercurrent carries her away. Faith rises to the surface coughing and screaming and flailing until another wave forces her under and pulled further from Hope. Hope's unable to swim and helplessly watches Faith taken from her.

'Dear God, what do I do?'

Luke's unaware since he's travelled a good distance from the unfolding danger. His attention is drawn to a group of people pointing towards Hope.

'Is something swimming near shore again?'

Luke's focus shifts from the water to Hope. *'Hope's actin' odd.'*

Faith's no match to fight the churning sea while it pulls her towards the horizon and she disappears under the angry waves when Chester reaches Hope.

'I never learned how to swim 'n I'm too old to fight that anyway.'

Hope screams, "Won't someone rescue my daughter?", but bystanders remain planted onshore.

Chester wonders, *'Hope's usually watching Faith like a hawk.'*

Luke flashes past like a silent ghost while running at full speed.

'Luke's able to swim. Thank you, God.'

Luke dives beneath the large inbound waves and remains submerged in the turbulent water until resurfacing to search for Faith. He spots her head appear and disappear and swims in her direction. He struggles in his boots and clothing even though he's a strong swimmer.

'I've never encountered anything like this.'

Luke submerges after another wave drives Faith below the surface. *'I can't lose her.'*

He reaches out until his hands touch her and grabs hold and kicks hard to resurface. Faith coughs and sputters after swallowing water and wildly flails in all directions in a panicked state.

"Faith, I've gotcha."

Luke looks towards shore. *'Not good.'*

A large wave crashes over them and viciously spins them around. Luke hangs on to Faith and thinks. *'My clothes are weighing me down.'*

Faith clings to Luke while he attempts to sidestroke directly to shore only to feel resistance. Faith thrashes around and falls off and wraps her arms around Luke's neck nearly strangling him. Luke repositions Faith to try again. He rethinks his strategy to conserve energy.

'I can't fight the current and Faith. I'll tire out and we'll both drown. We're farther out than I thought. I need to find a break in the outbound current and not waste too much time or strength.'

Luke's strength is being sapped by the ordeal during the search for an escape from possible death. *'I can't let Faith die like this.'*

Waves crash over Luke. *'Damn. I'm strugglin' too much 'n I need to keep Faith calm and not let my clothes sink me.'*

Luke's exhausted when he finally finds calmer water. *'I need help.'* "Faith, I promise we'll get out of this." *'Is that a promise I can't keep?'*

Luke relies on his training to save Faith and digs deep to overcome the burn in his joints. *'Either I save us or we drown. No one's helpin'.'*

Luke's energy is drained beyond training levels and starts accepting failure is possible. This makes him furious and decides not to let the forces of nature defeat him. Luke slips below the surface but holds Faith above the waves in his weakened state. He kicks hard to resurface and hears Hope calling out.

"Hold on, Faith. Luke'll save you."

Hope's encouragement pushes Luke to use his remaining strength to make a last ditch effort to reach shore. He's thankful when his feet touch the sandy bottom and struggles to stand to carry Faith to safety.

"You're safe, Faith." *'I can't believe we made it.'*

Hope waits frantically at water's edge and grabs hold of Faith. "Thank God you're safe. I don't know what I'd do if anything happened to you, Pecan."

Hope embraces Faith and both cry uncontrollably. Luke stumbles backwards into the water before moving sideways onto the beach. He staggers away from the watery beast that tried to destroy him and Faith.

THIRTY-FOUR

Luke's breathing is labored and his eyes are red from the salt water. He waves several people off looking to check on him. *'I don't need your help now assholes.'*

Luke drops to his knees. *'I need to stand 'n stay strong for Hope 'n Faith.'*

Hope and Faith are surrounded by people and hotel workers bring towels to Faith and Luke. Chester emerges from the group to approach Luke.

"Thanks for savin' my grand-daughter."

"I did what needed doin'."

"I never learned to swim."

Hope exits the crowd with Faith and spots the college girls approaching Luke. *'What do they want?'*

She shoots them a dirty look.

"We're sorry we were so bitchy 'n rude. We've been drinkin' all week. Some of us have nieces and nephews, and siblings. We could imagine how terrible this could've been if he weren't with you."

Hope's expression softens. "Thank you. That means a lot to me."

"Y'all've got a good man. Take care of him like he takes care of you and your daughter. I hope I find someone like him."

Luke's voice is hoarse. "Enjoy your weekend."

Chester discerns, *'Luke's plum tuckered out.'*

Hope hands Faith to Chester to stand in front of Luke. "I can't thank you enough for savin' Faith."

Luke simply nods and isn't ready when Hope lunges to hug him. She leans back before firmly pressing her lips against his for a long sweet kiss. Luke feels a renewed energy from Hope's soft lips touching his. Faith loudly exclaims, "Momma, you really kissed Luke. Again. What does that mean?"

Hope takes Faith back, "Um, uh, nothin' Pecan. I'm thankful Luke saved you. I got caught up in the moment."

One woman comments, "That's no thank you kiss. That's a marry me kiss."

Hope glances at the group before looking into Luke's eyes staring deeply at her. He's thinking, *'Is this what forever looks like? I never felt this with Linda.'*

Hope composes herself. *'My head's swirling.'* "We should head home now."

Faith gives out immediately. "Momma, you promised you'd get me new t-shirts on Padre Island."

Hope stares into Faith's imploring eyes. "It's a bad idea now, Pecan."

Faith's determined not to let the traumatic event cancel a shopping trip. "Momma, are you gonna break your promise to me?"

Chester offers a potential alternative. "We'll go but keep away from the water. We can still enjoy our time here."

Luke recalls college kids stories about Padre Island after spring break. *'What's there exactly?'*

Chester calls Hope into the room after noticing Luke's bloodied gauze. Luke's wearing only a towel when Hope enters the room.

'I'd steal Luke's towel if we were alone.'

Hope's gaze shifts from Luke's torso to his arm. "Did you rip my stitches out?"

"Faith may've helped." *'Hope's never worn jean shorts, sandals, or a stylish white crop top before. That's a Holly outfit.'*

Hope and Luke head to the lobby. Chester informs Hope to bring jeans, flannels, and boots for her and Faith when they return. They head out on US-181 to TX-286 and TX-358 which crosses over Oso Bay. John F. Kennedy Memorial Causeway travels over Corpus Christi Bay to the island side and becomes Park Road 22. They stop at Ocean Treasures Gift Shop built to look like a sand castle with oversized starfish and sand dollars imbedded into the walls. Large seashells, a sea turtle, and two sets of dolphins leap above waves. The centerpiece is a large mermaid seated in a white piece of thorny coral.

Luke thinks, *'This place was made for Faith.'*

Chester takes pictures of Hope and Faith with the oversized sea art. Hope buys several new shirts and shorts for Faith while Luke notes the store's stocked with ocean related items and interesting oddities.

'Faith sure is happy.'

Faith leads Luke around the store so Hope pulls Chester aside.

"I dread goin' near the water again, Chester."

"We'll be fine daughter. We'll stay away from the water 'n enjoy the beach. Luke'll keep Faith safe. He'll watch her closely."

Chester calls Hope daughter whenever she needs extra assurance.

"I hope you're right."

"Look. Luke's stickin' to Faith here."

They have lunch at Texas Mesquite Barbecue and Grill. Its maroon shaded brick exterior gives way to a lighter toned interior with diverse pieces of art and pictures on the walls. Chester points to the replica storefront of Luckenbach's Post Office.

"That's exactly how it looks."

Luke smirks. "Kinda small, don'tcha think?"

"Shut up wise-ass."

Hope giggles at their light-hearted banter. *'I'm glad Luke's here.'*

Park Road 22 leads to a sign announcing they've arrived at the Padre Island National Seashore. Hope pulls over so Chester can take their annual picture.

"Momma, can Luke be in the picture too?"

"Um, I guess so." *'A picture of Luke would remind me of more heartache if he leaves.'*

Hope pulls into the Malaquite Visitor Center lot and they walk down a wooden pathway to the beach. Hope stops to take a deep breath. *'I hope Chester's right 'bout this.'*

Faith chases Hope across the white sand while Luke takes his boots and socks off and stops when his feet touch the sand. *'This sand is much softer than at the hotel.'*

He scans the white sandy beach stretching on either side while an offshore storm creates strong winds and larger waves in the Gulf of Mexico. Chester comments, "No one's swimmin' in those whitecaps."

"It's rougher here."

"It can be completely calm too."

Chester settles in at a picnic table with a book while Luke sets off to sort out thoughts. *'I kinda like bein' in a picture with Hope 'n Faith.'*

Luke looks back at Hope and Faith playing. *'What if I leave? What if I stay? What chance would we have to become a family? Is that what my life's missing?'*

Hope sees Luke calmly strolling near the crashing waves and shudders. *'How can Luke get close to the water now? I'll never go near the water again. What's Luke thinkin'?'*

Luke's relaxed stride conceals his inner turmoil. The wind blows his hair around under his cowboy hat. *'Passing NAS Corpus Christi felt oddly familiar. It feels more like home here than Illinois ever has. I feel connected to these waters. Lake Michigan never felt like this.'*

A low flying P-3 Orion approaches NAS Corpus where pilots have been trained since 1941. *'This reminds me when dad was stationed at NAS San Diego.'*

Hope and Faith rejoin Chester. "Hey Hank, Hope 'n Faith are back. We'll talk more later."

"How can Luke get so close to the water?" Hope shivers while looking at Luke outlined against the water. *'He seems comfortable near water.'*

"Luke's able to swim. The water's not a threat to him." *'Or is he makin' peace with the devil?'*

"I'll never go near water again."

"Me neither, Momma."

Hope recalls the woman's comment about her kiss with Luke. *'Do I want that with Luke? Why does Luke have to be so close to the water?'*

Luke realizes Hope's looking at him. *'I wish I mattered more. I feel small 'n insignificant 'n worthless.'*

Chester studies Luke while he returns when Hope and Faith stroll down the beach. *'Luke's furrowed brow is tellin'. He's got a lot on his mind. He is watching Hope 'n Faith.'*

Luke compares the desolate sandy mounds of greenery and grasses against the white sandy beach.

'Faith's clearly skittish near water now. I'll fix that right quick while we're here.'

Luke waits for Hope and Faith to return. "Hope, could I take Faith for a walk?"

Hope nervously answers, "I don't know." *'Chester said Luke'll keep Faith safe.'*

Faith takes Luke's hand to answer the question. "Let's go."

"Don't go far, okay."

Luke reassures Hope. "Don't worry. Faith's safe with me."

Hope notices Chester's slight nod. "Okay, I'm trustin' y'all."

"Alright Miss Faith, let's walk 'n talk."

Chester's amazed Hope permits Faith to go with Luke. *'Hope's never trusted anyone off the ranch with Faith.'*

THIRTY-FIVE

Luke glances back at Hope periodically while maintaining a safe distance from the shoreline.

'Luke's keepin' Faith clear of the water.'

Hope's keenly watching when Luke edges closer to the water. *'Faith's too busy talking to Luke and not paying attention.'* "Luke's too close to the water. That's not bein' safe."

"Hope, Faith's safe. Don't worry."

Faith finally notices they're near the water. "I'm scared."

"Do you trust me, Faith?"

Faith's voice conveys her panic. "I wanna go back."

Luke kneels to look into Faith's fright-filled eyes staring at the waves.

"Luke, I trust you but I wanna go back now."

"Nothin' bad's gonna happen. I promised your mom I'd keep you safe. I wanna show you that, okay."

Luke smiles to ease Faith's fears. Hope's sidetracked by Luke's caring gesture.

'How does Luke know to get down on Faith's level?'

"Faith, I'm not afraid of the water, you know why?"

"Why?"

"Because I respect its power. I wanna teach you that too so you're not afraid. Let's walk to the really shallow water, okay."

"I don't want to."

"Faith, do you wanna be afraid of the water? Or wouldja rather play in it still?"

"I do wanna play in the water still."

"Okay, follow me."

They walk into the wave residue and Luke rapid fires questions. "Are you okay? Do you feel afraid of this much water? Is there any reason to be afraid? Does it feel good on your feet?"

Chester grins, *'Smart lad.'*

Hope reacts differently. "Luke's disrespectin' me. Faith's in danger."

Chester stops Hope from walking towards them. "Don'tcha see what Luke's doin'?"

"He's scarin' my daughter."

"Nope. Actually, the opposite. What's he doin' out there?"

Hope's flustered. "I don't know."

"What did I teachya after fallin' off a horse?"

"Hold the reins tighter?"

"Yes, but no. I toldja to get back on the horse. Why?"

"So I wouldn't be afraid of the horse."

"Yup. Luke's gettin' Faith over her fear of the water."

"He should've asked first."

Chester chuckles, "They're fine. Look."

Faith's unsure at first but realizes the bigger waves can't reach her. "Luke, I'm safe here, aren't I?"

"Yes."

"The water feels good on my feet."

"Exactly. You don't need to be afraid of the water. You should respect it though."

Hope watches Faith smile and weave in and out of the water with Luke. *'Faith's smiling. Luke's so good with her.'*

Faith finally returns to Hope and happily exclaims, "Momma, I'm not afraid of water anymore."

Hope hugs Faith. "Yikes. Faith, you're all wet."

Luke approaches to hear Hope declare, "You shoulda told me what y'all planned to do out there."

"Wouldja let me do it?"

"No! Of course not."

Luke grins, "Then I'm glad I didn't ask."

Chester chuckles, "Better to ask forgiveness than permission."

Hope's unamused by Chester's comment.

"Momma, can I take swim lessons 'n swim like Luke?"

Hope glances at Luke. "I think we need to take swim lessons."

"Yippee. I'm gonna swim like you, Luke."

Luke's happy to see Faith's reaction to swim lessons. "Great. I'll have a swim buddy again." *'I miss our swim time, dad.'*

Luke looks at the incoming waves until Hope speaks.

"Pecan, stay with Chester. I wanna talk with Luke, okay."

"Okay Momma."

'Oh boy, I stepped in it now.'

Hope motions Luke to follow her. "I grew up around horses. I never learned to swim. I see that needs to change."

Luke opens up. "I learned when I was two. I had no fear of water. We had a kiddie pool at N.S. San Diego. My parents had to watch me at all times so I wouldn't drown. My dad finally took me to the community pool and threw me into the deep end and waited before jumping in next to me. That scared the heck outta me."

Luke's childhood account shocks Hope. "I'd never go near water again after that."

"I struggled to keep my head above water until my dad reached out to hold me. It was part of the lesson. He asked if I ever wanted to be that afraid again. I said no. Of course. So he taught me to swim as long as I respected the water."

"That can't be true."

"It is. I'm not recommending that approach but it worked for me. My dad 'n I swam a lot until…"

Luke's voice trails off and his expression saddens. Hope reaches out to touch his arm.

"Are you okay, Luke?"

Luke's shaken by the memory until looking at Hope's hand. *'I'm glad I shared that with Hope.'* "I miss my dad 'n mom. They died when I was young."

Hope recognizes Luke's forgotten he'd told her that before. Her voice conveys distinct pain and anger. "I got dumped on Chester's doorstep. He and Millie adopted me and raised me as their daughter. I never knew my parents. I didn't try findin' them after learnin' the truth. I felt abandoned. All I know is my mom brought me to the ranch. The hawk's feather in my hat fell on me when Chester took me into his arms. It was Chester's hat till he gave it to me. I've never known anything about my dad."

'So that's why Hope wears that old beat up hat.'

"Maybe your mom wanted you to have a better life?"

"She could've left a note to explain that. But she hated me and dumped me on strangers."

"I'm sorry you never knew your parents."

Hope's oddly confused. "Why're you sorry?"

"At least I knew my parents. I know they loved me. I have those memories to hold on to." *'Hank's right. It doesn't matter where I live. We carry memories everywhere.'* "I don't remember anything from when I was really young. I know we moved a couple times."

"You did have that."

"Hope, you grew up in a stable home surrounded by love."

Hope looks back at Chester. "The ranch has been good to me. And Faith too. It's shaped my life positively. How did your parents die?"

"I, I don't wanna talk about it, not yet."

Luke's eyes reveal he's reliving the trauma.

"I'm sorry I asked. I'll listen if you're ever ready to talk about it. Or share anything else." *'It must've been terrible.'*

Luke locks eyes with Hope and nods. *'Hope's offered twice to listen.'*

"About that kiss."

Luke cuts Hope off. "You overreacted in the moment. You didn't mean it."

"Luke, I…"

"I get it, Hope. I'm not the right guy. I'm not from Texas. I'm not a real cowboy. I'm not Wyatt."

'Why did Luke bring Wyatt up?' "I, I have Faith to consider." *'I'm afraid to let you in then have you leave. Wyatt might be the past. You might be the future. I don't know.'*

Hope's thoughts trouble her on the walk back. *'The rough water and the beach's tranquility match my life right now. Is Luke wrong for me? I'm not sure anymore. Can Wyatt still be right? Luke's beginning to feel comfortable. In a good way.'*

Chester suggests another activity. "Let's ride along the beach."

"We didn't make reservations."

"You didn't."

"But you did?"

"Yeah buddy I did."

"Still sneakin' things in. Your friend runs the company."

"Yup. So change and enjoy."

Luke and Faith ride along the shoreline. He's lost in thought but focused on Faith. Hope guides her horse along the beach away from the water. Faith leads Luke's horse into the water so their hooves splash water everywhere and laugh while Hope has a realization.

'Faith brings out a happier side of Luke.'

Hope requests Snoopy's Pier as a supper stop before returning to the hotel to enjoy the sunset on the beach to end Saturday. Sunday's spent at the South Texas Botanical Gardens and Nature Center and Hurricane Alley Waterpark. Faith plays games with Luke on the drive back before falling asleep on him. Hope quietly observes them. *'I'd like to trust someone enough to fall asleep on them.'*

Luke's cognizant Faith's unlocking a long forgotten side of him. Chester's wondering what's causing Hope's unusual silence.

'I think I need to talk to Hope. Millie was better at this.'

Faith gives Luke a long hug before he gets out of the truck. "I love you, Luke. Thanks for takin' care of me 'n Momma."

Luke exits the truck and Hope gives him a wave before he heads to the bunkhouse. Luke looks back only once and sees Hope's disappointed expression as does Chester.

"You good?"

"Yeah." *'I should've hugged Luke. I should've said somethin'.'*

Chester remains in the truck long enough to share a thought with Hope. "Don't let the past get in the way of reality's gift. You've got things to consider, don'tcha? I'm here if ya wanna talk."

"Thanks. I may take you up on your offer when I'm ready."

Wyatt confronts Luke in the bunkhouse. "Hope's my girl. Don't be gittin' any ideas 'bout her."

Luke slams his fist into Wyatt's face. "I'm in no mood for your bullshit."

Wyatt staggers to his feet. *'Shit, that hurt. Luke really could've knocked Ben out.'*

"That's me holdin' my temper. Don't push me again."

THIRTY-SIX

Luke's saddling horses Monday morning when Colt arrives and threatens him. "Stay away from Hope, asshole. Or else."

"Get lost, dumbass."

"I'll have y'all taken out."

"Your record ain't so good there."

Luke's arrogance irritates Colt. "Hope'll return to her senses 'n me once you're gone."

"Hope's a strong independent woman who decides her own life choices. Wyatt's who you need to worry about, not me. Maybe I'll stick around 'n watch the show."

Hope speaks up behind Colt. "Colt? Why are you here?"

"Uh, Hope, I didn't know you were here."

"So you're not here for me?"

Colt's panicked expression precedes his slow reply. "I, uh, I was thankin' Luke for savin' Faith."

Hope frowns. "How would you know about that?"

"Word spread 'round the ranch."

"We're kinda busy today. Luke's been properly thanked. *Sort of. More kissin' would've been nice though.*'

Hope sees Luke's mischievous grin. "Colt invited me for a beer and datin' advice."

Colt scowls when Hope laughs. "I need to get goin'. I have a flight. Hope, we'll catch up later over dinner."

"I'm eatin' here tonight. The Longhorn need vaccinatin' today. Some other time."

Colt quietly warns Luke, "Hope's my girl. Back off."

Luke's response sends a message. "Hope's not your girl. You don't own her. She's not an object. Do you think of her that way?"

Hope smiles after hearing Luke's statement. Wyatt further embarrasses Colt.

"Hope's not a trophy. She's a Texas queen. I'll treat her as such."

Hope recalls, *'Wyatt 'n Colt never got along.'*

Wyatt approaches Hope. "I'm workin' alongside this beauty today. How's Faith?"

Colt's clearly dejected while leaving.

"Faith's good. She wants swim lessons now. I need to set up for work."

Luke comments, "I could teach Faith. I promise I won't throw her in the deep end."

Hope smiles, *'Luke's showin' interest in Faith.'* "I trust Faith with you, Luke. We'll talk at supper." *'Colt didn't ask how Faith was.'*

Wyatt walks Hope to her truck. "I may be outta line but Faith wouldn't've nearly drown if I were with you instead. I'd've been next to you helpin' out."

Hope's expression sours. *'Does Wyatt have a point? I didn't think about that. Did Luke distract me?'* "We've got work to do."

Ben studies Hope's interaction and notes her troubled look when she leaves.

"Wyatt, where's Hope goin'? We're settin' up for the Longhorn."

"Not sure. Hope said she'd be back soon."

Hope drives to Lakeline Mall to meet Jubilee and JeniMay at Jubilee's office.

"Is Wyatt right? Was I distracted by Luke?"

"Wyatt wasn't there 'n don't know the facts. Y'all're askin' an impossible question to answer."

Jubilee adds, "Be thankful Luke was there to save Faith. Why're ya askin' what if questions?"

JeniMay challenges Hope. "Do you really watch Faith every single second?"

"Of course. You know that."

"So guys' crude comments don't distract you for several seconds?"

"Maybe. But Faith's close by."

"Was Faith nearby this time?"

"Yes."

"So Luke bein' there didn't matter. Be glad y'all ain't mournin' the loss of your daughter."

"If Luke weren't there…"

"Dammit Hope! Stop! You're arguin' stupid hypotheticals. See a potentially good man."

"This is why I stay closed off. Wyatt did ask how Faith was doin'. He seems to care about her. Is that a sign he's back for me?"

Hope's crazy thought process aggravates JeniMay and Jubilee.

"Bullshit! Wyatt wants you outta your jeans. He sees what he left. You're drivin' me crazy."

"Me too."

"Luke's risked his life for you and Faith. He wasn't asked to, right? Maybe that's the sign y'all should focus on. If that's not love I don't know what is."

"Luke doesn't love me. He doesn't see me that way."

"JeniMay's right. You won't accept Luke might be right for you. Here's an idea, have supper with Wyatt tonight. See how you feel 'bout him after the weekend with Luke. Take notes."

JeniMay speaks bluntly. "Colt, Sam, 'n Wyatt look at you like hungry wolves wantin' to strip you naked to get what they want. Luke's eyes show a lovin' side exists. You keep denyin' it. And him. He won't make a move on you. He will leave for that reason."

Jubilee comments, "Neither Luke or Wyatt knew Faith existed. Luke cares about Faith. Does Wyatt? You're just meat to feed Wyatt's sexual desires. Nothin' more."

"Luke's gonna leave eventually. It doesn't matter if I have feelings for him."

"I knew it! You do have feelin's for Luke. Finally, you admit it. Luke'd stay if y'all asked him to."

"Beth said the same thing."

"What? Beth? Wait. How long have you had feelings for Luke?"

"Can we drop this? Luke'll leave 'n everything'll return to normal."

JeniMay sighs. *'Hope's frustrating. She's not gonna change her mind unless somethin' major shifts her feelings.'* "Your life's never been normal. Look at this from a different angle. Nothing's guaranteed. You know that."

"My love for Faith's guaranteed. Nothing or no one'll change that."

Jubilee carefully chooses her next words. "Faith's gonna grow up 'n have her own life. You'll be more alone then. We'll always be here for you. But if we get married 'n have families we won't be so readily available then."

Jubilee's factual points affect Hope. "I haven't thought about Faith growin' up."

"She's gonna whether ya like it or not. Faith's happy 'round Luke. More than the guys at the ranch. Faith's different around Luke. Good different."

"The guys are stayin'. Luke's leavin'."

"Are you sure? No. Quit hidin' behind past events. Wyatt left you once already. Luke ain't left yet. He might not either."

"Luke says he's leaving."

"You've never changed your mind?"

"Remember freshman year? Wantin' to go to Hollywood after the school play."

"That's different. I liked bein' on stage. I thought I might like actin'."

Hope, ya had one line. Chester 'n Millie letcha have it when ya told them your idea."

"At least I didn't try movin' to Dallas when Bobby Young left."

JeniMay gets defensive. "I was seven. Thank you very much. And Bobby was so cute."

Jubilee laughs at the forgotten memory. "He was cute. I remember you walkin' down the driveway and then havin' to ask your dad where Dallas was."

"Yeah, he drew me a map too. I still wonder if he was serious."

All three women laugh at the old memory.

"We've had some really good times, haven't we? Friends for life, right?"

"Of course, Hope. No matter what happens or what changes for any of us."

JeniMay quickly adds. "Includin' men coming into our lives. Some sooner than others."

Jubilee inserts her correction. "Including the right men coming into our lives. And stayin'."

Hope frowns, "Are we back to that? I thought we were done with that."

"Fine. Can we talk about Bobby Young? I wonder if he's still hot."

Hope throws a proverbial bucket of cold water on JeniMay's dream boy. "Naw. He's probably fat 'n bald now. And lives with three cats."

"That's not funny, Hope. Don'tcha dare mess with my forever love."

Hope returns to the ranch with thoughts about supper with Wyatt. *'Maybe Jubilee's right. I need to figure this all out.'*

THIRTY-SEVEN

Hope returns and heads for the pasture where Chester's explaining what's happening to guests.

"Drovers pushed Longhorn to other pastures or to market. Their biggest fear was drowning and stampedes."

The wranglers drive the Longhorn into a wide alley then through a narrow alley to a head gate and into a squeeze chute to allow Hope to vaccinate them. Beth arrives with Faith later and Faith immediately seeks Luke out. Luke spots Hope smiling and talking to Wyatt and hugging him once the work is done. *'They're happy together.'*

Hope thinks, *'Supper with Wyatt'll help answer questions. Of course Faith's found Luke.'*

Holly's in Chester's office when Hope enters. "Hi Holly. Chester, thanks for watchin' Faith so Wyatt 'n I can have supper."

Holly quips, "Gonna saddle up some romance? Good for you, Hope."

"We're just talkin', Holly. That's all."

"Don't stop short of the goal line 'n miss the real fun."

"Alright, enough. I don't need to hear 'bout either of you 'n your love life."

"Grand-daddy, only one of us has a love life. For now."

Hope tracks Luke down to talk to him. "Luke, somethin's come up 'n I need to change my plans this evening."

"Yeah. I know. You're eating with Wyatt."

"How would you know?"

"Wyatt told me."

"Oh. I wanted to tell you first. But Faith's stayin' here."

Luke's tone turns cold. "Hope, your life's none of my business."

"I'd like to hold off tellin' Faith 'bout swim lessons. You might still leave if Joe's caught soon, right?"

"Right. If Joe's caught soon."

Luke starts to walk away but turns around. "You could just be honest 'n say you don't trust me. I might stick around since Chicago's got nothin' for me anymore."

"Why would you stay?" *'Or who would you stay for?'*

"Ranch life's growin' on me."

Wyatt disrupts their conversation. "I'm lookin' forward to supper with you, Hope."

Hope detects a tone in Wyatt's voice and notes his sideways glance at Luke. "Wyatt, it's just dinner. Nothin' more."

"If you say so, darlin'."

"I'll let you two figure this out."

Wyatt notices Hope's long gaze at Luke while he departs. "He's a loser, Hope. Forget about him."

"You don't know him. I'm not sure I know you anymore either."

Wyatt arrives with a bottle of red wine and a bouquet of flowers. "I'm willing to put the effort in to be with you again."

"That's nice. Thank you."

Wyatt pours a second glass of wine for Hope while dinner's cooking.

"I really shouldn't. I don't drink much anymore."

"You're not drivin'. Relax. Enjoy."

"Maybe you're right." *'One more glass won't hurt. Anymore'll make me frisky like whiskey makes me wanna fight.'*

Wyatt sneaks more wine into Hope's glass when she's not paying attention. "I really have missed you." *'Parts of you more than others.'*

"I never forgot you." *'I remember how good you were in bed 'n enjoyin' your body.'* "My biggest mistake was leavin' you."

"You're just sayin' that."

"Hope, I still love you. I always have. That's what broke up my marriage. I had to admit that to myself, then to Alison, my ex-wife."

Wyatt moves closer to put his arms around Hope.

'What's happenin'? Could Wyatt 'n I get back what we had and build the life I wanted so long ago?'

Wyatt kisses Hope's lips and feels her press against him. Hope gives in to her body's neglected desires and kisses more passionately. Wyatt begins unbuttoning her shirt. Wine influences Hope's impulse to allow Wyatt to continue until her shirt falls to the floor along with her bra. Hope feels Wyatt's strong hands caressing her tender breasts. Wyatt enjoys the moment. *'I've missed these big bouncin' beauties.'*

Hope moans when Wyatt's lips touch her nipples. "Oh, Luke. Don't stop."

Wyatt halts after Hope's slip up and leans back while his hands remain on Hope's breasts. His eyes travel from her chest to Hope's eyes and return to her breasts.

"I'm Wyatt."

Hope realizes Wyatt's hands are fondling her bare breasts. *'This is a mistake. This can't happen. Why did I say Luke's name?'* "I'm not ready, Wyatt."

Hope reaches for her shirt to cover her naked torso. *'Not with you.'*

"C'mon Hope, we've screwed like crazy. This ain't nothin'."

"We need to go slow. I need to get to know you again."

"You know me. This feels right." *'Your tits feel right.'*

"It's just been Faith 'n I for so long."

"I'll help raise Faith." *'You can raise parts of me.'*

"Faith'll be home soon. You need to leave. I need time to think."

"We can finish what we started first."

Wyatt attempts to pull Hope's shirt away. "C'mon. I've missed you. I've missed your body. Luke's not stayin'. I am."

Hope's impacted by Wyatt's bitter remark. "He told me he might stay."

Wyatt lets go of Hope's shirt. "Fine darlin'. I'll be waitin' at the ranch for our next date."

Luke sees Wyatt return.

"Hope's better lookin' naked now than before. You wouldn't know that, wouldja?"

Luke's silence disguises his emotional reaction. *'Hope chose Wyatt already. Maybe I'll stay for Jazzy.'*

Ben notes Hope seems distraught when he drops Faith off and sends Beth to talk to her.

"You got naked? With Wyatt?"

"Not naked. Wyatt only took my shirt off. That damned wine. I didn't even have that much to drink."

"Hope, y'all could've got buck naked and let Wyatt wreck ya."

"I'm not ready for that."

"Or maybe Luke should wreck ya?"

Beth sees Hope's expression change. "What?"

"Why would you say that?"

"I don't know."

"Beth, I said Luke's name while Wyatt was sucking my nipple."

"Whoa! Hold on. You said Luke's name?"

"Yes."

"Hope, that's telling."

"Luke's still leaving."

"Hope, your heart's tellin' ya somethin' you can't deny anymore. Wyatt's probably tellin' Luke he's bedded you down already."

"Why would Wyatt do that?"

"Eliminate competition. You ain't makin' Luke wanna stay. He'll think ya want Wyatt 'n bolt."

"How do you know when you like someone? Or know if they like you?"

"Honey, if you can't answer that question by now, I can't help ya. Who ya talkin' 'bout?"

"You know who?"

"Truthfully, I don't. Wyatt? Luke? I'm not sure you know which means they don't either. Y'all need to talk them."

"I can't control how I'm feelin' about Luke anymore. I said his name while I was with Wyatt. What does that mean?"

"Do I really need to explain that? You're more hopeless than I thought, Hope."

"I wish I knew the right choice."

"I think you do. Butcha won't choose. Or accept the answer."

"I thought about Luke while watchin' the sunset. Thanks to Corpus." *I do miss Luke. But could he really love me?*

THIRTY-EIGHT

"Chester, where's Luke? I need to talk to him."

"He 'n Wyatt are bringin' in a trail ride."

"Great." *'Chester put 'em together.'*

Hope sees a parked Harley. *'Jazzy's here too. Is Luke spendin' time with her? He's treatin' her differently now. They do have things in common. Do he 'n I?'*

Wyatt rides to Hope and dismounts while Luke tends to the horses to avoid Hope. Wyatt returns to the barn with Hope.

"Ben, where's Luke?"

"He left to change his shirt."

Holly enters seeming perplexed. "Have you seen Jazzy?"

Ben answers, "Not for some time now."

Luke removes his shirt on the stairway and opens his door. He's stunned to find Jazlynn lying completely naked on his bed.

"Hey cowboy. Ride me for a quickie then we'll wear each other out later."

Jazlynn's pleased Luke's unblinking gaze stays on her and spreads her legs wider. "I got my nose pierced. Ain't it sexy?"

Luke's eyes drift to the small silver ring with turquoise inset midway. *'That does look sexy. Along with the rest of Jazzy.'*

"How'd you get in here?"

"Does that matter? How 'bout you get in here."

Jazlynn runs her hand along her vaginal area. "I shaved my kitty. Come pound me."

Luke views Jazlynn's muscular yet sexy body. *Jazzy's hotter 'n hell.*

"Admit it, Luke, y'all want me as much as I want you. I see it in your eyes."

Would it matter if I hook up with Jazzy now? Hope's gettin' naked with Wyatt.

Jazzy stands and walks to Luke to kiss him. "Touch me everywhere."

Luke lets his hands reach out and begin to explore Jazlynn's body and hears her moan as he touches her shaved pelvic area. Luke's finger feels her moistness as it enters her which induces Jazzy's explicit request. Hope's voice interrupts his thoughts.

"Luke, are you here?"

Luke's mind goes blank. *Why's Hope here?*

Jazlynn joins Luke in the hallway as Hope comes into view. "Come back later. Luke's makin' my kitty purr."

Hope's shocked expression speaks volumes. *Beth's right. I waited too long. Luke can do better than Jazzy though. Did I push him to her?*

Luke glances at Jazzy. *Wyatt's got Hope. Jazzy's still interested in me.*

"I came back to change my shirt. This one ripped. We ain't done nothin' yet."

"Yet?" *Luke's considerin Jazzy.* "I wanted to talk to you but I see you're busy."

Luke feels vindictive. "I have work to finish. Unless Jazzy has something in mind?"

"Jazzy? Really?"

"I never had a chance with you, Hope. Why do y'all wanna talk to me? You're with Wyatt."

Luke hands his torn shirt to Jazzy and retrieves a new one. He passes Hope while pulling the new shirt on. "You two play nice. Hope, maybe we'll talk if you're not busy gettin' naked with Wyatt."

Jazzy declares, "Hope, y'all got laid? Finally."

"What? No. I'm not sleepin' with Wyatt. Not yet." *Shit! Why'd I say that?*

Jazlynn throws the shirt at Hope after Luke slams the outer door shut. "Make yourself useful. Fix this when y'all ain't got your arm up a horse's ass. I screw, I don't sew."

"Shut up, Jazzy. Or I'll put my boot up your ass 'n leave it there."

"I'd rather let Luke use somethin' else."

Hope turns and leaves to prevent doing something she'll regret. *'Puta.'*

Luke finishes his task and goes to the gym with Jazlynn. He allows her to be more affectionate during the workout and afterwards at the ranch. Hope brings Luke's mended shirt back the next day and hands it to Katie.

"Here's Luke's shirt. I sewed the rip."

"That was nice of you."

Katie sets the shirt on the back of the couch. Jazlynn enters and notices it.

'Hope actually fixed it. I'll let Luke think I did.'

Katie sees Jazlynn leave with the shirt. *'Where's she goin' with that?'*

THIRTY-NINE

Tension builds between Hope and Luke during the next few days. Chester underhandedly schedules them to work in the riding barn together alone.

"Luke, Jazzy's not right for you."

"Why do you care? You settled on Wyatt."

"I haven't settled on Wyatt. Or anyone. Yet. *Luke thinks I'm with Wyatt already.*"

"Rumor has it y'all're gettin' naked with him."

"Who told you that?"

"Does it matter?"

"I'm not getting naked with Wyatt. Not fully." *Shit, why'd I say that?* "You're screwin' Jazzy."

"I haven't been naked with Jazzy. She got naked but we ain't screwed yet. Maybe I oughta."

"You'd hit a new low if 'n ya do."

"Yeah, well the one I thought I wanted ain't an option."

"Like who?"

"Don't matter now. She's lassoed by a cowboy now."

Does Luke mean me?

Hope processes Luke's words. *'Luke doesn't sound happy to be with Jazzy. He sounds angry.'* "Jazzy's thinkin' 'bout herself. That's who she is."

"So what. Wyatt hammerin' you into your mattress."

Hope slaps Luke out of frustration. He impulsively reacts and places his hands on Hope's cheeks and softly kisses her lips. Hope gazes into his eyes afterwards.

'Why did Luke do that? Why did he stop?'

"I figured I'd get one last kiss in."

Hope slaps Luke again and steps back. "How dare you! Would you like to be treated that way?" *'That was the most romantic thing y'all could do.'*

"You'd never do that to me. Or anyone else. It's not you. Honestly, I'd like to feel that kinda passionate love from someone."

Hope feels challenged to disprove she's incapable of being passionate. She wraps her arms around Luke's neck and delivers a long message sending kiss. Hope steps back and locks eyes with Luke.

"Don'tcha dare say I can't be passionate." *'I wish we continue this. You're makin' me feel things I've never felt before. Physically and emotionally.'*

Wyatt enters with several guests while Hope's stepping back. She glances at him. *'Wyatt didn't see that, did he? Do I care if he did?'*

Wyatt approaches Hope for a hug and kiss. "How's my hot-lookin' honey?"

"We shouldn't do this in front of guests."

"Why not? They do it in front of us."

"It's not professional, Wyatt."

"You wouldn't do it with anyone else in front of guests, wouldja?" *'Wyatt saw us.'*

Luke speaks up. "Hope's a beautiful woman. Treat her with respect."

Jazlynn comments behind Wyatt. "Are y'all makin' a move on Wyatt's girl? Goes against the cowboy code." *'Wyatt's never cared 'bout that code with me. He still rides me hard 'n gets me wet.'*

"Luke, my kitty'll fulfill all your desires."

Hope hears Jazlynn. *'Luke hasn't slept with Jazzy yet. Why not? I haven't with Wyatt either.'*

"Jazzy, I'm not qualified to date Hope. She's made that clear 'n she's with Wyatt anyway. I thought there coulda been somethin' but I was wrong."

Luke storms out of the riding barn. Jazlynn remains long enough to verbally jab Hope.

"You coulda had Luke. But y'all shot at him 'n insult him. I'm not sendin' mixed signals. I want him."

Jazlynn glances at Wyatt. *'Y'all'll get dumped faster 'n a wife in a whorehouse when Hope finds out you've cheated with me. Luke'll be all mine by then.'*

It occurs to Hope that Wyatt's return eliminated her chance with Luke. *'Luke admitted he was interested but I waited too long. Even Jazzy knew Luke liked me.'*

Hope checks on Patsy and the foal to avoid Wyatt and Jazlynn. *'Should I go after Luke?'*

Luke enters the rodeo barn and begins tossing hay bales around until Ben questions his actions.

"Whoa, hoss, what'd those bales do to you?"

"Y'all go about your business 'n leave me alone 'n we'll get along just fine."

"Lordy, Lordy, y'all sound like a true Texan."

"Hope's made it clear I ain't one of you."

"Hope don't know everything."

Ben notices movement by the door. "Hope, we were just talkin' 'bout you. I told Luke he's soundin' like us now."

Luke's statement gets Hope's full attention. "I can't return to Chicago but I can't stay here either."

Ben asks, "Aren'tcha stayin' for Jazzy?"

Hope appears nervous. "What about me? And Faith?"

"Yeah. I don't break promises. Jazzy might be the only other reason now. I was wrong to think someone else might be interested. Finish this up."

Ben looks at Hope while Luke departs rapidly. "Did Luke just give me an order?"

Hope's unfocused and doesn't hear him. *'Luke won't stay for me now, would he? I can't ask him to stay. It has to be his decision, right?'*

Katie notices Hope entering the house seeming upset. "What's troublin' ya, Hope?"

"Um, nothin'."

"That's not the face of nothin'."

"I don't think Luke should date Jazzy."

"Does it matter? Y'all're all hot 'n heavy with Wyatt."

"Why do you say that?"

"That's what Wyatt's spreadin' 'round the ranch."

"It's not entirely true. Things started happenin' but I stopped it." *'By sayin' Luke's name.'* "I may've lost any chance with Luke now."

Katie hears Hope's admission. *'Ah, the truth's comin' out now.'* "Who cares? You're back with Wyatt."

Hope and Katie step onto the deck and witness Jazlynn handing Luke's shirt to him. He hugs her and heads towards the house.

"Jazlynn was nice enough to fix my shirt."

"Jazlynn didn't…" Hope pauses, *'It doesn't matter.'* "Katie, I'll talk with you later. I need to get Faith."

Katie waits until Hope's far enough away to get Luke's attention. "Jazlynn didn't mend your shirt. Hope did. Just so's ya know."

CHAPTER
FORTY

Chester updates Hank on developing situations before texting Hope to meet in his office to iron out a scheduling conflict. *'I know Hope's busy with work and Faith's school shopping.'*

Hope informs Chester she can meet mid-morning. Luke interrupts their meeting.

"I, uh, howdy Hope."

Hope stands and coldly states, "Chester, we'll finish this later. I have a horse to deworm."

"Thanks for fixin' my shirt. Katie told me you did it, not Jazzy."

"Whatever."

Luke follows Hope out. "Why are you mad at me? I haven't done anything wrong."

Hope spins around. "For what it's worth, I'm not mad at you." *'I'm mad at me for lettin' you get to me. I'm mad because you admitted you like me.'*

Luke's puzzled while Hope continues to her truck. *'Was Hope sincere? I wish she'd be honest with me. I didn't do anything wrong.'*

Wyatt intercepts Hope, "Let's take a walk. Add a little romance to it."

"What've you been telling people? And Luke."

"A gentleman doesn't kiss 'n tell. I ain't said a thing to Luke or anyone else. Luke's with Jazzy anyway." *'Whatever keeps Luke away from you.'*

"I need to go."

Hope's conflicted. *'How can Luke stay after wantin' to leave for so long? After Wyatt returns. Why? Is he serious? Do I want Luke to leave? Or stay?'*

Hope starts her truck but decides to find Holly. "Are you busy tonight, Holly? Could we go for supper?"

"I'm swamped. I swear, Grand-daddy thinks I work here."

"You do work here, remember, guests, activities, shoppin' trips. Ring any bells?"

"Don'tcha dare use that four letter word in my presence. It's evil. I'm open tomorrow."

Hope smiles. "Hey, I work too. See you tomorrow."

A woman enters with several other guests. "Luke's gonna be mine for a night. I'll show him why a rich man married me."

Hope's smile disappears. *'I need to stop lettin' Luke get to me or just let him in. Should I tell him how I feel? What would happen? I'm too afraid to find out.'*

The woman catches Hope staring at her. "You don't approve? No. I've seen that look before. You want that cowboy too, don't you?"

Holly interjects, "Hope ain't been interested in guys since her divorce."

"It's not my first rodeo to bed down a young buck. Try stealing him if you can."

Holly laughs, "Fat chance that'll happen."

"You don't look like competition. You're beautiful, stunning even, but your eyes lack hunger. You look lost, unsure, perhaps even unwilling. This blonde, she's my competition. She has a hungry look like me."

Holly reveals a truth. "I brought Luke here."

Hope exits silently and finds Ben before reaching her truck. "Luke knows he can't date guests, right?"

"We've talked about this. Luke's not an official wrangler. Chester's banned Luke from Holly."

Ben mulls over Hope's odd behavior after she leaves. *'What's with Hope lately?'*

Holly and Hope go to dinner the next evening. Holly recounts Luke's encounter with the woman.

"She was relentless. I took notes. That's sayin' somethin'."

Hope responds, "I'm not interested in Luke's exploits with other women. Or with you."

Holly changes topics and they catch up on each other's life for the remainder of the evening.

"I'm glad we did this, Hope. It's been too long. I know you're busy with Faith 'n work. Now ya have Wyatt too. How's that goin' so far?"

"I'm not sure about Wyatt. I don't know if we still have what we did."

"Hope, you get a second chance with the man who stole your heart. Take a chance."

"Wyatt stole my heart. But he ran off instead of marryin' me."

"He came back. That's like a fairy tale come true." *'Luke'll focus on me better.'*

Hope ponders Holly's viewpoint. *'Wyatt did steal my heart. But he broke it too. And my trust in men. Then I met Joe 'n settled. I can't go through that again. Luke's pullin' at my heartstrings 'n makin' me feel things I'm not sure I want to anymore.'*

Chester greets Hope and Holly when they return. "You two look happy. Hank's comin' to supper tomorrow and asked if you 'n Faith can make it too."

"We'll be here."

Hope arrives early the next evening. "Where's Hank?"

Chester enters the room. "His card game's runnin' long. He's fixin' to clean up 'n ain't leaving money on the table."

Faith asks, "Where's Luke?"

Holly walks in, "Luke's late. He's on a private trail ride with that married woman."

Chester responds, "She's paid extra for a private ride. Requested Luke too."

"She wouldn't take no for an answer, right?"

"Gee, I wonder why she asked for Luke to escort her alone."

Chester mistakes Hope's concerned expression. "Luke's not gonna get lost out there. He's learned the trails well enough by now."

'He might know that woman well enough by now too.' "Luke doesn't know why he's out there."

"Luke understands. The woman paid handsomely. Not sure why?"

Hope mutters, "She has her reasons."

Chester questions Hope. "Y'all know somethin' I don't, Hope?"

'Why did I say anything? What do I say now? Chester'll think I'm crazy.'

"No. I'm sure everything's fine." *'I hope.'*

Chester's focus shifts with Hank's arrival. "About time."

"Howdy Chester. Monique's here to help. Y'all get to enjoy my company tonight."

Chester rolls his eyes. "Y'all're gittin' worse with age."

"You're just jealous."

"Yeah, I'm jealous."

Hope notices Monique's fixated on her despite the guys surrounding her. *'Why's she lookin' at me?'*

"Monique volunteered to come to supper tonight."

Hope half-heartedly smiles at Hank and thinks, *'Sure. Look at the guys fawnin' all over her.'*

Jake approaches Monique. "Howdy. We ain't had a chance to meet yet."

Katie's amused Monique seems unfazed, *'She's gotta be used to this.'*

Hope's troubled expression gets Katie's attention. *'What's up there?'*

Katie examines Hope studying Monique. Hope's contemplating, *'Monique appears disappointed for some reason.'*

Hank proclaims, "The cowboy's wanna meetcha, Monique."

"Yeah, because of my personality."

Hank chuckles while making mental notes before waving Hope over. "Catch me up on things, Hope."

FORTY-ONE

Luke's stressed as he enters late for supper until seeing Hank. "Howdy old timer. Are they outta Jell-O again? Chester's got plenty."

Katie chuckles, *'Luke gets away with insultin' Chester when the others can't.'*

"Heard y'all ain't cuttin' the mustard 'n needed a good whoopin'. I brought reinforcements."

"Luke, you made it."

"Oh, hi Monique. Didja draw short straw again?"

Hope spots a sparkle in Monique's eyes. *'Is that why she looked disappointed before?'*

"What's on your cheek, Luke? You're not cheatin' on me, are you?"

Luke brings his hand to his face. "I need to wash up but I wanted to report in."

"Is that lipstick?"

Hope's question gets Chester's full attention with a telling glance before glaring at Luke.

"What the hell happened out there?"

"It's not what you think, boss."

"Enlighten me."

"It's a thank you kiss."

Holly fuels the fire, "Way to go, Luke."

"We're talkin' 'bout this after supper. Clean up 'n change."

"Yes sir. Faith, am I sittin' next to you?"

"Of course. And Momma too."

"Yes ma'am. I'll be back."

Wyatt arrives and sits next to Hope. Hank stirs the pot.

"Monique, sit next to Luke also."

"I'd be glad to."

Luke returns to find Monique next to his spot and Wyatt by Hope. *'Hank's smirking, Faith's mad, Hope's upset, and Monique's happy. What's goin' on here?'*

Hope subtly studies Monique's gaze at Luke. *'Great. Monique's interested in Luke too. I need to decide what I want.'*

Wyatt grins while Chester interrogates Luke. "Why'd you let a guest kiss you? You know my rules."

Hope's relieved. *'Good. Luke can't date guests.'*

"Chester, no rules were broken. The ride went off without a hitch. We talked about life's direction and choices."

Hank interrupts, "Did you help somebody today?"

Luke responds, "Don't sound so surprised, Hank."

Hank grins after Luke's testy remark. Chester growls, "I hope that woman got what she paid extra for."

Hope tenses up. "Without crossin' lines."

Holly cheerfully adds, "Unless legs were uncrossed."

Chester barks, "Not funny, Holly."

Luke firmly states, "The guest got what she paid for, sir." *'That didn't sound right.'*

Monique inquires, "Could Luke give me a private ride too?"

Jake jumps in, "I'm better qualified, Monique."

"Thanks, but I think Luke's the right one."

Hank's watching Hope's flustered reaction. *'What's she thinkin'? I'll check after supper.'*

Faith's protective outburst surprises everyone. "Luke's too busy. He's my friend. He hasn't even had time for Momma 'n me lately. Right Momma."

Luke corrects Faith. "I'm never too busy for you, Faith. Or your mom. You're the busy ones."

"But you're like family now."

Faith's inclusion of Luke as family stuns the room until Chester responds.

"Y'all're right 'bout one thing, Faith. Luke stops workin' to spend time with you."

Luke's unsure how to interpret Faith or Chester. "I haven't had family for a long time."

Hope hears Luke's sorrow vocalized before responding, "Luke can't be part of the family if he's leavin'."

"I appreciate your thought, Faith. Your mom's right, I'm not part of this family."

Wyatt states, "I'll be part of your family, Faith."

"Momma, I want Luke to stay, not Wyatt."

Hope counters, "Faith, Luke's not from here. He's not stayin'."
'Faith's too attached to Luke. Or is she sayin' what I won't?'

Luke thinks, *'Hope sounds like she wants to get rid of me. Because of Wyatt.'*

Monique asks, "Where are you from?"

"I'm from up north."

"Dallas?"

Luke chuckles. *'That's what up north means to a Texan?'* "No, farther north, like Chicago."

"Hank never told me that."

Hope interrupts, "Why would he?"

"I ask Hank about Luke so I know what interests him. I do that with residents, especially ones without family anymore. They feel appreciated and necessary still."

Chester's impressed Monique tries improving the resident's lives. Hope feels slightly threatened that Monique's approach shows she cares about Luke.

'Monique's kind-hearted and sincere. That could win Luke over. She's a little young though.'

Hank corners Hope after supper. "Y'all okay?"

"Yeah, I'm good." *'Why can't I flirt like Monique? Or Holly? Or Jazzy?'*

Hope looks at Luke. *'He's not leadin' Monique on or flirting back. He keeps lookin' at me. Why?'*

Luke whispers to Monique, "How well do ya know Hank?"

"Monique, remember who brings you here."

"Remember who sneaks you extra cookies, Hank."

"You wouldn't."

"Maybe I should reconsider your dietary habits."

Hank sits back and pouts. "Fine. Only 'cause I ain't found where y'all hid my cookie stash."

"And ya won't. Unless maybe I could get a date with Luke."

Chester chuckles. *'I like Monique. She's got gumption.'*

Hope misses Hank's imperceptibly slight nod to Chester.

"Monique, do you have a car?"

"Yes."

"Terrific. I'll inform Hank when Luke's available. Hank's impossible without his cookies."

"Thank you, sir. I didn't think that'd work."

Chester idly glances at Hope and Luke. *'Hank's wantin' to see if Hope'll open up to Luke. If she's truly interested. I'm not sure this'll work.'*

Wyatt comments, "Jazzy's got competition. Hope, he's beneath you anyway."

Everyone stares at Wyatt.

"C'mon, y'all know it's true. Hope's too hot for him. She needs a real cowboy."

Hope shocks the room. "Maybe Wyatt's right. I should find out if Wyatt 'n I still have somethin'." *'I'm also interested in Luke but do I have a chance with him?'*

Faith's defiant, "Momma, y'all oughta give Luke a chance too. He helps me. He's good to you."

Luke considers his situation. *'I'm between a rock 'n a hard place. What do I do?'* "Wyatt, Hope's a beautiful woman. You don't seem to see that. Hope deserves a good man, no matter what else he is."

Hank's impressed Luke defends Hope. *'That threw Hope for a loop. She's not committed to her statement about Wyatt.'*

Hope's quiet for the remainder of the evening. *'I can't look at Wyatt or Luke. Two men, two choices. Either could be right. Or are both wrong?'*

Wyatt's frustrated Hope ignores him and further irritated by Jake's question after Hope and Faith depart.

"Was Hope jealous Monique got a date with Luke?"

Hank's answer is tinged by annoyance. "Jake, y'all got so much to learn. Monique, it's time we left. I have things to figure out."

Chester wonders, *'Did Hank's plan go sideways?'*

Luke stops Hank. "Can we talk first?"

Chester nods. "Use my office."

"I'm confused, Hank. Weren't you tryin' to push me towards Hope? Now, I'm goin' on a date with Monique. I opened up to Hope in Corpus. Now I'm gettin' shut out."

Hank's quiet at first. *'Luke's farther along than I thought. Hope might be as well.'* "Enjoy your date with Monique."

"I don't know if I want to."

"Luke, how do you feel? Honestly."

"Honestly? I think I'm fallin' for Hope. I shouldn't though. It's clear she's not interested. Maybe leavin's better at this point. I could try workin' things out with Linda."

"Slow down, Luke. Things might not be what they seem to be."

"How do you know you've met someone you can spend your life with?"

"When y'all start askin' questions like that. Trust yourself. You familiar with the expression 'bout leadin' a horse to water butcha can't make 'em drink?"

"Yeah."

"People don't always say things 'n make decisions they mean to follow through on. One day at a time." *'I didn't sense conviction in Hope's invite to Wyatt.'*

FORTY-TWO

Hank coordinates Monique's date with to Luke to coincide with Hope being at the ranch.

"This better not hurt Hope."

"This'll help Hope. Jazlynn didn't make Hope do anything. Monique might."

"What about Wyatt?"

"Hope's actions 'n words tell me she's considerin' Luke as well 'n Luke admitted he's got feelin's for Hope."

"This seems awful sneaky."

"Says the man who secretly investigated Luke."

"Don't judge me. He was a stranger. Still is, sorta."

"Butcha trust him, don't ya?"

"I do trust him. He's proven trustworthy too many times."

"Luke looks at Hope like you 'n I looked at Millie and Sally."

"It's a stretch to make that comparison. Luke's more open with you."

"I've never threatened jail."

"What? How'd you know that?"

"Oh, I've heard 'bout your threats. Luke knows hittin' Ben was wrong 'n he's smarter than he shows. That's what's so confusin'. He's lived a tough life for no real reason. Hope might bring him 'round. He could reciprocate that with her."

"Why use Monique as a pawn?"

"I'mma bit conflicted 'bout that. Monique's a perfect plot twist in my diabolically well-meant plan."

"Monique could get hurt."

"Naw. Our package delivery guy's clearly caught her eye. He just ain't asked her out yet. I'm fixin' to change that. She's only just met Luke 'n he'll become yesterday's news."

"Hank, y'all got way too much time on your hands."

Monique arrives as Hope exits the rodeo barn. They study each other until Luke steps from the bunkhouse wearing a maroon button-down shirt and jeans. Luke examines Hope's expression before she turns away.

'Why's Hope lookin' sad? She's got Wyatt.'

Luke glances at Hope once more after getting into Monique's car. *'What's Hope thinking about?'*

Holly diverts Hope's attention. "Hey, Hope, I've got somethin' for ya. From a guest."

"I'm not interested in what some guy's sayin' 'bout me."

Holly hands over the envelope. "It's from that married woman."

Hope hesitates before taking the envelope. "I'll read it later. I forgot to tell Chester somethin'."

Chester's on the phone when Hope enters so he holds his hand up. Hope opens the envelope while waiting and begins reading. 'I don't know your name. Luke's a good, honest man who deserves a good woman. I got half-naked and threw myself at him.'

Chester gets Hope's attention so she puts the letter away.

"Didja need somethin'?"

"I forgot we need to switch Wednesday 'n Thursday next week."

"Noted."

Wyatt knocks and enters, "Everything's set for tomorrow."

"Good. Thank you."

"Is Wyatt free for dinner tonight?"

Chester mulls over his answer. "I guess so."

FORTY-THREE

Luke reviews his date with Monique in the solitude of his room. *'Monique's nice but somethin' was missin'. She's funny, witty, smart, 'n pretty. I got no spark. I should've been honest with Hope. I've pushed her to Wyatt like I pushed Linda to Robert. Monique wants a second date. What do I say? I have things in common with Jazzy 'n she's my age. Hope's not a choice now.'*

Luke feels a deflated sensation after realizing he'll miss Faith. *'Who am I kiddin'? Chester'd never let me date Hope. I need air.'*

Luke heads to the rodeo barn. "Hiya, Bullet, did they feedya enough tonight?"

Hope picks her shirt and bra off the living room floor the next morning. Curiosity compels her to read the woman's letter. 'I got naked and threw myself at him.' Hope pauses, *I'm sure Luke enjoyed her.'* She continues reading, 'Luke made me put my clothes on. He said I should respect myself and my marriage or let my husband go if I didn't love him. Luke showed I was cheating myself out of a good life. He called me selfish. Luke said he'd never cross a line with a married woman. He also said his heart belongs to someone at the ranch. Even if she doesn't want him. If you're that woman, if you feel anything for him, take a chance to win his heart. His eyes told me he loves someone. You're eyes had that look too. Luke's a good man.'

Hope begins crying, *I've blown it. Wyatt wouldn't've been here last night if I read this already. I could've stopped Luke 'n Monique.'*

Jubilee and JeniMay meet Hope at the gym but they're skeptical when Luke and Jazlynn walk in. Hope declares, "I didn't know they'd be here. Honest."

JeniMay expresses her disbelief. "Jubilee, this is too coincidental, right?"

Jubilee nods, "You were rather insistent we come here. I see why?"

"No. Really. I need to talk to y'all. I can't do that now."

Jazlynn spots the three women in the weight area. "Keep up if y'all can, girls."

Hope sighs, *'I don't need this.'*

Luke notices Hope's angered eyes after Jazlynn's challenge. *'That's not good.'*

Jazlynn's small form fitting black shorts and tiny matching sports bra is the opposite of Hope's modest dark blue sweat pants and light blue t-shirt. Hope even regrets her appearance compared to JeniMay and Jubilee's sporty outfits.

'I look frumpy. Luke won't notice me in these.'

Jubilee and JeniMay notice Luke's not so subtle glances towards Hope between sets with Jazlynn.

"Luke 'n Jazzy are datin', right?"

"I don't know if they're datin'."

"And Hope, you're with Wyatt, correct?"

"I'm not datin' Wyatt."

Hope watches Luke assist Jazlynn. *'That could be me.'*

All four women watch Luke pick up the hundred twenty pound dumbbells and complete twelve reps. Jazlynn high fives Luke afterwards.

"Holy shit, Luke. Y'all made that look too easy. I've got some easy fun for y'all as well."

Jazlynn runs her hands seductively across her body. *'Why's Luke resisting me? We should've hooked up already.'*

Hope prepares for her next set but finds it's too easy. "I'm gonna try for a new PR. Spot me."

"Nope. We're not strong enough."

Jubilee approaches Luke. "Can you spot Hope?"

Jazlynn hisses, "We're busy. Go away."

"I'll be right back, Jazzy."

Hope observes Luke. *'Luke seems happy with Jazzy. But he's willing to help me.'*

"Let me helpya."

"Okay. I wanna try for two reps."

"Uh-uh. Go for as many as possible. No limits."

"I don't know."

Luke encourages Hope through each rep. "C'mon Hope, keep pushin'. I'm here for you."

Hope achieves six reps and stands up and receives a high five from Luke.

"Good job. I knew y'all had more in ya."

"Thanks, I couldn't've done that without you, Luke."

Luke hugs Hope, "Anytime. I'll always help you. I'm here for you."

JeniMay and Jubilee listen to Luke along with Jazlynn's response.

"I can do that. And more."

Luke responds, "Jazzy, it ain't a competition. No one can be stupid 'n risk gettin' injured. You're both strong."

FORTY-FOUR

Hope confesses to JeniMay and Jubilee when they leave the gym.

"I have somethin' to tell ya."

They listen to Hope's sordid disclosure.

"You did what?"

"What's gotten into you?"

"I don't know. I'm so confused about Luke 'n Wyatt."

"Fine. But y'all're startin' to act like Holly. Gettin' naked with any guy all of a sudden."

"I wasn't naked. I took my shirt off to see what Wyatt would do."

JeniMay states, "Lemme guess, he happily played with your big titties."

"No."

Jubilee and JeniMay look disbelievingly at Hope.

"Okay, yes, he put his hands on me."

"Did he kiss you first?"

"No. He tried sucking my nipple but I pulled away."

"Why? You've already been with Wyatt. Don'tcha still love him?"

"I started thinkin' 'bout Luke. I wanted Luke touching me."

"Hope Cooper! Tell Luke how y'all're feelin' already. Take a risk 'n get laid by the right guy."

"Yeah, don't let the wrong guy screw ya. You're not Holly. Or have you changed?"

Hope shoots a concerned look at JeniMay. "No. I'm not like Holly."

Jubilee states her thought. "It's okay if y'all wanna ride Luke hard all night every night. I get it. He's a hunk. Is that why you took us to the gym? To work off sexual frustrations? That makes more sense."

"I swear I didn't know they'd be there."

JeniMay sympathizes with Hope. "I do understand how you feel. I felt better but sleazy after hookin' up with Colt. But it helped me decide what I want. I don't want random hook-ups. I want something meaningful again. You need to decide who you want or lose them both. Give Luke the same chance you're giving Wyatt 'n see what happens. See how you feel. See if you pull away or not."

Hope seems sad after JeniMay's suggestion. *I want Luke to touch more than my body.'* "It doesn't matter. Luke wants Jazzy. Or Monique."

Jubilee disputes Hope's statement. "Don't bet on it. Luke's trainin' with Jazzy but he didn't try gettin' cozy with her between sets. He didn't hesitate to spot you. And he hugged you."

"Yeah, he said he's here for you. He didn't say that to Jazzy."

"Luke said he's here for you twice."

"Take the hint already."

Holly watches Jazzy kiss Luke during their drop-off. *'That bitch. Is she stealin' my Luke?'*

FORTY-FIVE

August bows out to September's fresh new energy. Corporate outings use cowboy tasks for unique problem solving exercises to challenge rigid minded individuals. Seasonal events also keep the ranch bustling. Luke's willingly spending more time with the Twisted Live Oak wranglers now that they accept him. Hank shifts Luke's attitude with one particular conversation.

"Luke, howya doin' after six months on the ranch?"

"Good. I still wonder 'bout goin' back to Linda."

"I see. Y'all can't let go of the past. That's why you won't succeed."

"What do you mean?"

"You tried bein' perfect for Linda but it's an impossible goal to reach. You failed 'cause you weren't bein' you. Y'all're doin' that here now. Be real. Be honest. See how that works. Hope would appreciate that. Linda, Chicago, that's the past. Your future's here."

"I'm not sure about that."

"Exactly! You won't accept the possibility. You'd rather doubt a wise old man's advice."

"What should I do?"

"Y'all know the answer. I've given you the tools to build a new life. Use 'em."

"Shouldn't you and two buddies be headed to a manger somewhere?"

"Ha ha. I'm wise. Y'all're a wise-ass."

Wyatt hears their conversation and waits until Luke leaves. "Hey, old man, leave Hope outta this. She's mine. Stop interferin' or somethin' terrible could happen to y'all."

Katie listens to Wyatt's threat. *'Oh Wyatt, Luke'll catch wind of this.'*

Hank laughs, "Boy, let me tell ya what, I've been through hell 'n back. You don't scare me."

"I oughta."

Hope's struggling with work demands, Faith's schooling, and Wyatt's constant presence in her daily life. Wyatt's frustrated circumstances prevent his succeeding at bedding Hope down. Chester updates Luke on Faith's progress in school.

"Faith's doin' well in third grade. Hope said homework's goin' better now."

"Great. I'd help but Wyatt's probably doin' that."

"Hope ain't datin' Wyatt."

"Their together all the time."

"Hope told me Faith's angry Wyatt's around so much. By the way, Faith's mad at you too."

"Me? Why?"

"For datin' Monique."

"First, how would Faith know?"

"Kids hear things. Adults talk, kids listen."

"Or they're told things. I'm not datin' Monique. I'm gonna end it."

"Why?"

"She's nice but there's no spark. Not like someone else."

"I've noticed you 'n Jazlynn gettin' along. Somethin' brewin' there?"

"Nothing serious. We're just trainin' together."

"What about returnin' north?"

"I might stick around. But that's not my decision."

Luke's comment silences Chester.

'Maybe Chester's already decided my fate.'

Chester doesn't pursue Luke's potential person of interest but updates Hope afterwards.

"Luke offered to help Faith with homework unless he's been replaced by Wyatt. Luke's not crossin' lines if you're datin' Wyatt."

"I'm happy Luke's still willing to help Faith. I'm not datin' Wyatt. Who's sayin' that? Besides, Luke's datin' Monique, or Jazzy. *Time with Wyatt's not like before. He's not the same.*'

Chester notes Hope's resistance to committing to Wyatt but acknowledges Luke's willingness to help Faith. "Luke mentioned he'd rather date someone else. He seems happy goin' to the gym with Jazlynn."

'Is Luke my second chance at love? Or is it Wyatt? Have I missed my chance with Luke?'

"Chester, I need to call a client. I'll call ya later, alright."

Hope hangs up and calls Beth. "I need your advice about Luke."

"Lordy woman, I've toldja a hundred times to talk to Luke. The worst that happens is he says no."

"I'm not sure I want an answer."

"You're hopeless."

"Attitude isn't what I need. I need your support."

"Hope, y'all've helped me realize how lucky I am with Ben lovin' me. I've run outta ways to get through to you. I'm glad I'm not dealin' with datin' drama 'n bullshit."

"Beth, Ben would die without you."

"No. Ben would die for me. Like I'd die for him. You could have that too. You won't take that chance."

Hope sighs, "I feel I got walked into that."

FORTY-SIX

Hope and Faith unexpectedly show up at the ranch. Faith seeks Luke out immediately.

"Luke, I've missed you. Let's play a game together."

Luke spots Hope approaching, "I'm not sure that's why you're here, Faith."

Hope pauses briefly, "I, I, uh, I have something for you."

"Me? Don'tcha mean Wyatt?"

Hope walks to her truck and returns with one hand behind her back. "I'd like to say sorry for bein' so confusin' and give you this."

Luke's dumbfounded when Hope hands him a single red rose. He's silent until Faith speaks up, "Momma wanted you to have a rose from our garden. Isn't it pretty?"

"Thank you. Yes. I wasn't expecting this."

Wyatt sees Luke with a rose near Hope. "What the hell's this?"

He furiously approaches them. "Get away from her. I'll bust your ass. Hope's mine."

Katie hollers out, "Wyatt, y'all like to threaten anyone who threatens your chance with Hope. Y'all threatened Hank because he gave Luke good advice about Hope. Now you're threatenin' Luke 'cause ya think he's givin' Hope a rose."

Hope speaks up, "I'm givin' Luke a rose. To apologize for me bein' me."

Luke focuses on Katie's intended slip up. "You threatened Hank? An old man. For offerin' his two cents to me. Start runnin'. Now!"

"You can't be serious."

Wyatt sees Chester, "Rein him in. Show him whose boss."

"You heard him. Y'all best start runnin'."

Wyatt realizes he's in trouble and turns to escape impending danger. Luke drops the rose to pursue Wyatt and crashes into him and forcefully kicks Wyatt's ribcage. Air is expelled rapidly from Wyatt's lungs and leaves him moaning and wheezing.

"You best shape up or ship out, Wyatt. Any more threats 'n I'll order Luke to beat the shit outta you, got it? Hope, come riding with me. Faith, stay with Luke. Luke, pick up your rose."

Ben approaches, "Did I miss the fun? Boss, the limo bus'll arrive 'round 8:00."

"Right. We'll get the guests off for the train ride to Burnet."

A male guest jokes with Chester, "The train station? How far from civilization are we going?"

Chester frowns, "Mister, our train station's just round the bend a bit. I'd be in jail or dead if I ran my ranch that way. That's not real, it's all for ratin's. Y'all'll come back alive 'n well."

Luke and Faith play with Austin after Hope and Chester ride off. Chester's dog trainer has already taught Austin to shake paws, roll over, and to play dead on command to entertain guests as well as basic commands. Scooter's in the rodeo barn when they enter to feed apples to the horses.

"Still workin' on that personal project?"

"Yup. I'll finish today. How 'bout you two? Whatcha up to?"

"Enjoyin' the peace 'n quiet 'n some fun."

Hope returns to ask Faith to go riding so Luke saddles a horse and watches them ride out to Chester.

Scooter comments, "Chester's aware there's a storm brewin' that might wet the guests on their Hill Country outing."

"A thunderstorm'll ruin Faith's day. I love the sweet smell of inbound rain."

"You care about Faith, don'tcha?"

Luke remarks an hour later after hearing a rumble of thunder, "That's not good."

"Hope'll have her hands full calming Faith down."

"Storms are cool though."

"Faith'll disagree."

Luke recalls forgotten memories until Scooter calls out, "Here they come."

Luke comments while preparing the stalls, "I guess my ride's gettin' cancelled?"

"You wouldn't say that a few months ago."

"Ridin' horses is relaxing."

Scooter snorts in disbelief, "Who are you and what happened to the real Luke?"

"Haha. I'm more real now than then."

"Burnet's got indoor activities for the guests."

Dark clouds conceal the sun but not Faith's terrified expression. Luke hears Faith's question, "Momma, are we gonna make it? I wanna hide in the house."

Thunder covers Hope's answer ahead of more lengthy lightning bolts crackling and dancing across the sky. Chester attempts to settle Faith down.

"Faith, you're safe."

Luke grabs the reins of Faith's horse when she enters the barn. "Faith, do thunderstorms scare you that much?"

"Yeah."

"What makes 'em scary?"

A blinding streak of lightning races from ominous clouds to the ground nearby to produce an earsplitting crackle and roar of thunder. Faith screams and covers her ears.

"It's too loud."

Chester counters, "It's the angels bowlin' in Heaven."

Luke offers another option. "Faith, could I show you somethin' cool 'bout storms?"

Hope notices Faith's fear get sidetracked by curiosity. "Like what?"

"We'd need to go the deck. If that's alright with your mom?"

"Pecan, I'm here, okay." *'What's Luke up to? Can I trust him?'*

Luke, Faith, and Austin run to the deck in the heavy drizzle. Chester sees Wyatt running towards the barn.

"What the hell're ya doin' here, Wyatt? You're supposed to be on the train."

"I switched with Henry. I wanted to stay with Hope 'n Faith today."

"Henry's supposed to be at his momma's birthday party. She's been real sick this year 'n they want to celebrate her recovery. Shit! I've gotta fix this. You don't make decisions."

"I have more experience. I have seniority."

Chester furiously cuts Wyatt off. "Your dumbass don't carry any weight here. You can't even pull rank on Luke. Comprende! Henry's not missin' the party."

Wyatt sees Hope's disgusted look while Chester walks away. "Really?"

Hope follows Chester. Wyatt considers his predicament. *'I'm not below Luke. Shit, this is gonna be a long day.'*

Hope notes Faith's intrigued by Luke's animated gestures. "Whaddya think Luke's sayin'?"

Chester responds. "No clue."

Hope observes, *'The storm's on top of us 'n Faith's sittin' still.'*

"Thanks Ben." Chester hangs up. "Beth's bringing Ben his wallet. She'll bring Henry back."

"Good."

Faith focuses on Luke pointing to the clouds from the edge of the deck and seems fascinated and smiles after the next flash of lightning. Hope's shocked. *'What's Luke tellin' Faith? Thunder 'n lightning don't scare her now?'*

Katie's listening at the door. *'Luke's good to Faith. He's smarter than I figured. Explainin' the scientific side of a storm to Faith. Hope should be considerin' Luke, not Wyatt.'*

"That's why storms don't have to be scary. Like the water, respect Mother's Nature power 'n know the real dangers. Chester's right too. Angels are bowlin' in Heaven. My dad told me the same thing. Dads don't lie to their children, right? So it's gotta be true."

"Luke, bring these umbrellas to Hope 'n Chester. I'll mind Faith."

"Yes ma'am."

Hope sees Faith clap during Luke's approach while thunder booms. "What did you say to Faith?"

Heavy rain begins rhythmically pounding the barn's roof.

"I explained how a storm works."

The trio returns to the house.

"Momma, Luke taught me to like storms."

"I see. How'd he do that so quickly?"

Hope's amazed by Faith's sudden transformation. "I can't believe it."

Chester's astonished. "How in blazes didja do that?"

"I did what my dad did. I explained how storms happen and its nature's way of showin' off."

Hope and Chester are speechless. Chester removes his hat to scratch his head.

"So much for the Longhorn's stampedin' 'n angels bowlin'."

"Grand-daddy, Luke said it's also the angels. Right?"

"Right, Faith."

Wyatt runs from the barn and attempts to impress Chester and Hope. "I double checked the stalls. They're secure."

"Scooter 'n I already checked 'em. Both barns."

Luke pauses. "Faith, I feel closer to my dad during storms. I pretend he's talkin' to me. Just very loudly."

Wyatt mutters, "That's stupid."

"I think that's special."

Wyatt notices Hope's side-eyed glance. *'Hope's not buyin' this bullshit, is she?'*

Chester recalls Hank's early assessment of Luke. *'Luke is smarter than he lets on 'n far more caring too. His brooding eyes disappear around Hope 'n Faith. 'Cept when Hope pulled her gun on him.'*

Hope's thoughts distract her. *'Faith always gets Luke's full attention. Luke could be the man I've always wanted. I thought it was Wyatt. But to see them together. Why can't I just ask Luke out? Or him ask me out?'*

Hope takes a step and slips on the wet deck and nearly falls. Luke reaches out to catch her from behind and everyone notices his hands land on Hope's breasts for several seconds. Luke adjusts his stance to prop Hope up. They both blush beet red.

"I'm sorry. I didn't mean for that to happen."

Hope smiles shyly. "I know. It's okay. You kept me from fallin'." *'Or maybe y'all just helped me fall for you? I enjoyed your hands on my body.'*

Katie chuckles. *'That's one way to keep Luke on the ranch. Luke's eyes tell me he wants more than Hope's body.'*

Luke has his own thoughts. *'I'd like to do that all the time. Chester'd never let me date Hope. She means too much to him. I think I've fallen in love with Hope.'*

FORTY-SEVEN

Chester calls Hank during the third week of September. "This ranch has gone to hell in a hand basket."

"What's goin' on? Y'all finally run it into the ground?"

"Holly's mad at Jazlynn for stealin' Luke away. Even though Luke ain't datin' Jazlynn. Wyatt's mad at Hope because she's showin' interest in Luke. Wyatt's mad Luke won't leave. I think a fight's brewin' between 'em. Most surprisin' is Luke. He's gotten ornry these past few days. I'm not sure why."

"He ain't said anything to me. Wonder what's on his mind?"

Chester idly questions Hope. "Y'all do somethin' to make Luke onry?"

"Me? No, I haven't done anything." *'Wait, its September. Luke said somethin' 'bout gettin' moody around now.'* "I might know. Let me ask him something."

Hope waits for Luke to return from a trail ride. "Luke, can we talk privately?"

"What did I do now?"

"Luke, its September, you're grumpy. Y'all're missin' your parents, aren'tcha?"

"How do you know…? Wait, you remember that?"

"I do."

Hope hugs Luke. "Y'all ain't alone, Luke. I'm here for you. We all are."

"Thanks. That means more than you know."

"I may have an idea, remember."

"Yeah, I do."

September turns to October. The guest count dwindles which allows wranglers to spend time away from the ranch. Danny and Kyle entertain guest around evening campfires with sing-a-longs. The duo changes words or tempo which throws people off with hilarious results. Chester's kept them on the ranch for their musical talent. Holly still tempts Luke despite losing hope she'll win him over. She finds Luke in Chester's office.

"Luke, let's enjoy nature to its fullest in the pasture. If'n ya know what I mean?"

"Holly, Chester'd shoot my ass off if I touch you. At least Hope has enough self-respect not to chase a guy like me. Chester wouldn't let me date either of you."

Hope stops in the hallway to listen to Luke. *'Is Chester the reason Luke's never tried askin' me out?'*

"Hope's tryin' to rebuild her life with Wyatt anyway."

Hope's stunned by Luke's comments. Chester enters the house.

"Is Luke in my office?"

"Um, yeah."

"Good. I've got somethin' for him to do."

Holly makes a snarky comment when Hope follows Chester into the office. "Grand-daddy, Luke's tryin' to get Hope to ask him out."

Chester looks at Luke. "I doubt that. Scooter needs help in the ridin' barn."

"Yes sir."

Chester examines Hope. *'Hope seems confused 'bout somethin'.'* "Hope, grab Luke, I forgot to tell him something."

"Can Holly get him. I gotta get Faith."

"I asked you. Now git."

"Yes sir."

Hope retrieves Luke and departs.
'I didn't know Hope was here. Did I screw something up?'
Hope calls Beth. "I heard somethin' today."
Beth listens while Hope explains what she heard. "Does he want you to ask him out?"
"I don't know. Maybe?"
"What did you do?"
"Nothin'. I left."
"Opportunity knocks and you leave the door shut. What's wrong with you?"
"I didn't know if Luke was bein' serious. He was talkin' to Holly."
"Okay. I'll give you that. Butcha won't know if you don't give Luke a chance."
"I need to pick Faith up."
"It's one excuse or 'nother with you. Luke won't ask you out. Chester's seen to that."

FORTY-EIGHT

Chester calls Hope after she's left. "Hope, would you like to go to Marble Falls this weekend for the Sweet Berry Fall Festival?"

"Yay. We have so much fun there."

"Oh, Faith, y'all're in the truck too."

"Grand-daddy, could we bring Luke?"

Hope interjects, "You mean Wyatt, right?"

"No. Momma, I wanna bring Luke. I'll have more fun with him 'n you. Not Wyatt."

"I doubt Luke wants to go with us." *Or at least with me.* "Besides, Luke works this weekend."

Chester asserts, "I make the work details. Wyatt'll take Luke's tasks. It's a date."

'Why did Chester say it's a date?'

Chester deftly words his next comment. "Should Luke know he's got a date with you 'n your mom?"

"Don't be silly, Grand-daddy. Luke can only be Momma's date, not mine."

"Your mom may not want that."

'Is Chester makin' fun of me? What does he mean?'

"Grand-daddy, let's surprise Luke, okay."

Saturday morning Chester instructs Faith, "Find Luke 'n tell him we need him here right now. Y'all can surprise him."

Faith's holding Luke's hand when they return. "Okay Grand-daddy, can I tell him now?"

"Yup."

"Luke, you're comin' to Marble Falls with us."

"Chester, I've got a ton of work today."

"Fine. Your choice. Stay 'n muck stalls or have fun with Faith."

"Um. Well, Faith wins."

"Good answer. Wyatt's gettin' your workload today."

"So where are we going?"

Faith answers, "Marble Falls. It's lots of fun."

"By the way, Hank set Monique up with their delivery guy."

Chester watches Luke and Hope's reaction. *'They both look relieved.'*

"Monique's a nice girl. I hope he treats her well."

Hope's silent. *'Good. Monique's out of the picture.'*

Faith heads straight to the pumpkin patch and chooses the largest one. "Grand-daddy, I'd like this one. Please."

Hope inquires, "Pecan, why do you always ask Grand-daddy to buy your pumpkin?"

"Momma, you 'n Grand-daddy spoil me. Butchy'all try teachin' me lesson's about life 'n money."

Chester's amused and Luke laughs while Hope composes herself. "That's not true."

Chester shrugs, "From the mouths of babes."

"Pecan, I just want you to understand, oh, I see where I'm goin' with the rest of my point."

Faith giggles and hugs Hope. "Momma, I know you love me and wanna spoil me."

Luke studies Hope's reaction. *'Hope wants to laugh 'n cry at the same time.'*

"Alright Luke, load this big 'ol pumpkin into that there wagon. We'll weigh it and bring it to the truck."

Luke playfully groans, "There's always a catch with you."

Chester informs Faith, "This pumpkin weighs six pounds more than you."

"Can you handle this, Luke?"

Luke takes Chester's keys, "Yeah, I got this."

He glances at Hope, "Don't worry. I won't steal Chester's truck. I save that honor for you."

Hope realizes Luke's poking fun at her. "I'm not worried."

"No?"

"You'd never abandon Faith."

"I'd never abandon you either."

Hope bites her lower lip and brushes her hair behind her ear before Luke turns to leave. A middle-aged man with a slightly graying beard approaches while Luke's gone.

"Hi, I'm Richard. You're about the prettiest lady I've ever seen. I'd like to take you on a date and get to know you better."

Hope notices Richard's eyes continually drop to her chest. "I'm here with my daughter. Not to pick up men."

"I love kids. I have three of my own."

Luke sees Hope with a man while walking back. *I can't compete for Hope. I don't have anything to give her.*

Hope subtly gestures for Luke to return while noticing his dejected expression.

Luke notes, *'Hope looks anxious.'* "Hi honey, who's your friend?"

"Um, he's not my friend."

Luke's smile fades to a glare while putting his arm around Hope's waist. Richard excuses himself and hurries off.

'I guess Hope felt threatened.'

Hope breaks free from Luke causing Chester to clear his throat. "What was that?"

"It's a defense mechanism to ward off unwelcomed men. I'll teach Faith one day."

Luke hears Hope's explanation. *'Hope used me to chase the guy off.'*

Chester eyes Hope indignantly. "Hope, daughter, walk with me."

Hope hears Chester's blunt tone. *'That sounds ominous.'*

The two walk out of earshot. "Hope, Faith won't learn anything good from that. More importantly, what message did y'all send Luke?"

"I don't understand. I didn't tell Luke anything."

"Faith'll learn to let others handle her problems. And Luke thinks you used him to get rid of that guy."

"I didn't do any of that."

"You moved away without thankin' Luke. You made him feel worthless."

"I wanted Luke's help. That's why I called him over."

"Hope, y'all try hard to be strong 'n independent which is fine, most of the time, but y'all ain't let anyone in or appreciate most any man's help. Luke ain't happy. Didn't you see his reaction."

"I didn't mean to hurt Luke. I…" *I'd like Luke's help more often. I like Luke.'* "What do I do?"

Chester glances at Luke. "That's your decision, not mine. Hope, if there's somethin' between you 'n Luke, or Wyatt, be honest with them, and yourself. Luke's proven his worth to me."

Hope stares at Chester. "I'm not sure I'm ready."

"You won't know till ya try."

Hope frowns while looking at Luke.

'Hope's mad I'm here. Like every other time.'

Faith regains Luke's attention before Hope approaches them. "Luke, the next place is a lotta fun."

"Yeah, what's that?"

"We're gonna get lost."

"Lost? That don't sound fun."

Hope giggles, "Faith means the corn maze."

"Oh. That does sound fun. Maybe I oughta wait here though so you and your mom can do it."

Hope speaks assertively, "Nonsense. Y'all're goin' with us."

"Would you hold my hand, Faith? So I'm not scared."

"Momma'll hold your hand too."

"I don't think your mom wants to." *'There's no guy to chase off.'*

Hope glances at Chester. *'Chester's right. I push people away.'* "C'mon big baby. I'll hold your hand."

Luke's face lights up when Hope takes his hand. "We'll protect you. Act up 'n you'll get a timeout."

Luke whispers loudly, "Your mom's kinda mean, Faith."

"You have no idea."

"Hey, little missy, who's side are ya on?"

"I'm warnin' Luke to behave."

They wander through the corn maze until Luke lifts Faith up onto his shoulders to guide them out. A game attendant calls out as they pass his booth, "Hey there little lady, how 'boutchur dad win a prize for y'all?"

"Yeah, Dad, win me a prize."

Faith's response concerns Hope. Luke doesn't hesitate and approaches the booth and wins a stuffed zebra for Faith. Faith turns to Hope, "Look Momma, a zebra."

"I see. Why did you call Luke dad?"

"Momma, Luke's not my dad but he acts like it 'n I appreciate what he does for me. Don't you?"

Hope's momentarily speechless.

"That's sweet." Hope glances at Luke. "Luke, can we talk?"

'This'll be bad.'

Hope leads Luke away from Chester and Faith. "I'm sorry Faith called you dad."

"I'm flattered but I know Faith didn't mean it. It bothers you though. I'll say somethin' to Faith."

"No. Don't upset Faith." *'Faith's right, you act like her dad.'*

Luke's uneasiness is conveyed in his voice. "I didn't mean to overstep."

"You didn't overstep." *'Faith 'n Luke worry about each other.'*

Luke notices Hope's eyes become inquisitive.

"Faith's concerned about you. She enjoys what you do for her. You really do care 'bout her, don'tcha?"

Luke smiles, "Faith's wonderful. The jury's out on her mother still. She likes to shoot first 'n walk away."

Hope playfully swipes Luke's arm. "Funny. Y'all're never gonna let me live that down, are ya?"

"Probably not."

"Fair enough."

Chester studies Hope's interaction with Luke. *'Hope's far more relaxed with Luke than Wyatt. Maybe she's finally acceptin' someone could be part of her life again. Could Corpus, Monique, Jazlynn, and Faith be pushin' her in a new direction, a better one?'*

Hope recognizes Luke's jabbed her for moving away after he chased Richard away and returns to Faith and whispers into her ear. Faith glances at Luke and nods.

'What are they up to?'

Hope and Faith take Luke's hands and lead him to a particular craft booth.

"Pick any sand jar y'all want. My treat. With Faith's permission. Get something to brighten your room."

"What? No. It's not necessary."

"Luke, pick one."

Luke spots a jar and points, "Okay, I'll take that one. The one with blues and greens is perfect. It matches the pretty eyes of two special beautiful women."

Hope catches her breath and turns away while blushing. Faith calls her out.

"Momma, why are your cheeks red?"

Chester decides how their outing finishes. "We'll pick fresh apples 'n berries for pies 'n snackin'."

Cody stirs things up between Luke and Wyatt the next day. "Hey Luke, how'd your date with Hope go?"

Luke notices Wyatt focus on him. "It wasn't a date. Faith invited me."

"Right? Maybe you'll find what I have with Jubilee."

Wyatt speaks up, "Hope's my girl. Not his."

"I'm surprised that worked out. Jubilee hit on me first. Y'all're second fiddle. I turned her down."

"Shut up! You lost. Deal with it."

"I was bein' generous. Deal with that."

Cody's about to lose his temper until Hope calls Luke's name. "Luke? Luke, come here please."

Wyatt intercepts Luke at the door. "She's mine. Remember that."

"Luke, help move something for me."

"Wyatt, y'all're about to find out why the devil stays in hell when I'm around."

Hope sees Luke emerge from the barn, "Bring these supplies to the barn. Please."

Wyatt steps forward, "I'll help ya, Hope."

"No. I want Luke's help."

Cody hollers out, "Hey, maybe you 'n Hope'll be a thing."

Luke laughs, "Nah, Hope shot at me."

Cody chuckles. "Hope missed ya. I've seen you look at her. Don't tell me you ain't interested."

Luke's cheeks redden before slowly heading towards Hope.

"These are for the rodeo barn. I need to talk to Chester."

Cody notices Luke glancing at Hope and amused Wyatt's irritated while Hope walks away. Cody observes Hope look back several times at Luke before reaching the deck. *'Huh. Is Hope actually interested in Luke?'*

FORTY-NINE

Wyatt's frustration builds thinking he could lose Hope to Luke. "Asshole. I'm gonna teach you not to butt into another guy's business."

"Wyatt, don't make a stupid choice that'll hurt you, not me."

Wyatt pulls his gun on Luke but immediately hears Chester. "Drop it, Wyatt. Or that's the last move you'll make."

"Dammit Chester, quit interferin' in my business."

"I'm gonna do ya one better, Wyatt. You 'n Luke are gonna beat the hell outta each other in the rodeo corral 'n finish this feud."

"I'm not fightin' Luke alone. He'll win that fight. That's not fair."

"But pullin' a pistol on him's fair? Alright, we'll even the odds. Call in some buddies to help ya."

Wyatt calls several friends to meet at the ranch the next day. Luke leads the group into the arena and lets them surround him. Chester invites the remaining guests to watch.

"This is how my cowboys settle disputes."

"Why in there?"

"Nowhere to run."

One guy moves in on Luke and falls from one punch. Wyatt shouts, "He can't fight all of us at the same time."

Wyatt and four guys rush Luke simultaneously and regret being in the arena within a couple minutes after Luke's abilities are ruthlessly displayed. Wyatt comes to a couple minutes later and feels pain like he's never felt before.

Wyatt spits a tooth out, "Shit, what didya hit me with."

"Hatred 'n aggravation."

Chester announces, "This stops here 'n now."

One guest has videoed the fight without asking if he could. Wyatt's thoughts revolve around revenge for getting hell beat of him in front of the guests and his friends.

October and the season near an end and Chester informs the wranglers, "Y'all're good to go out Saturday night 'n have fun. Scooter 'n I'll entertain the guests with campfire stories."

"So the guests'll be unsupervised after their hosts fall asleep at seven thirty."

The guys laugh at Chester's reaction instead of Jake's humorous dig which hangs in the air like cooked salmon.

"Congratulations Jake, you've volunteered to clean cabins with Holly on Sunday."

"What? No way! I'm takin' Sunday off."

The guys laugh more when Chester's stern look elicits Jake's response. "Yes sir. I'll gladly help Holly."

"Alright, back to work. We've still got guests."

"Luke, go fix the kitchen sink. Katie has snacks to prepare."

"Yes sir. I'm on it."

Katie's happy when Luke repairs the leak. "Thanks Luke. It's a chore to continually empty buckets. Are ya fixin' to join the boys this weekend in town?"

"I doubt it. I haven't been invited."

"They're last minute planners. Say yes 'n have fun."

"I ain't sure I'm safe hangin' 'round 'em."

"You're soundin' more Texan. Which ain't a bad thing."

"I would've disagreed months ago." *It's not so bad soundin' like these people.'*

Hope brings Faith to enjoy the pool Saturday afternoon. Chester watches Ben and Faith lead the foal around the arena.

"Grand-daddy, I've decided a name for the foal."

"Thank goodness. I thought we'd have to call it Nameless after the town."

"Don't be silly. I wanna name it Whiskey."

"Whiskey? Why?"

"It's the same color as your drink and he has a little kick in his step."

Chester's concerned expression makes Ben laugh. "How would Faith know that?"

"I explained your drink of choice. We think the foal matches whiskey."

"I see. Alright, Whiskey it is."

Katie brings snacks for Hope and Faith at the pool. "Faith, you look like a fish in the water."

Hope shares, "Faith's enjoyin' the pool more now."

"I think the guys are invitin' Luke to go out tonight."

"Where are they goin'?"

"No clue. They haven't decided yet." *'Y'all wanna join 'em?'*

Jake stops to say hello. "Lookin' good, Faith. I like the foal's name. I've gotta finish before we go out."

"Where ya headed? Who's going?"

"Most of us. Luke's goin' too. I'll teach him to dance pretty girls 'round the floor. Who knows, maybe he'll meet someone tonight."

"That's what you do, Jake."

"Yes ma'am. Luke might let loose tonight at High Hope's Saloon."

"Luke's too sophisticated for that place."

"Hope, y'all're usin' big words again. I don't know whatchur talkin' 'bout."

"You know exactly what I'm talkin' about."

Jake glances mischievously at Faith. "Your momma's mean."

"Momma's not mean, she's just tough. Be glad you don't live with her."

"Whose side are you on, young lady?"

"Yours Momma."

Luke checks on Faith and notices Hope's rodeo buckle on her jeans lying across a lounge chair. "How long was your barrel racing career, Hope?"

"Momma, you were a barrel racer? Can I be one too?"

Hope's irate expression informs Luke he's asked the wrong question. "Faith's never known 'bout that."

"I didn't know that. I'm sorry."

"You knew to stay quiet but you opened your big mouth. I didn't want Faith knowin' for years yet."

Luke departs hastily after Katie motions him to leave.

"Hope, Luke didn't know. It's my fault. I mentioned your rodeo career but didn't say to keep quiet."

Hope hisses angrily. "I don't care. He shoulda known I want Faith stayin' focused on school."

Luke finds Jake, Jesse, Jack, Wyatt, and Cody in the riding barn cleaning saddles. "Sheesh, Hope got mad because I asked about her rodeo career."

"Didja ask in front of Faith?"

"Yeah. What's the big deal?"

"Hope didn't want Faith knowin' and become another Holly."

Wyatt remarks, "I'm glad I'm not in your boots. Hope's insufferable when mad. I know."

Jake adds, "Hope's probably madder 'n a hosed down hornet's nest. She warned me never to say anythin' 'bout her rodeo days."

"I thought about stayin' here tonight. Now I think I'll join y'all at the bar."

Jack laughs, "Who knew the High Hope's Saloon would be safer than here?"

Billy warns, "Hope might could shootcha. We oughta sneak you outta here 'n away from her wrath."

Ben and Jack remain home. Jubilee informs Cody she'll be late.

"I invited Hope but she's mad 'n seems like she wants to kill someone. I'm gonna talk to her then meetcha at the bar."

Cody alerts her, "Good luck. She's mad alright."

Henry and Billy pull short straws to become the designated drivers for the evening.

"Well, Henry, hopefully sober's entertainin' tonight."

FIFTY

Luke enters High Hope's Saloon feeling subdued. *'Should I'd've talked to Hope?'*

Several young ladies run up to Jake and ask him to dance. "Ladies, there's enough of me to go around."

Billy notes Luke's mystified expression. "Jake's quite the dancer."

One young woman eyes Jake's belt buckle.

"Excuse me, sweetheart, the Jakester's eyes are up here."

"But the fun's down there."

"C'mon, let's go dance. We'll get horizontal later."

Luke rolls his eyes and scans the area. Guys are mostly dressed in jeans and button-downs ranging from plain to rather fancy. Women wear outfits ranging from scantily clad for attention to boots, jeans or skirts, and button-down shirts or t-shirts. The Twisted Live Oak group splits up to either go look for dance partners or find a table before congregating by the restaurant. Luke's bar instincts kick in walking around the honky tonk.

'I don't need any drama tonight. What would Hope wear?'

Luke examines red, white, and blue neon beer signs and notices one brand's turned off and covered with a towel. Posters of Red Dirt and traditional country musicians adorn the walls. Luke recognizes most of the names due to his time on the ranch. Billy introduces Luke to the owners.

"Luke, this is Clem 'n Bud Thomson. Katie's Bud's daughter. They grew the High Hope's outta a small food joint."

Bud's eighty-nine years old and enjoys running the saloon with Clem along with his two sons, Buck and Hoyt. Clem's a year younger and his daughter, Dottie, helps organize weekly talent and promote acts who go on to succeed around Texas and the country. Clem's son, Johnny, helps market the Saloon locally and nationally to bolster tourism support.

"Bud 'n Clem grew up with Chester."

Luke shakes hands with the men. "It's nice meetin' ya." Luke grins, "My condolences for knowin' Chester that long."

Bud smiles, "I like y'all already, son. Who's drivin' tonight?"

"Henry 'n I drew short straws, sir."

"Well, we've got plenty of pretty ladies to keep y'all happy on the dance floor. Luke, nice meetin' ya. Don't be a stranger."

"I won't, sir."

Billy leads Luke to the tables the Twisted Live Oak pulled together to rest at between dances.

"The High Hope's launches Texas 'n Red Dirt musicians Nashville passes on for bein' too country. Bud 'n Clem don't book most Nashville acts unless they truly represent country music. That means steel guitar, fiddle, banjo, harmonica play here. And people sing with a twang 'n wear boots, jeans, 'n cowboy hats. No skinny jeans 'n fancy shoes allowed here. You won't ever hear hip hop or rap here either. It ain't country. See that banner?"

Billy points up over the stage. The banner reads, **'We don't support Nashville pushin' soulless music without country sounds. That don't fly in the heart of Texas.'**

Texas and Red Dirt musicians offer beer salutes to the banner before shows. Billy points out the restaurant.

"Tell 'em your with the Twisted Live Oak. We have an account here."

Luke nods.

"Find me if ya have any trouble."

A cowboy approaches Billy. "If it ain't the sissy boys who run pony rides at the circus."

"Shut up, Travis. We wrangle just like you do."

"If you say so."

Travis walks away laughing. Billy remarks before heading for the dancefloor, "He's a huge dick."

Jack approaches Luke, "Y'all can hit him anytime."

"Weren'tcha stayin' home with Rosa?"

"Rosa cut me loose for a couple hours after findin' out I've been stuck workin' with Holly 'n she's got a new book to read."

Luke approaches the counter and studies the menu. Several choices stand out. 'Fat Chance Burger. No Chance Cheeseburger. Slim Chance Fries. Outofyerleague Chili.'

He re-reads the last one several times before realizing the play on words ties into the saloon's name. The middle-aged woman behind the counter scrutinizes Luke.

"Could I get the cheeseburger 'n fries? And put it on the Twisted Live Oak Ranch account. Please."

The woman eyes Luke momentarily before informing the cook.

"Excuse me, ma'am. You didn't ring that up."

"Nope 'n I won't. I know who you are. I know whatcha did."

Luke's eyes widen. "I've never been here before. I didn't do anything."

"I'm Susie Mitchell. My daughter, JeniMay is Hope Cooper's best friend. You saved Hope."

Luke worries aloud, "I don't want anyone here knowin' that? It'll cause trouble in a place like this."

"Your secret's safe. Go sit. I'll bring your food out. Y'all ain't gettin' charged on my watch."

"I can wait here."

Susie sternly orders, "I said go sit."

"Yes ma'am."

Jack questions Luke when he returns. "Was Susie hasslin' ya?"

"Nope. All's good." *I hope.*

Cody, Jubilee, and JeniMay arrive, "Howdy, mind if we sit with ya?"

"The ladies can. Y'all ain't one of us elites."

Cody grins while they sit down. JeniMay looks around.

"Where is everyone?"

"Jake, Jesse, and Kyle'r dancin', Henry 'n Danny are orderin' liquid courage 'n Wyatt's 'round here somewhere."

Billy approaches to Jack's reprimand. "Sorry, this table's for real cowboys."

"Ha ha. Y'all heard Travis, didn't ya? Rosa had enough of your sorry ass already?"

"Nope, she sent me to babysitcha."

"Good luck."

JeniMay stands close to Luke. "Wouldja like to dance?"

Cody questions Luke. "D'y'all know how to dance?"

"Not even one step."

JeniMay leans closer, "I could teachya. Y'all gotta learn to two-step if you're livin' in Texas."

"I've got two left feet when it comes to dancin'."

"C'mon. Let me teachya."

Jubilee's concerned until JeniMay mouths something to her before leading Luke to the floor. She attempts to show Luke the two-step but Luke's herky-jerky movements crack the guys up.

"Luke fights better 'n he can dance."

JeniMay puts her arms around Luke when a slow song starts. Jack walks up halfway through. "Luke, y'all best come get your food before the guys eat it."

JeniMay's annoyed not to be able to finish their dance not knowing two sets of eyes have watched from across the room.

"Are your toes okay, JeniMay? Sorry I stepped on them a few times."

"Hey, you tried. That's what matters."

JeniMay sits next to Jubilee and whispers, "Other girls can't meet Luke if I keep him preoccupied."

"Good idea."

"And maybe guys'll notice me if I'm with someone."

"JeniMay, you get noticed."

Cody suddenly speaks loudly, "Hold on. Why'd your food get delivered to the table?"

"My mom's bein' nice, Cody. Its Luke's first time here. I told her to help him out."

Luke mouths thank you to JeniMay. Jack groans, "Oh boy."

Luke notices Holly and Jazlynn looking at him. "Oh shit."

Cody's evil half smile precedes his irritating comment. "Y'all can get different dance lessons with them."

"I don't need trouble tonight."

"Maybe y'all should've invited 'em too?"

Jake adds, "Y'all met Holly at a bar, right?"

Jack leans back and chuckles, "Holly might leave ya alone. She's got her male buckle bunnies here."

"Buckle bunnies?"

Jubilee explains, "That's a rodeo term cowboys use to describe girls followin' the rodeo circuit to pick up cowboys."

JeniMay continues, "Holly reversed it 'n has guys chasin' her. You know that. You're one of 'em."

Jubilee and JeniMay listen to Luke's response. "Hell no! Holly approached me. I never chased her."

JeniMay whispers to Jubilee, "We're right. Holly chased Luke."

Luke speaks up, "Can I leave?"

Billy delivers the bad news. "We come together, we leave together."

Holly and Jazlynn walk up to the table. "Hey Jack."

Jack tips his bottle towards Holly.

"Luke, you're lookin' good. How 'bout a dance tonight? We didn't finish our last one. We had a horizontal selection on our mind, didn't we?"

Jazlynn offers her own option. "You 'n I could get close 'n let nature take over."

Luke's eyes dart around as if he's trying to find an escape route.

"We'll be waitin' over there for ya, Luke."

Holly and Jazlynn give Luke come-hither glances with bedroom eyes while sauntering away. Jack's sarcastic comment frustrates Luke. "We're havin' fun, how 'bout you, Luke?"

"I shoulda stayed at the ranch. I'd be better off there."
Cody states, "Hope's mad atcha. You'd be dead there."
"Hope left. Faith's not feelin' good."
Luke thinks, *I didn't say goodbye to Faith. Or Hope.*

FIFTY-ONE

Hope frets over Faith possibly having the flu and Luke vanishing. *'Luke didn't say goodbye to Faith. Damn those insensitive bastards. Assholes. I should've apologized to Luke. Katie didn't warn Luke not to say anythin' 'bout my rodeo career in front of Faith. I feel worse than she does. I might've really pushed Luke away this time.'*

Hope worries more when JeniMay texts Holly and Jazzy are making suggestive offers to Luke.

"Terrific. I just handed Luke to them before taking a chance. They've never pushed him away or made him feel like shit."

Beth checks in with Hope. "How's Faith feelin'?"

"Her stomach hurts but hasn't thrown up yet."

"You sound stressed. You okay?"

"Luke's at High Hope's with the guys."

"I heard. Good for him."

"No. Holly 'n Jazzy are there too. After I treated Luke poorly earlier. Again."

"I'll come over if y'all wanna go talk to Luke."

"You know Faith only wants me when she's sick."

"Looks like you'll be single forever."

"I don't need that right now, Beth."

Several guys in Holly's group glare at Luke. *'Maybe I should walk back to the ranch.'*

Jack texts to warn Ben that trouble may be brewing for Luke ahead of Hope calling Beth back.

"Beth, I really screwed up. I've lost any chance with Luke. I let pride stop me from apologizing to Luke before the guys snuck him off the ranch. Faith's upset he didn't even say goodbye. Now he's at High Hope's and all those girls that go there. And Holly 'n Jazzy."

"Hope, breathe. Calm down. Talk to Luke in the mornin'. It ain't like he's gettin' married tonight. Explain everything to Luke. I mean everything. Luke's passed on every possible chance with Jazzy 'n Holly. I don't know why."

"That's not comfortin', Beth."

Beth intentionally pushes Hope's buttons. "It's not meant to be. Y'all've made your bed. Now y'all gotta lie in it. You get mad at Luke for the dumbest things. I don't think you even like him. Just the idea of Luke is enough for you."

"I do think I could be happy with Luke. He makes me feel things I ain't felt before. That's scary. Losin' him to Holly or Jazzy scares me more. I could love Luke."

"Remember that for the mornin'. Get some sleep."

Hope's unable to sleep. *'I wanna talk to Luke. But am I too late?'*

FIFTY-TWO

Luke turns down several pretty women asking for dances. Jack questions him.

"Luke, what gives? Y'all're turning down hot sexy women tryin' to getcha on the floor. Texas women'll get offended."

"I'm not lookin' to encourage Holly or Jazzy." *A fight'll land me in jail.*

"Alright. Or maybe the right Texas lady ain't here to dance with?"

Luke wonders, *'Would Hope dance with me again?'* "Who'd that be?"

JeniMay murmurs to Jubilee, "I have an idea."

Jack points to the dance floor when the next song starts. "Us Texas cowboys call this a spectator sport."

Mostly women fill the floor and start line dancing. Jubilee and JeniMay jump up to join in.

"See what I mean."

Luke spots a couple bouncers flexing for women and acting tough in front of guys. *'Idiots. That starts fights.'*

Laurie arrives and recognizes Holly's scheming expression as she prepares to initiate her own game.

"Can you avoid trouble for one night, Holly? Let's catch up."

"There won't be any trouble if things go my way. Hold my hat."

Holly heads for Luke while Jazlynn remains with Wyatt. Holly slips behind Luke to take his hat and put it on. Billy calls her out. "Holly, what're ya doin'?"

"Y'all know a girl takes a cowboy's hat when she's interested in him."

Luke glares and snarls, "Give my hat back. I've never heard of that."

Billy states, "It's a thang."

Holly pretends to give Luke's hat back only to shift and sit in his lap to kiss him. Luke stands and sends Holly tumbling to the floor.

"How dare you! How dare you refuse me! Y'all know damned well what a girl takin' your hat means."

Luke wipes his mouth and stares at Holly. "I don't wantchur kiss or you takin' my hat."

Jake stirs the pot. "I've never seen anyone refuse Holly before."

Luke's anger shifts to Jake. "Shut up. I'm not goin' to jail over something stupid."

Holly feigns a hurt expression towards her friends approaching the table. A heavy set guy with a foreboding expression leads them. "Holly, y'all okay?"

"Bobby, Luke didn't wanna kiss me."

Jubilee glances at JeniMay, "We better move."

Bobby's attention turns to Luke. "What's wrong with you? Holly not pretty enough?"

Luke remains quiet. *'I know Bobby's type. Itchin' to fight for no reason.'*

Bobby's wearing overalls and a dark blue t-shirt on his roughly six-foot three inches and just over three hundred pound frame. Bobby was a defensive lineman through college but his quick temper and failed drug test ended his NFL tryouts. Now he works for his dad's construction company. Bobby shoves Luke backwards with his large crooked index finger.

Holly thinks, *'Luke's gonna regret refusin' me now.'*

Luke pleads, "Please don't do that."

"I'm gonna crush ya like a bug."

Luke remains passive and sounds non-threatening while avoiding eye contact. Jack's puzzled and wonders, *'Is Luke afraid?'*

Bobby shoves Luke harder.

"I'm askin' you to stop."

Bobby's emboldened by Luke's non-combative reaction. "Who said he could fight? You afraid of me? You oughta be."

Cody thinks, *'Luke's lost his nerve.'*

Luke's fully focused on his antagonist when Bobby moves in. He's aware of his surroundings but music fades to silence and people become blurred. *'This is it. Bobby's hell bent on fightin'.'*

Luke analyzes Bobby's movements while tuning out distractions.

"I'm gonna beat some sense into y'all."

Luke unblinkingly locks eyes with Bobby. "You can try. I'm not afraid of you. I'm afraid of me."

Jack notices Luke shifting and pulls Jake back. "Move." *'Luke's more aggressive now.'*

"Why?"

Cody's thought changes, *'Luke's settin' Bobby up.'*

Luke restates, "I'm not lookin' for trouble."

"Too late. It's found you."

Bobby's right fist swings upward in a wide arcing motion. Luke leans back to avoid it. Bobby's infuriated by Luke's calm demeanor and throws another punch. Luke effortlessly sidesteps this one. Jack observes, *'Luke's not fightin' but he ain't runnin' either.'*

Bobby growls after being humiliated in front of everyone. "I'm gonna crush you through the floor."

Luke assesses Bobby. *'He's like the rest. Too much talk, not enough skill. Big 'n stupid.'*

Bobby initiates his next punch until Luke abruptly strikes at Bobby's face with two expeditiously explosive punches. His head violently snaps back before crumbling to the floor unconscious. Jack watches Bobby collapse. *'I was wrong. Luke's not timid.'*

Danny and Kyle loudly exclaim, "Damn!"

Everyone realizes Bobby's not getting up. Holly slips away before the bouncers find Bobby lying on the floor gushing blood from his nose and mouth.

"Who did this?"

People gather nearby once word spreads Bobby's been knocked out. Laurie disbelievingly pushes her way through the crowd.

"Who knocked Bobby out?"

Several guys point at Luke.

"Thank you. He's been needin' that for a long time."

Laurie returns to Holly. "Here's your hat. Luke ain't interested. Get the message."

Holly realizes Laurie's disappointed. "I don't know why Bobby acted like an ogre."

"Nice try. Bobby deserved it but not that way."

The bouncers unceremoniously dump Bobby into a truck bed to be taken home while the guys settle in at the table.

"Bobby's been nothin' but trouble for years. That was fun to watch."

Luke's relieved but baffled when Jake boisterously exclaims, "Whoa baby! She's an in-betweener."

Jesse notices a particular girl, "She's an in-betweener for sure."

"What the hell's an in-betweener?"

Jake explains, "It's a girl ya wanna get between her clothes and skin."

Luke rolls his eyes. "You're both somethin' else. You know that?"

Jake puffs his chest out. "That's what the ladies tell me."

"The one's runnin' from ya?"

"Shut up. I'll bust ya up."

Jake notices Luke move and shrinks into a ball with his arms over his head. "Don't hit me. I'm kiddin'."

Jesse laughs, "Jake, y'all're three breadsticks short of a full box. Luke'll kick your ass."

Luke glances at Jack who shrugs, "Welcome to our world."

'Our world? I like belongin' here. More than I ever did in Illinois. I can't go back. I don't wanna leave. Even if Hope's not interested.'

Luke helps Jake up. "You ain't the sharpest knife in the drawer, are ya?"

Jake's harassed until two women walk by and tips his hat to them. "Ladies, the cowboy in me wants to be the cowboy in you."

They huff disgustedly but make eyes at Luke.

"How are you still single, Jake?"

"It's a mystery, ain't it?"

Jack's assessing Luke's dismissal of two more women's subtle advances. *It ain't normal. What's the reason?'*

Jake scans the crowd and spots a young lady walking towards the bar. "She's a P.F.A.D."

"A what?"

"A PFAD."

Luke's uncertain but inquires, "I'm gonna regret this, but I'll bite. What's a PFAD?"

Jake grins, "Pretty From A Distance. Or a PHAD."

Luke chuckles. "Jake, that's actually clever. Rude, but clever. I love you like the brother I never wanted from the mother I never met."

Jake laughs and heads for the bar to escort the girl to her table and then the dance floor. Luke comments, "I guess everyone gets lucky once in a while."

Billy adds, "Even a blind squirrel gets lucky and finds a nut."

Luke laughs at Billy's comment. Jack reveals, "Jake's known her for years. She likes his simpleton vulgarity."

Luke listens to Kevin Fowler's 'Texas Forever' on the drive back to the ranch. *'I wish I were Texan. I might have a chance with Hope then.'*

FIFTY-THREE

Scooter discovers several Longhorn next to the guest lodges in the morning. Ben supervises Luke during the roundup to push the strays back to the herd.

"Y'all've gotten good ridin', Luke."

"Blame Chester. I've ridden every day which got me over my fear of horses."

Chester's raspy voice booms from Ben's walkie-talkie. "Are y'all done yet?"

"Yes sir."

"Good. Send Luke to my office. Now!"

"Chester sounds pissed. Why?"

Ben ponders Chester's tone. "Not sure. Somethin's buggin' him though."

"Y'all know him better 'n I do."

"Why's Chester need you ASAP?"

Luke shrugs.

"We've got this. Go see what he needs."

Luke returns to the barn. Scooter rushes over. "Get yourself to Chester's office lad."

"I need to undo the saddle."

"Get goin' already."

Luke exits the barn and worries when Katie appears relieved to spot him entering the house. Luke knocks on the closed office door and hears Chester's gruff command. "Git in here. Now!"

'Why's he so ticked off?'

Holly's antics come to mind. *'Great. Chester's probably aimin' his gun at the door.'*

Luke slowly cracks the door open and sees Chester's irritated expression. *'Not good. But no gun.'* "You wanted to see me, sir."

Chester leans forward to rest his arms on the desk. "Ask your question already."

Luke notices Chester's eyes aren't fixed on him. "I don't have a question."

A woman's exhausted voice speaks from behind the door. "Didja meet anyone?"

Luke steps in to find Hope fatigued and slumped over in the chair by the door holding a white envelope. Her reddened eyes contrast the dark swollen areas under them.

'Faith must've kept Hope up all night. Is she wearing my mood ring?' "How's Faith? Is she feelin' better?"

Hope weakly smiles. "She's better. Thanks. She's upstairs sleepin'." *'Luke still cares about Faith even if I screwed everything up.'*

Hope hesitates before repeating her question. "Didja meet someone last night?"

Luke glances at Chester. "I don't understand. What's goin' on?"

Chester's exasperated and stands to confront Luke. "Just answer Hope's question."

Luke's perplexed. *'How do I answer Hope?'*

"I'm steppin' out. You two figure this out. Today. Now. Whatever this is. I need Luke fixin' fence. Hope, don't take another eight years to explain yourself. Got it?"

Luke opens his mouth but gets cut off.

"I'll return with my two cents. Quit actin' like stupid teenagers. Talk like adults."

Luke stares at the door after Chester exits and slams it shut. Hope's long buried inner desires attempt an emotional escape while standin to face Luke.

"What's going on, Hope?"

Hope feels dizzy and collapses into the chair. "I'm so tired I might not make sense right now."

"We can talk later if Faith's made you that tired."

Hope's eye shimmer with a new energy. *'Luke's bein' considerate. Or is he tryin' to get rid of me?'* "Faith didn't make me tired. You did."

"Me? How? We weren't together."

'Exactly.' "Did you hook up with someone?"

"What? No. Why?"

Hope nervously admits her true feelings. "Luke, I like you. I've tried not to. I can't stop how I feel."

Luke's stunned and stares deeply into Hope's green eyes. *'Hope likes me?'*

Hope takes a breath. *'Here comes the rejection.'* "I'm afraid of gettin' hurt again. But I wanna get to know you better. If you'd like that too? If I'm good enough for you?"

Luke speaks one word at first. "Oh." *'Hope thinks she's not good enough for me?'* "Hope, I'm not good enough for you. You're perfect. And you have Wyatt."

"You'd rather be with Holly or Jazzy, wouldn't you?"

"What? No. Holly tried kissin' me last night and got a guy knocked out for it." *'Why'd I say that?'*

"Holly 'n Jazzy are prettier than me. They always get the guys."

Luke locks eyes with Hope and speaks resolutely. "There's one guy they're not gettin'."

"Who?"

"Me!"

Hope questions Luke. "Why not? They know what guys want."

Luke boldly states his point. "They don't know what I want."

Hope's eyes twinkle. *'I'm so relieved.'* "What do you want?"

"Truthfully, someone absolutely gorgeous. Mature. Real. Someone who has fun along with a serious side. A woman who understands real love and doesn't play emotional games. She's considerate and knows how to treat someone special."

"You've thought about that before." *'Luke knows what he's lookin' for.'*

"Has anyone ever met your list of qualifications?"

Luke nods and slightly tilts his head. "Once. Possibly a second time. But she's hard to read."

Hope slumps in the chair. "You mean Jazzy, don't you?"

Luke considers Jazlynn's circumstances before answering. "Jazzy's not hard to read. I did consider her for a bit."

"JeniMay'd like to make you happy."

She's nice but not the person I'd stay for."

"Who'd make you stay? Wait, don't tell me. Tell her."

"You don't have a clue, do you?"

Luke reaches out to touch Hope's shoulder. "Hope, I like you too. I'd stay if you'd ask me to."

"Really?"

"Yeah. But I'm not one to play games or share someone datin' someone else. The first time you give me the silent treatment instead of talking things out would be the last time. I've learned the importance of communication in a relationship. I can't read minds."

Hope gazes into Luke's eyes. "What about everything I've said 'n done to you?"

"Honestly, Hope, I don't think I'm good enough for you or Faith. I…"

Chester barges in, "Alright, here's the deal. Hope likes you. You seem to like Hope. What're you two gonna do about it? You're drivin' me crazy 'n I'm too old for this shit."

Hope smiles at Chester.

"What? What's wrong with you?"

Hope's gaze returns to Luke. "Y'all're right. But how would you know?"

"For God's sake. Hope, y'all ain't really been hidin' it. I've seen y'all sneakin' looks at each other for some time now. Hell, you gave Luke the once over twice his first day here."

Hope blushes after Chester's revelation.

"Yeah, I noticed that."

Hope's embarrassed she was caught. *I wasn't that obvious, was I?*

Luke's eyebrows rise up. "Oh? Is that so?"

Chester restates his question. "What are you two gonna do now?"

"We're not sure yet."

Chester rubs his eyes with his thumb and finger. "For starters, y'all got a reservation at Oasis for supper to discuss all this and watch the sunset over Lake Travis."

"Oasis doesn't take reservations."

"I know the owner, remember. You'll have a table with no disturbances. Now, I need Luke fixin' fences. Y'all can pick him up later."

Hope smiles, "That's very kind, Chester. Thank you."

Chester replies, "Are you kiddin'? It's time to end this runaround two-step between you two. Y'all've been hangin' onto the past too long. Live in the present. Look towards the future."

Luke pushes his luck. "Um, Chester, could I do something with Hope first?"

"Hurry up."

Hope's emerald eyes shyly flicker with anticipation and uncertainty. "Yes Luke?"

"Could I kiss you without any excuses?"

Hope nods breathlessly and lightly bites her lower lip. *'Luke wants to kiss me.'*

Luke steps closer and locks eyes with Hope before gently placing his hands on her blushing cheeks. Hope shudders and closes her eyes when Luke leans in for an affectionately romantic kiss. Luke's lips tenderly touch Hope's soft, sweetly glossed lips to bond the pair in a heartwarming new beginning. Hope feels a tingling sensation travel up and down her body and shivers with delight.

'I've never felt like this before.'

Luke lowers his arms to wrap Hope into a strong hug to continue kissing her passionately. Hope melts into the strength of his embrace and enjoys feeling his muscular body holding her. *'I feel safe in Luke's arms.'*

Hope wraps her arms around Luke's neck. *'Is this true love? It's overwhelming.'*

Chester shakes his head. "Dear God! What have I done? I'll be dealin' with this now."

Hope and Luke start laughing. Hope eagerly steals another kiss from Luke. "Get your work done." *'I have a date with Luke.'*

Chester instructs, "Hope, bring Faith here for a sleepover. Luke, finish 'round four so y'all have time to get ready for your date with Hope. Sunset's 'round 6:45."

Luke smiles, "Yes sir." *'I never thought I'd have a date with Hope.'*

Ben's organizing supplies when Luke enters the barn. "What happened?"

"I'll tell ya later. Let's fix those fences."

Ben smiles. *'Uh-huh. Luke's got lipstick on his lips.'*

Holly spots pink lipstick smeared on Luke when he enters the guest office. "Holly, it's safe for the guests to go outside."

'Only one person I know wears that shade. Why's it on Luke?'

FIFTY-FOUR

Faith jumps from Hope's truck. 'Yippee. I'm havin' a sleepover tonight."

Luke emerges from the bunkhouse in black jeans, boots, and cowboy hat along with his green button-down shirt. He stops in his tracks when he catches sight of Hope in a beautiful white dress with a blue floral pattern and her black boots and black felt cowboy hat. She's wearing a small amount of make-up and a sweet honeysuckle fragranced perfume which delicately hangs in the air. Luke's pleased expression inexplicably changes to concern.

'Oh God. I'm goin' on a date with Hope.'

Hope worries, *'Oh no. Luke doesn't like my outfit. He's changin' his mind. I shouldn't've listened to Beth 'n Faith.'*

Luke's expression doesn't convey his thoughts. *'Hope's gorgeous in that dress. Am I worthy?'* "Hope, you're all kinds of beautiful."

Luke's heart beats faster while his smile returns. Hope blushes, "No I'm not."

Hope covers her cheeks with her hands while Faith runs to Luke. "I helped Momma with her outfit."

"You chose well, Faith."

Luke hugs and kisses Hope. "Is it okay that I did that without askin'?"

Hope giggles, "Yes Luke, it's okay. You don't need to ask. I hope I'm not always blushin' 'round you."

"I hope you do. I'm nervous. Are there special rules to take a beautiful Texas woman on a date?"

Chester speaks up, "Yup. Get her home by ten. Behave or y'all'll be answerin' to me. Got it?"

Hope responds to Chester's threat. "Oh my God! Chester, I'm a grown woman. I can take care of myself." *'I'll let Luke take care of me too.'* "Why would you say that?"

"That's my job. Luke, remember what Bob 'n I told ya the first day if ya got outta line?"

"Sue'd have your hide on the barn wall if'n y'all shot me."

"No."

Hope's questioning expression entertains Chester. "Do I wanna know?"

"Nope."

Luke states, "I'll treat Hope like the Texas queen she is."

"You better. Or else."

Hope shoots a telling look at Chester. "Alright. We're leaving now. Faith, be good for Grand-daddy."

"I will Momma."

Holly sees Hope dressed up and Luke getting into her truck. *'What's goin' on?'*

Cody's whistle has Wyatt join the guys at the rodeo barn door.

"Why's Hope lookin' hotter 'n a two dollar pistol?"

Cody answers, "Rumor has it Luke's got a date with Hope."

"Over my dead body."

"Y'all may wanna rethink that thought."

Hope starts the truck as a song starts. "Luke, listen to this song but don't take it the wrong way, okay."

Luke nods and hears a duet sing about setting pride aside to express their love to each other instead of saying goodbye. They reveal they'll seal the deal on their relationship that night.

"The song's called 'Oh Tonight' by Josh Abbott 'n Kacey Musgraves. I'm not pushin' for anything but I'm willing to get to know you better 'n see where this goes."

Luke senses Hope's nervous. "I understand. I'm willing to let someone, you, have an honest chance to get to know me."

Hope realizes Luke's equally nervous. *Luke's willing to chance possible heartache 'n rejection.'*

Luke marvels at the size of The Oasis On Lake Travis while the manager shows them to their table.

"Hope, we haven't seen you in a while. How's Faith?"

"She's grown since y'all last seen her."

Luke asks, "How big is this place?"

"It's over thirty thousand square feet, multi-leveled, and we're about four hundred fifty feet above the lake. Please enjoy you meal and the sunset."

Hope comments as they sit down. "We do things bigger in Texas, don't we?"

"And then some."

"Oasis is known as the Sunset Capital of Texas."

"That's some view. It's almost as breathtaking as you, Hope."

Hope reacts shyly before Luke follows up with a kiss.

"You messed up my lipstick. I'm gonna freshen up, alright. I'll be right back."

Several men in suits watch Hope pass their table. One stands to block Hope's path when she returns.

"Join me for dinner. Then we'll talk about you being dessert."

"I'm not sure my date would like that."

"He doesn't need to know. I'll give you what he can't."

"True. You look like a disease carryin' rat, asshole."

The man roughly grabs Hope's arm. "Puta. Bitch. Nobody insults me. Learn your place around a man."

"The lady knows her place. It ain't with you."

The guy spins around to face Luke.

"This bitch needs a lesson taught to her. Walk away. I'll hurt you otherwise."

"Hope, do y'all need a lesson tonight?"

"No!"

I agree."

Luke delivers a very painful message while grabbing the man's crotch. "Bother my lady again 'n I'll go next level, understand?"

The man emits a tortured howl while his friends watch him drop to his knees and fall over.

"All y'all understand as well?"

The men nod and look at their friend curled up on the floor. Hope adds, "He's lucky Luke got him first. I'd've shot his balls off 'n turned him into a gelding."

Luke kisses Hope before pulling her chair out to return to enjoying each other's company during dinner.

"I could get used to bein' your lady." Hope sips on her wine. "Kiss the wine from my lips."

Luke smiles and shares a sensual kiss with Hope ahead of expressing his main concern.

"I'm worried I don't have anything to offer you in a relationship. Faith as well."

Hope gazes into Luke's hazel eyes. *'Luke's scared to let us down.'* "Faith adores you. You're so good, supportive, 'n helpful with her."

"What can I possibly offer you?"

'Luke feels vulnerable.' "You offer me somethin' I've never really had. You care about me 'n take care of me 'n protect me without bein' asked to. I miss you when you're not around."

"You miss me?"

"You sound shocked. I've never dated a man before. I've chosen boys, I see that now."

Luke reveals, "I miss you too."

"Oh?"

"You're beautiful, successful, why would you miss me. Other people don't."

Hope comprehends Luke's alluding to Bob's comment regarding no missing person's report. "It's their loss. My parents didn't miss me either. Chester 'n Millie are my parents."

"I wish I'd've met Millie."

"She'd've loved you."

Luke smiles. "From what I hear, she was amazin'."

Hope wipes a tear away, "She was. I miss her."

"I worry you 'n Wyatt'll get back together."

Hope stares at Luke before answering. *'I don't think so.'* "I think, no, I know Wyatt 'n I are done. He's not the same person I loved."

"I'm not competin' with him if y'all still want him."

"I loved Wyatt and thought I felt loved. I thought I knew what love was. Till now."

"Hope, I don't easily trust people. I stayed closed off even with Linda. I didn't give an honest effort for a good relationship. That's what broke us up. I don't wanna do that with you."

"Luke, what broke you 'n Linda up?"

'How do I answer without scarin' Hope?'

"Don't answer. That was too personal 'n rude to ask on a first date." *'I upset Luke but I don't want to make Linda's mistakes.'*

Luke's answer relieves Hope's fears. "I was the reason. I didn't give a hundred percent. Hank showed me we would've failed anyway. Linda focused more on her career than our relationship. We didn't have enough in common to offset our differences."

"Luke, I own my veterinary clinic" *'Could I be too similar to Linda?'*

"I know. But you make time for other people. Especially Faith and the wranglers."

"Faith's my daughter. I have to make time for her."

"No. You don't. I've seen people ignore their own kids and not be present for them. Some've torn the kids down instead of havin' their backs. You don't let work consume you."

"Faith does that." *'Did that sound like I won't have time for Luke?'*

Luke chuckles, "Faith's supposed to come first. You're a great mom. You make time for your girlfriends, the wranglers, and Chester. You have balance in your life."

Hope laughs. "Balance? Some days I don't even know my own name."

"So you're a parent. Look, I was in a bad place when I got here but I was drawn to you. Even after you shot at me. Twice."

"I was mad at you."

Luke smiles, "I get it now. I never felt the way I did when I first saw you. Actually, that's not true. There was one other time but I screwed that up. I don't want to this time."

'Luke's had a past love. Like I did with Wyatt.'

Luke continues, "I wanted to be around you but pulled away. I was confused 'n wanted to leave the ranch but you kept drawin' me in and breakin' down my defenses. It scared me."

'I can't believe what Luke's saying.'

"Your eyes expressed something the day I tried leaving the ranch. You threatened me but your eyes made me want to stay. Your gun had nothing to do with that. Back then, I felt dead inside and would've been happy if you shot me dead."

Luke's candid admission stuns Hope.

"I was breakin' down your defenses? You were breakin' mine down too. How could you read my eyes 'n know what I was thinkin' or feelin'?"

"My training taught me to read people, to understand who might be first threat."

"Oh? So I was a threat? Is that what I'm hearin'?"

"You were pointin' a gun at me."

"Fair point."

"I've learned to read people in most situations. Mostly."

"You hurt Ben 'n I grew up not trustin' most men."

"You made that very clear."

"Luke, I'll admit I think y'all were cute when I first saw ya."

"I'm amazed I caught your eye. I was a mess. Honestly, I thought the iceberg showed more compassion to the Titanic than you showed me."

Luke pauses when Hope looks down. "Hope, are you okay?"

"I was emotionally closed off. I thought I controlled my life, Faith's life. I see I don't control much at all. It was a horrible wake up call."

Hope's eyes meet Luke's again. "You've been forcin' me to reconsider my choices."

"I never wanted to force you to do anything."

"It's okay. You've helped me."

"I never felt I controlled anything. Here, in Texas, ridin' horses, learning the Cowboy Code, understanding Cowboy Up, it's all changed me, my thinking. Chester 'n Hank might've helped a little too."

Hope laughs, "So Texas changed y'all for the better. Texas looks good on you."

"That's horse manure."

"You've proved me wrong 'bout you becomin' a cowboy 'n I'm okay to be wrong this one time." *'I married someone I never should've said I Do to. Faith's all the good that came from that. Luke 'n I seem to understand each other. That makes him a better choice, right?'*

A bell rings to announce the beginning of sunset. Luke stands behind Hope by the railing with his arms around her to watch the fiery red ball sink beyond the hilly terrain west of Lake Travis. He shifts to be next to Hope and she realizes Luke's looking at her in the blazing scarlet glow.

"You're missin' the beauty of a Texas sunset."

"No. I'm watching a beauty in a Texas sunset."

Hope blushes, "Stop it."

The dusk's brilliance fades and the darkening night closes out another day in Texas.

"This reminds me of Corpus. And the most beautiful woman there."

Luke kisses Hope gently and fondly recalls their morning kiss. *'That was the most electrifying kiss I've ever had. It was beyond any I've ever had in my life.'*

Hope's phone rings. "It's Chester."

"He probably wants to gloat. Answer it."

Hope's smile fades. "We need to get back to the ranch."

Luke's baffled. "What's wrong? Is Faith alright?"

"Faith's fine. We need to leave. Now."

Hope's alarming reaction concerns Luke while she pulls him to her truck at a hurried pace. Hope's head swivels left and right as if she's searching for someone.

FIFTY-FIVE

Hope pulls her gun from the console safe and lays it on her lap.

"What's goin' on, Hope? What did Chester say?"

"They spotted Joe near Austin. He blamed me for his business failing. Now his house is gittin' foreclosed on."

Hope speeds through winding roads to return to Faith.

"Slow down. The Twisted Live Oak's the safest place for Faith to be. Let's get there alive."

Hope slows down after Luke's reassurance. "You're right."

Luke hugs Hope before entering the house. "Don't panic Faith. Take a deep breath and relax. You're safe. We're safe. I'm here."

"Thank you, Luke."

Hope breathes deeply to hide her worries before entering the house and helping Faith get ready for bed. Chester knows Hope's stressed.

"Stay here, Hope. Sleep in the guest bedroom tonight."

"Thanks Chester. I'd like that."

Hope grabs some sweatpants and a t-shirt to sleep in and Luke attempts to alleviate Hope's tenseness when she returns.

"Should we hit the gym?"

Hope weakly smiles while her mind churns with troublesome thoughts. She fears Luke will leave due to her sordid past wrecking their date. Her voice conveys her apprehension. "I'm sorry my past ruined our date. You must think all our dates'll be like this."

"Hope, your past kept me here. I'm not goin' anywhere. Joe hasn't changed anything."

Chester listens in, *'Luke sounds determined to stay and help.'*

"I'm afraid you'll change your mind 'n leave."

"Hope, I'm not leaving you. I like you. And Faith. I like the ranch. Chester's debatable still."

Hope laughs while gazing into Luke's eyes.

Chester snaps, "Watch it! Bob can still make that visit we discussed."

"I'm exhausted. Would you mind if I lay down."

Chester responds, "Get a good night's sleep. You'll feel better in the morning."

Wyatt barges in and heads straight at Hope. "I heard you had some trouble. I'm here to help."

Chester glances at Hope before speaking to Wyatt. "It's under control."

Hope hugs Luke and adds, "I'm okay. Luke's here."

Wyatt shoots a dirty look at Luke. "I'd take better care of you, Hope. I've known you longer 'n know what you need."

Hope kisses Luke and rests her head on his shoulder. *'I've missed this.'* "Luke knows what to do."

Chester sees Hope yawn. "Time to go, Wyatt."

"Could Luke sleep on the couch? I'd feel safer if he's here tonight."

Hope's imploring eyes inform Chester she wants Luke nearby.

"I don't see a problem with that."

Hope answers in her sweet, husky drawl. "Thank you. And Luke, thank you for stayin' here tonight. It means a lot to me."

Wyatt's disgusted to be dismissed by Hope. Luke notes exhaustion and relief force Hope's eyelids to close halfway.

FIFTY-SIX

Luke slips outside to perform katas to exercise stress and tension from his muscles after a sleepless night on the couch. Hope finds Luke's gone when she comes to check on him.

'Where's Luke? Did he leave?'

Chester sees Hope in the living room. "Luke went outside earlier."

"Oh. Okay."

Wyatt hears Luke enter the bunkhouse. "What game are ya playin' with my woman?"

"I could ask you the same. Hope's not your woman. She's not mine either. I don't own her."

"I'll figure out a way to get rid of you."

"Good luck with that. I've got work to do, don't you?"

Chester calls Luke to the house when Bob stops by to share information he's learned overnight.

"It looks like Joe's returned to Mexico."

"Are you sure?"

"Two former employees informed me Joe contacted them to say he's done here."

Hope's relieved and examines Luke. *'Luke looks like he didn't sleep last night.'*

Bob continues, "It looks like y'all won't need to stay after all, Luke. Joe's not a threat anymore."

Chester watches Luke's expression sour. *'Luke's actin' like he's been insulted.'*

"I promised Hope I'd stay till Joe's caught. I don't break promises."

Hope reaches for Luke's hand. "Luke has a new reason to stay."

Bob replies, "Oh. I see."

Luke studies Bob. *'Bob looks agitated.'*

"Those jackasses that shot at the ranch were part of some militia group outta Arkansas. They randomly picked the ranch for target practice while hidin' out here."

"I best get back to work. I reckon Wyatt's missin' me."

Hope kisses Luke before he leaves. *'I'm happy I had a date with Luke. I hope we have many more.'* "Luke, Wyatt 'n I are done. I haven't said as much to him yet. But I will."

'Why hasn't Hope said anything to Wyatt yet?'

FIFTY-SEVEN

Faith continually checks on Luke's whereabouts on Halloween.

"Hope, does Faith know about Joe's threats?"

"No. Why?"

"She keeps looking for me."

Hope giggles. "I might've told Faith the costumes scare you."

"Ah, funny."

"Truthfully, Faith's happy you're here."

"I'll share any day with Faith. And you."

An approaching woman calls out to Hope after Luke pulls Hope in for a kiss.

"Hope Cooper, where've you been hidin' this fine lookin' stallion?"

Luke blushes from her compliment.

"Hi Suzie. This is Luke. He's here to carry Faith home when she's done trick or treating."

Luke glances at Hope, "Yes ma'am. I'm Hope's pack mule."

Hope kisses Luke's cheek. "You are my pack mule."

"As long as I get your kisses."

Suzie comments before leaving, "I like this new Hope. Keep him around. He's good for you."

"I agree."

"Faith's one happy girl around you."

Luke puts his arms around Hope. "And what about this girl? Are you happy too?"

Hope answers with a passionate kiss until Faith returns to show all the candy she's collected.

November's cooler weather is offset by warm encounters between Hope and Luke. Their time is spent with Faith, time at the gym, and other dating activities. Hope invites Jubilee and JeniMay to some of their workout sessions but Luke refuses to let the guys to join him.

"Luke, why can't the guys come too?"

"They'll turn everything into a competition. Someone'll get stupid then get hurt."

Jazlynn and Holly enter the gym during a group outing. Jazlynn shoots a glaring look at Hope. Jubilee remarks, "Jazzy's bitter to lose Luke to Hope."

Hope asks, "Does Jazzy need your help, Luke?"

"Her trainer's here. You have my full attention."

JeniMay and Jubilee make goofy lovey faces and gestures at Hope when Luke's not looking. They laugh at Hope's attempts to quietly stop their childish behavior. Holly heard Hope had Chester's permission to go out with Luke but didn't believe it. She storms into his office when she returns.

"What the hell, Grand-daddy?! Y'all're lettin' Hope date Luke? But not me? That's not fair."

"Calm down, Holly. And don'tcha dare take that tone with me or I'll putcha over my knee 'n straighten y'all out."

"I saw Luke first. Hope shouldn't get any chance with him."

"Holly, you'd use him up quicker than an old sock full of holes gettin' respun for yarn. Luke 'n Hope might be good for each other."

Holly stomps out fuming. "I won't let this happen." *I'm not losin' Luke to Hope.'*

Jazlynn's doubly upset. *'I get any guy I want. I'm not lettin' Hope win this time. I'm losin' a good trainin' partner.'*

Jazlynn vents to Holly. "Hope ain't stealin' Luke away. She's not in my league."

Holly verbally attacks Jazlynn. "Y'all tried stealin' Luke from me with the gym excuse."

Wyatt confronts Hope while she tends to Patsy. "Y'all ain't pickin' that city slicker dipshit over me, are ya?"

"Wyatt, calm down."

"Calm down? No way. I returned to make you mine. Not lose to an asshole."

"Luke's got more class and cares for me more than you ever did."

"Yeah? Until he leaves ya. Then you'll come crawlin' back to me."

"Luke would've left already if he were gonna. He's promised to stay 'n I believe him. You left me, remember."

Wyatt's frustration boils over and physically lashes out and shoves Hope to the ground which tears her shirt. "You bitch. You're mine." *'I'm beddin' y'all down, no one else.'*

Ben enters and charges Wyatt after hearing his comment to Hope. Ben knocks Wyatt down and stands over him. "I oughta beat the shit outta you. Literally."

"Whoa, Ben, hold on. I'm sorry. I didn't mean to do that. I lost control."

"Don'tcha ever touch Hope again. Or I'll end you. Better yet, I'll let Luke."

Hope speaks while standing up. "Don't tell Luke. Wyatt didn't mean to do that."

Wyatt's relieved Hope defends him. *'I meant it. But not for anyone to see.'*

Ben glances at Hope. "I'll stay quiet. Unless somethin' else happens. Got it."

Wyatt nods and stands while Hope adjusts her torn shirt around her. Luke catches sight of Hope walking to her truck and notices her ripped shirt and worried expression.

"Ben, what happened to Hope? Her shirt looked torn."

"She's fine. She, uh, got caught on a nail."

Ben thinks, *'Luke doesn't believe me. Luke oughta know the truth.'*

Luke heads to the rodeo barn and hears Wyatt on his phone.

"Yeah, I pushed the bitch. Tore her shirt. Got a quick look at her tits again. She'll come 'round 'n dump that dumbass. Talk to ya later, Cole."

Luke clenches his fists but slips out to confront Ben. "You lied! Why? Wyatt hurt Hope, didn't he?"

"He didn't hurt Hope. He shoved her down 'n ripped her shirt. Hope made me promise not to tell ya. She's afraid what y'all might do."

"Wyatt's got a lesson comin' on. My way."

"I'm not stoppin' ya."

Luke's waiting by Wyatt's truck that evening. Wyatt pauses when he sees Luke but reveals he's armed before moving in. Luke speaks quietly. "Y'all enjoy hurtin' women?"

"Get out of my way. I've got somewhere to be."

Luke raises his hands and steps aside. Wyatt grins. "Asshole." *'You're all talk.'*

Wyatt regains consciousness next to his truck feeling as if a bus hit him. He struggles to his feet and drives off. He's late returning to the ranch the next morning with darkening eyes and a taped up nose. Ben smirks at Luke while Chester chides Wyatt for his facial condition.

"Drinkin' more than ya can handle? Whaddya run into? A truck? And how many times?"

Wyatt growls, "Luke hit me, sir. For no reason."

"Simmer down. Now what reason would Luke have to hitcha?"

Hope's told about Wyatt's appearance. *'Luke found out. I won't lie to Luke but I won't bring it up either.'*

FIFTY-EIGHT

ope, Faith, and Luke find Hank on the deck after an afternoon ride. Luke trots Waylon over to Hank.

"Howdy Hank. What do we owe the pleasure of your company?"

"Sharin' supper 'n a chat about life with a certain someone."

Luke smirks mischievously, "Chester's too old for that talk."

"You're not."

"Haven't all your talks been about that?"

"Yup. Have y'all been listenin to my wisdom?"

"Yes sir. Whether I wanted to or not."

Randy's fast approaching truck interrupts their light-hearted banter. Randy stops short and gets out and points a nine millimeter pistol at them.

"I'm here for Chester. I'll shoot anyone tryin' to stop me."

Luke dismounts. "This ain't the way to solve problems, Randy."

Chester appears on the deck and aims his rifle at Randy. Hope attempts to guide Faith to safety.

"Drop it, Chester." Randy's aim shifts to Hope. "Or the girls get the first rounds."

Luke assesses Randy. *'Shit. Randy's drunk.'*

"I'll shootcha both off your horses."

Hope's terror filled eyes dart back and forth between Luke and Randy. Luke winks at Hope and stuns everyone with his next words.

"Set your rifle down, Chester."

"He'll shoot all us if I do."

"I'm not lettin' that happen."

Chester reluctantly complies. "Luke, y'all best know what you're doin'."

Randy refocuses on Luke. "You ain't got a gun. How're ya gonna stop me?"

"Push your luck 'n y'all'll find out."

"Like this?"

Randy's aim shifts and shoots at Willie's hooves so he rears up to throw Faith off his back. Hope screams and jumps off Patsy. A second shot stops her when it strikes the ground near her boots.

"Damn. I was aimin' to shootchya, bitch."

Randy's next shot bloodies Chester's arm when he reaches for his rifle. "Uh-uh. Back off asshole."

Chester observes Faith lying on the ground and Hope terrified nearby. *'Luke has no idea what he's doin'.'* "I should've shot the bastard."

"Hope and Faith would've been dead already."

Randy aims at Luke. "You're dead if I squeeze this trigger."

"Walk away, Randy. While you can."

"Or I can finish you off. Then them."

Luke speaks calmly. "Hope, check on Faith."

"It's the last thing she does."

"Naw. Your beef's with Chester."

Randy mutters, "Women 'n kids suck the life outta ya."

Luke worries when Randy fires a shot at the house and hears Katie scream then go silent. *'It's time to end this.'*

Chester threatens Randy. "I'll kill you with my bare hands if you've harmed Katie."

Katie steps onto the deck with a bloodied shoulder and slumps into a rocker. Katie's appearance distracts Randy long enough for Luke to close the distance between the two men. Luke and Randy struggle for the gun until two shots end the altercation. Luke releases his grip on Randy and steps back. Randy staggers backwards and drops to his knees and mumbles, "You shot me."

"No, asshole, you shot yourself."

Randy's left shoulder is painted blood red from two seeping wounds. Luke's holding Randy's pistol. Hope runs to Luke's side. "Faith just had the wind knocked outta her. Luke, you're shot!"

"I'm not shot. I'm pissed this asshole tried ruinin' our day."

"Your shirt's bloody. We need to stop the bleedin'."

"I'm fine."

Chester calls Bob while examining Randy. "We've got multiple GSW's. Randy's shot clean through. Send two ambulances."

Hope tends to Katie while Luke mercilessly ties Randy's hands behind his back.

"You're hurtin' my shoulder."

"Here's something for the pain."

Luke knocks Randy out with a single anger driven punch. When Randy regains consciousness Luke warns, "Y'all should've walked away, asshole. Next time you'll be diggin' for six 'n I'll putcha there."

Hope hears the fury in Luke's voice. *'Luke's madder 'n I've ever seen.'*

Bob and two ambulances arrive followed by several more squads. Chester pulls Hope aside before he and Katie are loaded into one ambulance while Randy's put into the other. Chester returns later that day and calls Hope and Luke into his office.

"Luke, y'all're gonna start trainin' with firearms."

"Why? I disabled Randy. I'm capable without a gun."

Chester looks at his sling. "Your luck nearly ran out today. Three people got shot. Should've been only one."

Luke's annoyed his fighting skills are being dismissed until realizing Chester's point. *'Hope 'n Faith could've been killed today.'*

Chester looks at Hope. "Take Luke to the range." He looks at Luke. "In fact, you teach Luke to shoot."

Hope disagrees, "Luke should learn from an instructor."

Chester studies Hope. "Y'all're a qualified instructor. And a marksman. Who's better than that?"

"Luke, I'd like to talk to Chester privately."

"Sure."

Luke steps into the hallway so Hope can close the door.

"You've trained everyone on the ranch. Why're ya fightin' me on this, Hope?"

"Luke's different."

"How so?"

Luke's a guy. You know how guys react when a woman's better at somethin'."

"No. Enlighten me."

"Guys don't want girls that're better 'n them. At anything."

Chester comprehends Hope's message. *'Hope's past taints her judgement.'*

"Luke's not most guys. Take him to the range 'n git him squared away."

"But I…"

"We'll discuss this further later."

Hope drives Luke to the local gun range.

"Travis, this is Luke. He needs an instructor for shootin' lessons."

"Hope, you should teach him. You're qualified 'n y'all're better 'n I am."

Travis shows Luke several pistols. He chooses a 9mm Glock Gen4 pistol with a fifteen shot magazine.

"Let's head to the range so you get a feel for the kickback with the first clip."

Hope giggles after Luke's poor performance. "You completely missed the target. Good thing you can fight."

Travis adjusts Luke's stance. "Anticipate the recoil."

Luke looks at Hope, "I suppose you can do better?"

'Shit. How do I handle this? Travis knows I don't miss. Luke may not like my shootin' ability.' "Are you sure?"

"Yup. I doubt you can hit the broadside of a barn door. Y'all did miss me that first day."

"Step outta that box." *'Luke'll see how good I am.'*

Luke winks at Travis when Hope falls for his taunt. Hope forgets Luke's seen her shoot while putting on glasses and ear protection. Travis sends the target out and Hope rapidly shoots off nine rounds.

'Doubt me, will ya?'

Travis brings the target back for Luke to inspect. The bullseye's just a hole. Luke casually comments, "Just lucky."

Hope's flustered. "Just lucky? Are you serious?"

Luke's smirk indicates he's egging her on.

"Are you seriously messin' with me? While I'm armed? I can't believe you."

"The gun's empty. I'm safe."

"For now."

Travis laughs, "Hope, I think Luke knows how good y'all are."

"I see. You think you're funny. Here's funny."

Hope compares Luke's target against hers. "Still think I can't hit the side of a barn door?"

Luke shrugs while Travis sets up with another target. Luke does slightly better and comments afterwards, "I'm safe with you. Unless I'm the target."

Travis chuckles. "Hope's a crack shot. She'd turn ya into Swiss cheese."

Hope's discomfort is revealed after Travis' compliment.

"Hope, it's okay to be better than I am. I don't have a problem with that."

Hope stares at Luke. "Why would you say that?" *Does Luke know what I told Chester?'*

"Be proud. You've worked hard to be this good. You've earned it."

Hope's relieved. "Do you really mean that?"

"Yes. I'd support you to be the best at anything. Even if it means you'd be better than me. You deserve respect for your accomplishments."

Travis agrees. "Hope, you're a fierce competitor with a compassionate side. Your rodeo days and shootin' skills are expert level and you own a successful business."

Hope replies, "Joe hated I could shoot better 'n him."

"Joe's an idiot. I'm not Joe."

"No, Luke, you're not. But guys've never liked me bein' better or smarter at anything."

Luke states, "Hope, that's the difference between men 'n boys. You're special and should be treated as such."

Travis shares a parting comment. "Hope, I think ya got a keeper here."

Hope smiles, "Luke y'all deserve a true Texas reward. We're goin' to Whataburger."

Luke's confused when they arrive at the restaurant until Hope explains, "Us Texans consider Whataburger as part of the four food groups. People get married at Whataburger 'n it's a first stop after bein' outta state."

Luke comments after enjoying his meal, "I'd definitely come back here."

"Then you'd best behave."

"I'd ask Faith to come here."

"Don'tcha dare use my daughter against me."

"You're invited too."

Luke realizes Hope's misunderstood him. "Hope, I don't mean I'd use Faith against you to get something. I meant I'd like for all of us to come here."

"Oh. That's different then."

Katie returns after two days in the hospital. She and her husband are watching a movie when Hope and Luke enter the family room.

"Good timing, Hope."

'What does Katie mean?'

A woman's voice sings in the background about not being perfect but strong enough for her and her love and not being like the others. Katie catches Hope and Luke exchange a glance.

"How's Luke's shootin' practice comin' along?"

"Luke's come a long way. He's figured out which end to hold."

"They really oughta label those things."

"Luke, be a dear, fetch me 'n Steve some sweet tea. Thanks."

"Yes ma'am. Comin' right up. How ya feelin'?"

"Randy missed an artery. It hurts but I'll heal. Quicker with that sweet tea."

"Alright. I'm goin', I'm goin'."

Katie waits for Luke to leave. "Hope, how are things between you 'n Luke?"

Hope pauses, "I've never felt like this before."

"How's Faith with this?"

"Faith's never been happier." *'She's always known Luke's special. She wants me to see that too.'*

"Good. How's Luke really doin' at the range?"

"Luke's improving' so fast. Travis introduced him to new weapons."

Hope's unable to bring Luke to the range every time but calls Travis for updates. "Howdy Travis, how's Luke doin' in your opinion?"

"Hope, Luke's improving so fast. It's off the charts. He's disciplined. Like he's had specialized training."

"Luke's mentioned martial arts training."

"He's cold, calculating, 'n handles the Mossberg 88 shotgun and Rugar AR-556 rifle expertly. His trainin' goes beyond normal levels."

"How 'bout Luke's mental state with firearms? Is he cocky or reckless?"

"Luke's unique."

"Why do you say that?"

"He's serious about learnin'. He respects weapons. He's protective."

'Protective. Respectful. That's Luke.' "Luke hates fighting. He knows it's necessary at times. He didn't wanna learn to shoot."

"Luke seems hesitant but understands death's possible when the trigger's pulled."

"He fought five guys to protect me."

"Luke would kill if necessary to protect someone."

"Thanks Travis." *'He's killed to protect me.'*

"Hope, Luke gets a special look in his eyes lookin' at you. I feel sorry for anyone tryin' to hurtcha. Or Faith. He won't show mercy."

"You're more right than you know."

Luke approaches training with weapons with a serious mindset. He understands the ominous reason. He's dangerously proficient with staffs, throwing stars, swords, nunchakus, and his hands. Each weapon can end a life. The ranch forced that experience on him.

FIFTY-NINE

Luke continually challenges Faith to think through homework problems to find answers and assists only when necessary. Faith worries Chester and Katie when she appears to pull away from Luke and Hope while they're together. Katie wonders, *'Is Faith changin' her mind?'*

Katie questions Faith while they're alone. "Faith, is everything okay?"

"Yeah. Why?"

"You seem upset Hope's with Luke."

"No. I'm happy. Momma needs time alone with Luke to like him like I do."

Faith's explanation surprises Katie. "You're not feelin' left out?"

"No, why would I? Luke 'n Momma spoil me all the time. Maybe Luke'll wanna be my daddy."

"You have a dad."

"I want a good daddy. Like my friends."

Katie informs Hope of Faith's sneaky plan.

"I was wondering about all the sneaky encouraging comments from her."

Ben's concerned Luke would leave if Faith became a handful and sends Beth to meet with Hope.

"How's things goin' with Luke?"

"Good so far."

"Is Luke someone to start datin'?"

"Why're ya askin' that? Do you know somethin' I don't?"

"No."

"You've been pushin' me to talk to Luke for months. Now y'all sound like you want me to pull the reins back."

"I'm just lookin' out for ya. Luke seems nice but he could still leave. You rushed when you married Joe. I don't wantcha repeatin' that mistake."

Hope bristles at Beth's insinuation. "Luke's nothing like Joe. How dare you even think that!"

"Whoa! Hold on. I'm just makin' sure y'all're thinkin' clearly this time. I'm on your side."

"It doesn't seem like it. I'm a grown woman. I'm gettin' to know Luke more every day. He's been hurt like I have but he's bein' honest with me. I'm not pushin' for anything he doesn't want to share yet. I'm not tryin' to ruin my chance with him."

"Okay. Good. I want to see you happy. I'm here if you wanna talk."

"Your support means a lot but trust me with Luke. My eyes are open. And so's my heart."

SIXTY

Luke watches a Monarch Butterfly flutter past on a warm breeze headed for a yellow flowering Cassia bush. *'Thanksgiving Eve is very different here.'*

Luke spots a green anole dart out nearby to catch a pesky fly. *'Chicago's cold. Everything's dead. Butterflies, dragonflies, and lizards still move 'round here 'n I don't hafta wear a winter coat.'*

Katie observes Luke's serene moment on the deck. *'Luke might've found peace.'* She steps outside. "Mornin' Luke. Do ya need anything?"

"Mornin' Katie. I should be askin' you that. How's your shoulder?"

"Better. I hate this sling."

"Can I ask you a question?"

"Shoot."

"When's Texas at its prettiest?"

"I'm biased. I'd say every day. For tourists, I'd say springtime when the Bluebonnets 'n wildflowers are bloomin'."

"I didn't pay attention this spring."

Katie's husband joins her with two cups of coffee. "Here darlin'. Howdy Luke. Whatcha up to?"

"Howdy Steve. Enjoyin' some peace 'n quiet."

"Luke, Texas is prettiest when you're starin' into your loved one's eyes, right honey?"

"You're so right, darlin'."

The harmonious sounds of birdsong and buzzing insects enhance the tranquil morning until several horses snort and whinny. Luke stands, stretches, and tips his hat. "That's my call to let the horses exercise."

Luke heads for the barns. *'March seems like a lifetime ago. I don't feel lost anymore. I have two good reasons to stay now.'*

Billy, Cody, Henry, and Jack are brushing horses before sending them out.

"Hey Luke, we're goin' out for a drink tonight. Wanna join us?"

'I am accepted here.'

Hope interrupts the moment. "Luke, I have a question and I want an honest answer."

"Okay."

"Are you gonna leave me?"

Luke comprehends Hope's stressed before giving his answer. "Yes, Hope, I'm gonna leave you. When a raindrop can return to a cloud."

Hope's expression turns from dread to joy after grasping Luke's message and hugs him. "Thank you."

"The guys asked if I wanna join 'em tonight."

"Go. Enjoy. I'll miss you but have fun. We'll have tomorrow."

"Are you sure?"

"Yes. Have fun, but not too much, alright."

"Y'all're so bossy."

"You're spendin' too much time with Faith. Y'all sound like her."

"Don't worry. I'll come home to you."

Luke awkwardly corrects his verbal blunder. "Er, you know what I meant."

"I know what you meant. What you said, it sounded nice."

Luke's called to the office to go over the books with Steve Wright, Chester's accountant. Steve's impressed by Luke's math aptitude and comments after Luke returns to the barns.

"That boy could put me out of a job."

Chester chuckles. "Nah. I've got other plans for him."

Kyle and Henry volunteer to be designated drivers while the guys drink since they have early morning hunting plans.

SIXTY-ONE

Luke breaks away from morning tasks to say hello when Hope and Faith arrive early on Thanksgiving Day. Jake comments to Ben, "Who could've predicted that?"

"Life's full of surprises."

Hope helps Katie with her special brunch before watching the parade. Afternoon temperatures rise into the low seventies for the group ride. Chester pulls Luke aside before the 'Give Thanks' ride.

"Luke, you need to be happy to be successful in life. In order to be happy you need to accept your true self."

Chester pauses for dramatic effect. "Y'all're gittin' to be valuable to the ranch. I wantcha to know that."

"That means a lot. Thank you. I feel part of the ranch now. I was hated in the beginning."

"You weren't hated."

Luke raises an eyebrow.

"Maybe you were hated at first. Especially by Hope."

"Lookin' back, I kinda deserved it, didn't I?"

"Yup."

Luke notices Dottie's acting odd while saddling her. "Hope, come here, Dottie's not right."

Hope approaches and stands in front of Dottie to talk softly and put her arms around Dottie's neck for a couple minutes. Dottie leans heavily against Hope.

"You're learnin' to read horses, Luke. Dottie's tense and needs attention before the ride."

"How'd you know to do that?"

"I've grown up with horses. I understand them better 'n men. Horses get apprehensive at times."

Chester's first to share his thanks in the open pasture. "I'm thankful for everyone and everything in my life and this ranch. And watchin' the Longhorn game tomorrow."

Hope inquires after Luke seems puzzled. "Are you okay, Luke?"

"I remember my dad watching Longhorn games. And Navy games."

Hope smiles, "Your dad had great taste."

Chester's reaction to Luke's comment goes unseen. *'Luke's unaware 'bout parts of his life.'*

Hope adds, "I might have everything I need to be thankful for. Finally."

Wyatt rolls his eyes when Luke thoughtfully replies, "I'm beginning to think so too."

"Really?"

Faith honestly expresses her desire loudly, "I still want a rabbit."

Hope hides her smile. *'Faith's already earned her rabbit.'*

Faith asks to assemble a puzzle with Hope and Luke afterwards then requests that Luke read a bedtime story. Hope's happy to watch Luke give Faith his full attention. *'Luke's truly a godsend.'*

Friday's split between work and the Longhorn game. Chester takes Hope, Faith, and Luke out to dinner and it begins raining on the way home. Hope winks and takes Luke's hand when they get out of the truck.

"Faith, go inside with Grand-daddy. We'll be in soon, okay."

"You want an umbrella?"

"No."

Luke listens to rain droplets softly cascading through Live Oak leaves while Chester leads Faith inside.

Hope suggests, "Let's take a walk."

"In the rain? Without an umbrella?"

"That would ruin the romantic mood I'm tryin' to set."

"I don't wanna ruin that. Can I ask why we're takin' a romantic walk in the rain instead of on a sunny day?"

Hope's voice softens, "Because I've never done it before."

Luke squeezes Hope's hand. "You are now. I won't argue your reasoning."

Hope pulls Luke close by the rodeo barn and delivers a kiss full of desire. "Luke you can touch me anywhere. My body is all yours."

"I've wanted to but didn't want you thinkin' that's all I want."

Hope gazes into Luke's hungry eyes before his passionate kiss precedes his hands wandering around Hope's sensuous figure. He listens while Hope softly moans when his hands caress her breasts. Hope's hands travel down to Luke's butt.

"Mine. All mine."

Luke laughs, "I knew it. You only want me for my body."

Hope grins. "Maybe. Maybe not."

"I'm not a Texas cowboy but I'd like to become someone special for you, Hope."

Hope's taken back by Luke's honestly worried statement. "Luke, a cowboy does what's needed when needed without lookin' for attention. A job well done is its own reward to a cowboy. You've acted that way here on the ranch. With Faith. You are special to me."

"Am I?"

"I was so wrong to say you couldn't become a cowboy. You've proven to be everything I've always known a cowboy to be. Caring. Considerate. Honest. Able. Protective. Loving. You've been all that and so much more. You're as much a cowboy as any wrangler here."

"I don't know what to say."

"I'm sorry I was so mean for so long. You didn't deserve that."

"Yeah, I did. Y'all didn't know me then. I hurt Ben. I let guilt control my emotions and thoughts."

Luke pauses, *'Whoa, that's rather profound.'* "Maybe that's what drew me to you. We've both had guilt and anger affect decisions and choices."

"You could be right. Okay, let's go inside and warm up."

"Do we have to?"

"Yes, yes we do. I need to get Faith in bed."

"True."

"Hope, are you sure 'bout this? I don't know what I offer you."

"Should I choose Wyatt?"

"Um, no."

"Luke, I'm sure. You have more to offer than you realize. And Faith thinks you hung the moon."

Chester notes a new spring in Hope's step. *'Hope lights up like a town square Christmas tree around Luke.'*

SIXTY-TWO

Chester's request to meet off the ranch puzzles Hope.

"Hope, how'd you feel about Luke carryin' a gun?"

"Why?"

Chester pauses, "How much do you trust Luke?"

"Are you askin' for my opinion?"

"Yes."

Hope doesn't hesitate to answer. "I trust Luke completely. He's saved my life. He's saved Faith. Luke's so good to her. He's earned my trust. And you know my history on that subject. Luke's stood up for the ranch hands. I'm fine if Luke carries a gun."

"Good. My decision's based on your answer. You're well-bein's first and foremost for me."

Luke's concerned when Chester calls him to the office mid-afternoon and sees Hope standing next to the desk with a serious expression.

"This doesn't look good."

Chester speaks first. "We discussed a matter involving you. Hope'll explain why you're here."

Luke's confused expression makes Hope smile. "Luke, Chester 'n I decided you should carry a gun."

Luke quietly absorbs Hope's announcement.

"I don't need a gun." *'Do I?'*

Chester interrupts, "Luke, y'all ain't up north anymore. People 'round here settle disputes with guns."

"People up north use guns too."

"True."

Hope comments, "Luke, I want you protectin' Faith 'n I the best way possible. I trust you."

Luke's overwhelmed by Hope's trust in him. "I can't even argue that."

Chester responds, "No, you can't. We don't need your luck runnin' out."

Luke thinks, *'I've never felt needed like this before.'*

Chester switches topics. "Faith brought up Enchanted Rock. Hope, wouldya like to bring Luke to experience more of what Texas has to offer?"

Hope smiles and answers, "Yes. I'd like that very much."

"Enchanted Rock? Is that an amusement park?"

Chester's entertained by Luke's incorrect guess. "Nope. But y'all'll enjoy it with Faith."

"Faith'll be so excited."

"Faith's here? I haven't seen her."

"Faith's helpin exercise Whiskey with Ben."

Hope and Luke head for the riding barn.

"Faith, should we take Luke to Enchanted Rock?"

Wyatt scowls when Faith squeals excitedly. "Yippee. I'd like that a lot."

Hope smiles while Faith celebrates. *'Faith's so happy 'round Luke.'*

"Luke, we're gonna have so much fun together."

"Are there monsters and dragons there?"

"No way. That'd be too scary."

"I don't wanna go then."

"Really?"

"Nope. I'm pullin' your leg, Faith."

Hope enjoys Luke's playful interaction with Faith. *'Maybe I have found a man who could become Faith's dad. Because he wants to.'*

Hope and Faith sleep at the ranch that night. "We'll be gettin' up early. They only let so many people in at a time. The Bluebonnets 'n Indian Paintbrush bloomin' make the spring drive prettier."

"Katie was saying that the other day."

A replication of the Alamo frames a driveway entrance gets Luke's attention as they pass by.

"The Alamo means a lot to Texans, doesn't it?"

"Yes."

Luke spots the earthy hued dome and a line of cars not long after sunrise. Faith leads the way after they park and points to a particular location.

"We're goin' up there."

Luke studies the pink granite batholith. "I don't think you can climb that."

"Faith's a mountain goat up there."

"Try keepin' up with me, Faith."

Faith yells when Luke starts running. "Hey, wait for me. No fair. You didn't say go."

Hope calls out, "Wait for me."

Luke grins after slowing down. "Y'all'll need to keep up with me."

Hope reaches them and states, "I'm with two mountain goats today."

Faith leads Luke up and down rocky formations jutting out as the trio ascends over four hundred feet to the top. Luke studies his surroundings.

"That's steeper than it looks but this view's amazin'. It's beautiful but I feel like I'm on the moon."

Hope gazes deep into Luke's eyes. "Yes, it is and it does."

Luke kisses Hope before continuing to view the rocky formations, prickly pear cactus, and bluestem grasses dotting the pink-hued dome. Green spikey Rock quillwort grows in transient vernal pools.

"There's a few things to see."

Faith and Hope lead Luke to a specific location and point to large rocks nearby.

"Whaddya see?"

"Two big rocks."

"Yes. And?"

"Hold on. They look like the number ten. Cool."

Faith takes Luke to the edge of a vernal pool. "Do y'all notice anything?"

"It's a puddle. Wait. What's moving? Are those shrimp? How'd they get up here?"

"Birds eat eggs and poop 'em out here. Then the eggs hatch."

Hope takes Luke's hand. "There's somethin' else you should see."

"Lead the way."

Faith points out a nearby area.

"What am I looking for?"

Hope hints, "Think ocean."

"The ocean? We're on a small rocky mountain."

Faith adds, "Keep lookin', Luke."

Luke scans the area again. Wait, is that a seal? It looks like a seal resting over there."

Faith moves ahead to explore. "Stay where I can see you."

Hope's expression turns serious. "Why'd you save me?"

"What?"

"That day in the parking lot. Why did you save me? You could've run 'n left me with those guys. I shot at you. You didn't care about me then."

Luke examines Hope's green eyes before pointing at Faith. "That's the main reason right there. I wasn't lettin' Faith grow up without a mom. I couldn't letcha get hurt. I don't run from those situations."

Hope throws her arms around Luke's neck for a long unyielding hug. "I was so mad at Chester for mentioning Faith around you."

"It helped save you."

"Thank you."

"I don't know how to explain it. It was like I had a special connection to you."

Hope kisses Luke passionately.

"Boy howdy. I'll tell ya that every day if it'll get me kissed like that, darlin'."

Luke pauses, "Sorry, I forgot you don't like bein' called that."

"I don't like just anyone callin' me darlin'. You can. And y'all'll keep gettin' my kisses anyway."

"That reminds me. Don'tcha owe Sam a date still?"

Hope answers quickly, "Sam'll never get that date."

"You two'd make beautiful babies."

Hope responds after Faith calls to Luke. "Faith saved your hide, mister."

Luke notices Faith's standing next to a stack of rocks. "Didya build that, Faith?"

"Yep."

"I see others did the same thing. Awesome."

"Let's build one together."

"Alright."

Hope laughs when Luke stacks rocks only to have them topple over."

"This ain't so easy."

Faith helps Luke stack rocks into a decent little tower.

"Not bad for a beginner, Luke."

"Thanks, Faith. Betcha can't catch me."

Faith chases Luke until he lets her catch him. Hope watches Luke pick Faith up and swing her around and hugs her. *Luke makes Faith feel so special. And me too.*

Faith enjoys having someone to chase around the rocky terrain. Hope's eyes well up with tears knowing Faith's happy to play the game with Luke.

'Faith's bonded with Luke. He's so kind 'n caring.'

Hope's heart races when Luke returns to hold her hand. Faith finally proclaims, "Momma, I'm hungry. Can we go eat?"

"Yes Pecan, we can."

Luke surveys the buttonbush, switchgrass, and muhly grasses along with Live Oaks scattered below during the descent. He points out a Spiny Lizard basking on a rocky ledge before it disappears. Several Rock Squirrels scamper about while Bewick's Wrens, Carolina Chickadees, and Yellow-rumped Warblers sing and chirp. A small group of deer leap and run off into the distance near the bottom and

Luke spots an armadillo as well. Hope comments, "They're nocturnal, it's rare to see them now."

Hope heads north on TX-16 to eat at a quaint restaurant on Main Street in Llano. "Faith loves the buttery buns here."

Hope and Faith bring Luke to their favorite shops on the south side of the Llano River. Hope buys Luke a t-shirt that states, 'I wasn't born in Texas but I got here as fast as I could'. Luke winks at Hope before kissing her inside the charming little store. Hope strongly feigns false indignation for his simple kiss.

"Y'all, that's not good enough. You can do better 'n that."

Hope continues her upset pretense through the doorway until Luke reaches for her hand and gently squeezes to get her attention to pull her close. He wraps his arm around Hope's waist and swings her around to dip her backwards. Luke places his hand on Hope's shoulder and plants a long passionate kiss on her pink-tinted lips. A stranger hollers his approval as their kiss ends. Hope gazes affectionately into Luke's eyes while being helped to her feet and barely whispers, "Oh my."

"Is that better?"

Hope lovingly nods while recovering from Luke's surprise kiss. Faith questions Hope.

"Momma, is that what you wanted?"

Hope smiles and rests her head against Luke's shoulder and slides her hand into his back pocket. "Yes, Pecan, that's the kinda kiss I wanted."

The trio walks down to the river bank. Luke spots more rock piles.

"Faith, let's build another rock pillar. But we should include your mom this time."

"Yeah. Let's all build a huge one together."

"Okay, then we'll head home."

Hope glances at Luke. *'Home. Could Luke be my home?'*

Faith sleeps during the drive back to the ranch.

"You tuckered Faith out today."

"Faith tuckered me out too."

SIXTY-THREE

"How was Enchanted Rock?"

"Fun. Not what I expected."

Luke understands why he's training with firearms. *'I need to protect Hope 'n Faith any way possible.'*

Wyatt approaches Luke on the way to the bunkhouse. "Turn around Wyatt."

"Look asshole, you're not gettin' with Hope if'n I can help it."

"You can't help it. It's Hope's choice. Not mine. Not yours. Just hers. Get outta my face."

Wyatt throws a punch only to feel Luke's hand grab his throat.

"Listen dumbass, I will end you. Y'all're a gnat to me, a pest that needs crushin', understand?"

Luke throws Wyatt backwards and walks into the bunkhouse.

Chester calls Luke to the office the next morning. "Take my truck 'n bring this to Hope's office."

"Yes sir." *'A chance to see Hope. She's won my heart but I can't say that yet.'*

Luke drives to Hope's office only to find her in the arms of another man. He sets the carton down and leaves. *I'm not lettin' Hope play me like Linda did. I don't need to see them kiss.'*

Luke returns to the ranch while bitter feelings of agonizing betrayal are revived. *'Linda cheated on me. I'm not lettin' Hope cheat on me like Linda did. Wyatt 'n this guy can protect her.'*

Chester catches sight of Luke traveling fast up the driveway trailing a dust plume.

"Why're ya drivin' like Earnhardt's number three at Talladega? I called Hope 'n found out she never saw you."

Luke glares at Chester, "Hope's seein' someone else."

"No she's not."

"I saw her huggin' another guy through the door. I got cheated on once already this year. Ain't gonna go for two."

Chester notes Luke's distressed state. "I'm callin' Hope to figure this out."

"Go ahead. I'm leavin'."

Wyatt hears their verbal exchange and grins. *'Didn't think Hope would chase the asshole off all on her own?'*

Luke's packing is slowed when Scooter appears to discuss upcoming tasks before leaving for Ireland. Chester knocks on Luke's door.

"Hope's not seein' anyone. 'Cept you."

"That's not what I saw."

Luke hears Hope's voice a couple minutes later. "Luke, I need to talk to you. Privately."

Hope spots Luke's suitcase on the bed. "Don't you dare leave me when I need you most! When Faith'll need you."

Chester worries when Luke angrily explodes. "Get out! I don't ever wanna see you again."

Hope and Luke are shocked by Chester's verbal rage. "Watch your tone mister. Don'tcha dare lift a finger against Hope or y'all ain't leavin' here alive."

Hope thinks, *'Chester sounds like when I was attacked.'* "That wasn't what you think. That was Joe's brother. He was threatenin' me."

Luke's expression alters but his attitude remains. "It looks like you were cheatin' on me. Like Linda did."

"I'm not cheatin'. I've letcha into my heart, Luke."

"How do I know you're not lyin'?"

"I wouldn't let Faith down like that."

Luke's anger softens after Hope's statement.

"You promised to take care of me until Joe's caught. I'm hoping for much longer."

"Linda strung me along 'til she found someone better. What if you're doin' the same?"

Hope recognizes why Luke's so angry. "I'm not Linda. I'm not like her. I don't want anyone else. Not even Wyatt. I wish y'all'd've stopped Ryan from hurtin' me."

Hope starts crying. "I care about you, Luke. I don't wanna lose you. I'm…"

Luke's silent even after Hope rushes at him and throws her arms around him. "Please don't leave me. There's no other guy. I don't want anyone else. I…I…I like you, a lot." *I love you. I can't tell you that yet.*'

Hope releases Luke and sobs uncontrollably. *'This could be my only chance to keep Luke in my life. I'm falling in love with him. Can I tell him without scaring him? Or me? Joe's still ruinin' my life if Luke misunderstands all this.*'

Luke suspiciously asks a question. "How do I know I can believe you?" *'Hope's reaction is similar but different than Linda's.*'

Hope peers into Luke's eyes. "You're the only man I want in my life. In Faith's life."

"I'm stuck here. You go wherever whenever with whoever you want. Even Wyatt."

"I'm not cheatin' on you. Wyatt has no chance now."

Luke examines Hope's moisture laden emerald eyes steadily gazing at him. *'Hope's not lookin' away. She seems truly sad. Her shoulders are slumped. Hope's not lyin'. I waited too long to give Linda a second chance. I won't make that mistake with Hope. She's tellin' the truth.*'

Luke pulls Hope into a comforting hug and hears her breathe a sigh of relief before looking into his eyes again.

"I won't hurt you, Luke. I promise. Stay. Please stay."

"I believe you."

Luke gives Hope several small kisses. "Is that enough kisses to make everything better? Or would you like more?"

Hope smiles. "Yes please. More kisses please."

Chester's happy to see Luke holding Hope's hand while approaching the house. *I'm glad they've worked that out. Hope loves Luke.'*

"You two've taken a big step forwards."

Luke responds, "I'm glad I'm wrong this time."

Hope snuggles against Luke on the couch and gazes lovingly into his eyes. "I'm glad you're here."

Katie watches Hope. *'Hope's reactin' to Luke unlike any other man in her past. Her eyes sparkle like stars. Wyatt's never made Hope this happy.'*

SIXTY-FOUR

Holly enters and sees Hope and Luke cuddling. "What the hell? This is bullshit. I brought him home. Not her."

Chester attempts to speak.

"Save it Grand-daddy. I see who the favorite is."

Holly stomps off to collect clothing to keep at Jazlynn's. *Luke's supposed to be my hook up. I'll break 'em up 'n get Luke back.'*

Holly and Jazlynn scheme how to end Hope's budding relationship with Luke. Holly brings Jazlynn and Colt to the ranch a couple days later to stir up trouble.

"Jazzy, Colt, settle in, I have a few things to get."

Chester hears Holly and steps out of his office. "Holly, I need to talk to you before y'all leave."

Holly stands at attention. "Yessir."

"Don't annoy me."

Holly knows how far she can push Chester without getting kicked off the ranch. Chester rolls his eyes when he sees Colt and Jazlynn. "No trouble, got it?"

"Chester means you, Jazzy."

"No. He means you, Colt."

"I mean all y'all."

Jazlynn leans against Colt and smirks when Hope enters the house. "Um, hello, CJ, Jazzy. Are you two datin'?"

"We're consoling each other for the loss of our true loves. Until you come to your senses."

"Colt, I'm happy with Luke. You've lowered your standards and boundaries."

"Grief'll do that."

Luke sneaks in behind Hope. "I'm happy you're happy with me."

"Shouldn'tcha be workin' in the barns?"

"Yep. I just wanted to say a quick hello."

Jazlynn stands with a devious expression after Hope kisses Luke. "Remember this, Hope. Luke's seen me naked first 'n called me pretty as a peach. I see it in his eyes he wants to hook up with me again."

Hope becomes concerned. "Luke, do you still want Jazzy?"

"Jazzy's tryin' to get a rise outta us. I didn't hook up with her. And I don't wanna now."

"Your eyes spoke to me at the pool. You couldn't keep 'em off my naked body."

Hope pulls away from Luke. "I can't believe it. You do still want Jazzy, don'tcha?"

"What? No! Nothin's happened with Jazlynn. It never will."

"I thought I could trust you. I'm not sure I can. They'll keep chasin' you. I need to pick Faith up. I need to leave."

"Hope, I want you, not her. C'mon, you've got nothin' to worry about."

Katie hears everything and spots Hope leaving. *'Hope's chance for love can't end like this.'*

"Y'all're ugly disgusting human beings. Hope's finally found someone who makes her happy 'n your repulsive game is ruinin' that."

"Katie, I don't care if Hope gets hurt."

Jazlynn glances at Luke, "No one knows how I've been hurt. No one's understood me." *'Would Luke tell anyone?'*

Katie notices Jazlynn's fearful look at Luke.

"Luke, since you'll be free tonight, we can hook up."

Katie studies Luke's reaction as he turns to leave. Colt delivers his own parting shot.

"Hope knows who she can trust. It ain't you. Go home Yankee. You don't belong here."

Luke clenches his fists but exits the house. Katie enters Chester's office.

"I'm on the phone. What's goin' on out there?"

"Hope's lettin' someone interfere with her thoughts 'n feelings. She needs guidance to continue her relationship with Luke."

"Those two gotta learn to work through problems themselves."

"I have an idea. It's a little sneaky and underhanded."

"I'm listenin'."

Chester and Katie enlist the wranglers along with Beth, Jubilee, and JeniMay to show Hope what she has with Luke. The guys drop hints to Luke as well to remind him he's lucky to be dating Hope. Jubilee and JeniMay nudge Hope to keep an open mind about Luke.

"Luke's never made any attempt to date Holly or Jazzy. Even after goin' to the gym with Jazzy. He may've considered her for a moment but said he can only take her in small doses."

Beth speaks bluntly to Hope. "Hope, I love you but you're a moron."

"What the hell? You're supposed to be my friend."

"I am your friend. I'm tellin' you y'all're 'n idiot. You're blowin' a chance at love."

"Luke doesn't love me."

"No? Why do you think he's still here?"

"He just wants to score with me then move on."

"Luke has Jazzy or Holly for that. He's not lookin' for that with you. He hasn't taken them up once. Luke's more like Ben."

"No one's like Ben."

"Luke cares about you and Faith like Ben cares about me and our daughters. There's love in his eyes when he looks at you. Don't throw that away."

"He's gonna leave."

"No. You're pushin' him away. You've never asked him to do one thing. Look how much he's done compared to Colt, Sam, Wyatt. None of 'em add up to what Luke's done. And Joe, well, let's not even go there."

Hope rolls her eyes which fuels Beth's frustrations. "Never mind. Blow any chance at somethin' you've been wantin'. The right guy's here but not for much longer, probably. Go back to Wyatt. You don't want love. I'm done tryin' to help ya. I'm goin' home." *I'm so sick 'n tired of Hope not seein' blessin's in her life. Like Luke.'*

Beth storms out. Hope's left to sift through thoughts, emotions, and Beth's heated observations. Hope watches Faith sleep that night.

'Luke's been good to Faith and me. Was I too hard on him for what happened with Jazzy? He didn't start anything with her. Luke has done more for Faith than Colt, Sam, or Wyatt combined.'

Faith stirs and settles again once she grabs the stuffed elephant Luke won her.

'Beth's right. I'm gonna lose Luke if I don't get past my fears.'

Hope calls Chester in the morning. "Could I talk to Luke today?"

"That's Luke's decision. I'll ask 'n letcha know his answer. Y'all shit on him again and made him feel small 'n unimportant."

"I didn't mean to. I'm coming anyway."

Hope sees Wyatt first. "Wyatt, do you have a minute? Please."

"I'm busy."

"Wyatt, I'm sorry. I didn't mean to lead you on. I got swept up by the past we shared and thought we could get it back."

"We can, Hope"

"No, I was wrong."

Luke spots Hope talking to Wyatt and turns for the riding barn. *'Hope's goin' back to Wyatt.'*

Hope realizes the optics don't look good. *'Dammit. This made things worse.'*

"I gotta go, Wyatt."

"Luke's done with you. He plans to leave."

"Not if I can help it."

Chester steps out on the deck. "Hope, come here. Now."

'Crap. That's not good.' "I need your help, Chester."

"No. You need a butt whoopin' for your behavior."

"I don't wanna lose Luke."

"Could've fooled me."

"Help me. Please."

"If y'all're serious 'bout Luke, go after him. Take a ride. Get away from everything 'n everyone. But it's his decision. I'm not gittin' in the middle anymore."

Ben watches Hope run to the riding barn while calling Luke's name. "Luke, Luke, I need to talk to you."

"I'm busy. We've got nothin' to talk about. You're back with Wyatt."

"No. What? No! I need to apologize."

"I have horses to take care of. Everyone else is busy. Just go already. Find Wyatt."

"Luke, I don't want to fight with you. I am willing to fight for you."

Hope's phone pings. She looks at the message and turns her phone around to show Chester's text. 'Ride Waylon. Talk to Hope. Clear the air 'n decide after that.'

Luke flings the mucking rake against the wall. "Fine. Let's get this over with. I've got work to finish. I don't know why we're doin' this."

Luke's voice cracks to reveal sorrow and bitterness.

Hope thinks, *'This is gonna be tough.'*

Wyatt walks in. "Dump this asshole already. Send him packin'. Come back to me like y'all want to."

"Not now, Wyatt. I wanna be alone with Luke."

"Nope. He's goin' in the trash where he belongs."

Wyatt rushes at Luke. Luke sidesteps him and drives his elbow into the center of Wyatt's back. He drops immediately to the ground and groans in agony. "My back."

"Luke, didja injure him?"

"Take care of him 'n find out. You know you want to."

Luke returns to the rake while Hope observes Wyatt moving his arms and legs. She does a hurried examination and finds Wyatt's not seriously hurt.

"You're lucky Luke didn't cripple you."

Hope turns to see Luke leaving the barn. "Luke, stop! We're not done. Not by a long shot. I'm not givin' up on what we've started."

Hope races to get in front of Luke and puts her hands on his chest to stop him. "I do trust you. It's me I haven't trusted. I need to work on that. You've been honest 'n good with me. And so good with Faith."

"You 'n Linda got strange ways of treatin' men. She slept with another guy 'n still said she loved me."

"I'm not like Linda. Don't compare me to her. I'm sorry I hurt you. I thought I was protectin' myself. My divorce cut me deep 'n I'm still workin' through a minefield of hurt 'n mistrust. Let's go ride 'n talk."

Hope tells Luke much of what she wants him to know on their ride. "I want us on the same page. I'm excited to share Christmas and New Year's with you. It's only been me 'n Faith and the ranch but not someone special."

"Those are family days. I'm not family here. I'm not sure I'm anything here anymore."

"Yes you are, Luke. You mean more here than you know. We could be family."

SIXTY-FIVE

Hope's anxiety level rises and falls like a roller coaster ride while overcoming her fears. December's temperatures drop and rebound while Luke's receptive to the ranch, Hope, and Faith becoming permanent aspects in his life. Hope teases Luke physically and emotionally and encourages the same from him with the potential for more passionate interactions.

Luke wakes early Christmas morning to exercise and care for the horses before church. Danny and Kyle arrive late after oversleeping and find Luke's nearly done. Cody and Jubilee also enter the riding barn.

"Y'all're nearly done? Sheesh! I came to help."

"Jealous? I'm better 'n you now."

"It's a sin to mess with someone on Christmas Day."

"I got this. Y'all head inside."

Luke finishes and changes for breakfast and church. Hope and Faith warmly welcome Luke before service starts.

"Merry Christmas, Luke."

"Merry Christmas, Hope, Faith."

"Santa came to my house last night."

"I knew he would. You've been a good girl."

The group returns to the ranch for Katie's Christmas brunch. Faith runs to Chester's Christmas tree surrounded by gifts.

"Momma, look. Santa came here too."

"Pecan, do you really need any more presents?"

Faith places her hands on her hips and gives Hope a questioning look. "Momma, I'm a kid. There's never enough presents."

Everyone laughs.

"I told Santa not to overdo it this year."

Chester grins, "Santa forgot."

"I'm gonna find all mine."

Chester sips his coffee. "I remember someone else bein' like that."

"Yeah, Holly."

"And you."

Faith shoots a suspicious glance at Hope. "Grand-daddy, is that where I get it from?"

"Yup."

Luke watches the scene and decides to share a thought with Hope. "I wanna tell you somethin'. But don't worry."

"That sounds ominous."

"I think I need to return to Chicago to clear things up with Linda. Like you did with Wyatt. What do you think?"

"I don't know."

Hope frets while Faith hands gifts out until noticing a red envelope propped against the tree stand.

"This has Luke's name on it."

Luke's surprised. "Me? Are you sure?"

Hope realizes, *I didn't even get Luke a card. Now he's thinkin' 'bout Linda.'*

Luke inspects the envelope and looks at Hope. She hesitantly shakes her head.

"I didn't get anything for anyone. I wasn't expecting this."

Chester speaks gruffly. "Just open the dadgum thing already."

Luke opens the envelope and pulls out a card with a snowy landscape on front and quietly reads what's written inside. His eyes dart from Chester to Hope to the card's message again. Hope feels a chill run up and down her spine.

'I don't like the look in Luke's eyes.'

Faith breaks the silence. "What does the card say?"

Hope studies Luke's concerned expression and swallows hard. *'I don't think I wanna know.'*

"Um, okay. It says Merry Christmas. You've earned your release from the Twisted Live Oak Ranch."

Jake hollers, "Best gift yet."

Luke scowls at Jake before asking, "Does this mean I can leave?"

Hope's heart stops. She's clearly distressed knowing Luke's brought up Chicago and Linda. Chester mercifully ends the suspense.

"It's your choice. Y'all don't hafta leave."

Hope's green eyes reveal her dread while Luke ponders his decision. *'Hope seems afraid I'll leave. That's good, right? It means she cares. I'd rather stay.'*

Everyone's guessing during Luke's prolonged muted state. Especially Hope.

'Is Luke gonna leave me 'n Faith? I can't read his eyes.'

Luke's serious tone conveys his decision's conviction. "Chester, I'd, well, I'd like to stay if that's an option."

Jake's disappointed. "Shoot. I'm stuck with him."

Luke's eyes lock on Hope during Chester's response. "That settles that. Faith, couldja get the box Santa hid in the tree?"

Faith peers into the branches. "Hey, there is a box in here. With Luke's name on it."

Luke takes the box and lifts the lid and pulls out an ornament which matches Hope's and Faith's. His name's written decoratively in silver glitter on the shiny blue globe. Hope's emerald eyes shimmer while she cautiously approaches Luke with a small optimistic smile.

"Have I received my real Christmas present? The one I didn't know I needed. I'm sorry, I didn't get you anything. I thought you'd leave after my behavior."

"I think I got two presents today."

Luke hugs and kisses Hope. Faith's unable to stay quiet.

"Does this mean Luke's stayin'?"

Hope glances at Faith. "Yes Pecan. Luke's stayin'."

"Yippee! I get another Christmas present. Luke's a real-life cuddle bear. Promise me you're stayin' at the ranch, Luke."

Luke seems suddenly angered. "I can't do that, Faith."

Hope questions Luke. "What? Why not?"

Luke unexpectedly extends his right arm and makes a fist. "Faith, promises sometimes get broken."

Everyone's fascinated when Luke sticks out his pinky finger. "Let's pinky swear. Y'all know you can't break a pinky swear, right? It's forever."

"That's right, Luke."

Hope watches Luke and Faith pinky swear before Luke wraps her into a strong hug. Faith struggles to speak.

"Luke, I can't breathe. You're squeezin' me too tight."

"What? Squeeze tighter. Okay."

"No. I'm not a toothpaste tube."

"I promise I'm stayin' at the ranch."

Hope adds, "We both get to enjoy our cuddle bear a lot more." *'Faith risked gettin' hurt but stayed open to new possibilities knowing Luke might leave.'*

"Faith, help me find the perfect spot for my ornament."

Luke smiles when Faith points to an open spot next to hers and Hope's. *'Chester left room for mine.'*

Hope notices a tear fall down Luke's cheek. "Luke, what's wrong?"

"Nothing. I feel like I belong somewhere. Like I'm home. Finally."

"You are home."

Chester addresses Faith. "I think one gift was left in your room."

Hope smiles and takes Luke's hand. "C'mon. Let's watch this together."

Faith enters her room and yells, "Momma, I love you so much."

The trio reappears. Luke holds a cage with a baby rabbit inside. Katie hands Luke another envelope.

"Ben 'n Beth asked me to give this to you."

Luke opens the envelope and quietly reads the message before re-reading it aloud. "Remember who you were. Think about who you are. Keep working towards who you want to be. Merry Christmas."

Chester comments, "Wise words to live by. You've walked a hard road but God's been there every step of the way to bring y'all here."

Jake pipes up, "I swear God hates me."

Luke retorts, "God hates that ya swear."

Katie watches Hope during the day. *'Hope's happy but tense.'*

Hope follows Katie to the kitchen. "What's gnawin' atcha, Hope?"

"You know me too well."

"Y'all should be over the moon Luke's stayin'."

"Luke brought up his ex. But that's not all. How do I say this?"

"How 'bout honestly."

Hope hesitates, "I think I'm in love with Luke."

Katie's stoic expression matches her tone. "It's about time y'all figured that out."

"What should I do?"

"First, be honest with yourself. Next, be honest with Luke."

"I'll sound like a lovesick teenager."

"Good. Nothin' wrong with that. I still act like that 'round Steve."

"What if Luke doesn't feel the same way?"

"Honey, are y'all that blind? Luke looks at you like a man in love. Has been for months.

"I'm scared, Katie. I did this before."

Katie cuts Hope off harshly. "With the wrong damned men."

"You sound like you know Luke's the right one."

"Luke's far better than Joe, Wyatt, or anyone else by the way he's treated you. You shot him but he's never really put you down. No one's looked at you like Luke does."

"Could I write it down, put it in an envelope, Luke can read it when I'm not around?"

Katie pauses. "No. But you've given me an idea which might work better."

Hope calms down after listening to Katie's idea before re-entering the living room.

"I'm gonna discuss a few things with Luke on a ride. We'll all ride after that."

Hope smiles, "Givin' Luke the talk?"

Chester grins, "I might start with that."

"Can I come too? Luke can ride me back to the house."

Hope nods, "Sure."

"Alright, c'mon Faith. We'll saddle horses 'n bring her back."

Luke rides up on Waylon. "As promised. One special girl returned to another special girl. Don't miss me too much."

"I'll miss you as much as I want to."

Luke smiles, "Fair enough."

Chester takes Luke into the pasture while Hope and Faith head indoors. Hope notes Luke glances back at her. Faith returns to her new bunny while Hope walks to the window. Wyatt intercepts her, "Y'all're makin' a mistake choosin' him over me. He's not good enough for you."

"Wyatt, you're lucky Luke didn't severe your spine. Or worse. He letcha off easy. Thanks for considerin' me incapable of makin' good decisions."

"He ain't that tough."

"Luke's tougher 'n all y'all."

Hope looks out the window before Luke and Chester disappear. *'Luke asks my approval before doin' anything with Faith. He respects me.'*

Hope's lost in thought and doesn't hear Katie. "Whatcha lookin' at?"

Katie's second attempt breaks Hope's trance. "Hmmm, what?"

"They sure sit horses good, don't they? Who'd've thought Luke could be a cowboy nine months ago?"

Hope faces Katie. "Luke is a cowboy, isn't he?"

"I remember someone declare Luke'd never be one."

Hope smiles weakly. *'I'm embarrassed I misjudged Luke so badly.'* "I didn't know him back then."

"Howya feelin', Hope?"

"Happy. Scared. Excited. Terrified. Hopeful."

"Good. It means you care."

"I always could come to you if I couldn't go to Millie or Chester."

Katie smiles, "I'm always here if y'all wanna talk."

Hope nods while Katie supportively touches her shoulder before returning to the kitchen.

'Love could come to Hope if she stays outta her head and outta her own way.'

SIXTY-SIX

Luke observes the Hill Country greenery with more experienced eyes while a southerly breeze swishes through leafy Live Oaks and Ashe Junipers, also known as Cedars by the locals. Prickly Pear cactus and large Agave the guys also call Century Plants dot the landscape.

"Those Cedars'll be makin' people miserable soon with their greenish-yellow pollen explodin' to cover everything. We call it Cedar Fever. Begins roundabouts now 'n goes through February."

The sinewy trunks and branches of the cedars fascinate Luke. *It reminds me of an Orangutan's outstretched arms.*

"Do you understand what it means to be Texan?"

Luke shrugs. "Not really."

"It ain't about the drawl, boots, or jeans. Real jeans, not designer jeans. It ain't about cowboy hats or sittin' high on a horse like this."

"I'm confused. Isn't that bein' Texan?"

"Nope. That represents Texas. Bein' Texan is bein' proud of our state 'n country. It's not gittin' pushed 'round or lettin' someone take what belongs to you without a fight. We ain't lettin' anyone tell us how to live our lives. It's about bein' true 'n honest to yourself and everyone around you. It's havin' the right to bear arms to defend yourself and your loved ones. It's bein' there for people. Everyone forgets Texas became its own Republic after defeatin' Mexico in 1836. Hence the Lone Star state."

Chester pauses to catch his breath.

"Bein' Texan's becomin' your best every day for yourself and God. He gives all this so we can do as we please. People get uncomfortable nowadays hearin' that because politicians 'n people are tellin' 'em we should hate God and America's freedoms. Go live in Russia, Cuba, or somewhere like that for a year. It'll change your mind right quick."

Luke wonders, *'Why's Chester talkin' deep about Texas and bein' Texan?'*

"I was born in a different time. I'm baffled by what's happenin' now. Y'all can get back money, friends, things ya lost, but y'all can't get freedom back once you lose it. People nowadays are givin' it up left, right, 'n down the middle 'cause of lies."

Luke ponders Chester's points.

"Outsiders don't understand our pride for Texas. We push freedom here with fewer restrictions. We certainly don't want lyin' politicians controllin' us. Most politicians are power hungry 'n have their own interests in mind, not ours. Us Texans are born with a spirit y'all don't find anywhere else."

Chester pauses, "Do y'all have any questions?"

Luke shakes his head. *'What do I ask after that?'*

Life's road is full of forks to challenge us. We need to be brave enough to make the right choices if'n we want what's good for us. That helps us determine what direction to travel. This ranch, Hope, Chicago, these are forks in your road. Forcin' y'all to choose how to live your life. And where. And who with. I think if y'all really loved that girl up north you'd've never left her. And you'd've left here if Hope hadn't won your heart already."

Chester's bold honesty stuns Luke.

"I never tried bein' better for Linda. I never set goals. I'd like to be better for Hope. And for Faith."

"Be better for yourself first."

"Why here? Why now?"

"Love. True love inspires us to change so we don't disappoint someone special. Happened to me with Millie. It's happenin' to you with Hope."

Luke glances at Chester. *'Chester's giving me permission to be with Hope. But why?'*

"I'm done ramblin'. Consider it my gift today. Be happy, live life to the fullest. Stop punishin' yourself."

Luke nods acknowledgement. "I do like it here. I haven't admitted that before. I feel connected here somehow. The horses've even become likable. I didn't think that was possible."

Chester laughs before sharing another serious thought.

"You know Hope's worked hard to build a successful practice, right?"

"Yeah, I know."

"Hope still wants to be cared for."

Luke's unsure what Chester's alluding to. "I know Hope's life ain't been as easy as I thought but how do you mean? I understand why she treated me so badly for so long."

"Good. Now what exactly are y'all gonna do about Hope?"

"I'm not sure. We've been honest with each other. I know how I feel about Hope but I have doubts about me. About a good future for us. Am I good for Hope 'n Faith? I don't want to fail them."

Chester replies, "Here's my two cents on that. Regrets'll eatcha alive. Success is the result of a hundred percent effort."

"I see your point."

Chester bluntly asks, "Do you love Hope?"

"Yes."

"Worryin' accomplishes nothin'."

Chester's quiet until they reach the barn.

"Luke, love yourself for who you are 'n someone'll love ya wholeheartedly. Accept your faults knowin' y'all can change 'em. Let go of anger. Accept the good, bad, and pain you'll deal with and life changes for the better. Bad happens but it can be turned around to somethin' good. Life's a never-ending lesson about change."

Luke's unaware of the full extent of Chester's message. Luke notes Chester's expression at the stairs.

"Y'all've got somethin' else to say. It shows on your face."

'Luke reads me too well.' "If ya live in fear, you're livin' in the dark. If you're not afraid to feel pain then you're also able to live life fully."

"Sounds like that sums up life in a nutshell."

"Shut up, smart ass. I've been busier 'n a cat coverin' crap on a marble floor educatin' y'all on life. Chase your dreams. Make 'em come true."

Hope smiles when the men enter the house. Luke stops by the door to study Hope's brilliant green eyes.

'I don't think Hope's looked at me quite like that before.'

Hope approaches and takes Luke's hat and sets it on her long wavy black hair. Luke takes in the sight.

"I was told if a woman wears a cowboy's hat it means she's interested in him. Is this true?"

"It's very true in this case."

Luke tips the hat back and leans in to sweetly kiss Hope before wrapping her up in his arms. Hope feels an incredible and undeniable new attraction to Luke.

'This is how love's supposed to feel.'

Hope quizzes Chester during the afternoon ride. "Why's Luke ridin' Waylon instead of you?"

"Luke can handle Waylon. I trust 'em together."

They check the Longhorn paddock before returning to the barn. Hope watches Luke rub Waylon's neck before leading him into his stall.

"Chester, Luke doesn't fear horses anymore, does he?"

"Naw. You'd think he grew up 'round 'em, wouldn'tcha?"

"You have a knack for trainin' people."

Luke winks at Hope. "I'll join ya after takin' care of the horses."

Holly arrives alone to celebrate her birthday but her sulking attitude mutes the festive atmosphere. It's clear she's unhappy to see Hope with Luke and half-heartedly participates during her cake presentation. Holly brings Faith a gift but nothing for anyone else. She shows little interest for Hope's generous gift card to her favorite clothing store.

"Hey sis, let's go shopping together soon, okay."

Holly bitterly responds, "We'll see."

Hope asks Chester about Holly's standoffish behavior when they're alone in the kitchen. "Why's Holly so upset tonight? It's her birthday."

"Holly's mad you're datin' Luke."

"I should talk to her, right?"

Hope cautiously approaches Holly. "Can we talk? What's troublin' you, Holly?"

"Don't act all innocent. I've got nothin' to say to you. I just wanna get through this 'n leave. Jazzy's got somethin' better planned."

Hope returns to Chester. "Is Holly mad 'bout me 'n Luke?"

"Holly's pissed about somethin' I'd never let happen. Her 'n Luke's like a dog that won't hunt."

"I feel bad. Am I a terrible sister?"

"No. You're living the life you're meant to."

Holly leaves without saying goodbye to anyone.

SIXTY-SEVEN

Chester analyzes Hope and Luke's body language throughout Christmas day. *'They can admit lovin' each other but not to each other. The past has gotta be gettin' in the way.'*

Chester takes matters into his own hands. "Hope, Luke, I'd like to see you in the kitchen."

They're confused when he closes the door.

"Have y'all heard the expression the road less travelled?"

Hope and Luke nod.

"Do ya understand what it means?"

Luke's ready to respond but pauses, "No. I don't actually."

Hope agrees. "I've never given it any thought."

"Here's my take on it."

Luke glances at Hope with a wry little smile. "Oh oh. Here comes another Chester lecture."

Hope giggles until seeing Chester's glare. "Oh, you're serious."

"Both of ya shut up 'n sit down and listen!"

They answer as one. "Yes sir."

Hope sits and reaches for Luke's hand.

"Too many people fail to step outside their comfort zone. New roads if you will. They stop chasin' dreams 'n settle for a life they think gives 'em security but lets dreams die long slow deaths. They hate their jobs but refuse to change outta fear of failure. They don't challenge themselves to reach new goals 'n create a better life."

Luke shifts in his chair. *'That's meant for me.'*

"These people merely survive, sort of, until they die under a pile of regrets."

Chester watches Hope lean against Luke.

"There's a smaller group who continually take risks to reach new goals and seek rewards life offers even if they occasionally fail. This is the road less travelled. They don't let life just happen."

Hope glances at Luke while thinking, *'Where's Chester goin' with this? I usually recognize his point already.'*

"You've lived guarded lives. You're both at crossroads. A road to Damascus moment. Understand upcoming choices 'n figure out what's right 'n wrong for the present and future. Leave the past behind y'all. Think. Talk. Decide whatchy'all want next."

'Ah. There it is.'

Chester leaves the kitchen so Hope and Luke can decipher his message. Luke notices Hope's preoccupied gaze.

"What was all that about?"

Hope shakes her head while multiple thoughts surge through her mind. *'I know what Chester's tellin' me. It's about my future. With Luke. I need advice from Katie 'n Beth.'*

Luke approaches Chester after everyone leaves. "Can I talk to you in your office?"

"Sure, what's up?"

Katie sneaks over after Luke closes the door over. *'I'm curious what Luke's gonna say.'*

"I've been thinkin' about what you said earlier."

"Good. You should."

"I'm worried."

"What's to worry about?"

"Everything. I can't support Hope or Faith. How can I stay here knowing that? I could be the worst thing to happen to Hope."

Katie's disgusted when her phone rings and has to scurry away to answer. *'Damn. I'll miss Luke's conversation.'*

"Luke, y'all ain't the worst thing to happen to Hope. Joe was. Are ya suddenly able to see the future? Do ya know something now you didn't earlier?"

"Chester, I'm broke. I have no job. I don't own anything. That's not a good future."

"Hey, whoa, hold up."

"Technically, I'm not taking care of myself here. How can I take care of anyone else? That's irresponsible."

"Y'all're overthinkin'. You're bein' responsible. Live one day at a time. See what happens. Tomorrow's unknown until its yesterday's news. Get some sleep. We've got a busy week."

Katie barges in after Luke leaves.

"Who lit your butt cheeks on fire?"

"Are you really gonna let Luke leave? After everything that's brought him 'n Hope together."

"It ain't polite to eavesdrop."

"You're gonna let Luke skate outta here."

"Just how much of our conversation didja hear?"

"Enough."

"So you heard Luke bein' responsible? And me tellin' him to take it one day at a time?"

Katie's attitude shifts while exiting the office but returns a moment later.

"Now what?"

"I come in peace. And on behalf of Hope."

"How so?"

"Keep Luke busy this week."

"Y'all know the final week's always busy."

"Hope's fixin' to figure how to tell Luke somethin' important. She needs time to prepare."

"Done."

The workload exhausts the guys during the week but New Year's Eve comments pop up daily. The younger guys debate which bars to go to while the rest look forward to quiet nights with spouses and family. Ben's curious what Luke has planned.

"How ya gonna celebrate your first New Year's Eve in Texas?"

"I don't know. I don't have a car, money, or anywhere to go."

"What about Hope?"

"She hasn't mentioned anything. She has Faith to consider. We haven't talked much this week."

Ben pauses, "Hope 'n Faith usually come here. Talk to Hope."

"I'll call her later."

Luke calls from Chester's office. "Howdy Hope. Do you have New Year's Eve plans?"

"Yeah. Faith 'n I have plans tomorrow night."

"Oh, okay. It's kinda late askin' for a date anyway."

Hope giggles. "Luke, we're comin' to the ranch. Chester hasn't toldja yet, has he?"

"No. He seems to've forgotten that detail. I'm lookin' forward to seein' you and Faith. I miss you."

Luke informs Ben. "Chester's forgotten to tell me Hope 'n Faith will be here tomorrow."

"Chester's messin' with ya."

Hope arrives early and happily kisses Luke. Faith gives him a dirty look and points to her cheek.

"Ahem."

"Don'tcha worry Miss Faith, I'd never forgetcha."

Luke picks her up and blows a raspberry against her cheek. Faith squeals with delight.

"That's not what I wanted."

"Excuse me. The little lady knows what she wants."

Luke gets two thumbs up after kissing each of Faith's cheeks.

"I've missed ya both. We've been busy. And tired."

Hope notes, *'Luke's mentioned twice how he's missed me, us. Could this be the last year I'm livin' like this?'*

"We've missed you too." Hope glances at Katie. "We can only stay till ten o'clock. I have something to do tomorrow."

"I'll take what I can get."

Luke enjoys the evening with Hope and Faith. He gives each a kiss after walking them to Hope's truck.

"Happy New Year."

Chester meets Luke at the door. "I've got a task for you early tomorrow."

"Good thing I'm not stayin' up late then."

Luke misses Chester's sly smile after turning towards the bunkhouse.

Two Mourning Doves greet Luke from the deck overhang the next morning. "You two again?"

He realizes Hope's truck is parked out front. *'Hope must be dropping Faith off.'*

Luke hears a ruckus occurring upstairs before entering the kitchen. "Should I go help?"

"Nah. Hope 'n Faith are rearrangin' the bedroom a bit. They've got it."

Luke eats and washes his plate and waits for Chester. Hope, Faith, Ben, and Chester finally come down to find Luke sitting on the couch. Hope catches sight of Luke and takes in a deep breath and lets it out before approaching with an apprehensive gaze. Hope shares a small kiss before pulling away.

'Hope's wearin' make-up. And perfume. What's she doin' today?'

Luke's concerned after Hope's cool greeting. Chester and Ben head to the office to talk.

"Everythin' could change 'round here today for Hope 'n Luke."

"I'm crossin' my fingers. They deserve it."

"They've travelled bumpy roads. Started off hatin' each other before learnin' to be open with each other. And trust each other, I hope. Hank's known how to push Luke outside his comfort zone for positive results. He's had a special connection with Hope her whole life to get her through tough times."

Luke stares at Hope. *'I love Hope. And Faith. How do I tell her?'*

SIXTY-EIGHT

Luke's unaware Hope's arrived specifically to see him. Beth and Katie have coached Hope about her future and now she stands nervously in front of Luke wearing a light pink pearl snap button-down shirt, Wranglers, and her boots.

'Luke's gotta wonder why I'm wearin' make-up 'n perfume.' "Luke, I'd like your help today."

"I'd love to but Chester's got work for me today."

Chester and Ben exit the office. "Ain't I taughtcha anything? Y'all go help the lady when she asks."

Ben grins, "I'll manage withoutcha today. Go."

Luke responds positively, "Ya don't need to tell me twice." *I'm closer with Hope in ten months than four years with Linda.'*

Luke's enthusiastic reply soothes Hope's nerves. Chester winks supportively when Hope glances at him before pulling on her fleece lined Wrangler jacket.

'I hope this works. Hope finally admitted how she's feelin' 'bout Luke to me. She ain't given a man a chance in years.'

Luke's curiosity takes over, "What am I helpin' ya with today?" *'Hope's dressed too fancy for ranch work.'*

"I, uh, have somethin' in town to do."

Hope merges onto U.S. 183 which prompts Luke to ask, "Is this for the ranch?" *'We're headin' south.'*

"Possibly."

Luke rethinks the situation. *'This sorta feels like a couple's outing.'* "Is this a work errand?"

Hope worries, *'Don't ask too many questions. I'm barely holdin' myself together as it is.'*

Luke's quiet when they merge onto I-35 and exit on Sixth Street. Hope sighs nervously.

'Hope's awfully tense. Why?'

Luke notices the closed businesses. "I spent my first day in Austin here."

Hope smiles shyly. "We're almost there." *'Is Luke thinkin' about Holly?'*

Luke inquires after Hope turns left onto Congress Avenue. "Are we touring my route of Austin?"

"Are we?" *'And where you met Holly. Stop it, Hope. Get a grip. Luke's here with me. Don't blow this.'*

Hope drives several blocks south of the Colorado River and backs into a parking spot near a couple of cars. She takes a deep breath and slowly lets it out. "We're here."

Luke joins Hope on the sidewalk in front of a woman's clothing store and looks around. "I'm confused. Why are we here?"

Hope shivers while reaching for Luke's hand when a passing cloud obstructs the sun's warming rays.

"Are you cold? Take my jacket too."

"I'm okay. I'm not cold." *'I'm nervous.'* "Let's walk."

Hope leads Luke back towards the river.

'Where's Hope takin' me?'

Luke spots a sign for coffee as they near the corner of Congress and James Street. *'Did Hope drive us here for coffee? We could've stayed at the ranch for that.'*

Luke looks past the large red sphere on the roof and through Live Oaks at Austin's skyline. He refocuses on the coffee house name. *'Jo's Coffee.'*

Hope turns the corner and spots several people standing near the wall and grows annoyed. *'This can't be happenin'. I came early to prevent this.'*

Hope's grip tightens on Luke's hand. *'Why are these people here?'*

Luke's concerned. *'Why's Hope so upset?'* "We can go somewhere else."

Hope barely looks at Luke.

'Are we here so Hope can dump me in the city?'

Hope's relieved when the people depart the area. Luke asks, "Am I in trouble?"

"No. Everything's good. I'm just bein' silly, I guess."

Hope's erratic behavior worries Luke.

"Follow me. Please."

Hope's pleading green eyes passionately implore Luke to follow her. Luke's perplexed by Hope's smitten gaze when they lock eyes.

"Where?"

Hope leans against the wall by some words painted on it but Luke's focused on Hope.

'Hope's acting really strange this mornin'.'

Luke ignores what he perceives to be graffiti and watches Hope's expression turn fearful.

'Luke's not happy.'

Hope glances at the words and back at Luke. His eyes shift to the wall. *'i love u so much'.*

Luke's stunned and re-reads the words and glances at Hope. She's anxious, frightened and ready to burst into tears.

'Luke doesn't feel like I do. He doesn't love me.'

Luke slowly processes Hope's gesture until comprehending her romantic act and smiles. *'Hope loves me.'* Exhilaration replaces Luke's worries and strongly hugs Hope and feels her heart pounding and body trembling. He places his hands on Hope's flushed cheeks and leans in to sweetly kiss her. The sun breaks through to brighten the moment.

'Does Luke understand what I'm sayin'?'

Hope's emotional roller coaster ride through uncertainty to worry to fear and anxiety turns to relief and elation.

"I like you too."

"What?"

Hope experiences near heart failure after realizing Luke's less than favorable remark. Her joy diminishes to disbelief until Luke smiles and speaks again.

"Gotcha! I love you too."

Hope punches Luke's arm.

"Ouch."

Luke grins mischievously while rubbing his arm. "I had to get even for you shootin' me."

Hope interlocks their fingers to hold hands while Luke gazes into her sparkling green eyes.

"Are you sure about this, Hope? You've been through a lot."

Hope treasures Luke's loving gaze. "I couldn't've done this if I wasn't certain."

"I'm speechless. Nobody's done anything like this for me."

"There's somethin' else I hope you agree to."

Luke's spellbound by Hope's soft, sweet Texas drawl. "I'll agree to whatever you ask."

Hope whispers into Luke's ear, "Take me home 'n let me wear my lipstick off on you and become your lover."

Luke looks deeply into Hope's twinkling eyes. "Really?"

Hope bites her lower lip. "Yes."

Her shy smile grows while trying to keep eye contact with Luke's hungrier loving gaze. She takes his hand to return to the truck.

"You drive. I know you won't steal my truck."

"Nope. Just your heart."

Luke unlocks the truck and opens the door but pulls Hope close. "Wouldja hold it against me if I toldja y'all had a beautiful body?"

Hope catches Luke off guard when she wraps her legs around his waist and her arms around his neck.

"How's this for an answer."

Luke instinctively places his hands on Hope's butt to keep her from falling. Hope feels chill bumps and lovingly kisses Luke.

"I love your answer."

Hope feels a long forgotten yearning while Luke's hands are below her beltline. *Luke can give me chill bumps any time.*

"Take me home. I'll make you a very happy man."

"I'll make you a very happy woman too."

Luke helps Hope into the truck and she places her hand on his right knee and moves it until her fingertips run up and down his zipper. Hope feels Luke's physical reaction to her touch.

"Touch me everywhere you want to." *'We can't get home fast enough.'*

Hope exclaims, "I love you! I'm in love with you, Luke."

Luke thinks, *'Hope's Texas drawl never sounded softer, sweeter, or more angelic.'*

"I love you too."

Hope surprises Luke in the driveway. "Faith's stayin' at Chester's tonight."

"So we have all day and night alone together?"

"Yes. I'm all yours all day 'n night."

SIXTY-NINE

Hope's undoing Luke's belt and jeans and pushing his jeans down before the door's fully closed so her fingertips touch his hardened shaft. Luke unbuttons Hope's shirt.

"It has snaps, just rip it off lover."

Luke uses one quick motion to separate Hope's shirt from her body and let it fall to the floor. His eyes drop down to Hope's bare chest to admire her ample, perfectly shaped breasts.

"I didn't wear a bra so you can touch me quicker."

Luke gently caresses Hope's breasts. "I have been wantin' to get you naked."

Hope moans with delight.

"That sounds wrong. I don't want you thinkin' I only want your body."

"I've been wantin' you naked too."

Hope's eyes close partially while enjoying Luke's hands on her body. "I began wonderin' if y'all wanted me naked like you did with Jazzy."

"Don't mention her. There's no comparison."

Hope's confidence soars after Luke's statement. *'Luke's makin' me so wet. I want him heart, soul, and body. Bein' topless with Luke is way better.'*

Luke's eyes lock on Hope's eyes before continuing to admire her curvaceous body. "You're so beautiful. I'm so in love with you too."

"Luke, I'm so wet 'n ready. Take me to bed."

Hope yearns to endlessly please Luke and let him fulfill her sexual desires. Luke undresses Hope and watches her take his hands and put them on her breasts again.

"Touch me. Love me."

Hope strips Luke while his hands explore her bare body. His hands travel downward to Hope's hips and vaginal area. Hope moans pleasurably when Luke's finger tenderly touches her inner velvety moistness. She removes his hand after a couple minutes of utter bliss.

"Let's continue this in my bedroom. Do anything you want with me."

Luke affectionately places his hand on Hope's waist and guides her upstairs. He picks Hope up and sets her down on the bed and lies on top of her.

"I'm happy I'm naked with you, Luke."

"All day 'n all night."

Hope shudders and blushes. "I can tell you're happy bein' naked with me." *'It feels so good bein' completely naked with Luke.'*

"I don't wantcha wonderin'."

Luke holds Hope's hands and stretches his arms out to touch the headboard and passionately kisses her soft pink lips for several minutes.

'Luke'll make me climax with his kisses.'

Luke shifts to kiss Hope's cheeks, then her nose. Next he kisses her chin and watches her smile after each attentive kiss. Luke kisses her neck and nibbles her earlobe which induces another pleasurable moan. Hope's moans intensify when Luke kisses each erect nipple before kissing his way down her stomach. He releases Hope's hands and places his on her graceful thighs before repositioning to spread her legs apart.

'I've dreamt of Luke doin' this. I never thought it would happen.'

Hope quivers when Luke's lips touch her vaginal area to build further arousal and cause Hope to surrender all control and inhibition. Luke listens to Hope beg him not to stop his erotic oral foreplay while enjoying a sensual phenomenon she's never experienced.

"Don't stop. Keep doin' whatchur doin'."

Luke willingly satisfies Hope's request. Her body tingles from head to toe while placing her hand on Luke's head to encourage him. Hope moans with pure pleasure and passion while climaxing and enjoys Luke pleasing her for several more minutes. She pulls Luke up to kiss him wildly and releases all inhibitions to allow an animalistic combination of love and lust take over after tasting Luke's moisture laden lips.

"Luke, did you enjoy that as much as I did?"

"More than you know."

Hope's next kiss conveys her carnal desires. "Do that to me again. Please."

Luke smiles, "I'll do that every day if you'd like."

Hope whispers sexily, "Hey cowboy, how 'bout slidin' your big gun into my holster 'n firin' off a few rounds?"

Hope's reddening cheeks enhance her erotically captivating smile. "I can't believe I just said that."

"Say that to me every day for the rest of our lives together."

Hope's eyes possess a burning desire. "Luke, I'd like you here with me for the rest of my life. Not a short time."

Luke gazes at Hope. "I'm yours forever, Hope."

Hope feels Luke shift and readily guides him inside her willing body. She feels his hardness penetrate deeper to initiate a blissful experience Hope thought she'd never feel again. *I've missed this. I want this forever with Luke.'*

Luke's intense gaze matches Hope's yearning and strong desire for his loving affection. Hope's moan full of pure ecstasy entices her to pull Luke down while aggressively thrusting her hips upward. Luke's rapidly driven deep inside to begin sharing their first sexual encounter together. Hope worries after they finish their initial saturated moments of climaxing passion. *'Was I good enough?'*

"Luke, I'm nervous. Was I any good? I haven't done this in over eight years."

"Hope, I've never felt so close to anyone like I do with you. That's the best sex I've ever had."

"You're not sayin' that to make me feel better, are ya?"

"I wouldn't say it if it weren't true."

"Luke, be honest, do you only want me for my body?"

"Yes, I want your body. I don't apologize for that."

Hope attempts to move under Luke. "But I also want you for more than this. I'd like to build a life with you. And Faith."

Luke's lovingly spoken words relax Hope. "I believe you. Because you included Faith." *Wyatt never did that.*

"I do want this every day. And walks in the rain. And everything else we do together. I pray you'll wanna spend your life with me."

"Luke, I love you. I want to spend my life with you. And I'd like this every day too."

Hope passionately kisses Luke. "I'll be your lover for life. Especially if y'all keep doin' what you just did. I'll never leave you."

Luke smiles and kisses Hope. "That sounds good to me. This feels good too."

"Chester had his reasons to keep you at the ranch. I have my own reasons to keep you here."

"Hank's babblin' and Chester's decision got me thinking 'bout stayin'. I learned there was more to you than I first thought. I'd've never been here if Ben hadn't put me on Bullet."

"Ben putcha on Bullet? That's how you were in a restricted area."

Hope's comment reveals why she reacted the way she did for so long.

"You didn't know that? That explains a lot." Luke chuckles, "These past ten months in Texas have been the craziest of my life."

Luke pauses to reflect on those changes. "I nearly didn't board the bus that brought me here."

"I'm glad you did."

"It's like something made me get on."

"Now you're here. With me."

Hope's hands glide up and down Luke's muscular back. Luke shudders when Hope plays with his hair.

"I need to cut my hair. It's too long."

Hope gives out. "Don'tcha dare! This suits you. I like it this way. Y'all're way more sexy wearin' your cowboy hat now. You're like a cowboy and a medieval knight. You're my handsome cowboy knight."

Hope's other hand travels downward. "And you've got a great lookin' ass. I love it. And you."

Luke shudders while Hope's fingers softly touch him. She whispers after feeling his physical reaction.

"You have something I'd like to enjoy again."

"Are you ready for it again?"

Hope rolls Luke over to get on top of him. "I'm beyond ready. My turn on top. Enjoy me as often as you'd like."

Luke remembers his dream from months ago. *'Did I dream this? Did I know my future already?'*

Hope's long black waterfall curls fall around Luke's face while she gazes down at him. Luke's wanting eyes look into hers while his hands lovingly caress her breasts. Hope leans down to kiss Luke and playfully purrs for him.

"I'm so happy right now."

Hope's sultry expression and sexy green eyes mesmerize Luke. *'Hope's eyes hunger for passion and love.'*

Hope positions herself so Luke re-enters her for more love making. She excitedly informs Luke, "It's like a big, hard stick of dynamite exploding pure pleasure deep inside me when you climax."

"I'm so turned on too."

Hope's heart beats faster from Luke's deep loving touch inside her and releases an erotic groan while physical desires intensify.

"You make me wetter than I've ever been."

"I'll make you wet as often as you want."

"Every day. Please. I've missed this. It's so much better with you."

"Is once a day enough?"

"No. I want more than once a day. If that's okay with you?"

Luke embraces Hope and kisses her until she asks, "Are y'all hungry for somethin'? Besides me? I wanna stay naked all day."

"My love", *'That sounds so good to say'*, "I wantcha naked all day too. We can get a snack and enjoy each other for dessert."

Hope leads Luke to the kitchen. "What if someone sees us naked?"

Luke nibbles Hope's earlobe and kisses her neck. "Let 'em see what they can't have."

Hope strokes Luke's hardened shaft. "Hey cowboy, wanna share this with me again?"

Luke places his hands on Hope's waist and moves her backwards against the counter. "Let me in."

Hope sits on the edge of the counter and spreads her legs and erotically groans while sexually engaging Luke again. She pulls Luke closer and rhythmically gyrates her hips against his to enhance her erogenous reaction until climaxing. Hope whispers, "I'll never look at my kitchen the same way again."

Luke smiles when Hope whimpers when he separates from her.

"Y'all know how to make me happy, don'tcha Luke?"

"I'm learnin' what you like. And how much."

Hope's expression turns worrisome. "Luke, am I askin' for too much sex?"

Luke laughs. "I'm a guy. There's no such thing as too much sex. Especially with a drop-dead gorgeous woman like you. That I'm in love with. I might want sex when you don't."

"Don't bet on it. I've missed this. And you're so much better than I imagined. Yes, I've imagined havin' sex with you."

Hope feeds grapes to Luke before teasing a banana with her hands and blushes afterwards. "Look what you do to me. Joe never seemed to want me very much. I thought he cheated on me because I wasn't good in bed. I thought that's why Wyatt left too."

"There's nothin' wrong with you, Hope. You're sexy, beautiful, sensual. I can't get enough of you. I love you."

"Do you mean that?"

"No."

Hope's pleased expression disappears until Luke expands his answer.

"I'm in love with you. Not just for your looks. You make me feel loved. And alive. And wanted. And heard."

"You do think I'm pretty, right? Wyatt's always callin' me hot."

Luke kisses Hope and holds her close. "You're more than pretty or hot. You're beautiful, gorgeous, stunning, breathtaking. A Texas smokeshow with a heart of gold."

Luke kisses Hope's lips then her neck before bending down to kiss her erect nipples and return to her lips. Hope's come get me smile precedes her invitation.

"I'm ready for you again, lover. Come get me in our bedroom."

'Hope said our bedroom.'

Hope seductively lies down and spreads her legs to welcome Luke inside her again. "I want you so much."

Luke listens to Hope's guttural groan laced with passion after she wraps her legs around him. "Do this with me forever."

Luke issues an order. "Unlock your legs."

'Oh oh, did I do something wrong?'

Hope uncrosses her legs and gets surprised when Luke brings her feet up to his shoulders to create more stimulation.

'Luke feels like he's gettin' bigger inside me.' "I've never done this before. I like it."

Hope passionately moans while Luke thrusts hard and deep until reaching another climax. *'Luke wants me as much as I want him. I see it in his eyes.'* "I'll try any position with you."

"Let's try every position together."

Hope imagines what her sexual future will be like with Luke. Her thoughts produce new desires to discover what's she's been missing. *'I feel so close to Luke emotionally. I'll try anything with him.'*

"Luke, I've never wanted to be with anyone as much as I want to be with you." *'Not even Wyatt.'* "Can we stay naked forever? Sheesh, I sound like Holly now."

"Except you want a lastin' relationship with one person."

"Could we cuddle on the couch?"

"Sure. Do you wanna get dressed?"

"No way. Let's be naked on the couch." *'I wanna erase any memory of Wyatt 'n me on that couch.'*

"I like how you think."

Luke notices Hope's odd expression. "Did I say somethin' wrong?"

"No."

Hope pulls a soft blanket over them. Luke's hands begin exploring her body.

"That's not cuddlin'. That's foreplay."

Luke smiles, "You cuddle you way, I'll cuddle my way. Or should I stop?"

"Don'tcha dare."

Hope's hand travels down to Luke's groin while kissing him. He pulls Hope on top of him and mischievously orders her, "Make me happy. Here. Now."

Hope doesn't hesitate to lower her hips against Luke and enjoy his shaft's insertion once again. "My kitty's so wet. I've never done this on a couch before."

Hope happily moans and rides up and down on Luke until their steamy sexual encounter moistens the couch. "We just christened my couch. This gets better 'n better with you."

Hope pulls Luke to the kitchen. "Fruit's not gonna cut it. I wanna do this all night."

Luke helps cook the meal and enjoys kissing and feeding Hope and being fed. Hope leads Luke upstairs and announces, "This is where we'll continue our naked fun."

Hope moves ahead of Luke and climbs onto the bed on her hands and knees and looks over her shoulder with a wanting expression. "I'm ready for another position with you, big boy."

Luke smiles and moves in behind Hope. "I'll make you happy every way possible. And forever too."

"I'd like that. Make me yours 'n I'll make you mine."

Luke enjoys making Hope moan while running his hand through her silky black hair. "You're so sexy."

Hope lowers her head and flings it back to let her hair fly in all directions. Luke playfully tugs on it while Hope drops her head down.

"Oh. You do have control over me, don'tcha? What wouldja like me to do, lover?"

Luke places his hands on Hope's hips and thrusts deeply. "Enjoy every moment with me."

"Mmmmm, ooooh. I am."

Hope's sweet voice resonates with desire while Luke causes another ultra-moist reaction. She utters a sexually explicit request to further arouse Luke and feels his physical response.

"I love hearing your beautiful pink lips say that. Say it again."

"Really? You'd like to hear me say that again?"

"Yes. If you want to. And I'd like to say it to you too."

"Go ahead. Turn me on."

Hope lies next to Luke afterwards and gazes into his eyes. *'Luke loves me. And he wants me to be me.'* "How's my lipstick, lover?"

Luke glances at Hope's lips. "It looks good to me."

Hope yearns for more sex. "Good. I'm not done lovin' on you today."

"I'd make ya put more on if y'all'd worn it off already. I'm not done lovin' on you either."

"I like your thinkin'."

"I love how you love me."

Hope snuggles against Luke's muscular body. *'I'm enjoyin' raw pure intimacy with Luke.'*

"You could choose any man, Hope. I feel lucky to be here with you. I'll do what it takes so you feel the same about me."

Hope's hug tightens.

"I felt so alone and lost when I got here. This feels like home with you."

"I'm overwhelmed. I do understand. I'm surrounded by friends 'n family at the ranch. But I felt like somethin' was always missing. I didn't wanna be a one-night stand or a temporary trophy for some boy but I didn't think I deserved a good man to love me. I realized I could be loved after you saved me. Faith not bein' afraid of you showed me somethin' but I'd been so angry and confused for so long I didn't notice immediately. You broke my barriers down and made me want love again. To let a man love me."

"I do love you. Faith's a great kid. She's so smart and funny. You've done a wonderful job raising her."

"It's more her doing than mine."

Hope clasps her fingers with Luke's and begins crying without warning. Luke pulls her close and kisses her cheek and forehead. *'Hope might be experiencing an emotional release like I did.'*

Hope's thinking, *'I want Luke in my life. And my body. I've kept my guard up for so long. Luke challenged me in all the right ways.'*

Luke reasons, *'Hope won't run if I share everything with her.'*

Hope wipes away tears and smiles. "You must think I'm a crazy emotional girl."

"Quite the opposite actually. You've been through a lot 'n now you're lettin' your guard down. It's overwhelming, isn't it?"

"How could you possibly know that?"

Luke speaks softly, "It happened to me. I finally had to admit to what was true after you broke my walls down too."

Hope optimistically gazes into Luke's hazel eyes. "Does that mean we're meant to be? Forever and ever?"

"I've never felt this before. Hope, you inspire me to be a better man. I thought I knew what love was. You've shown me a whole different side. I meant what I said at the wall today. Nobody's ever done anything like that for me before. The sun wasn't the only light to shine on that moment."

Hope's quiet before acknowledging, "It's the same for me. I got married too young. I thought it was the right thing to do until it all fell apart. Then I got pregnant with Faith. Truthfully, it was fallin' apart long before that. I couldn't admit that though. Chester tried makin' me think before I got married."

"Chester does share advice whether it's asked for or not. But he has helped me. Hank too. Have we gone through what we did to get here and see everything clearly?"

Hope contemplates Luke's assessment of everything. "I agree."

Luke notices Hope's expression change from serious to playful. "Y'all know where I'd like to be right now?"

"Where?"

"Underneath you. If that's okay?"

Luke rolls Hope onto her back and enjoys watching her provocatively spread her long slender legs. "Mount me, lover."

Hope's deeply hidden seductive side longs to repeatedly arouse Luke's sexual desires. *'I understand Holly 'n Jazzy better.'*

"I love hearin' your sweet Texas drawl sayin' that."

Hope wraps her legs and arms around Luke. "I'm yours forever if you'll have me."

Luke views Hope's sparkling green eyes. "Try gittin' rid of me."

Hope's tone turns serious. "No way! I don't wanna lose you."

Luke and Hope wear each other out until finally falling asleep.

SEVENTY

Luke wakes to Hope's soft kisses and smiles at her lying naked in the early morning light with her hand on his exposed groin.

'Hope's so beautiful and irresistible like the first day I saw her. Her waterfall curls are still eye-catching'

Luke realizes something. *'I slept. I didn't have my nightmare.'* "I'd like to wake up and see the sun shine on you every day."

Hope smiles. I'd like that too. After a night full of sex."

"Wakin' up to sex sounds good too."

Luke caresses Hope's breast while she strokes his hardening shaft. Her expression implores for more.

"I'm ready for you, lover."

Luke presses his lips against Hope's and moves with her so she's on her back.

"I'm ready for you."

"You want me as much as I want you."

"My kitty craves your lovin' touch, my love."

Hope feels Luke's strong chest against her. "I'm so wet. I feel like a sex-crazed teenager again."

Luke appreciates Hope's hungry gaze during two romantically engaging encounters. "You're gorgeous anytime but seein' you naked on messed up sheets makes you even more desirable."

Luke slides off the bed and entices Hope to follow him to the bathroom. She's uncertain when Luke leads her to the shower.

"Do I smell?"

Luke laughs. "No."

"Why are we in here?"

Luke turns the water on. "I'm gettin' you wet inside 'n out."

"Are we gonna shower together?"

"Yup. And have sex."

"I've never done this before."

Luke kisses and maneuvers Hope into the shower to allow the warm water to cascade over them. Hope gleefully convulses while Luke begins washing her erogenous areas with her sponge as the steam accentuates the heat of the moment. Luke gently caresses Hope's body and receives a passionate kiss as Hope's desires are heightened before she eagerly reciprocates the loving gesture with Luke. Hope's erotic impulse overtakes her and turns around and leans forward and utters an explicitly lustful request. Hope shamelessly repeats her request while Luke's large shaft deeply enters her while his hands explore her body. He holds Hope's hips to enhance her pleasure while her shyness is overruled by her sexual yearnings. Hope graphically expresses her wants and desires several times during this steamy new experience.

"Can we do this again?"

Luke thrusts deeply to finish. "Yes. We'll definitely do this again."

"You're like a volcano erupting inside me. I love it."

They kiss and hug while drying each other off in the warm, humid setting.

"Luke, you can absolutely enjoy me anywhere, anytime, anyway. Don't hesitate. I won't say no. I promise never to keep sex from you. I want it as much as you do."

"Hope, you'll only need to look at me or touch me and I'll be standing before my jeans hit the floor."

They finally dress to eat breakfast. Hope chooses a cotton dress and shyly glances at Luke while setting their bowls in the sink. She smiles with freshly painted lips.

"I'm in love with the most beautiful woman in the world."

"I accidently on purpose forgot to put panties on."

Hope watches Luke move behind her to press against her body. Hope spins around and drops to her knees and undoes Luke's jeans and looks up to see him smiling. She lightly strokes Luke's erect shaft before using her mouth to pleasure him and listen to his happy moans. Hope stands and kisses Luke.

"I promise to fully deliver next time but I want somethin' else again."

Luke pushes Hope towards the wall and lifts her dress. Hope raises one leg around Luke while they kiss.

"Put your hands on my ass. Drive me wild."

Luke eagerly complies and presses his hips against Hope's and induces erotic groans while repeatedly penetrating deeply. Hope wraps both legs around Luke to share her exhilaration until climaxing. Hope drops her feet down to the floor and crouches down to lick Luke's erection.

"I feel like bein' as naughty as I can with you. I hope that's okay."

"As long as I'm allowed to be naughty too."

Hope holds her hand out. "Pinky promise."

Luke pinky swears and squats down once Hope stands and runs his tongue over her vaginal area. Hope retrieves a small lacey sexy white thong.

"Holly bought this after my divorce. I've never worn them. Until today."

Luke watches Hope slip them on under her dress. "I'm not sure how long I'll allow you to wear those."

Hope grins, "You can remove 'em anytime y'all want to."

Luke leans against Hope to let his hand travel down under her dress and move the thong sideways and slide his finger inside her.

"No fair, lover. Y'all know how much I want you."

Hope's passionate kiss backs up her message. Luke locks eye with Hope afterwards.

"Darlin', you must miss Faith. We'll enjoy the day with her. Then each other again tonight."

"I do miss Faith. Can we go get her?"

Hope takes Luke's hand to lead him towards the front door. *I've never been so happy. I've finally found true love. Nothin' can ruin this moment.'*

Luke considers his future. *'I'm finally somewhere I can call home with someone I truly love.'*

Hope's reaching for the door knob when the door explodes in on them to disrupt their blissful mood. The door splits into two main pieces. One half forcefully crashes against Hope's head. She cries out in pain while stumbling backwards and falling over the side of the chair behind her. A large menacing man enters the house swinging a baseball bat and strikes Hope's shin and fractures her tibia. Hope's agonized shriek distracts Luke while he's instinctively blocking the other half of the door. A second man laughs at Hope's pain-filled screams and delivers a dizzying blow to Luke's head with his bat. Luke's attention remains on Hope falling to the floor in excruciating agony and the first man moving towards her. Luke's dazed and graying out but his hazy mind has one thought.

'I have to stop them from hurtin' Hope.'

EPILOGUE
COWBOY WITHIN
LOVE CONQUERS ALL

Luke's alone on the deck contemplating his emotional state after experiencing death again.

'I don't know how to feel. Could I stop that from happening? Life's different now. What do I do?'

Hank worries about Luke's mental state more than his physical wounds. Faith exits the house and sits on Luke's lap and leans against him.

"I miss Momma. Do you miss Momma too?"

"Yes, Faith, I miss your mom. But she's with Chester."

Luke reflects on the assault against Hope and wonders, *'Why was Hope targeted for such a violent attack?'*